Glittering parties
passiona...

Regency

HIGH-SOCIETY
AFFAIRS

They're the talk of the Ton!

The Sparhawk Bride
by Miranda Jarrett

&

The Rogue's Seduction
by Georgina Devon

The *Regency*

HIGH-SOCIETY AFFAIRS

Regency

HIGH-SOCIETY
AFFAIRS

*Miranda Jarrett &
Georgina Devon*

M&B

*M&B™ and M&B™ with the Rose Device
are trademarks of the publisher.
Harlequin Mills & Boon Limited, Eton House,
18-24 Paradise Road, Richmond, Surrey TW9 1SR*

First published in Great Britain in 1998 and 2002

REGENCY HIGH-SOCIETY AFFAIRS
© Harlequin Books S.A. 2009

The publisher acknowledges the copyright holders of the
individual works as follows:

The Sparhawk Bride © Susan Holloway Scott 1995
The Rogue's Seduction © Alison J. Hentges 2002

ISBN: 978 0 263 87557 7

052-0909

*Printed and bound in Spain
by Litografia Rosés S.A., Barcelona*

The Sparhawk Bride

by

Miranda Jarrett

For Kathleen,
With affection and regards.
The Perfect Roommate and the Other Blonde.

Miranda Jarrett considers herself sublimely fortunate to have a career that combines history and happy endings – even if it's one that's also made her family far-too-regular patrons of the local pizzeria. Miranda is the author of over thirty historical romances, and her books are enjoyed by readers the world over. She has won numerous awards for her writing, including two Golden Leaf Awards and two *Romantic Times* Reviewers' Choice Awards, and has three times been a Romance Writers of America RITA® Award finalist for best short historical romance.

Miranda is a graduate of Brown University, with a degree in art history. She loves to hear from readers at PO Box 1102, Paoli, PA 19301-1145, USA, or at MJarrett21@aol.com

Prologue

"Look at them, Michel!" whispered Antoinette Géricault urgently. "Look at them and remember all they have stolen from you!"

Her fingers clenched the boy's shoulders tightly, her nails sharp through the worn linen of his shirt. But Michel did not flinch. He deserved whatever discipline *Maman* gave him. Hadn't she proved to him times beyond counting that he was wicked and shiftless, scarcely worth the toil it cost her to feed him? If she didn't love him so much, she wouldn't bother to correct him or strive so hard to make him worthy of his heritage.

And of her. He must be worthy of *Maman*'s love, for she was all he had.

"Look at them, Michel!" Her breath was hot on his ear as she leaned farther over his shoulder and out the single window of the attic room they shared. "*Mon Dieu*, that they should come here to my very doorstep after so many years! Look at all they have, while you must go wanting!"

The English family was leaving the sloop now, lingering on

the gangway for their last farewell with the captain and crew. They were treated more as honored guests instead of passengers, and why shouldn't they be? They were handsome and prosperous, well dressed and well fed, from the broad-shouldered father to the small, plump mother with a baby in her arms and four more children gathered around her.

The oldest boy, the one who looked to be Michel's age, tugged on the leash of a rambunctious black puppy, all floppy ears and buggy-whip tail. The boy bent to pat his back, and the puppy licked his face in a wet, sloppy kiss. The mother laughed, her head tipped back so her merriment rang out clear to Michel's ears, and with her free arm reached out to fondly hug the boy's shoulders.

"Look at her, the shameless English whore!" whispered Antoinette furiously. "Look at how she can laugh at the suffering she has brought to us!"

Michel looked at the other boy, forcing himself to share her outrage. *He* would never have a puppy. There was scarcely enough bread for *Maman* and him, let alone for a dog. *He* would never have a coat of blue superfine, or a three-cornered beaver hat with a silk cockade, or shoes with brass buckles, or a leather-covered spyglass to tuck nonchalantly beneath his arm. With shame he thought of his single pair of breeches, too short now to tie at the knee, his darned thread stockings, the worn shoes with the mismatched laces that he'd stolen from the feet of a drunken sailor.

He would never have two brothers to jostle and jest with the way this boy was doing. His father would never crouch down to point out something high among the mast-filled skyline of the harbor, something just for the two of them to share. His mother would never embrace him like that, openly, for all the world to see.

And his *Maman* never laughed....

"I did not know there was a daughter, too," his mother was

muttering. "Evil little creature, born of their sins. May she perish from the same shame that her father brought to me!"

Before this, Michel had not noticed the little girl, hidden from his sight by her mother's skirts until she skipped forward to throw her arms around the puppy's neck. Though she was scarcely larger than the dog, she showed no fear of it, shrieking with delight as the puppy tried to lick her face, too. The hood of her cloak slipped back and Michel could see her face, her round, rosy cheeks and her laughing eyes, her black hair charmingly tousled, the promise of her parents' looks already confirmed in her beautiful little face.

Unconsciously Michel inched forward, drawn by the spell of the small girl's happiness even from this distance. Beside him his mother smiled with grim approval.

"You will not forget now, will you, Michel?" she whispered, almost crooning. "You will never forget them until justice is done. For that man is Gabriel Sparhawk, and he is the one who murdered your father."

Chapter One

Newport
Colony of Rhode Island
and Providence Plantations
1771

He hadn't meant to come here to the house, not on the night of the wedding. If anyone recognized him, he could be dancing at the end of a rope before he knew it, and then how would justice be served?

Another carriage stopped before the house, and Michel Géricault shrank back into the shadows of the tall hedge. More wedding guests—more red-faced, overdressed Englishmen and their blowsy ladies—braying to one other as they tried and failed to ape their betters in London.

Mon Dieu, *how foolish they all were, these* Anglais, *and how much he hated them!*

The front door to the house swung open, candlelight flooding into the streets. Instead of the servant Michel had expected, the unmistakable figure of Captain Sparhawk himself appeared, his broad shoulders silhouetted in the doorway as he welcomed the newcomers to his daughter's wedding. After a week of watching the man, following him like a shadow from his home to his countinghouse to his ships, Michel could look at Sparhawk now almost impassively, without the white-hot fury he'd felt at first. It was better this way, much better. He'd long ago learned that passion of any kind led to the kind of carelessness he could ill afford tonight.

Farther down the street he heard a woman's soft laughter and the footsteps of her companion on the brick sidewalk, and swiftly Michel eased deeper into the tall bushes that formed the hedge. He was in an empty, formal garden now, between a *parterre* of roses and an arbor of clematis and honeysuckle with a lady's teakwood bench. Beyond that the clipped lawns rolled clear to the very edge of the harbor itself. From inside the house came the laughter of the guests, mingled with the more distant sounds of hired musicians tuning their instruments. Somewhere upstairs a tall clock chimed the hour: eight bells.

He should leave now, before it was too late. Only a fool would stay.

But from here Michel could see through the open windows into the house and the parlor itself, and like the set of a play when the curtain first rises, the scene beckoned him to stay, to watch. On a laden supper table in the center of the room sat the wedding cake, raised high on a silver epergne festooned with white paper lace and chains, and on another table was arranged a display of wedding gifts, a king's ransom in silver glittering in the candlelight. A score of candles lit in an empty room, the finest white spermaceti, not tallow; that alone was an unimaginable extravagance.

A coarse, vulgar display, a barbarous English show of wealth without taste. They said Captain Sparhawk had spared nothing to celebrate his favorite daughter's marriage. What price would he offer, then, when the chit vanished without a trace?

A flicker of white in the moonlight at the far end of the house caught Michel's eye, a pale curtain blown outward through an open window. But why only that window, on a night as still as this one, unless the curtain was being pushed by someone within? Warily Michel touched his belt with the pistols and knife, and swore softly to himself, wishing the street were clear so he could retreat through the hedge.

But to his surprise, a lady's leg came through the window next, a long, slender leg in a silk stocking with a green fringed garter, followed by its mate as the young woman swung herself over the windowsill and dropped to the grass. Cynically Michel wondered if it was her father or, more likely, her husband that she'd escaped, and he glanced around the garden again to see if he'd somehow overlooked her waiting lover.

The girl paused long enough to shake out her skirts, her dark head bowed as she smoothed the cream-colored sateen with both hands, then hurried across the grass with a soft rustle of silk. As she came closer, the moonlight caught her full in the face, and unconsciously Michel swore again.

She froze at the sound, one hand raised to the pearls around her throat as her startled gaze swept the shadows until she found Michel.

Startled, but not afraid. "You've caught me, haven't you?" she asked wryly. "Fair and square. You must be one of my brothers' friends, for I don't believe I've met you, have I?"

"But I know you," he said softly, his voice deep and low, his accent barely discernible. It had been nearly twenty years, yet still he would have recognized her anywhere. "Miss Jerusa Sparhawk."

"True enough." She bobbed him a little curtsy. "Then you must be friends with Josh. He's the only one of my brothers I truly favor. As it should be, considering we're twins. But then, I expect you knew that already."

Michel nodded in agreement. Oh, he knew a great many things about the Sparhawks, more than even she did herself.

"Miss Jerusa Sparhawk," she repeated, musing. "I'll

wager you'll be the last to call me that. While you and all the others act as witnesses, in a quarter hour I'll become Mrs. Thomas Carberry."

Her smile was dazzling, enough to reduce any other man to instant fealty. He'd heard much praise of her beauty, the perfection of her face, the flawlessness of her skin, the vivid contrast between her black hair and green eyes and red mouth, but none of that praise came close to capturing her charm, her radiance. Easy even for him to see why she was considered the reigning belle of the colony.

Not that any of it mattered.

She was still a Sparhawk.

Still his enemy.

"Is this really the great love match they say?" He didn't miss the irony that she'd mistaken him for a guest, let alone a friend of her brother's, and trusted him to the point of not even asking his name.

Like a pigeon, he thought with grim amusement, a pretty, plump pigeon that flew cooing into his hands.

The girl tipped her head quizzically, the diamonds in her earrings dancing little fragments of light across her cheeks. "You dare to ask if I love my Tom?"

"Do you?" He was wasting time he didn't have, but he wanted to know exactly how much suffering he'd bring to her family this night.

"Do I love Tom? How could I not?" Her smile outshone the moonlight as her words came out in a tumbled, breathless rush. "He's amusing and kind and, oh, so very handsome, and he dances more gracefully than any other gentleman in Newport, and he says clever things to make me laugh and pretty things to make me love him even more. How could I not love my darling Tom?"

"Doubtless it helped his suit that he's rich."

"Rich?" Her eyes were innocently blank. "Well, I suppose

his father is. So is mine, if you must put so brass a face on it. But that's certainly not reason enough to marry someone."

"Certainly not," agreed Michel dryly. She'd never wanted for anything in her sweet, short life. How could she guess the lengths she'd go to if she were cold enough, hungry enough, desperate enough? "But if you love him as you claim, then why have you run from your own wedding?"

"Is that what you believed I was doing? Oh, my!" She wrinkled her elegant nose with amusement. "It's Mama, you see. She says that because I'm the bride I must stay in my bed-chamber until the very minute that I come down the stairs with Father. If even one person lays eyes upon me before then, it's bad luck, and I'll turn straight into salt or some such."

Another time, another woman, and he might have laughed at the little shrug she gave her shoulders and the sigh that followed. Another time, another woman, and he might have let himself be charmed.

She sighed dramatically. "But I *would* want a rose from this garden—those bushes there, the pink ones—to put in my hair because Tom favors pink. Banished as I was, there was no one else but myself to fetch it, and so you found me here. Still, that's hardly running off. I've every intention of returning the same way I came, through the window into my father's office and up the back stairs."

"Don't you fear that they'll miss you?"

"Not with the house full of guests that need tending, they won't." Restlessly she rubbed her thumb across the heavy pearl cuff around one wrist, and, to his surprise, Michel realized that much of her bravado was no more than ordinary nervousness. "The ceremony proper won't begin until half past eight."

No matter what she said, Michel knew time was fast slipping away. He'd dawdled here too long as it was. His mind raced ahead, changing his plans. Now that she'd seen him, he couldn't afford to let her go, but perhaps, in a way, this would be even better than what he'd originally intended. His fingers brushed against the little vial of chloroform in the pocket of his coat. Even *Maman* would appreciate the daring it would take to steal the bride from her own wedding.

The *Sparhawk* bride. *Mordieu,* it was almost too perfect.

"You're not superstitious, then?" he asked softly, easing the cork from the neck of the vial with his thumb. "You don't believe your mother's unhappy predictions will come true now that I've seen you?"

She turned her head, eyeing him with sidelong doubt. "You'll tell her?"

"Nay, what reason would I have to do that? You go pick your roses now, *ma chère,* and then back in the house before they come searching for you."

Hesitancy flickered through her eyes, and too late he realized he'd unthinkingly slipped into speaking French. But then her doubt vanished as quickly as it had appeared, replaced by the joyful smile he was coming to recognize. With a pang of regret that caught him by surprise, he knew it would be the last smile she'd ever grant him.

"Then thank you," she said simply. "I don't care which of my brothers is your friend, because now you're mine, as well."

She turned away toward the flowers before he could answer. Her cream-colored skirts rustled around her as she bent gracefully over the roses, and the sheer lawn cuffs of her gown fluttered back from her wrists in the breeze as she reached to pluck a single, pink rose.

So much grace, thought Michel as he drew the dampened handkerchief from his pocket, so much beauty to mask such poisoned blood. She struggled for only a moment as he pressed the cloth over her mouth and nose, then fell limp in his arms.

He glanced back at the house as he carried the unconscious girl into the shadow of the tall hedges. There he swiftly pulled off her jewelry, the pearl necklace and bracelet and ring, the diamonds from her ears, even the paste buckles from her shoes. Whatever else they called him, he wasn't a thief, and he had pride enough to leave her jewels behind. He yanked the pins from her hair and mussed the elaborate stiffened curls until they fell in an untidy tangle to her shoulders, shading her face. With his thumb he hurriedly smudged dirt across one of her cheeks and over her hands, trying hard not to think of how soft her skin was beneath his touch.

She was a Sparhawk, not just a woman. Think of how she would revile him if she knew—when she learned—his father's name!

He used his knife to cut away the bottom silk flounce of her gown, baring the plain linen of her underskirt, which he dragged through the dirt beneath the bushes. Finally he yanked off his own coat and buttoned it around her shoulders. As he'd hoped, the long coat covered what remained of her gown, and in the dark streets, with her grimy face and tousled hair, she'd pass for one more drunken strumpet from the docks, at least long enough for him to retrieve his horse from the stable.

Briefly he sat back on his heels and wiped his sleeve across his forehead as he glanced one last time at the candlelit house. The girl had been right. No alarms, no shouts of panic or pursuit came through the open windows, only the sounds of laughter and excited conversation. It took a moment longer for him to realize that the loud, rapid thumping was the beat of his own heart.

One last task, that was all, and then he'd be done.

Swiftly he retrieved the rose she'd picked from where it had fallen and laid it across the pile of her jewelry. He dug deep into the pocket of his waistcoat until he found the piece of paper. With fingers that shook only a little, he unfolded and stabbed the page onto the rose's thorns so that the smudged black *fleur de lis* would be unmistakable.

The symbol of France, the mark of Christian Sainte-Juste Deveaux.

A sign that Gabriel Sparhawk would read as easily as his own name.

And at last Maman would smile.

Chapter Two

It was the rain that woke Jerusa, the rattle of the heavy drops on the shingles overhead. Still too groggy to open her eyes, she rubbed her bare arm against the damp chill and groped for her silk-lined coverlet. She knew she'd left it on the end of the bed last night, there beside her dressing gown. Blast, where was it? Her blind fingers reached farther and touched the sharp prickle of musty straw.

"Whatever you're seeking, it isn't there."

She turned toward the man's voice, forcing herself to open her eyes. The world began to spin in such dizzying circles that she swiftly squeezed her eyes shut again with a groan. Now she noticed the foul taste in her mouth and how her head ached abominably, as if she'd had too much sherry and sweetmeats the night before. She must be ill; that would explain why she felt so wretched. But why was there straw in her bed and a man in her bedchamber, and where *was* that infernal coverlet?

"There's no call for moaning," continued the man unsympathetically. "No matter how badly you feel now, I do believe you'll live."

He wasn't one of her brothers, he wasn't Tom, and he certainly wasn't her father, yet still the man's voice seemed oddly familiar, and not at all reassuring. Uneasily she opened her eyes again, this time only a fraction. Still the world spun, but if she concentrated hard she found she could slow the circles until they stopped.

What she saw then made even less sense. Instead of her own bed with the tall posts in the house where she'd been born, she lay curled on a heap of last summer's musty straw in the corner of a barn she didn't recognize. Gloomy gray daylight filtered halfheartedly through cracks in the barn's siding. There were none of the familiar sounds of Newport, no church bells, no horses' hooves and wagon wheels on the paving stones, no sailors calling from the ships in the harbor, nothing beyond the falling rain and the wind and the soft snuffling and stamping of the horses in the last two stalls.

Nothing, that is, beyond the man who sprawled in his stocking feet on the bench beneath the barn's single window, watching her intently over a copy of last week's *Newport Mercury,* his boots placed neatly before him. She guessed he was not so much older than herself, still in his twenties, but though his features were regular, even handsome, there was a grim wariness to the set of his wide mouth that aged him far beyond his years. The gray light brought gold to his hair, the only warmth to be found in his face. Certainly not in his eyes; how could eyes as blue as the sky be so cold?

"Who are you?" she asked, her confusion shifting to uneasiness.

He cocked one skeptical brow. "You don't remember, my fair little bride?"

"Bride?" She pushed herself up on shaky arms and stared at him, mystified. Surely she wasn't married to a man like this one. "When was I—"

And then abruptly she broke off as everything came rushing back to her in a single, horrible instant. Her wedding to Tom, the tears of joy in her mother's eyes and the pride in her father's as they'd left her alone in her bedchamber, how she'd climbed from the window to find a rose for her hair and instead found herself in this man's company. She had been fooled by his plain but well-cut clothing and his ready smile, and she had believed him to be a guest at her wedding. She had trusted him, for then he had seemed trustworthy, even charming. Now he seemed neither.

Frantically she threw back the rough blanket that had covered her and saw the soiled, tattered remnants of her wedding gown. Gone was the pearl cuff that Mama had given her as she'd dressed, and her hands flew to her throat, bare now of the necklace that had come from Tom.

"You've not only kidnapped me but robbed me, as well!" she gasped, struggling to rise to her feet. "I demand, sir, that you take me back home at once!"

"So that your father can see me hung?" His smile was humorless as he refolded the newspaper and tossed it onto the bench beside him. "I'm afraid that won't do, Miss Jerusa. And try not to be so imperious, *ma chère*. You're scarcely in a position to make demands."

The sheer lawn fichu that had been tied across her neckline had vanished, as well, and Jerusa was shamefully conscious of how his gaze had shifted from her face to where her stays raised and displayed her half-bare breasts in fashionable *décolletage*.

Swiftly she snatched up the blanket and flung it over her shoulders. "My father *will* see a rogue like you hung, you can be mightily sure of that! If you know who I am, then you know who he is, and he won't stand for what you've done to me, not for a moment!"

He clucked softly. "Such wasteful, idle threats, *ma chère!*"

"You're French, aren't you?" Her green eyes narrowed. "You speak English almost as well as a gentleman, but you're *French*."

He shrugged carelessly. "Perhaps I am. Perhaps I merely prefer the French manner for endearments. Does it matter?"

"It will to my father," she said warmly. "Father hates the French, and with good reason, too, considering all they've tried to do to him. Why, he's probably already on his way here, along with Tom and my brothers, and I don't want to even consider what they shall do to you when they arrive and Father learns you're *French!*"

"'When they arrive.' That, *ma belle,* is the real question, isn't it?" He reached into the pocket of his waistcoat to pull out his watch and held it up for her to see. "It's half past six. Nearly a full night and day have passed since we departed Newport together, and still no sign of any of your gallant knights. So how does it matter if I am French or English or dropped to earth from the moon itself?"

She clutched the blanket more tightly, trying to fight her rising panic. She'd no idea so much time had passed, and she thought of how worried her parents must be. And Tom. Lord, how he must be suffering, to have her vanish on the night of their wedding!

"Have you at least had the decency to send some sort of note to tell them that I am unhurt?" There were so many perils that could befall a woman in a harbor town like Newport, and she hated to think of her poor mother imagining every one. Without thinking, she touched her bare wrist where Mama's bracelet had been before she remembered bitterly that this man had stolen it. The pearl cuff had been special, a gift to Mama on her own wedding day, which she had given, in turn, to Jerusa. "You can't possibly know the pain you've caused my family!"

"Ah, but I do." His expression was oddly, chillingly triumphant. "But you can be sure I left behind a message that your father will understand."

"Then they will come," she said, as much to convince herself as him. "They won't abandon me. They'll find us, wherever you've taken me."

"I'm sure they will," he said easily, stretching his arms before him. Though he wasn't much taller than Jerusa herself, there was no mistaking the strength in his lean, muscled body. "In fact I'd be disappointed if they didn't. But not here, and not so soon."

"Where, then?" she asked, her desperation growing by the minute. "When?"

"Where I please, and when I say." Those cold blue eyes never left her face as he tucked the watch back into its pocket, and he spoke slowly, carefully, as if she were a child he wished to impress. "Remember, sweet Jerusa, that it's my word that matters now, not yours. I know that will be a difficult lesson for a Sparhawk, but you seem a clever enough girl, and in time you'll learn. You'll learn."

But she didn't want to learn, especially not from him. Jerusa shivered. How much longer could he intend to keep her his prisoner? It was bad enough that she had passed a night alone with him when she'd been drugged into unconsciousness, but what would he expect tonight, when she was all too aware of him both as her captor and as a man?

"If it's money you want," she said softly, "you know my father will pay it. You already have my jewelry to keep for surety. Let me go free now, and I'll see you're sent whatever else you wish."

"Let you go free?" He looked at her with genuine amusement. "Not a quarter of an hour ago you were ready to lead me to the gallows yourself, and now you ask me to trust you?"

"I didn't mean it like that. I meant—"

"It doesn't matter what you mean, because I don't want your money. I didn't want your baubles, either, which is why I left them behind." His voice slipped suggestively lower. "It's you I want, Miss Jerusa Sparhawk. You, and nothing else."

She didn't ask why. She didn't want to know. All she wanted now was to go home to her family and to Tom and forget that she'd ever set eyes on this horrible Frenchman. How had the most glorious day of her life disintegrated into this?

She should have known he wouldn't bargain with her, just as she shouldn't have trusted him in the garden in the first place. She wasn't sure if she believed him about the jewelry, either, though it would be her luck to have stumbled into a man too honorable for theft but not for kidnapping.

Luck. She remembered Mama's half-serious warning as she'd helped Jerusa dress: bad luck to the bride who let the world see her in her wedding finery before she was made a wife. Jerusa had scoffed at the time, but look what had happened. Was there ever a more unfortunate bride?

Unfortunate, homesick and more frightened than she'd ever been in her life.

She stared out the little square window, struggling to keep back the tears. A man like this one would only mock her if she wept, and no matter how bleak her situation was, she'd no wish to give him that pleasure. She'd given away too much already.

Far better to remember that no matter what else happened she was still a Sparhawk, and Sparhawks were never cowards. Hadn't Mama herself fought off a score of French pirates to save Father long ago, before they were married? Mama wouldn't have stood about wringing her hands until she was rescued. Mama would have found a way to help free herself, and so, decided Jerusa with shaky resolution, must she.

The rain had stopped, and a milky-pale sun was sliding slowly through the clouds toward the horizon. One night, one day. How far from Newport could they be? The land through the window was a fallow, anonymous pasture that could have been anywhere on the island. The key would be to find the water, Narragansett Bay or the Sakonnet River, for either would take her back to Newport. Even though she wasn't a sailor like her brothers, she'd grown up on Aquidneck Island, and she was sure she'd be able to recognize nearly every beach on it. Certainly she'd have better bearings than some cocksure bully of a Frenchman.

Now all she had to do was get away from him.

"I don't feel quite well," she announced, praying she sounded convincing. "Whatever smelling stuffs you used to force me to sleep—I fear they've made me ill."

He sighed with exasperation. "If you're going to be sick, then use that bucket by the stall. Don't foul the straw if you can help it."

"It's not that," she said quickly. She felt herself blushing furiously from excitement, fear and embarrassment. "It's that I must use the privy."

He muttered to himself in French, and though she didn't understand the words, Jerusa knew well enough that he was swearing.

She bent over from the waist, rubbing her stomach. "Truly. If you please, I must go."

"You're not going alone." With another sigh he leaned forward to pull on his boots.

Jerusa saw her chance and seized it. She raced to the barn door, shoved it open just enough to slip through and raced outside. Swiftly she pushed the door shut and threw the long swinging bolt into the latches, barricading the Frenchman inside. With a little laugh of giddy exhilaration she turned and ran, away from the barn, the privy and the burned-out ruin of a house. She didn't recognize the farm, or what was left of it, but that didn't matter. Before her, to the east, lay the pewter gray of the water, and her salvation.

Without buckles, her shoes flapped awkwardly around her heels, and she kicked them away, and when the wind dragged the heavy blanket from her grasp and off her shoulders, she left that, too, behind, running as fast as she could down the narrow, overgrown path to the shore. One last windblown rise lay before her, then the sharp drop to the beach. She slipped and skidded on the wet grass and tall reeds lashed at her legs, but still she ran, her tattered skirts fluttering around her in the wind. The path turned to sand beneath the ruined stockings on her feet, and before her, at last, were the beach and the wide river that emptied into the bay.

Or was it? Confused, she paced back and forth along the water's edge, trying to make sense of what she saw. The sinking sun to the west was behind her, so this should be the eastern shore of Aquidneck, with Portsmouth across the river in the distance.

But this short, sandy beach was all wrong, the distance to Portsmouth too far across the water. Jerusa shaded her eyes with the back of her hand and squinted at the horizon. Instead of the narrow tip of Sakonnet Point, which she expected, she saw what looked like two islands: Conanicut Island then, with Dutch beyond to the north, and a barren lump of stone that must be Whale Rock.

And there, to the east, washed in the pale light of the setting sun, was Aquidneck Island, and Newport.

"Newport," she whispered hoarsely, the full impact of what she saw striking her like a blow. She wasn't on her island any longer. She was on the mainland, an endless, friendless world that before she'd only seen from a distance, the same way that she was now gazing at her home. Her home, her family, her own darling Tom, all so hopelessly far beyond her reach. "God help me, if that's Newport, then where am I?"

"Aye, ask your God to help you," said the Frenchman roughly, "for you'll have precious little from me."

She turned slowly, rubbing away the tears that wet her cheeks before he could see them. His face was taut with fury, his blond hair untied and blowing wild around his face, and the pistol in his hand was primed and cocked and aimed at her breast.

"Don't try to run again, *ma chère,*" he said so quietly she almost didn't hear him over the sounds of the wind and the waves. "I'd far sooner keep you alive, but I won't balk at killing you if you leave me no choice. I told you before, it's you I want, Jerusa Sparhawk. Alive or dead, it's you, and nothing else."

Chapter Three

Joshua Sparhawk watched as his father, Gabriel, ran his fingers over the crumpled paper with the black *fleur de lis*. How many times, wondered Josh, how many times had his father touched that scrap of paper since Jerusa had disappeared last night?

"I just spoke with the leader of the last patrol, Father," he said wearily, tossing his hat onto the bench beneath the window. "They've searched clear to Newport Neck and back again and found not a trace of her."

"Not that I expected they would." Gabriel sighed heavily as he sank back against the tall caned back of his chair. Though his black hair had only just begun to gray at the temples and his broad shoulders remained unbent, he would be sixty next spring, and, for the first time that Josh could remember, his formidable father actually looked his age. "Whoever took her is long gone by now."

Once again he glanced down at the paper that was centered squarely on the top of the desk before him. To one side lay Jerusa's jewelry, her necklace, ring and earbobs tucked within the stiff circle of the pearl cuff. On the other side was the pink rose in a tumbler of water, the fragile flower's petals already drooping and edged with brown, an unhappy symbol for the Sparhawk family's fading hopes.

"But we had to be sure, Father." Josh frowned, unwilling to share Gabriel's pessimism. If the black *fleur de lis* held some special significance, then he wished his father would share it with the rest of them. He still couldn't quite believe that Rusa was gone, that she wouldn't yet pop up from behind a chair to laugh at them for being such hopeless worrywarts. "There was still a chance we'd find her somewhere on the island. They had at most an hour's start on us. How far could they go?"

"Halfway to hell, if they had a good wind." Gabriel glared up at Josh from beneath the bristling thicket of his brows, the famous green eyes that he'd passed on to his children as bright and formidable as ever. "I told you before that the bastards came by water, and left by it, too."

Unconsciously Josh clasped his hands behind his back, his legs spread wide in the defensive posture he'd used since boyhood to confront his father. He was doing his best to find his sister; they all were. But Father being Father and Jerusa being the one missing, even Josh's best would never be enough.

"You know as well as I that we've checked with the harbormaster and the pilots, Father. We've stopped and boarded every vessel that cleared Newport since last night, and we've still come up empty-handed."

"Oh, aye, as if these bloody kidnappers will haul aback because we've asked them nicely, then invite us all aboard for tea!" In frustration Gabriel slammed his fist on the desk. "They knew what they were about, the sneaking, thieving rogues. They slipped into town just long enough to steal my sweet Jerusa, then slipped back out without so much as a by-your-leave. That jackass of a harbormaster was likely so deep in his cups he wouldn't see a thirty-gun frigate sail under his nose!"

"For God's sake, Father, they had less than an hour, and if—"

Abruptly Josh broke off at the sound of the voices in the front hall. Perhaps there was fresh news of his sister.

But instead of a messenger, only Thomas Carberry appeared at the door to Gabriel's office, pausing as he waited vainly for Gabriel to invite him in. When Gabriel didn't, Tom entered anyway, irritably yanking off his yellow gloves as he dropped unbidden into a chair.

Unlike the two Sparhawk men, unshaven and bleary-eyed after the long, sleepless night and day of searching, Tom was as neatly turned out as he'd been for the wedding itself, his hair clubbed in a flawless silk bow, and his linen immaculate. For his sister's sake, Josh had tried very hard to like Tom, or at least be civil to him, but to him the man was an idle, empty-headed popinjay, too concerned with dancing and the latest London novel. Of course the ladies fancied him to distraction, his sister most of all.

"Well, now, Captain," Tom began as he crossed his legs elegantly at the knee. "What word do you have of my bride?"

Joshua watched how his father lowered his chin and drummed his fingers on the desk, his expression as black as thunderclouds. If Tom Carberry had any sense at all, he'd be running for cover by now.

"*Your* bride, Carberry?" rumbled Gabriel. "Damn your impertinence, Jerusa's still my daughter first, and I'll thank you to remember it!"

Undeterred, Tom sniffed loudly, an unpleasant habit he'd developed from overindulging in snuff. "You make it rather hard to forget, don't you, Captain? But you've still not answered my query. Where's Jerusa?"

The drumming fingers curled into a fist. "Where in blazes are the wits your maker gave you, boy? Do you think we'd all be scouring this blessed island and the water around it if we knew where Jerusa was? Not that we've had much help from you, have we?"

"I'll beg you to recall, sir, that I ordered and paid for the handbills posting the reward for Jerusa's return. Nothing mean about that!"

"Oh, aye, nothing mean about that, nor meaningful, either!" growled Gabriel as he shoved back his chair and rose to his feet. "Ink and paper won't fetch my daughter back out of the air!"

"My point exactly, Captain. How, indeed, could a lady vanish into the very air?" Belligerently Tom sniffed again as he, too, rose to his feet. "Nor am I alone in my surmise, sir. There's others, many others, who shall agree, sir, that my bride's disappearance mere minutes before our union has a decidedly insulting taint to it. An insult, sir, that I've no intention of bearing without notice."

Josh grabbed Tom and shoved him back against his chair. As far as he could see, the insult was to Jerusa, and he'd be damned if he'd let anyone speak of his sister like that. "What the hell are you saying, Carberry?"

"I'm saying that I believe Jerusa's jilted me," said Tom, his words clipped with fury. He lifted both hands to Josh's chest and shoved hard in return. "I'm saying that her disappearance is merely a convenient manner of explanation. I'm saying that the chit's amusing enough, but neither she nor her dowry's worth—"

At once Josh was on him, driving his fist squarely into Tom's dimpled chin and knocking him to the floor. Tom's own blow went wild, but as he toppled backward he grabbed the front of Josh's coat and pulled him down, too. Over and over they rolled across the floorboards, whichever man was on top swinging at the other as they grunted and swore and crashed into furniture.

But while in height the two were evenly matched, Josh had long ago traded a genteel drawing room for the far rougher company on the quarterdeck of his own sloop, and Tom's anger and dishonor alone weren't enough to equal Josh's raw strength and experience. Finally when Josh was on top he stayed there, breathing hard, pinning the other man down between his thighs.

"My—my sister's too good for you, you stinking son of a bitch," he gasped, breathing hard as he raised his fist to deal one final blow to Tom's battered, bleeding face. "Why the hell didn't they take you instead?"

But before he could strike, Gabriel caught his arm. "Enough, Joshua."

He struggled to break his father's grasp, Gabriel's voice barely penetrating the red glare of his rage. "Father, you heard what he said—"

"I said enough, or you'll kill him, and the bastard's not worth that."

Reluctantly Josh nodded, and Gabriel released him. As he climbed off Tom, he flexed his fingers where he'd once struck the floor instead of Tom. His hand would be too raw to hold a pen tonight, and already his lip felt as if it had doubled in size from the swelling, but one look at Tom made it all worthwhile. No ladies would come sighing after that face for a good long while.

Slowly Tom crawled to his knees and then to his feet, swaying unsteadily but still shaking off Gabriel's offered hand as he headed to the door. He fumbled for his handkerchief and pressed it to the gash on his forehead.

"You're a—a low, filthy cur, Sparhawk," he gasped from the doorway, "an' so—an' so I'll tell th' town."

"Then go and tell them, Carberry," said Gabriel grimly, "but don't come back here. It was only for your father's sake and Jerusa's begging that I agreed to your wretched proposal anyway, and thank God I've broken the betrothal before it was too late."

"*You* broke it?" croaked Tom. "*I* came here t'end it!"

"My daughter didn't jilt you, Carberry, but I did. Now get out."

And this time Tom didn't wait.

Shaking his head, Gabriel went back behind his desk. From the bottom drawer he pulled out a bottle of rum, drew the stopper and handed it to Josh. "Don't let your mother see you until you've cleaned yourself up. You know how she feels about fighting."

Josh smiled as best he could and took the bottle. The rum stung his lip but tasted good, sliding and burning down his throat. This was the first time his father had ever shared the bottle from his desk with him, and Josh savored the rare approval that came along with the drink.

It was one of the quirks of his family that though he and Jerusa had been born together twenty-one years before, their positions were curiously reversed. Josh was the third, the youngest son, always trying to prove himself, while Jerusa was the first and eldest of his three sisters, the beautiful, irrepressible favorite to whom everything came so easily. Not that he'd ever been jealous of her; Jerusa was too much a part of him for that, almost like the other half of his being.

Lord, he hoped they'd find her soon.

His father left the bottle on the desk between them. "You've traded with the French islands, Josh. Ever heard of a pirate named Deveaux?"

Josh shook his head. "The name's not one I recall. Which port does he call home?"

"Once he sailed from Fort Royale on Martinique, but not now. I watched him take a pistol and spatter his own brains aboard the old *Revenge.* Your mother was there to see it, too, more's the pity." Gabriel sighed, his thoughts turned inward to the past. "Must be nearly thirty years ago, though I remember it as if it were yesterday. And that, I think, is what someone wants me to believe."

He picked up the paper in his right hand, and to Josh's surprise his father's fingers were trembling. "This was

Deveaux's mark, lad. All his men had it burned into their flesh, and anytime he wished to take credit for his actions he'd leave a paper like this behind."

"How could he have anything to do with Jerusa?" asked Josh. "You said the man is dead."

"As dead as any mortal can be, and his scoundrel crew with him. The ones that weren't lost in the wreck of his ship we took to Bridgetown for hanging. But now, Lord help us, I cannot swear to it."

Josh held his breath, waiting with a strange mixture of dread and excitement for what must follow. There were some stories of his father's past—and his mother's, too—that were told so often they'd become family legends. But most of Gabriel's exploits as a privateer he had kept to himself, and certainly away from the sons who would have hung on every heroic word.

Until now, when Jerusa's life might be swinging in the balance between the past and the present....

Gabriel reached inside the letter box on his desk. In his palm lay a second paper, faded with age but still a perfect match to the new one found with the rose. "Deveaux kidnapped your mother on the night of our wedding as she walked in the garden of my parents' house at Westgate. And everything—damnation, *everything*—about how Jerusa vanished is the same, down to this cursed black lily, even though there should be no one left alive beyond your mother and me to know of it."

Josh stared at the black lilies, his head spinning at what his father said. Whoever cared enough to come clear to Newport to duplicate his mother's kidnapping so precisely would want to see the macabre game to its conclusion.

"But obviously this Deveaux must have let you redeem Mother," he said, striving to make sense of the puzzle. "He didn't hurt her."

"God knows he tried. He would have killed us both if he could," said Gabriel grimly, "just as he murdered so many others. Christian Deveaux was the most truly wicked man I've ever known, Joshua, as evil as Satan himself in his love of cruelty and pain. When I think of your sister in the hands of a man who fancies himself another Deveaux…"

He didn't need to say more. Josh understood.

"I can have the *Tiger* ready to sail at dawn, Father," he said quietly, "and I'll be in Martinique in five days."

Chapter Four

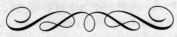

"If you're well enough to run away, *ma belle*," said Michel curtly, "then you're well enough to ride. We'll do better to travel by night anyway."

He bent to tighten the cinch on the first saddle so he wouldn't see the reproach in her eyes. Silly little chit. What did she expect him to do after she'd bolted like that?

But then, in turn, he hadn't expected her to run, either. He'd thought a petted little creature like Jerusa Sparhawk would whimper and wail, not flee at the first chance she got. And locking him within the barn—though that had made him furious, it also showed more spirit than he'd given her credit for. Much more. He'd have to remember that, and not underestimate her again.

Jerusa watched the Frenchman as he murmured little nonsense words to calm the horse. Kindness for the horse, but none to spare for her. He'd made that clear enough.

She forced herself to eat the bread and cheese he'd given her, even as she remembered that he'd threatened to kill her. Rationally she didn't believe he would, though she wasn't sure she had the courage to test his threat and try to escape again. If he didn't want her alive, he wouldn't have gone through the trouble to kidnap her in the first place.

But the ease with which he'd handled the pistols had chilled her. Most men in the colonies knew how to shoot with rifles or muskets to hunt game, but pistols were only used for killing other men. Because of her father's whim to teach her along with Josh, she was adept at loading and firing both, and good enough to recognize the abilities of others. The Frenchman was a professional. He could be a soldier, more likely a thief or other rogue who lived outside the law.

He turned back toward her, smoothing his hair away from his forehead. By the light of the single lantern, his blue eyes were shuttered and purposely devoid of any emotion as he studied her with cold, disinterested thoroughness.

Whatever he was, he wasn't a gentleman to look at her like that. She flushed, wishing she hadn't lost the blanket, but resisted the impulse to cover her breasts with her hands. Pride would serve her better. She wouldn't gain a thing with fear or shame. And at least if they traveled by night, then she'd be spared for now the question of where and how they'd sleep here together.

"Where are we?" she asked. "Kingston? Point Judith?"

"South." The truth was that Michel hadn't bothered to learn the name of the nearest town. Why should he, when he'd no intention of lingering?

"South?"

"South," he answered firmly. She didn't need to know any more than that.

"Well, south, then." Jerusa sighed. He'd been talkative enough in the garden. "Would it be a grave affront to ask how we came to be here?"

He didn't miss the sarcasm, but then, *humility* was never a word he'd heard in connection with her family. "By boat, *ma chérie,* as you might have guessed. We sailed here together by the moonlight, just you and I."

To do that the Frenchman must be a sailor, and a good one,

too, to make that crossing alone and at night. A sailor who could handle pistols: a privateer, like the men in her own family, or a pirate?

If she could only get one of those pistols for herself to balance the odds!

With an unconscious frown, she lifted a lock of her hair from her shoulder and twisted it between her fingers. Pistols or not, she wasn't accustomed to men speaking to her as freely as this, and she didn't like it. Moonlight and togetherness, indeed. As if she'd spend two minutes with such a man by choice.

"And these horses?" she asked dryly. "Did they have a place in our little ark, too?"

The corners of Michel's mouth twitched in spite of himself. The provocative image of the girl before him in the lantern light, her hair tumbled about her face and her elegant clothes half-torn away, was so far from old Noah's virtuous wife that he almost laughed. "These horses were here waiting for us, as I'd arranged."

"Then you planned all this?" asked Jerusa incredulously. "You *planned* to bring me here?"

"Of course I planned it." He slung the second saddle onto the mare. "Chance is a sorry sort of mistress, *ma chère*. I prefer to leave as little of my life in her care as I possibly can."

"But you couldn't have known I'd go into the garden!" she cried. "I didn't know myself! I went on an impulse, a fancy! You *couldn't* have known!"

He shrugged carelessly. "True enough. Originally I'd planned to take you from your new husband's coach on your way to your wedding night in Middletown. With the servants already waiting to receive you, there would have been only the driver and your pretty Master Carberry. His father's second house, isn't it, there to the east of the high road to Portsmouth? Not quite as grand as your own at Crescent Hill, but it would have been comfortable enough for newlyweds, and the view from the front bedchamber is a fine one."

She listened mutely, appalled by how familiar he was with the details of her life.

"It would have been dramatic, to stop a coach like a highwayman," he continued. "I would, I think, have quite enjoyed it. Yet finding you alone in the garden was far easier."

All of it had been easy enough, really. He'd spent so much of his life at the hire of whoever paid the most, listening, watching, making himself as unobtrusive as possible until the last, that learning about a family as public as the Sparhawks had been no challenge at all. No challenge, but the reward that waited would be far sweeter than all the gold in the Caribbean.

He smiled briefly at Jerusa over the mare's chestnut back. "True, I don't care for chance, but if she casts her favors my way I won't turn my back, either."

"You would never have succeeded!" she said hotly, insulted by his confidence. She might have been disarmed by his smile in the garden, but not now. "The Portsmouth Road isn't Hounslow Heath! If the coachman hadn't shot you dead, then you can be sure that Tom himself would have defended my honor!"

He cocked one brow with amusement. "What a pity we didn't have the chance to test his mettle, *ma petite*. You could have been a maid, a wife and a widow in one short day."

She opened her lips to answer, then pressed them together again with her rebuttal left unspoken as she realized the reality of what he'd said. Tom was the most genteel man she'd ever met, a gentleman down to the cut-steel buckles on his polished shoes. His elegance was one of the things she loved most about him, perhaps because it made Tom so different from her wilder, seafaring brothers.

But that same gentility wouldn't have lasted a moment against the Frenchman. He might not kill her, but somehow she didn't doubt that he would have murdered her darling Tom if he'd raised even his voice to defend her. He would be dead, and she would still be a prisoner.

She laid the bread on the bench beside her, the crust now as dry as dust in her mouth. *A maid, a wife, a widow.* Thank God she'd gone to the garden, after all. That single, pink rose might have saved Tom's life, and under her breath she whispered a little prayer for him.

Michel watched how the girl seemed to wilt before his eyes. Perhaps she truly did love Carberry, though how any woman could lose her heart to such a self-centered ass was beyond reason. He'd seen Carberry only once from a distance, waving a handkerchief trimmed with more lace than a lady's petticoat as he climbed into his carriage, but that glimpse had been enough to turn Michel's stomach with disgust. *Merde,* he wouldn't have had to waste the gunpowder on that one; more likely Carberry would have simply fainted dead away on his own.

Michel glanced out the window. The clouds had scattered, and the moon was rising. Time for them to be on their way.

He reached into one of the saddlebags, pulled out a bundle of dark red cloth and tossed it onto the bench beside Jerusa. "I expect you'll wish something more serviceable for traveling. No doubt this is more common than you're accustomed to, but there's little place for silk and lace on the road."

She looked up sharply. "Where are we going?"

"I told you before. South."

"South," she repeated, the single word expressing all her fears and frustration. "South, and south, and south again! Can't you tell me *anything?*"

He watched her evenly. "Not about our destination, no."

She snatched up the bundled clothing and hurled it back at him. "I'll keep my own clothing, thank you, rather than undress before you."

He caught the ball of clothing easily, as if she'd tossed it to him in play instead of in fury. "Did I ask that of you, *ma chérie?*"

She paused, thrown off-balance by his question. "Very well, then. Dare I ask for such a privacy? Would you trust me that far?"

His fingers tightened into the red fabric in his hands. "What reason have you given me to trust you at all?"

"Absolutely none," she said with more than a little pride. "Not that you've granted me much of the same courtesy, either."

He didn't bother to keep the edge of irritation from his voice. "Whether it pleases you or not, Miss Jerusa, ours will not be an acquaintance based on trust of any kind."

"I'd scarce even call this an acquaintance, considering that I'm your prisoner and you my gaoler," she answered stubbornly, lifting her chin a fraction higher. "To my mind 'acquaintance' implies something more honorable than that."

"There is, *ma chère,* nothing at all honorable about me." The wolfish look in his blue eyes would have daunted a missionary. "Or hadn't you noticed?"

Heaven preserve her, how could she have missed it? "Damn you, what is it that you want?"

"I told you that before, too. I want *you.*"

"Want me for what?" she demanded. "For this? To haul about the countryside, to degrade and disgrace for your amusement? To—to be your mistress?"

There, she'd said it, put words to her worst fear, and the expression on the Frenchman's handsome face did nothing to reassure her.

"You mean do I plan to force you, *ma chère?*" He came slowly to stand before her, his arms folded over his chest and his words an odd, musing threat. "For that's what it would be, wouldn't it? I certainly can't envision you, Miss Jerusa Sparhawk, the most renowned belle in your colony, cheerfully offering a man like me the pleasure of your lovely body."

"No," she repeated in a whisper, looking down to her hands clenched in her lap. *"No."*

Her dark, tangled hair fell forward like a veil around her face to hide her shame. With a shy eagerness she had anticipated her wedding night, and the moment when at last she would be free to love Tom as his wife. Once their betrothal had been announced, she had breathlessly allowed him all but the last freedom, so that it had been easy enough to imagine their lovemaking in the big bed in his father's Middletown house.

"No."

But there would be no bliss in having her maidenhead ravished by a stranger, no poetry or whisper-soft kisses in a bed with lavender-scented sheets, none of Tom's tenderness or gentle touches to ease her nervousness.

All because, worst of all, there would be no love.

He took another step closer, his boots rustling the straw. "So then, *ma chérie,*" he asked, "your modest question is, Did I steal you away with the intention of raping you?"

Though dreading his answer, still she nodded, afraid to trust her voice. She knew she must not weep or beg for mercy, no matter that her heart was pounding and her breath was tight in her chest from fear. He was so much stronger, his power coiled tight and ready as a cat's, that she knew full well he could do to her whatever he chose. Here, alone as she was, far from friends and family, how could it be otherwise?

Her head bowed, and every nerve on edge, she waited, and waited longer. When finally she could bear it no more and dared to raise her head, his face was bewilderingly impassive.

"If that is your question, Miss Sparhawk, then my answer, too, is no," he said quietly. "You're safe from me. The world is full enough of women who come to me willingly that I've never found reason or pleasure to do otherwise."

Stunned, Jerusa stared at him. "Then you don't—don't want that of me?"

"I said I wouldn't force you to lie with me, not that I didn't wish to." Again he held out the bundle of clothing to her. "Now go dress yourself, there beyond the horses, before I decide otherwise."

Her eyes still full of uncertainty, Jerusa slowly took the

rough clothing from him. "But why?" she asked. "Why else would you—"

"Because of who you are, *ma belle,*" he said. "Nothing else."

Clutching the clothing to her chest, she rose to her feet and nodded, as if his explanation made perfect sense. As she walked past him he saw that she held her head high as any duchess, heedless of the ripped stockings on her bare feet or the tattered skirt that fluttered around her ankles. No, he decided, not like a duchess but a Sparhawk, for in her mind that would be better.

He watched as she went to the far end of the barn, to the last stall, and turned her back to him. She was tall for a woman, and the rough deal stall shielded her only as high as her shoulders. In preparation she draped the rough skirt and bodice and the plain white stockings he'd given her over the side of the stall, and then bent over, out of Michel's sight, as she untied her petticoats and stepped out of them.

Out of his sight, perhaps, but not his imagination. With a clarity that was almost painful he envisioned the rounded shape of her hips as she dropped the layers of skirts, the long, shapely length of her legs as she shook them free of the crumpled linen.

Oh, he wanted her, that was true enough. *Sacristi,* he'd wanted her from the moment he'd seen her climb through the window into the garden. But forbidden fruit always seems sweetest, and Jerusa Sparhawk was a plump piece treacherously beyond his reach.

Morbleu, would he ever have agreed to this, given half a chance to refuse?

He thought of the last time he'd seen his mother before he'd sailed north to New England. The nurse he paid to watch her had tried to warn him at the door that Antoinette was unwell, but his mother had overheard the woman's whispers and hurled herself at Michel like a wild animal, her jealousy and madness once again swirling out of control.

*It took him until nightfall to calm her, his soft-voiced reas-
surances as crucial to her fragile peace as the opium draft she
could no longer live without. The doctor had come, too, with
his wig askew and the burgundy sauce from his interrupted
supper speckIng the front of his shirt. He had clucked and
watched as his leeches had grown fat and sleek on Antoinette's
pale forearm.*

*"You must heed the warnings, Monsieur Géricault," whis-
pered the doctor with dark gravity. "When your travels take
you away, she is inconsolable. Her passions can no longer be
contained by one caretaker alone, and I fear, monsieur, that
she will bring harm to others as well as herself. If you will but
consider the care of the holy sisters and their asylum—"*

*"It would kill her," said Michel softly, gently stroking his
mother's brow so her heavy-lidded eyes would flutter shut. "As
surely as if you put a pistol to her forehead, this place you
speak of would kill her."*

"But, monsieur, I must beg you—"

*"No," said Michel with unquestionable finality. "My
mother gave everything she had for me, and now that I can, I
will do the same for her."*

*Later, much later, when the doctor had left and the nurse
had gone to the apothecary for more of the opiate in the thick
blue bottle, when Antoinette's breathing had lost its ragged
desperation and her ravaged face had softened with sleep,
Michel had sat by her bed in the dark and told her all he would
do in her name to Gabriel Sparhawk and his sons.*

*And somehow Antoinette had struggled her way through the
haze of the drug and her own unsettled mind to hear him.
Weakly she had shifted her head toward his voice, her face made
more ghostly by the mosquito netting that shrouded her bed.*

*"The girl," she rasped. "You will take the girl who is to be
wed."*

Michel stopped, wondering if he'd imagined it.

"The Sparhawk girl, Michel. Bring the little virgin bride here to Martinique, to me."

He hadn't heard her voice sound this lucid in years. But what she asked—dear Lord, what sense did that make?

"What would you want with her, Maman?" he asked gently. *"It's the old man you want to destroy, the captain and his sons. Why waste your vengeance on some petulant little girl?"*

"Because you will rob her of her marriage and her happiness the same way her father stole mine from me." Her dark eyes glittered, though whether with tears or anticipation, Michel couldn't tell. *"What you do to the men will be for your father's honor, Michel. But what sorrow you bring to this girl will satisfy mine."*

Michel sighed, his interest quickening as he watched the girl lift her arms to twist her hair into a lopsided coil, the lantern's light caressing the rising curves of her white breasts exactly as he longed to do himself. Damnation, how would he survive the next weeks, maybe months, that they would be together?

He'd found it easy enough to agree when his mother's request had been abstract, a faceless young woman he knew only by her family's name and a distant, childhood memory. In a way it even made sense, for what better lure for the Sparhawk men than to carry off one of their women?

But Michel hadn't bargained on the effect that Jerusa Sparhawk herself, in the very real flesh and blood, was having on him. It wasn't just that he desired her—what man wouldn't?—but, far worse, he almost felt sorry for her. And from long, bitter experience, he knew that pity was one thing he could not afford.

Especially not for the favorite daughter of Gabriel Sparhawk.

Jerusa tied the waistband on the dark skirt, smoothing the linsey-woolsey over her hips. As the Frenchman had warned, the skirt and bodice were not stylish, but the sort of sturdy garments that a prosperous farmer's wife might wear to market. The bodice was untrimmed and loose, the square neckline modestly high, and the skirt fell straight without a flounce or ruffle to give it grace. But both were new and clean, which was more than could be said for her wedding gown.

She sighed forlornly as she looked one last time at the filthy, tattered remnants of what had been the most lavish gown ever made by a Newport seamstress. She thought of how carefully Mama and her maid had handled the fragile silk as they'd helped her dress, and against her will tears stung her eyes.

Swiftly she rubbed her sleeve against her nose, ordering herself not to cry, and reached around to undo the tight line of lacings at the back of her bodice. Twisting awkwardly, she struggled to find the end of the cording, only to discover it tied fast in a knot at the bottom eyelet. Of course the maid would have done that with the slippery silk, just to be sure. How would she have known that Jerusa would be forced to untie it herself?

Swearing under her breath, Jerusa bent her arms back and tried again. If she could only ease her thumb beneath the cord she might be able to work the knot free that way. If only—

"Let me help you," said the Frenchman softly behind her, and she gasped as she felt his hand on her shoulder to hold her still.

"I can do it myself," she said quickly, her face hot with humiliation as she tried to edge away. "Please, only a minute more and I'll be ready."

"I've watched you struggle, *chérie,* and I know you cannot. You're trussed up tighter than a stewing hen for the kettle."

She gasped again as she felt the edge of his knife slide beneath the lacings, the blade moving carefully up the length of her back as he snapped each crossing of the taut cord.

"My mistake, *mademoiselle,* and you have my apologies," he said with mock chivalry. "I should never have expected a lady to be forced to dress without her maid."

"I don't have a maid," she said stiffly, grateful that her

back was still toward him so he couldn't see her confusion. He was right, she wouldn't have been able to free herself without his help, but for him to volunteer to do so like this was an intimacy she didn't want to grant. "My mother does, but I don't. I don't need one."

With the strain of the lacing gone, the silk bodice slipped forward off her shoulders, and she raised her hands quickly to hold it over her breasts.

"You don't need these stays, either." With a gentleness that took her breath away, he ran his fingertips from the nape of her bare neck, over the sheer linen of her shift and down the length of her silk grosgrain stays to her waist. "I'll warrant your waist is narrow enough without them, *ma chère*. I'll cut them away, too, if you wish."

"No!" Wild-eyed, she spun around to face him, clutching the bodice to her breasts. Her stays were her whalebone armor, her last protection against him. "That is, I thank you for your assistance, but no lady would wish to be—to be free."

His smile was dark and suggestive enough to make her face hot. "No lady would be here in an empty barn with me, either."

A score of tart rebuttals died on her lips as she searched his face. His blue eyes were almost black, half-closed as he met her gaze, the twist of his lips at once wry and very, very charming.

She'd spent all her life in the company of handsome men, and she'd believed there were few things left they could do to surprise or unsettle her. So why, then, did a single smile and an illicit caress from this one leave her feeling as breathless and blushing as this? He had kidnapped her and threatened to kill her, but this other, bewildering side of him and her own strange response frightened her most of all.

She swallowed, struggling to regain her composure. "As you say, no lady would be alone here with you or any other man. But you brought me here against my will and choice, and that changes everything."

"Does it, *ma petite?*" He reached out to brush away a single lock of hair that had fallen across her forehead.

Still clutching the bodice, Jerusa couldn't shove away his hand as she wanted. Instead she jerked backward and, to her horror, into the rough deals of the barn wall. He didn't move closer. He didn't have to, not so long as that same teasing, infernal smile played upon his lips to agitate her more than any other man she'd ever met. Dear Almighty, how had she let herself be cornered like this?

"You said I was safe with you," she said raggedly. "You said you wouldn't force me."

"Tell me, Jerusa," he said, his voice scarce more than a coaxing whisper. "Am I forcing you now?"

"I don't even know your name!"

"It's Michel. Michel Géricault. It would please me if you'd say it."

"I don't see why I must do—"

"Say it, *ma chérie.* I wish to hear it on your lips."

Unconsciously she moistened her lips with the pink tip of her tongue, and he thought of how much more than his name he wished to be there. Was she as aware as he was of the current of excitement running between them? Fear alone might have parted her lips and flushed her cheeks so temptingly, but he was willing to wager it was more than that.

Much more.

"Say it, Jerusa. Say my name."

Her eyes widened and she took a breath that was almost a gasp. "Michael Jericho."

"Nay, pretty Jerusa, say it not like an Englishwoman but a French one, instead." What the devil was making him do this to her, anyway? *Morbleu,* why was he doing it to *himself?* "You can, you know, if you try."

She shook her head. "I can't. Father wished me to learn French, but I've no gift for it."

"Merely the wrong teacher. Together we'll do our best to discover your gift and make your *papa* proud. Now try again, Jerusa. Michel Géricault. Softly now, with none of your English brittleness."

She swallowed again, and he watched the little convulsion along her white throat. "Michel Géricault."

"Perfection, *ma chérie!*" He smiled indulgently, the way a satisfied tutor might. "Do you think your *papa* would know my name when he hears it from you?"

"Does my father know you?" she asked breathlessly, so obviously reaching for a hope that was bound to be disappointed. "Is that why you've done this? My brothers and their friends are forever playing elaborate tricks and pranks on one another. Are you doing something in that fashion to my father? I've never heard him speak of you, but then, I don't know all his acquaintances, particularly since you're not from Newport."

Tricks and pranks! *Morbleu,* if it were only that simple!

"I doubt your father even knows I exist," he said softly, turning away to let her finish dressing. "I wished to be sure, that is all. But he'll learn my name soon enough, my dear Jerusa. Soon enough for us both."

They rode for the rest of the night, keeping to roads that followed the coast and were often little better than glorified paths, the remnants of the trails of long-gone Indians. The land on either side was often wild, unplowed pasture used for grazing and little else, dotted with clumps of rocky boulders and gnarled scrub pines, bent low by the wind.

They saw no one, and no one saw them. Though the moon lit their way, Michel kept the pace slow to spare both the horses and Jerusa. She didn't complain—in fact she'd spoken no more than a dozen words to him since they'd left the barn— but he noted with concern the way her shoulders sagged and her head drooped, and how too often she seemed to sway in the saddle from weariness. When they stopped to rest she was too tired to refuse his offer of help, and let him ease her to the ground without the protest he'd expected.

The first time he'd been wary, wondering if this was another ploy to throw him off his guard, but her exhaustion and despair were real enough. For all her spirit he had to remind himself that she was gently bred, and grieving, too, over what she'd lost. He also told himself he wasn't being protective, only practical. He couldn't afford to have her fall seriously ill while they traveled. Perhaps he would be pushing her too hard to try to make Seabrook by week's end.

Yet as Jerusa rode the little mare behind Michel's gelding, it was her heart that felt the most pain, not her body. Oh, her head still ached from the chloroform and every muscle in her back and her legs protested over being curled across the un-accustomed sidesaddle, but all that was nothing compared to the shame of what she'd let happen in the barn.

Michel Géricault had been right, absolutely, appallingly right: he hadn't forced her to do anything. She'd stood as still as if she'd been carved from marble and let herself be drawn into the lazy, seductive spell he'd cast with his voice and eyes alone. Without flinching she had let him cut her free from her wedding gown and trace his hand along her spine with a famili-arity that should have belonged to her husband, not her kid-napper. Without a murmur of protest, she had followed his lead, and obediently—even eagerly—recited his French name, as if it were only one more incantation in his unearthly litany.

She hadn't fought and she hadn't tried to escape beyond the single, pointless attempt. She hadn't even boxed his ears the way she'd done to other young men who hadn't dared half as much. And with her compliance she had betrayed not only Tom but her family's honor, as well.

She stared numbly at the Frenchman's back before her, the broad shoulders that tapered to a narrow waist and the dull gold of his queue, gleaming in the moonlight against his dark blue coat. If he had been just one more handsome man flirting with her, she could have tossed her head and walked away. She should have done it already, for every step the little mare took was another away from Newport.

She glanced back over her shoulder in the direction they'd come, and her fingers twisted nervously in the worn leather of her reins. She *could* do it. He didn't have her bound or tied to the saddle. She'd simply have to pick her best chance, that was all. Eventually they'd have to meet with other people, and then she'd be gone in an instant.

Not that she had a choice. Either she escaped, or she'd lose her soul along with her freedom.

Dear Lord, but she was tired….

"We'll stop here for now," said Michel, swinging easily from his horse. They were in a small copse of poplar trees sheltered against a rocky hillside, and the stream that ran beneath the tall grass was fresh, not tidal. "I doubt we'll find better, and besides, it's almost dawn."

She was asleep before he'd finished with the horses, curled on her side with the blanket wrapped tightly around her like a woolen cocoon. Asleep, with her face finally relaxed and her hair simply braided, she looked achingly young. For a long time Michel lay beside her and watched as the rising sun bathed her cheeks with rosy warmth, and he wondered how a man without a conscience could still feel so damned guilty.

He wasn't sure when he, too, finally slept, but he knew the exact instant he woke. The cold steel of the rifle's barrel against his temple made that easy.

"On your feet, you rascal," said the voice at the other end of the rifle. "On your feet, I say, or I'll shoot you where you lie."

Chapter Five

Jerusa's eyes flew open at the sound of the strange man's voice. This time she was instantly awake, shoving herself free of the blanket as she pushed herself up from the damp grass.

A man in rough homespun with a turkey feather thrust through the brim of his hat was holding his musket over Michel, the dull steel barrel only inches from his cheek. This was her chance, the opportunity she'd gone to sleep praying for, and eagerly she clambered to her feet, brushing the dew from her skirts.

"Not so fast, ye little hussy," said a voice behind her, and she spun around to see another, younger man with his musket pointed at her. "Ye wouldn't think we'd take the cockerel an' let the hen fly free, would ye?"

"But you don't understand," she said, favoring him with the most winning smile she could as she tried to smooth back her tousled hair. "You've done me a vastly great favor. You've rescued me, you see. I don't wish to be with that man at all."

The first man guffawed, and she turned to smile at him, too. He was obviously the father of the younger man, for both shared the same bristly red hair and eyebrows so fair as to be nonexistent. Sheep farmers, guessed Jerusa disdainfully, both from the men's clothing and the land around them, which was too rugged for cultivation, and she wondered if they sold their wool or mutton to her father for export. Maybe they'd be impressed by his name; they certainly weren't by her smile alone.

"Mighty cozy ye seemed for not wishin' to be with the man," said the father, "nesting side by side with him like ye was."

Jerusa gasped. "Not by choice, I assure you!"

"Choice or not, I know what my eyes seen," he answered, leering. "And there weren't much to mistake about what I saw."

"Not about that, no, but there does appear to be some confusion for you to be accosting us in this manner." Michel sighed, slowly raising himself to a sitting position with deliberate care so as not to startle the man with the musket into firing. "Or is it the custom in this region to waken travelers at gunpoint?"

"I'll do what I damn well please with those that cross my land," declared the older man promptly. "'Specially them that does it armed themselves."

"Ah, my pistol." Michel glanced down ruefully at the gun on the blanket beside him, almost as if he were seeing it for the first time. "But since when is a man not allowed to protect himself and his wife alone on the road?"

"Your *wife?*" Jerusa stared at Michel, stunned. "I'll thank you not to call me any such thing!"

"Hold yer tongue, mistress, and let yer husband speak!" ordered the older man sternly.

"But he's not—"

"I told you to shut yer mouth, woman, or I'll shut it for ye!" While Jerusa sputtered in relative silence, the man shook his head with pity for Michel. "There's nothing worse than a yammering shrew who don't know her place. But then, I warrant I don't have to tell ye that, sir, do I now?"

"Indeed you don't." Sorrowfully Michel, too, shook his head. "I was lured to wed her by her pretty face and her father's prettier purse, and now I'll pay until she nags me to my grave."

"'Lured' to wed me? *Me?*" exclaimed Jerusa. She knew exactly what he was doing, trying to play on the other man's sympathy as a kind of woe-is-me, beleaguered husband so he'd put down his gun, but still she didn't care for it one bit. *She* was the prisoner. The two men should be feeling sorry for *her.* "Since when did I lure you to do anything? Why, when I—"

"Hush now, dearest, and be quiet for this good man, if not for me." Michel smiled sadly at the man at the other end of the gun. "You can see why we keep to the back roads. In a tavern or inn, this sorry excuse for a wife thinks nothing of shaming me before an entire company. By the by, I'm Michael Geary."

"Oh, 'Michael Geary' indeed!" said Jerusa indignantly. "I'll Michael Geary you!"

With her fists clenched she charged toward Michel, intent on doing him the kind of harm she'd learned from having three brothers. How dare Michel do this to her, twisting around everything she said in the worst possible way?

But she hadn't taken two steps before the young man dipped the barrel of his musket across her shins, tangling it in her skirts so that she stumbled and nearly fell.

"There now, that'll teach ye to mind yer man," he said smugly as Jerusa glared at him. "Pa, too, considering as how he likewise told ye to stop yer scolding. My ma knows her place proper."

Jerusa began to answer, then stopped. She wasn't getting anywhere with these men, but perhaps the mother might be more willing to listen. Might, that is, if the poor woman weren't so thoroughly cowed by her dreadful excuse for a husband.

And the red-haired man was dreadful, a man who had made absolutely no attempt to help her when she stumbled, said not a word to chide his son for his treatment toward a lady, and who even now was heaping a shovelful of salt onto her wounded pride by slinging his musket over his shoulder and reaching his hand out to help Michel—*Michel!*—to his feet.

"The name's Faulk, sir," he said with enough respect to show that he'd swallowed Michel's ruse. "Abraham Faulk, sir, at your service, and that be Isaac. Bow proper to the gentleman, lad."

"My pleasure, Mr. Faulk." Michel shook the man's hand with just the right amount of friendliness and distance to prove that he was in fact a gentleman, but a good-natured one at that. An *English* gentleman, noted Jerusa glumly; now, when Michel's little slips into French could be most useful to her, he was speaking better English than King George himself.

In return, Faulk began bowing and grinning as if he were the one being honored. "Ye said ye was only guarding yerself with the pistol, sir, and so was I with my musket," he said apologetically. "These days I must be careful to protect my land and my flocks from rascals and vagabonds."

"No offense taken, Faulk, none at all. It's the way of the world, and a man must be careful." Unchallenged now, Michel bent to pick up his pistol and tuck it back in his belt. As he rose he glanced pointedly at Jerusa, enough to fan her anger afresh. "You have to guard what you hold dear."

Faulk nodded vigorously. "Ye shall come 'round to the house now, won't you, Mr. Geary?" he asked eagerly. "Just to prove there be no hard feelings? A taste of cider, or rum, if ye are of a mind?"

"How civil of you! We'd be honored, my wife and I both," said Michel warmly, "and if you can spare a handful of oats for the horses, why, they'd thank you, too."

Jerusa's eyes narrowed with suspicion. He had his gun back and they were free to go on their way. Why, then, would he wish to sup cider with a sheep farmer?

"A quarter hour or so, Mr. Faulk," continued Michel, "and then I fear we must be on our way. But a quarter hour would be deuced pleasant."

Jerusa watched how Faulk beamed at the Frenchman, her resentment simmering. She'd never met a man with such a gift for cozening and out-and-out lying. And charm: sweet Almighty, this Michel, or Michael, or whatever his name really was, could sell it from a wagon on market day. No wonder she'd trusted him in her mother's garden.

As if he read her thoughts, he turned and smiled, his eyes as clear and open as his conscience had no right to be, and his hand held out graciously to her. "Come along, dearest, we'll accept Mr. Faulk's hospitality before we're off again."

Dearest! Briefly Jerusa considered spitting on him, or at least calling him the worst name she knew.

"Now, sweetheart. We don't wish to keep Mrs. Faulk waiting on your fancy, do we?" Michel's smile faded a degree as an unspoken warning flickered in his eyes for Jerusa alone. If she was mentally calling him every foul word she could imagine, then she was quite sure from the expression in those blue eyes that he was thinking not a whit better of her.

But it was the reminder of Mrs. Faulk, not that silent warning, that made Jerusa force herself to smile and take Michel's hand. Surely the other woman would understand her plight. Soon, very soon, she'd be on her way home, and her smile became artlessly genuine.

She'd seen countless houses like the Faulks', a style that was common in the colony: a gray stone wall at one end, with the chimney and fireplace, and the other three walls covered by weather-silvered clapboard. The few windows were small and old-fashioned with tiny diamond-shaped panes and no shutters, and the battened door was so stout that it might have done service against King Philip's savages a hundred years before.

Though Jerusa had seen such houses all her life, she'd only seen them from a distance, usually from the window of her parents' carriage, and while Michel and Isaac led the horses toward the barnyard, she eagerly followed Mr. Faulk through the open door of the little house. On the threshold she paused for her eyes to grow accustomed to the murkiness, for while it was still afternoon out-of-doors, the sun scarcely penetrated inside the house, and there was little light beyond what filtered through the small-paned windows and the glow from the embers in the fireplace. The entire first floor seemed to be only this single room, a parlor, kitchen and bedchamber combined into one, with the sagging, curtainless bedstead in the far corner.

"On yer feet, Bess, we've guests," ordered Faulk sharply. "This be Mistress Geary, and she and her husband be stopping here on their journey to—where'd ye say yer was bound, mistress?"

"South," said Jerusa faintly. Did the house really smell so much like the yard outside, or was it her own clothing that still carried the scent of the barn where she'd spent last night?

"South," repeated Faulk with as much relish as if Jerusa had said London. "Now offer the lady some of yer cider, Bess, and be quick about it."

"Ah, don't ye be giving me orders, Abraham, 'specially not before a stranger." The woman came forward from where she'd been bending over a pot on the fire, wiping her hands on her apron. She was small and round, and clenched in her teeth was a white clay pipe, whose bowl glowed bright before her cheek. "Good day to ye, Mistress Geary, and pleased I am to have ye in my home."

"Thank you, Mrs. Faulk," said Jerusa quickly. "But before, uh, Mr. Geary joins us, there's something I must say to you alone that—"

"Ah, do yer husband be as full of his own wind and worth as mine, then?" The other woman laughed merrily, the embers in her pipe bobbing. "Ordering ye not to speak less'n it pleases him?"

Faulk snorted. "As it should be, Bess."

"And as it never will be," said Bess tartly, "least not in this house, Abraham!"

"Please, Mrs. Faulk, a word—"

"Pray, mistress, be seated before ye begin, and I'll fetch ye a cup of my own cider. Some say it's the best in this county or the next."

Swiftly Jerusa perched on one corner of a bench before the trestle table. "Please, Mrs. Faulk, there's something I would say to you that I'd rather Mr. Geary didn't hear. You see, I'm not—"

"Not what, sweetheart?" asked Michel as his shadow filled the doorway. "You know we've no secrets between us. What, then, did you wish to tell these good people?"

Jerusa only stared at Michel in rebellious silence. She still meant to tell the Faulks who she was, but now she'd have to do it before him, as well.

Not that Michel seemed the least bit discomfited, continuing on as if nothing were amiss. "I'm honored, Mrs. Faulk, to be welcome in your home," he said, gallantly bowing over the woman's hand as she held Jerusa's cider with the other. "How fortuitous that your husband came upon us!"

Mrs. Faulk giggled and simpered, and Jerusa watched with disgust. Oh, the Frenchman was handsome enough, but not so fair as to merit that degree of foolishness.

"Oh, Abraham prowls our land like a wolf himself," said Mrs. Faulk as, at last, she took back her fingers. "He must, ye know, to guard the flocks. Why, at market yesterday he heard of a man north of here lost a dozen prime ewes to thieves!"

"Nay, Bess, but that's not the best tale I brought home to ye!" said Faulk eagerly as he put a battered pewter tankard of rum and water into Michel's hand. "Tell them what I told ye first!"

"Oh, ye mean about the heiress what jilted her bridegroom!" The pipe in Mrs. Faulk's mouth bounced more fiercely. "Ye might not have heard this, ye being travelers, but two days ago a lass from one of the best families in Newport changed her mind and left her poor groom and half the town waiting alone before the minister! Jilted the man cold, she did, without leaving one word to comfort him."

"That's not true!" cried Jerusa, leaping to her feet. "I didn't jilt him, I swear!"

The only sound in the room was the pop and hiss of the fire.

Mrs. Faulk cleared her throat. "Not to shame ye, Mistress Geary," she said gently, "but ye must be mistaken. This girl we be speaking of is gentry, Captain Gabriel Sparhawk's daughter."

Faulk glanced uneasily from Michel to Jerusa. "True enough, mistress. I've seen Miss Sparhawk once with my own eyes, riding through the streets in Newport in an open carriage, a wonderfully proud beauty covered with pearls and plumes, like a very princess. And though you be a fine enough lady, mistress, ye don't be her."

"But I *am* her!" cried Jerusa indignantly. She'd never considered that they'd doubt who she was. "You must believe me because it's true! I couldn't possibly have jilted poor Tom the way you said, because I was kidnapped instead, carried away from my own house by that man!"

She swung around to point at Michel, half expecting him to turn and flee. What else could a man as low as a kidnapper do?

But Michel didn't run away. He didn't even look guilty. Instead, with a low sigh, he set the tankard with the rum on the table beside him and came to stand before Jerusa, his arms folded across his chest.

"Sweetheart, please," he said softly. "You promised."

"I never promised you anything!" answered Jerusa scornfully. "You're a villain, a rogue, a kidnapper, and I hope they hang you for all the grief you've brought my family!"

He sighed again, all resignation and patient sorrow. "My dear, the Sparhawks are not your family. Your parents live in

Charlestown, not Newport, and you can't have jilted your bride-groom because you've been wed to me these last three years."

"That's not true, none of it!" Fighting her panic, Jerusa turned from Michel to the worried, fearful faces of the Faulks. "Surely you'll believe me and take me back home! You must believe me! This man isn't my husband. He isn't even Mr. Geary!"

"Be easy now, mistress," said Mrs. Faulk cautiously. "Faith, I'd never have told ye the scandal if I'd known it would strike ye like this."

"But I *am* Jerusa Sparhawk!" Jerusa pressed her hands to her cheeks, desperate for the words that would make them believe her. Without the silk gowns and jewelry that had made such an impression on Faulk, words were all she had. "Gabriel Sparhawk's my father and Mariah Sparhawk's my mother. You've only to look at me to know it's true! I was born on the twelfth of April in 1750, the same day as my twin brother Josh, and I've two older brothers and two younger sisters besides, and, oh, everyone in Newport would know me. Everyone!"

Yet one look at the Faulks' faces told her they didn't.

"Please, please believe me!" she pleaded. "I need your help to return to my family!"

"I didn't hear nothing about a kidnapping," said Faulk with exaggerated care, staring somewhere past Jerusa's shoulder to avoid meeting her gaze. "Only that the bridegroom hisself swore he'd been left, and that that be the end of the match for him."

"Tom said that?" Jerusa shook her head, unable to accept such blasphemy. Even in nightmares, life didn't take such dreadful twists, and she felt herself sliding helplessly into the depths of her fear. "No, not my darling Tom! I love him, and he loves me. You must be wrong. You *must* be!"

"She's unsettled, that's all," explained Michel with a sorrow so genuine it left Jerusa speechless. There was a warmth to his eyes, a tenderness softening his hard-edged face that seemed too heartfelt to be playacting, and in spite of everything else he'd done to her, she felt the color warm her cheeks. She could, in that instant, almost believe he cared for her. Yet how could he be so sympathetic when all of what he said were lies?

"Most days she's perfectly well," he continued gently, "but on others, she believes herself someone else entirely. It will pass. It always does. Yet you can see now why I choose not to take the poor lass into public houses."

"Oh, God bless ye, Mr. Geary," murmured Mrs. Faulk. "What a terrible burden she must be to ye!"

"But it's not true," whispered Jerusa hoarsely. "God help me, none of what he says is true!"

Protectively Faulk rested his hands on his own wife's shoulders. "Is there aught we can do to help ye, Mr. Geary? Ropes or such to control her rages?"

Michel shook his head. "Thank you, no. She'll be well enough when there's just the two of us again. Once we're on our way, the breezes will help dispel her tempers, and she'll be meek as a new lamb."

He stepped forward and laid his hands on Jerusa's shoulders, an empty mockery of Faulk's own gesture. "Isn't that true, sweetheart? Shouldn't we be leaving these good people so you can feel better?"

Jerusa stiffened beneath his touch, but the fight was gone from her now. No wonder the Faulks believed him instead of her; he made sense, and she didn't. It wasn't just the plain clothing Michel had given her that made her seem less the "gentry" that Faulk had expected. It was instead the role Michel had chosen to play for himself, that of her caring, concerned husband, that made every word she'd said ring so false.

And even worse was realizing that he would do it again if she dared try to seek help from another.

"You will come with me now, won't you, dearest?" he said gently.

"Very well," she said, her voice so low that the Faulks

wouldn't hear her bitterness. She was still Michel's prisoner, true, but at least by accepting his will in this she could deprive him of the pleasure of having to carry her forcibly from the house. "Decide what you please, and I shall follow."

The moon was nearly risen before Michel stopped to rest the horses. Since they'd left the Faulks' farm, Jerusa had said not a word to him, and the silence between them had grown deeper and more uncomfortable with every step.

He tried to tell himself it was better this way. What was the point of listening to her ill-timed attempts at conversation or deflecting yet again the same questions she insisted on asking, which he'd no intention of answering? She was his prisoner, his hostage, his bait, his enemy. That she was also quite beautiful must be inconsequential. She was neither his friend nor his lover, and the sooner he remembered that and stopped thinking of her as a woman, the better for them both.

Easy to resolve, impossible to do. How could he ignore how neatly his hands fit around her waist as he helped her from her horse, or the way her scent filled his senses as she brushed against him? On her, even the unassuming clothing he'd bought seemed to accentuate the ripe, full curves of her body, and he couldn't forget the glimpse he'd had of her breasts, firm and lush, above her stays when he'd cut her from her tattered wedding gown. *Mordieu,* why was nothing easy where this woman was involved?

He watched her as she returned from the bushes, her eyes carefully downcast to avoid meeting his. At least this way he wouldn't have to pretend he wasn't watching her. In the moonlight her face was pale, her hair, in its loosened braid, a dark cloud around her shoulders. Maybe it was seeing her so often by moonlight that had unsettled him this badly.

Unsettled: that was how he'd described her to the Faulks, the same term the Parisian doctor from Port Royal preferred. What devil had put such a word into his mouth last night, anyway?

He held out a flask he'd taken from the horse's pack. "Mrs. Faulk's cider," he explained as she stopped before him. "She sent it along especially for you."

Jerusa glanced at the flask, reminded again of how easily he'd thwarted her at the farm. She didn't want the cider; she didn't want to take anything from him.

"Go ahead, *ma chérie*," he said, irritated by her silence. He'd expected her to be angry for what he'd done, but she'd no right to turn sullen. "I swear it's not poisoned. Not by me, or by Mrs. Faulk."

"A dubious recommendation," murmured Jerusa. Though the Frenchman's eyes were masked by the shadow from his hat, there was no mistaking his mood, surly and ill-humored. He hadn't shaved since they'd left Newport, and the dark stubble around his jaw only made him look less like the gentleman he'd pretended to be. "No doubt she thought her celebrated cider might benefit a poor, pitiful mad creature like myself."

"She believed you would enjoy it." Inwardly he winced at her words, shamed. He had never before used madness as a pretense, and he didn't know what had made him do it now. To draw from his own mother's distress to save a useless chit like this one, the daughter of Gabriel Sparhawk—*morbleu,* what had he been thinking?

"Indeed." Finally she took the flask, carefully avoiding touching his fingers, and swept back her hair from her forehead as she briefly lifted the flask to her lips to drink. "Then that was all Mrs. Faulk should have believed."

He shrugged. "She believed what she wished."

"What *you* wished, you mean," said Jerusa tartly. "There's a difference."

His mouth curved into a mocking smile. "All your life you've had everything your own way, haven't you, Miss Jerusa? How instructive for you to have it otherwise!"

She dismissed his question by ignoring it. "You don't care

for my questions, Monsieur Géricault," she said with icy politeness, "but can you please tell me why you told them what you did about me?"

"You left me no choice."

"No choice," she repeated incredulously. "Wasn't it bad enough to claim I was your wife without insisting I was witless, too?"

His jaw tightened. He wasn't accustomed to explaining his actions to anyone. It was much of the reason he'd been so successful. At least until now.

She sighed impatiently. "They were going to let us go free anyway. There was absolutely no reason for us to go traipsing back to their home. Except, of course, your great love for cider."

She shoved the flask back against his chest and turned away. Swiftly he seized her arm and jerked her back around to face him.

"I may not like your questions, *ma petite folle,* but you'll like my answers even less," he said, holding her fast as she tried to break free. "Do you flatter yourself to think I'd truly want you for my wife? But as my *wife,* you also have my protection. Didn't you notice how those men left you alone once I said you were a respectable woman? What do you think they would have done to you otherwise?"

"They were farmers, not brigands!"

"They were men, *chère.*"

"They would not have dared a thing when they learned who I was!" She struggled again, uneasily aware of the same odd sensations his touch had caused that first night in the barn. No matter how much he claimed to be her protector, she sensed that the darkness hiding within him could be infinitely more dangerous.

"But they didn't believe you, *ma chérie.* The Sparhawks are gentry. Even the Faulks know that, and only a madwoman would insist otherwise. I merely added to what you'd already begun."

Damn him, he was right. She'd put the doubts in their minds

from her first outburst. And if Michel hadn't graced her with the feigned respectability of being his wife, the suggestive leers of the two Faulk men could easily enough have led to worse. Any woman who'd let herself sleep beside a man in an open field was asking for it.

But she wasn't just any woman. She was Jerusa Sparhawk, and ever since she'd been born that had been enough. More than enough, really. There wasn't a person in Newport who wouldn't recognize the Sparhawk name, and treat her accordingly.

But she wasn't in Newport any longer, and with a handful of words and a few sighs, this Frenchman had managed to strip her of her name, of who she was and what she was. If she couldn't be a Sparhawk, what, she wondered unhappily, would be left?

Michel frowned, wary of her sudden silence. It wasn't like her to stop when she was as angry as she'd been, and he didn't like surprises. Where his fingers grasped the fine bones of her wrist, he could feel how her pulse was racing, only one sign of the coiled tension he sensed in her body. *Sacristi,* he should recognize it: his own body had been hard from the instant he'd first touched her.

"And consider the knowledge you gained, *ma chère,*" he said, his voice low. "If we hadn't met Mrs. Faulk, you wouldn't have learned of your faithless lover."

She gasped, appalled that he'd taunt her about such a thing. She'd thought of little else while they'd ridden, and none of those thoughts had been comforting.

Michel pulled her another fraction closer. "You don't deny it, then?" he asked relentlessly. "You believe what they said?"

"Why shouldn't I?" she cried as the tears burned in her eyes. "Unlike you, the Faulks had no reason to lie."

Michel, of course, had believed the story at once, remembering Carberry as a vain, self-centered fool. But he hadn't thought she'd accept it, too. A girl who'd had the world handed to her would expect the same perfection in her husband, and be blind to his faults if his fortune was substantial enough. From the way she'd defended Carberry to the Faulks, he'd thought she was.

Michel wouldn't have mentioned it otherwise. He was a hard man, a ruthless man when necessary, but he'd never considered himself a cruel one, and what he'd said to her had been heartless.

Morbleu, *Géricault, since when have you needed a heart?*

"You cannot understand," Jerusa was saying, her voice quaking perilously with emotion. "I *loved* Tom, and I thought he loved me more than anything. I thought he would love me forever. I thought—I thought—"

She broke off, closing her eyes as she bowed her head. He remembered how radiantly joyful she'd been before her wedding, how she'd brought him into her circle of happiness with a single, open smile, and he wondered if she'd ever smile like that again.

"Ah, *ma bien-aimée*," he said softly, "the man was unworthy."

"I'm not your wretched *bien-aimée!*" she cried, and a single convulsive sob racked her. "I'm not anyone's beloved!"

In her misery she twisted away from him, and, for the first time, the moonlight shone full on her anguish. He had seen this same look on her face before, when she'd finally realized the Faulks weren't going to accept her farfetched claim. Without the protection of her Sparhawk arrogance, she'd been lost and achingly vulnerable, and her eyes reflected the frightening depths of her desperation, mutely beseeching.

Only one other woman had ever looked to him for help like that....

He had answered Jerusa Sparhawk in the only way he knew how, using the words of compassion and excuses, the careful, quiet words to calm an unquiet mind.

The same way he did with his mother, his poor, lost *Maman*, who'd asked for nothing more than that he carry her vengeance to the family who'd destroyed her own life and love. Jerusa's family.

And because *Maman* wished it, Jerusa Sparhawk would be first.

No, *must* be first.

Michel released her arm, and she sank to her knees and buried her face and her tears in her hands. For his mother's sake, he knew he must leave the girl where she was, leave her to her misery and tears and the dew that would soak her skirts. The only son of Christian Deveaux would turn his back on her without another thought, except, perhaps, to consider how exceptionally easily he'd managed to crush his enemy's spirit.

But God help him, he couldn't do it. There was too much sorrow in her to bear alone, too much pain in her bowed, grief-stricken body. He'd fail his parents with his weakness, but he couldn't leave her like this.

Without a word, he bent to raise her back to her feet, gently turning her cheek against his chest, and held her, just held her, until her sobbing stopped and her breathing grew still.

And when at last she stood quietly in his arms, he prayed to God for forgiveness.

Chapter Six

Josh had barely climbed over the side of the Massachusetts sloop before he began firing questions at her captain.

"You're bound north from the sugar islands, aren't you?" he asked, his urgency turning a simple question into a demand. "What port, sir? Have you spoke any other vessels on your journey?"

"Stay a minute, Cap'n Sparhawk," said Captain Harris irritably. "You're racin' onward like the devil himself's licking at your coattails."

"He may well be." Impatiently Josh touched the guard of the cutlass at his waist. He wasn't accustomed to its weight there any more than he was to the unfamiliar bulkiness of the pistols beneath his coat, but his father had insisted that he take no chances. "I'm searching for a lady who's in great peril, Captain. Some bastard stole her bold as brass from her parents' house minutes before she was to wed, and I've reason to believe she was taken south, to one of the French islands."

"A stolen bride!" Harris whistled low under his breath, and the crew members around him strained their ears to hear more. "Sounds like the very stuff of ballads and plays, don't it?"

"Damn it, Harris, this isn't some bloody drinking song!" It

was frustration that made his temper so short, and Josh knew from the surprise on the other man's face that he'd spoken too sharply. The same thing had happened with the other three northbound ships he'd stopped and boarded when their captains had told him they'd seen no sign of either an English lady or a Frenchman.

But Josh couldn't help it. In the days since Jerusa had disappeared and before he'd sailed from Newport in the *Tiger,* there'd been no clue, no word from whoever had her, beyond that first tantalizing scrap of paper with the black *fleur de lis.*

Yet worst of all was how ready people—the same people who'd been his family's friends and associates for years—had been to believe Carberry's accusations instead of the truth. The man's battered face had brought him sympathy, not scorn, and while Josh didn't regret thrashing Carberry as he'd deserved, he would admit now that it wasn't the wisest thing he could have done.

If Josh had begun this journey determined only to rescue his sister, because of Carberry he now was forced to save his family's honor, as well. No one believed that Jerusa had been kidnapped. She had always been too pretty, too sought after, too envied for the gossips to leave her reputation alone once she had vanished. There were whispers of her running off with a wealthy young man from Boston, and a second tale involving a besotted, married shipmaster from Virginia. Whichever version, Jerusa had always left willingly, with her family's knowledge and consent. After all, this was New England, not Scotland in the time of Queen Bess, and abducting ladies from their weddings simply did not happen here.

But then, unlike Joshua, none of the gossips had seen his mother weeping in the doorway to his sister's empty bedchamber, or heard how his father's voice broke when he prayed for Jerusa's safe return during grace before supper. Nor had any of them stared out at the endless sea the way that he had, tormented by the dread that his sister, his twin, the other half of himself, was forever beyond his reach.

Yet he would know if Jerusa had come to harm. Somehow he would sense it deep inside the soul they'd once shared. Somehow...

"The Caribbean is a mighty big place, Cap'n Sparhawk," Harris was saying, scratching the back of his neck beneath his queue, "and there's a world of fine young women scattered about the islands there. How, then, would I know your kidnapped lady if I came upon her?"

"You'll know her," said Josh, his smile grim. "She's my sister, and she's my twin."

Chapter Seven

"I'm sorry, Mr. Géricault," called Jerusa, drawing her mare to a halt, "but I'm afraid we shall have to stop for today."

Frowning, Michel wheeled his gelding about. If he hadn't taken pity on her near the stream, she never would have dared to make this request now.

"That's for me to decide, *Miss* Sparhawk, not you," he said curtly, "and I say we still have farther to go before we stop."

"I'm not the one who's asking." Jerusa sighed, not missing the inflection he'd put on her name. She should never have allowed herself to be so shamelessly weak before him, weeping until he'd felt forced to comfort her. But what had been worse was that his arms around her had seemed so *right*, full of solace and understanding, as if he himself weren't the source of the same sorrow that he wished to ease. "It's my mare. She's pulling as if she's turning lame."

Before he could order her to ride on anyway, Jerusa slid from the saddle to the ground, her legs stiff and clumsy from the long ride. Thankful that her face was turned from Michel's critical eye, she winced and held tightly to the saddle for support as the blood rushed and tingled once again through her legs. She had always enjoyed riding before, but after the past three days she hoped she'd never see a saddle again.

Murmuring, she stroked the animal's velvety nose to reassure her before she reached down to lift the mare's right foreleg. "Though I can't see properly without a light, I think she must have picked up a stone."

"I'd no idea you were so familiar with stable-yard affairs, *ma chère,*" said Michel dryly, watching her obvious ease with the horse. Unexpected though it was, the fact that she was sensitive to the animal's needs secretly pleased him, her small, elegant hands moving so gently along the mare's fetlock to her hoof. "And here I've been tending the beasts all by myself."

"As children, if we wished to ride, Father insisted we look after the horses, too." Carefully she lowered the horse's hoof and stood upright, flipping her braid back over her shoulder as she looked at Michel over her saddle. He still hadn't dismounted, but then, he hadn't ordered her back on the mare, either. "Though Father's a sailor at heart, he does have an eye for a good Narraganset pacer, and the stable at Crescent Hill's generally full. When Josh and I were young, you know, he and I always had matching ponies."

"Pretty, privileged children on their ponies!" exclaimed Michel with withering sarcasm. It wasn't just the matching ponies themselves, but how they represented an entire blissful childhood that he'd never known. He'd first gone to sea with a drunken privateer when he was eight, and learned to kill to save himself before he'd turned ten. "How charming the effect must have been! That would, of course, have been during the summers you spent at Crescent Hill?"

Reluctantly she nodded, disconcerted again by how much he seemed to know of her family's life. "You don't exactly ride like a farmer boy tossed on the back of his father's plow horse, either," she said defensively. "You sit like a gentleman."

"I do many things *like* a gentleman, my dear Jerusa, but that doesn't mean I am one." He swung down from his horse, holding the reins in his hand as he walked toward her. "Is she really lame, then?"

"Nothing that a few hours' rest likely won't cure."

Michel swore under his breath. Why couldn't the mare have lasted one more night? Though the horizon was just beginning to gray with the light of false dawn, he had counted on riding at least for another hour. By his reckoning, they had one more night of traveling before they finally reached Seabrook and, God willing, Gilles Rochet and his sloop.

Unaware of his thoughts, Jerusa waved her hand in the direction they'd come. "I thought I saw a house there to the north when—"

"No, *chérie*, no houses," he said curtly. "I, for one, have no wish to repeat our performance with the Faulks."

Self-consciously she looked at the toes of her shoes. It wasn't what had happened at the Faulks' that she wished to avoid again, but what had followed. "I don't think that would be a problem, Mr. Géricault. The house I meant looked to be a ruin. Against the sky the chimney looked broken-down, and part of the roof gone. From the hurricane two years ago, maybe, or a fire, I don't know. But at least there'd still be a well, and maybe an orchard or garden."

"Is that so." Michel leaned his elbow across the sidesaddle, watching her. She'd just said more to him in the last two minutes than in the last two days, and though he rather enjoyed the change, it still put him on his guard. "Then tell me, *ma chérie,* exactly how you plan to try to leave me from this delightful ruin of a cottage?"

"Leave you?" Jerusa repeated, her face growing warm at the accusation, which, this time, was unfounded. She wished they could return to talking about the horse instead.

"Yes, yes, leave." He sighed deeply, in a way that made her think again of what it had been like to rest her cheek against his chest. "I hadn't expected you to give up just yet, you know."

"Then you have more faith in me than I do myself. I have neither food nor water nor money, I'm in a place I don't know, where no one knows me, and my horse is lame. You might not have bound me with chains or cords, Mr. Géricault, but what you've done has been thorough enough."

His smile faded as he listened. Though the bitterness was still in her voice, something else had subtly altered between them. He couldn't tell exactly what, not yet, but the change was unmistakable.

"No more of this 'Mr. Géricault,' *ma chère*," he said softly as he stepped around the mare's head to come stand before Jerusa. "Call me Michel. Please."

She twisted her reins in her fingers, shaking her head. The distance she earned by using that "Mr." was small and fragile, but with him she felt she needed every last bit, and she was almost painfully aware of the dark, inexplicable currents of emotion swirling between them now.

She forced herself to look away and to watch instead how her mare had begun to graze, tugging at the long wild grass that grew alongside the path. They had stopped near an old stone wall that was overgrown with a tangled mass of honeysuckle, and the sweet, heady fragrance of the white-and-yellow blossoms filled the air like perfume.

Michel clucked, and the mare's ears pricked up as she eyed him quizzically. In spite of herself, Jerusa smiled and let her gaze follow the mare's to the Frenchman. He stood with his hat in his hand, the pose of a careless supplicant, his hair pale gold in the fading moonlight and his blue eyes almost black, a half smile playing about his lips that was meant to be shared. With a start, she realized she'd never smell honeysuckle again without thinking of Michel Géricault. Would he, she wondered, say the same of her?

Whatever are you thinking of, Jerusa Sparhawk? This man is your kidnapper, your enemy! He deserves no place at all in your thoughts, let alone in your heart! The minute you can you'll escape and leave him as far behind as possible. Remember that, Jerusa, and forget these silly musings about honeysuckle and blue eyes!

"Come," she said, all too aware of how strained her voice sounded as she gathered the mare's reins to lead her. "We can't dawdle in the road forever."

But Michel didn't move from her way. "Perhaps, *ma chère*," he began softly, his accent seductively more marked. "Perhaps you don't run away because you don't wish to."

From the way her eyes grew round, Michel knew he'd put into words what she'd secretly feared. A lucky guess. But then, so much of what had happened with her *was* lucky, at least for him, and he didn't mean just how easy their journey had been, either. She was blushing now, her face so rosy her discomfiture showed even in the moonlight. Somehow he'd never expected the belle of Newport to blush at all, but he was glad she did, and gladder still that he was the reason.

"Of course I wish to return to Newport," she said, struggling to sound as if she meant every word. "I want to go back to my poor parents, my home, my—"

"To your marriage to a faithless, fashionable popinjay?"

She frowned, toying with the reins. "Tom will be fine once I speak to him and explain everything."

"'Fine'?" Michel raised one mocking, skeptical brow. "That is what you wish in your husband? That he be *fine?*"

"Well, he will," said Jerusa defensively. "Tom's the man I love and the one I intend to marry. Oh, stop looking at me like that! It's simply not something you would understand!"

"True enough, *ma belle*. All I can do is keep you safe."

She glanced at him sharply, unsure of what he really meant, but he'd already turned away, leading his horse back in the direction they'd come, and leaving her no choice but to follow.

Michel was being possessive, that was all, just like any

good gaoler would be with his prisoner. What else could he have meant by keeping her safe? Yet still her mind fussed and worked over the doubt he'd planted. The only thing Tom would ever fight to keep safe would be the front of his shirt, and then the enemy would be no more formidable than a glass of red wine. He certainly didn't seem eager to come to her rescue, and that hurt more than she'd ever admit to the Frenchman. But that was what she'd always wanted, wasn't it? A gentleman of wit and ideas, not some rough man of action?

Wasn't it?

Michel, too, had seen the abandoned house earlier from the road. As they drew closer, picking their way through the overgrown path, the burned, blackened timbers that remained of the roof and the broken chimney became more clearly outlined against the pale dawn. The gelding snapped a branch beneath its hoof and a flock of swallows rose up through the open roof, their frightened chatter and drumming wings piercing through the early morning.

He glanced over his shoulder at Jerusa, so close on his heels that they nearly collided. Considering what he'd said to her about Carberry, he'd half expected her not to follow at all. Though it would have been a nuisance to track her down again, he was glad for other, less appropriate reasons that she'd decided to come with him.

"No doubt now that it was a fire that drove them out," he said, stating the obvious. Though from the growth of plants and vines around the house, he guessed the fire must have taken place years ago. There was still a desultory pile of half-burned chairs and benches in the yard, and clearly no one had since returned to repair or rebuild. Unless, he thought grimly, no one had survived. "Are you sure you want to stay here?"

Jerusa sniffed self-consciously and smoothed her hair, still more disconcerted by the way she'd almost walked right into his back than the burned-out house before her. "Why shouldn't I? We've come this far, haven't we? If you don't want anyone seeing us, what better place could there be than this?"

"I meant, *ma belle,* were you willing to share your sweet company with whoever might have lived here before?"

"You mean ghosts?" She stared at him, searching his face to decide if he was teasing or trying to frighten her, and couldn't decide either way. She'd never met a man whose thoughts were harder to read. "You're asking if I'm afraid of *ghosts?*"

He shrugged, all the answer he'd give. He'd said too much already. But the ruined house still made him uneasy, the way any place destroyed by fire always did.

How many times had Maman *taken him to see the empty shell of his father's house, the tall chimneys and pillars now snaked with vines, the charred walls crumbling and the windows blind as unseeing eyes? She had meant the visits to inspire him, to show him how grandly his father—and she, too, briefly—had lived. Twenty years, and still she could recite the contents of every room like a litany, the paintings and silver and gilded furniture with satin coverings. She said his father had been a* grand gentilhomme, *a Parisian by birth, a man of the world with the fortune to support his elegant tastes. Even the ruin of his house showed that.*

But what Michel remembered most were the unearthly shrieks of the birds and monkeys within the empty walls, echoing like so many restless spirits, and the way Maman *had wept so bitterly at what she'd lost.*

"Well, if you hope to scare me away with tales of ghosts and goblins, you're wrong," declared Jerusa soundly. She felt she'd won a great concession from him when he'd decided to come here, and she wasn't about to give it up simply because he wanted to frighten her. To prove her point she walked around him, pulling the mare behind her as she marched up toward the ruin. "You've no good reason to believe that anyone died here, let alone that the house is haunted. Besides, what ghost would dare show his face on a morning like this?"

What ghosts, indeed, wondered Michel, painfully aware of the irony of what she said. But how much could she truly know? Had Gabriel Sparhawk bragged to her and the rest of the family of how he'd burned *his* father's great house to the ground?

"Here's the well, just as I said, and there's even a bucket, too," announced Jerusa as she looped the horse's reins around the well's post. "Though the house may be abandoned, I'll wager we're not the only travelers who've stopped here."

She shoved the cover back from the well, dropped the bucket inside and listened until she heard it hit the water with a distant, muffled splash. Next, to Michel's surprise, she threw her weight against the long sweep, as expertly as any farm wife, until she'd slowly raised the dripping bucket to the surface. With both hands she caught it and set it on the ground for the thirsty mare.

Satisfied, she wiped her palms on the back of her skirt as she watched the mare drink before she glanced back at the Frenchman. "You didn't think I could do that, did you?" she said smugly.

"I didn't think you *wished* to, no," he said gruffly.

"No, you didn't think I could, even if I'd wished to." She lifted her chin, her face lit with a triumphant grin and her hands on her hips. "You think I'm too much a lady to do such a thing. But I'm not nearly as helpless as you want to believe, and you'll see, I'll find the old kitchen garden, too. Whatever's left growing there is bound to be an improvement over your infernal old cheese and stale bread."

Before he could answer, she had disappeared around the side of the house, and he could hear her feet crashing through the brush as she began to run.

"Damned foolish woman," muttered Michel as he swiftly tied his own horse and hurried after her. Here he'd been dawdling with his thoughts in the past, and all the while she'd been planning to skip away from him again. Not that she'd get far. He'd seen how her legs had nearly buckled under her when she'd first climbed from the horse.

But on the other side of the house he found no trace of her beyond the ragged path she'd cut through the weeds, and when he pushed open the gate to the garden, the rusty hinges groaned in protest. An ancient scarecrow, the straw stuffing gone from its head and its clothes in tatters, beckoned limply to him. In the damp morning air, the charred timbers still smelled of smoke, and once again he fought back his own uneasiness. Why the devil had he agreed to come here, anyway?

"Michel!" Her voice was faint in the distance, edged with excitement, or was it fear? "Oh, Michel, come quickly!"

Morbleu, what had she stumbled into now? As he ran along the path she'd taken, his fears raced faster, first to coarse, leering countrymen like the Faulks, then to rootless sailors without ships, thieving peddlers, vagabonds and rogues, all eager to do her harm, to hurt her, to steal some of her loveliness with their filthy hands. Was this, then, how he kept her safe?

And, for the first time, she'd actually used his Christian name....

"Michel, here!"

He'd never heard that note in her voice before. With a pistol primed and cocked in each hand, he ducked instinctively behind the shelter of a twisted elm tree. Carefully he inched around it, knowing that surprise would be his best weapon.

But *mon Dieu,* he hadn't counted on being the one who was surprised, and certainly not like this.

There were no lewd farmers with muskets, no rummy sailors, no tinkers or vagabonds. Instead there was only Jerusa, washed in the rosy light of the rising sun, kneeling in the mud with her skirts looped up over her petticoats and picking wild strawberries as fast as she could. Her cheeks were flushed and her braid had come unraveled to spill little dark ringlets around her face, and her expression was a mixture of concentration and delight.

"Jerusa, *ma chère,*" he said, not bothering to hide his irritation. "Just what the hell are you doing?"

Jerusa sat back on her heels and grinned mischievously, tossing her hair back over her shoulders. She wasn't quite sure why she suddenly felt so giddy in the face of his drawn pistols; was it the irresistible joy of an early morning in June, or the strawberries, or simply that she hadn't slept more than four hours at a time since they'd left Newport?

"I'm picking strawberries," she announced, "as you can see perfectly well with the eyes the good Lord gave you. And what, pray, are you doing with those guns?"

From ill humor alone Michel briefly considered firing them over her head, but instead merely uncocked them and shoved them back into his belt.

Her grin widened, and she tossed a berry high into the air, meaning to catch it in her mouth the way Josh did. But because she kept her eyes on Michel, not on the berry, her catch became more of a grab, and instead of landing the berry neatly in her open mouth, she managed to crush it with her fingers against her lips. She gulped and giggled as the red juice dripped from her mouth and between her white fingers.

"They're very good, and vastly better than your moldy old cheese," she managed to say, still laughing. "Very sweet."

He was willing to wager his soul no berry could be as sweet as her lips would be to kiss. Her skirts gathered up to hold the berries in her lap gave him a tantalizing glimpse of her legs, clear to her garters, and even in mud-splattered white thread stockings, her calves and ankles were shapely enough to make him want to ease her skirts higher, above the smooth skin of her bare thighs until he might—

Morbleu, had she any idea of what she was doing to him?

If he'd any sense at all he'd take her by the arm and drag her back to the house and the horses and they'd ride until they reached Seabrook. Until he'd be too exhausted to even consider what his body was now begging him to do.

Hell, they'd be shoveling dirt onto his coffin and he'd still want her.

"Now it's your turn to catch, Mr. Géricault," ordered Jerusa, "and pray you do better than I."

She wasn't surprised that the Frenchman caught the berry in his hand, not his mouth, for she couldn't imagine him willingly doing anything that might make him look foolish. He never would. Men as dangerous as this one didn't take risks like that. He didn't even laugh. For that matter, she hadn't laughed with him, either, at least not until just now. Why should she, considering what he'd done—no, what he was still *doing*—to her life.

But sitting here in a strawberry patch with the warm sunshine to ease her fears, Michel Géricault suddenly seemed less of a monster and more of a man. Only a man, she thought with new determination, and she'd yet to meet a man she couldn't dazzle if she set her mind to it. Could he really be any different? Perhaps if she could beguile him into trusting her, he'd let down his guard long enough for her to escape.

She tossed another berry to him, and again he caught it, but this time as he bit into the fruit he smiled, a lazy, knowing smile, white teeth against his dark new beard, a smile that was more disconcerting than all his threats and guns combined. He would never be as handsome as Tom, but when he smiled, his face lost much of its hard edge and his eyes warmed, the blue reminding her more of a summer sky than winter.

With sudden shyness she ducked her chin, but still watched him from beneath the shadow of her lashes. He was the one who was supposed to be dazzled, not her. But for him to smile like that, maybe even he had felt the magic of this June morning.

"You know, Mr. Géricault," she began, "I could keep casting berries at you one by one all day. It's rather like feeding a goose."

As if to demonstrate, she tossed one more berry to him and clapped her hands when he caught this one, too. Yet she noticed how his eyes narrowed a fraction with a predator's watchful interest, and she realized how much he mistrusted even her playfulness.

Only a man, she reminded herself fiercely. *He was only a man....*

She forced herself to smile as brilliantly as she could. "But I do think, Mr. Géricault, we'd both find it a good deal more agreeable if I give you half of what I've picked all in a lot. Then we could sit on the wall and eat them in a halfway civilized manner at the very least."

What, he wondered cynically, was sprinkled on those berries to make her change her tune so abruptly? Oh, he liked it—he liked it just fine—but she was woefully mistaken if she thought he'd turn her loose for a few smiles and fluttered lashes. She might have been the reigning belle of her provincial little Yankee town, but beside the Frenchwomen he'd known, who'd raised flirtation to an art, she was only one more green, country virgin.

He held out his hand to her and helped her to her feet, enjoying her surprise at his gallantry. Her hand was so small in his, fine boned and fragile, exactly the kind of well-bred hand she would have, and he held it a fraction longer than he should, just long enough to disconcert her into tugging it away.

"As you wish, Miss Sparhawk," he said, trying not to stare at the way the berries had stained her mouth such a vivid, seductive red. "Not that a stone wall will be much warmer than the ground."

"Fine words, those, after you've made me *sleep* on the ground!" She perched on the wall, carefully keeping her skirt bunched to hold the berries.

"There was musty straw one night, too, as I recall." He sat beside her, close enough that her skirts ruffled against his thigh, and close enough, too, that her eyes widened uneasily. But she didn't move away, and to his amusement he wondered which one of them had won that particular point. "Yet I'll agree, *ma belle,* that the accommodations haven't exactly been fit for a lady."

Only a man, thought Jerusa as she struggled to keep her composure. *Only a man, even if he insists in practically sitting in my lap!*

Swiftly she reached up to pluck his hat from his head and began to scoop his share of the strawberries into the crown. "Then I suppose I must be thankful it's summer, not December or January, else my bed would be a snowbank."

"Ah, but consider, *ma belle,* that June in New England must be equal to December in most other places." He took his hat from her with a slight nod of thanks, as if he'd always used it as a serving bowl. That one, he thought wryly, he'd concede to her. "In Martinique a day like this would make the ladies run for their shawls and huddle next to a fire."

Her green eyes lit with genuine interest. "Is that where your home is? Martinique?"

"It has been," he said, purposefully noncommittal and already regretting that he'd volunteered as much as he had. "I've traveled many places, *ma chérie,* and seen many things."

"Men can do that, can't they?" Slowly she began to pull the leaves of the hull from the berry in her hands. Unlike every other man she'd known, this one didn't talk incessantly about himself. Could he really have that much to hide? "And have you a wife to keep your home in Martinique, Mr. Géricault?"

The idea alone struck Michel as so ridiculous that he didn't bother denying it. "You're an inquisitive little soul, Jerusa Sparhawk."

"Well, and why not? You already know everything there is to know about *me.*"

"Ah, but that's much of my trade, *ma chérie*," he said lightly. He could tell her that much, for she'd never understand. "Soldier-man, sailor-man, beggar-man, thief—I've tried them all, and more besides. Now I trade in secrets. For kings or governors, rich men or merely desperate ones."

"You're a mercenary?"

"I do the things that others haven't the courage to do. For a price, of course."

Again he flashed that lazy smile that made her wonder if he'd invented it all to tease her. It could be true; she'd certainly heard worse nonsense from men, and at least he didn't seem to be bragging.

She turned the hulled berry over and over in her fingers, her interest in eating it gone. "What," she asked softly, "was the price for kidnapping me?"

"My price?" he repeated, thinking of his mother's pale, tortured face against the rumpled linens of her bed. "My price for taking you, *ma chère,* was beyond all the gold in your precious Newport."

For a moment, just for a moment, she had truly thought he would tell her *why,* and disappointment turned her voice bitter. "All the gold in Newport won't restore my good name, either, not after I've spent so much time alone with you."

Strange how closely she echoed his mother's wish, to ruin Jerusa Sparhawk's honor as her father had done to *Maman,* rob her of the same hopes and dreams. All that remained was to bring the girl to Martinique for his mother to see her shame for herself.

It had all come to pass so easily; too easily, really, for him to feel any sort of satisfaction. That, he supposed, would come when he met with her father and brothers. What more could he want from her?

"So what will Carberry say, *ma fille,*" he said slowly, watching her reaction even as he wondered at his own, "when he learns of how we traveled together, ate together, slept together?"

Jerusa's face grew hot with humiliation at how much he was suggesting. "We—I've allowed you no liberties."

"I haven't taken any, either, *ma belle,* no matter how many opportunities you've offered to me."

Automatically she opened her mouth to protest, then stopped, speechless, and he knew from her eyes the exact, horrified instant she remembered how he'd first drugged her into unconsciousness, how he'd cut her clothing away, how she'd wept away her sorrow in his embrace. Any more opportunities like that and he'd qualify for sainthood.

"Your Tom would find you in exactly the same honorable state as he left you last. He would, at least, if he decides to welcome you back."

"Of course he will, once I talk to him." Jerusa's chin rose bravely. "Besides, Father will make him marry me."

"How wonderfully romantic." And how much like the Sparhawks, he thought cynically.

"But I love Tom!" she cried in anguish. "Nothing you can say or do can change that! I *love* him!"

Despite her brave words, Michel saw the hopelessness in the tears that made her eyes too bright. She had loved Carberry and now she'd lost him, but with the pride of her breaking heart she wouldn't let him go.

"I never said you didn't, *chérie.*" Gently he reached out to brush her cheek with the back of his hand, and he felt her quiver beneath his touch. "But do you love this selfish man enough not to care if he doesn't love you in return? Enough that you'll be content as another of his ornaments, one more pretty toy among his snuffboxes?"

His face was too close to hers, each word a feather-light breath against her skin. Other men in her past had sat beside her and she'd thought nothing of it. Other men had dared to touch her cheek, and she'd laughed and struck their hands away. But with Michel she was trembling, her heart pounding in her breast. The blue of his eyes was like a pool that drew her in deeper and deeper until she knew she was foundering, far over her head.

He turned his hand to cradle her face against his palm, his fingers carrying the masculine leather scent of his gloves and the horse's reins.

"Tell me, *ma chérie*," he whispered, his voice as soft as black velvet. "Do you love him enough that you'd settle for ashes when you could reach for the fire?"

And then his lips found hers, the way she'd at once desired and feared they would, and without further thought, her eyes fluttered shut. He kissed her lightly at first, his mouth barely grazing against hers as he let her grow accustomed to him. Gradually he increased the pressure and the pleasure with it, and she thought again of the bottomless pool, deep enough to swallow her up forever. And God help her, she didn't care. His lips were warm and sure on hers, the sensations heightened by the roughness of his beard on her skin, and, with a tiny gasp of surrender, her own lips parted for him, searching for more.

But instead she found nothing, the warmth and pleasure gone with his kiss. Confused, she opened her eyes. Though his fingers still held her face as gently as if he feared she'd break, his expression was distant, his eyes shuttered against emotion, the same lips that had kissed hers now set in a grim, impassive line.

"You have your answer now, Jerusa, don't you?" he said, shoving his hair back from his brow before he settled his hat. "Pick more berries if you wish. I'll be with the horses."

He turned and left her then, before he saw the bewilderment in her lovely eyes and before he was tempted to kiss her again.

One kiss was enough for them both. She had her answer, and he, God help him, had his.

Chapter Eight

Jerusa was dreaming.

She had to be, for she was ten years old again, and it was winter, and she was waiting on the back step to their house in Newport, hopping up and down to keep warm in the snow while Josh tried to hold the fuse straight on the little red Chinese firecrackers. It was past midnight, long past their bedtime, but because the new year was only minutes old and their parents and the other grown-ups were too busy drinking toasts and firing off empty muskets to notice, she and Josh had crept outside to set off the last of the firecrackers their older brother Jon had brought from London for Christmas.

"You must hold it steady, Josh, or I'll never be able to light it," she complained. In the streets others were setting off firecrackers, too, some loud enough to drown out the pealing of the First Day bells.

"You just hush, Rusa," ordered Josh, "and mind the striker, or we'll never be able to light it because you never made a blessed spark!"

But even as he spoke, the spark found the fuse, a bright flash along the tallowed cord, and Jerusa shrieked with excitement as Josh tossed the firecracker onto the paving stones. For an endless moment it lay rolling gently back and forth, and then with a mighty, deafening crash and a great burst of light, it exploded.

"Wake up, Jerusa!" called Michel. "Wake up *now!*"

She pulled the blanket higher over her shoulders and rolled away from him, her eyes still tightly shut. She wanted to stay with Josh and the snow and the firecrackers. There was another flash, and another firecracker exploded even more loudly than the first, and Jerusa smiled sleepily. Josh had sworn he'd only that one left from Christmas, the greedy little—

"*Morbleu,* woman, can you sleep through anything?" Michel grabbed the blanket from her shoulder and ripped it away. "You claim you're so blessed good with horses. I could sure as hell use your help now!"

"And I thought you could blessed well do everything yourself," grumbled Jerusa to herself as she sat upright, for he was already gone. They had decided to sleep in the empty barn, and she brushed at the bits of straw that clung to her skirt. "It can't possibly be time to leave yet, and I—"

But she broke off abruptly at the brilliant flash of lightning at the open end of the shed, followed by the immediate crack of thunder. Joshua's firecrackers, she thought, and then she heard the squeal of the frightened horses and the loud thumps and cracks as they panicked in their stalls. Dear Almighty, the horses!

Swiftly she pulled on her shoes and ran to the back of the barn to join Michel. He stood in the stall beside his horse, Buck, to hold him by the halter, stroking the gelding's shoulder and murmuring in French to calm him. But in the next stall Abigail was skittishly dancing from side to side, tossing her head and trembling with anxiety.

Hurriedly plaiting her own long hair so it wouldn't startle the horses, Jerusa glanced outside the barn's open doorway. Though there was no rain yet, the sky was nearly dark as night, the racing clouds a flat gray-green and the wind blowing hard enough to whip the trees like grass. No wonder the horses were terrified.

"Be careful, *ma chérie*," warned Michel softly without turning toward her. "That mare's so on tenterhooks now that she'd strike at her own shadow."

"Then that will make a pair of us," she murmured, grateful for his concern. She'd need it. At Crescent Hill the grooms were the ones who stayed with the horses during storms, not her, but she'd overheard enough stories of the damage a frightened horse could do to be wary herself.

Slowly she inched into the stall toward Abigail. "Pretty girl," she crooned softly. "I know you're scared, but there's not a thing out there that can hurt you. It's just wind and thunder, a whole lot of noise and show that doesn't amount to anything worth your notice."

The mare's ears pricked forward at Jerusa's familiar voice.

"That's it, girl," she coaxed. "You know me, I'm only Rusa, and you know I wouldn't tell you a word that's false, would I? Pretty, pretty girl."

With infinite care she reached for the halter, stroking the horse's forehead as she hooked her fingers beneath the leather straps. She was surprised to see that Michel had already saddled the horse. Though the storm made it difficult to gauge the time, she wouldn't have guessed they'd be set to leave so soon.

"There you are, Abigail. Easy as you please, pretty girl. Rusa didn't tell tales, did she?"

From the gelding's stall she heard Michel chuckle. "Ah, Buck, my fine fellow, perhaps you know. When will Rusa stop telling tales to *me*?"

"When will *I* stop telling tales?" she said, keeping to the same crooning tone she'd been using for the mare's sake. There was another brief flash of lightning, another fainter rumble of thunder, and though the horse trembled and whinnied uneasily, Jerusa still held firm. Perhaps the storm would miss them, after all. "Easy, pretty girl, easy. *I* never started telling tales, unlike certain Frenchmen, who can't begin to tell the truth."

Her baby name, Rusa, had sounded exotic and foreign the way he said it, so soft and slurred and indolent that she wished she'd never let him hear it; one more thing he'd stolen from her. He laughed softly again, and though Jerusa couldn't see his face, she could imagine his mocking smile well enough to make her cheeks grow warm.

"Ah, *ma chère,* I've never yet lied to you," he said with amused regret, which she was certain was quite false, "yet you will never believe me."

"Then tell me the truth. Tell me why you kissed me."

"So easy a test, sweet Rusa, so easy!" He kept her in breathless agony while he murmured to the gelding in French. "I kissed you because we both wished it."

"That's not true!"

"You see how it is? I could not be more truthful, and yet you won't believe me."

A fresh gust of wind rushed through the doorway with a swirl of leaves, ripped from their branches, and as the mare's nostrils flared, Jerusa caught the same scent of coming rain and salty air blown east from the sea. Abigail arched back, and Jerusa forgot answering Michel as she struggled again with the mare.

Then, from the yard outside, came a loud, sizzling crackle followed by a hiss like a hot poker in cold water, then the brittle explosion of splintering wood.

Her heart pounding, Jerusa whipped around toward the noise in time to see the last standing wall of the abandoned house burst into flames around the white ball of lightning. In an instant the dry timbers became a solid sheet of fire, the flames urged faster by the wind. As she watched, the first sparks spun through the curling smoke to the roofless henhouse, and that, too, soon grew bright with fire.

And directly to the west, next in the fire's path, was the barn.

Michel was shouting to her, but as she turned toward his voice, Abigail plunged back and ripped herself free of Jerusa's grasp. Frantically Jerusa lunged for the halter again, and as she did, the mare tossed her head and caught Jerusa's side beneath her raised arm.

Almost as if it came from someone else, she heard the odd, hollow sound she made as the wind was knocked from her. In disorienting slow motion she felt herself lifted from her feet and into the air, until, with a leaden thump, she fell to the hard earthen floor of the barn. There she lay, gasping for breath, every inch of her body hurting. But as she struggled to make her lungs work again, the only air she could find was acrid with smoke, burning her eyes and nose.

"Jerusa?" shouted Michel, fighting to control Buck. "*Jerusa!*" Where was the girl, anyway? Why the hell didn't she answer? The barn was filling with smoke from the burning house, and it would be only a matter of minutes before the wind would drive the flames this way. He tore his arms free of his coat and tied it across the gelding's white-ringed eyes.

"Come along, Buck, we've tarried here long enough," he said as he led the horse from the stall. They'd have to pass directly past the fire, and he prayed the horse wouldn't balk. "You're a brave fellow, and I know you can do it."

Coughing from the smoke, Michel guided the horse toward the door. Another flash of lightning, another deafening crack of thunder and he nearly lost his grip on the horse. He heard Abigail's terrified whinny, and in the split second of lightning, he caught a glimpse of the mare alone in her stall. But where the devil was Jerusa?

"Just a few paces more, Buck, a few more," he coaxed, and then they were out of the barn and in the yard. As swiftly as he could, he ran with the horse to a tree well beyond the fire's reach, to the east, and tied him there. At last the first fat drops of rain were beginning to plummet from the clouds to hiss into the flames, and as Michel raced back across the yard, he prayed the rain would end the fires.

He stopped at the door of the smoke-filled barn, tying his handkerchief over his nose and mouth. The mare would be easy to find, pinned by terror in her stall. But where was the girl?

He shouted her name again, and again came no answer. Maybe she'd already fled the barn, determined like every Sparhawk to save herself first, but even as Michel considered the possibility he dismissed it. Jerusa wouldn't do that. She'd come to care too much for that foolish mare to abandon her now. She had to be in here somewhere, hidden by the stinging, murky clouds of smoke.

Sacristi, why had he been burdened with a silly chit who'd risk her life for the sake of a secondhand horse?

He felt his way to Abigail's stall, stroking the trembling mare's foam-flecked neck as he covered her eyes with his coat the same way he had with the gelding.

"Where is she, Abigail?" he asked softly as he led her forward. "Where's our Jerusa, eh?"

The mare balked and shied, and then Michel heard the coughing. She was on her hands and knees on the floor, swaying as she struggled to breathe. He grabbed her around the waist, and she sagged against him, and together they staggered the last few feet to the open air.

Outside the barn, Michel pointed Abigail toward Buck, pulled the coat from her eyes and left her to join the gelding on her own. He slipped his arm beneath Jerusa's knees and carried her, still coughing, to the little stand of maples where the horses waited.

Gently he settled her on the grass, slipping his coat protectively across her shoulders as she still coughed and gasped for breath. Her eyes were red rimmed from the smoke, making the irises seem even more green by contrast, and the rain had flattened her hair and blotched the soot that covered her face. But because she was alive, to him she'd never looked more lovely.

"You'll be fine, *ma chère,*" he said, trying to smile. She had frightened him badly, more than the fire itself and more than he wanted to admit. He'd come so close to losing her, and though he tried to tell himself it was only for his mother's sake, deep down he knew the truth, and that, too, frightened him. "It hurts now, I know, but you'll be fine."

Jerusa nodded, all the answer she felt able to give. She sat curled over her bent knees, holding her side where Abigail's nose had struck her. Her lungs still stung from the smoke, but each breath seemed to come a little easier. She was sure her side would be purple and sore for at least a week, and she touched herself gingerly, praying she hadn't cracked any ribs. She wasn't about to complain to Michel and have him go cutting her clothes off again to tend to her.

She looked back at the fire, more smoke now than flames, thanks to the rain. The last wall of the house, the one that had been struck by lightning, was completely gone now, and only the stone chimney remained like a lopsided pillar against the sky. The rain had spared the barn, but, even with the wind, the air was still thick with the smell of burning wood, and she shivered as she thought of how near she'd come to dying through her own carelessness with Abigail.

Michel handed her a cup of water and she drank it gratefully, the well water deliciously cool as it slid down her raw throat. He, too, was smudged with soot, and one sleeve of his shirt was torn nearly the length of his arm. He'd lost the ribbon to his queue, which allowed his hair to fall loose around his face, and small black scorched spots left from cinders peppered his waist-coat. Whatever his reasons, he'd clearly risked his life for her, and no one else had ever done that. Certainly not Tom Carberry.

"There now, I told you you'd feel better," said Michel softly. With one finger he brushed a lock of her hair from her forehead. She was a brave little woman, he thought with fond admiration. He couldn't think of another who would have stayed with the horses, as she had. "No real damage, eh, *ma mie?*"

Though he smiled, weariness had deepened the lines around his eyes and made his accent more pronounced. She doubted he'd rested at all while she'd been asleep.

"Thank you," she whispered, her voice breaking. "You didn't have to come back for me."

"Don't thank me, *ma chérie*." He winked wickedly. "I came back for Abigail."

She tried to laugh, but all that came out was a croaking bark. "Then I thank you for Abigail's sake. She's unharmed?"

"She and Buck both. You can see for yourself how happily they're grazing now, without an anxious thought in their heads. Horses can be charming, useful creatures, but they're not particularly fearless in a fire."

"Who is?" Her smile faded as she pulled his coat higher over her shoulders. Though she didn't really need the coat's warmth, she wasn't yet ready to give up the security and concern—Michel's concern—it represented.

"You knew, didn't you?" she said quietly. "We didn't lose a thing because you had the horses saddled and ready, even though we weren't supposed to leave until dusk. Somehow you *knew*."

He shrugged carelessly. "A guess, that was all. The high ground, the fact that the house had suffered from fire before, something in the air that felt like a storm. But don't look at me like I'm a sorcerer, *chère*. If nothing had come of it, then I would have looked the fool, not the wise man."

Of course it had been more than that. From the beginning, the place had made him uneasy in ways he didn't want to explain. He looked past her to the smoldering ruin of the farmhouse and imagined again the empty, charred walls of his father's house.

No, he didn't want to explain that to her at all.

She brushed her fingers across the grass beside her and wondered what had made him fall silent. She wished he hadn't. The terror she'd felt when she'd been lost in the smoke was still very real, and talking had helped her forget. Talking to *him*.

"If you'll only take credit for saving Abigail's life," she said slowly, "and not mine with it, will you let me at least thank you for that?"

He raised his brows with feigned surprise. "A Sparhawk offering thanks? What's happened to your pride, Miss Jerusa?"

"Oh, hang my pride, Michel, and let me be grateful!" Before she lost her nerve she leaned over and kissed him quickly, her lips barely grazing his. She sat back on her heels, breathless at her own daring, and unconsciously licked her lips as if to taste the fleeting memory of his.

He looked at her blandly. "Were you telling the truth that time?"

"About what?" she asked, flustered by the way he seemed to be studying her mouth. "About being grateful?"

"Of course not, *ma chère*. About kissing me. That tiny *souffle* was so slight I'm not sure but that I imagined it entirely."

"You don't believe I kissed you?"

"I don't know what to believe, *ma mie*, not where you're concerned."

"It's not as if I'm in the habit of kissing every man I see, you know," she said indignantly. "But I'd have thought you'd have the decency to *believe* it when I did!"

He smiled with lazy charm, his teeth a white slash against his dark beard and soot-smudged face. She didn't have to defend herself so vigorously—he'd known from the start that her bumbling popinjay of a fiancé hadn't taught her a thing—but at least she'd forgotten entirely about the fire.

And so, for that matter, had he.

"I told you before, Rusa, I've never lied to you," he said. "Decency or not, I haven't begun now."

With an exasperated grumble she threw herself against him, seizing his shoulders to steady herself as she planted her lips soundly against his. There, she thought triumphantly, he wouldn't forget *that!*

But suddenly his mouth was moving against hers in a way she hadn't intended at all, surely, seductively, and she forgot all her triumph as his lips slanted across hers to deepen the kiss. She shuddered as his tongue invaded her mouth, teasing and tasting her in dizzying ways she'd never dreamed possible. Shyly she let herself be led, echoing and responding to his actions until she realized that he, too, felt this other fire flaring between them.

Her fingers tightened into the hard muscles of his shoulders beneath the soft lawn shirt, and when she felt his hands circling her waist and spreading across the soft curve of her hips, she let herself be drawn closer to his body, relishing the new sensation of him beneath her. She was alive, gloriously alive, and he had saved her for this. He pulled her back with him onto the grass and she kissed him hungrily, as if she were famished, as if she hadn't feasted on strawberries or—

Dear Almighty, what was she doing? Abruptly she tore her mouth away from his, pushing herself up on her arms to stare down at him. Her heart was pounding and her body ached in strange places that had nothing to do with her fall, and, to her shame, she realized she was sprawled across his body with her legs spread on either side of his.

"Oh, Michel," she said breathlessly, unable to think of anything else to say as the color flooded her face. "Oh, my goodness."

He laughed softly, and she felt it vibrate through her own body before she hurried to untangle herself from him. "Ah, Rusa, *now* I believe you've kissed me."

Chapter Nine

With the storm done, Jerusa scarcely met Michel's eyes as they prepared to leave. Even when for the first time he'd made a tiny fire so he could offer her tea, real, hot tea from his saddlebag, her thanks was no more than a swift, curt nod.

But he knew what she was doing as clearly as if she'd spoken. More clearly, maybe, than she did herself. Self-righteously she believed that he'd tricked her into kissing him so that she could blame him for the fact that she had enjoyed it as much as she had.

He hadn't been quite that devious, but he'd admit to taking advantage of the opportunities that life—and pretty, sooty women—offered him. Why shouldn't he? She *had* been the one to kiss him. What harm could possibly come from a single kiss?

At least that was what he tried to tell himself, and that was where his own confidence faded. Jerusa wasn't some merry barkeep's daughter or *femme du soir* who forgot each passing pleasure as soon as she found the next one. No, Jerusa Sparhawk was his enemy's daughter, and she was supposed to be his prisoner. So why the hell was he rolling around in the grass with her like some besotted farmer on market day?

But it was worse than that. Much worse. Kissing her was

unlike kissing any other woman in his life. She was hotter, sweeter, more fascinating, more beguiling. The innocent eagerness she'd shown with him today had very nearly shredded his self-control, the untapped passion of her lush young body crying out to be freed.

Yet if her passion could burn him with pleasure hotter than any fire from lightning alone, then it could also scorch a path to his soul if he let it. And he wouldn't. All he had to do was look at his mother to see the disastrous results of loving and caring. Love led to ruin and madness and pain that lasted forever, and he wanted no part of it. He'd spent his whole life carefully building a wall of indifference around himself as protection. He wasn't about to tear it down for the sake of one spoiled little English virgin who would cringe with horror when she finally learned who he was.

He looked at her graceful profile, staring resolutely ahead as she rode beside him. He must not forget who she was again. There would be no more kisses, no more dallying on the grass.

No more caring.

They had not been riding a quarter hour before they saw the dim shape of the other horses coming toward them on the road ahead. Four horses, guessed Michel, four riders, four men he'd no wish to meet, and he swore to himself.

Jerusa looked at him sharply. "What's wrong?"

"Company, *ma chère.*" He pointed toward the horizon ahead. "Four men at least coming our way. I know why we travel by night, but I'm not sure I want to know their reasons, too."

She understood at once; no decent men would be on the road at this hour. "We can run, can't we? The horses are fresh."

"In this open country? No, if we've seen them, then they've seen us, and there's no help but to meet them." He was glad he'd checked his powder after the rain. Not that he intended to use the pistols, but it was comforting to know the guns were there if he needed them. He sighed and smiled wearily at Jerusa. "You're not frightened, are you?"

She shook her head quickly, and he thought of how much she'd changed. Only a few days ago she would have been racing up to meet the others, shouting about how she was one of Newport's own anointed Sparhawks.

"Good girl. Let's pray they're as anxious to be on their way as we are."

As the two parties drew closer together, Michel slowed his horse to a walk and Jerusa followed.

"Good evening, sirs!" he called in his best bluff English. "Good evening, friends!"

The others slowed, too, then stopped. In the lead was a stout man whose white-powdered wig seemed strangely out of place on the open road as he stood in his stirrups to scowl down at them. The other three, servants or hired men, hung back a deferential distance. One more self-important provincial Englishman playing at being a squire in Connecticut, thought Michel irritably as he forced his face into a cheerful smile.

"My wife and I have passed through a dreadful storm not an hour ago," he said to the man in the wig. "Can you tell us, pray, if there's a decent inn or ordinary to be found in this neighborhood?"

"Do I look like an innkeeper to you, sir?" the other man demanded. "I am Dr. Richard Hamilton, sir, and I'll have you know you trespass on my land."

Briefly Michel lifted his hat from his head. "Michael Geary, sir, your servant, and my wife, Mrs. Geary. If we trespass, Dr. Hamilton, I assure you it is through no intention to do you harm."

Hamilton peered at Jerusa, striving to see her face, and it took all her resolve not to draw away. He might not have been the highwayman she'd feared, but still she didn't like him one whit, and she trusted him even less. When Michel had first spotted the other horsemen, she had fleetingly considered throwing herself on their mercy. Now, after meeting Hamilton, she was glad she hadn't.

"Mistress Geary, ma'am," said Hamilton with a grudging, cursory nod, before he turned back to glare at Michel. "What is your destination, Mr. Geary?"

"New York, sir, to visit my wife's people. We ourselves live in Massachusetts, in Essex County."

"Queer sort of business, hauling your wife on horseback about the countryside like some damned tinker." Hamilton grunted skeptically. "Why didn't you go by water, eh? And where are your trunks? Never in my days have I seen a lady travel without trunks."

"It's our trunks that are sailing south, Doctor," answered Michel easily. "We sent my wife's gowns and other such that she'll need to New York in my cousin's coaster, while we ourselves, sir, prefer to travel lightly by land. It's my wife's choosing, you see. She has not the constitution for sea journeys, nor can she abide the closeness of a carriage."

Jerusa listened in silence, amazed by the ease with which Michel spun one tale after another. Just as with the Faulks he had contrived to sound their better, now with this man he managed exactly to be a step or two lower, a prosperous tradesman, perhaps, or craftsman. He was so convincing that she almost believed it herself.

And so, more important, did Hamilton, who at last nodded. "Tell me, Geary. Did you pass a house afire to the east on this road?"

Michel's eyes widened with appropriate wonder. "Why, yes, sir, we did at that! We had stopped for shelter from the storm at a ruin of a farm, only to have the old house struck by lightning even as we watched. You've but to look at our clothing to see how near we were. A terrible sight, sir, awful to behold! Thank God in his mercy for sending the rain to douse the flames."

"And thanks to you, Geary, for saving us the trouble of going there ourselves." For the first time Hamilton's lips curved in a smile, or what in a man like him would pass as a pleasantry. "That makes five times in as many summers that lightning's found that spot."

"Five times, sir!" Michel whistled low under his breath. "Five times is cruel of fate indeed."

"'Twas nothing to do with fate," declared Hamilton with disgust. He turned in his saddle to stare contemptuously at one of the other men. "What kind of thick-witted oaf would choose the highest hill in the county to build his house? You deserved what the Lord sent you, Saunders, indeed you do, just as you deserved to lose the land itself. Be grateful I'm the one who bought it, else you wouldn't even have the right to work the miserable plot."

Saunders sank lower in his saddle with shame and misery, and Michel's initial dislike of Hamilton swelled. He hated men like this, men who thought that gold and land gave them the right to grind down and humiliate everyone else less fortunate.

"*'Vous êtes un sot en trois lettres, mon fils,'*" he said softly.

Hamilton jerked around to stare at Michel. "What the devil did you say?"

"'You're a fool in three letters, my son,'" he said levelly, translating for Hamilton's benefit. "Or four, in English. Molière. It seemed appropriate."

Jerusa almost gasped aloud. What didn't seem appropriate was Michel saying such a thing, especially if he was pretending to be a respectable tradesman. Hamilton was a contemptible bully, but that was no reason for Michel to insult him.

But for some reason Hamilton didn't seem to have even heard what he'd said. "No, before that, Geary," he insisted. "What did you say? Did you dare to speak like a worthless, frog-eating bastard in my presence?"

Jerusa saw Michel stiffen. "Molière was a Frenchman,"

he said softly, and to her ear he intentionally let his neat, clipped Boston tradesman's accent slide in favor of the softer French of his birth. "A French gentleman, a playwright and a genius."

"You're one of them, aren't you, Geary?" demanded Hamilton, his voice shaking with rage. "You couldn't rattle off their lingo so neat otherwise. I lost two sons to the French swine in the last war. Two fine, honest, English boys, dead because of you! And now you dare to come on my very land to mock me, nay, to burn and destroy my very property!"

Hamilton fumbled to unfasten his coat and Jerusa saw how swiftly Michel's hand slid down to his belt with the pistols. Dear Almighty, in another minute they'd begin shooting at each other, unless, unless…

"You believe my husband is French, Dr. Hamilton?" she asked incredulously as she urged Abigail forward between the two men. *"French?"*

Hamilton jerked his head back to look at her, his eyes popping beneath his brows, clearly annoyed that she'd dare interfere. "Aye, mistress, I do."

"Then you should consider your words before you speak, Dr. Hamilton," she said tartly. "My own father sailed in a privateer in the old French war, sending more than his share of Frenchmen to their graves in the Caribbean, and my brothers, too, whenever King George has given them the chance."

"Most admirable." Hamilton snorted with scorn. "How then do you explain your bastard of a husband's speechifying, eh? He prattles away in their infernal tongue as if he were born to it!"

She forced herself to laugh. "Then my husband has fooled you as he hopes to fool others. He has high-flown hopes to rise above his station, you see, and fancies that because the gentry speak French, then he shall, too. His teacher is but a dancing master on our street who feeds his foolishness for our hard-earned shillings."

Hamilton scowled beneath his white wig. "You speak the truth, mistress? You do not mock me?"

"La, it's he who mocks *me,* Dr. Hamilton!" she said with a toss of her head. She was sure now he believed her, for despite his scowl, his body had relaxed and lost its tension. "For myself, I would no more take a Frenchman for a husband than I would an ape."

"An ape, you say, my dear wife?" asked Michel, speaking at last. "Is that how you choose to think of me today?"

She couldn't miss the clipped edginess in his voice, or the way his pale eyes had narrowed to watch her. But was his irritation with her real, she wondered, or feigned like so much else he did and said?

She sniffed with what she hoped would pass for proper wifely disdain. Playing a shrewish wife might be a step up from playing a mad one, but it still wasn't particularly flattering. "Not so much an ape, Mr. Geary, as a fool. Why should I sit by meekly while you display your learning and get yourself murdered in the process? What would become of *me,* I ask you that?"

"Only what you deserve, my dear," answered Michel with irritation, implying he'd like nothing better. "Not that this fine gentleman wishes to hear it."

"He'll hear me whether he wishes it or not," she said sharply.

"But not unless I wish it, too, my dear Mrs. Geary." His eyes glittering with unspoken threats, he reached for her horse's reins and jerked them from her fingers. "No matter how ill-used you believe yourself, you're still my wife, and you still must answer to me. You've said more than enough as it is, haven't you?"

"But I—"

"Not a word more, my dear. Now you're coming with me." He jerked the reins so sharply that the mare lunged forward and Jerusa, caught off-balance, was forced to seize the horse's mane to keep from toppling off her saddle. "Good evening to you, Dr. Hamilton, and Godspeed."

Jerusa had no choice but to follow as Michel pulled her horse along with his. But she could choose to keep silent, too angry and humiliated by the way he'd just treated her to rejoice in the fact that they'd escaped Hamilton's wrath.

"If you wish to play the meddling wife, *ma chérie,* you shouldn't have stopped your quarreling so soon," said Michel as soon as they were out of earshot of the others. "They'll never believe I've tamed you this easily."

"*Tamed* me!" sputtered Jerusa indignantly. "No one has ever ordered me about like that for any reason whatsoever, let alone hauled me away in that shameful, degrading manner!"

"And what of how you treated me, eh? Carberry should thank me on his knees for saving him from a wife who'd use her husband with so little respect or kindness."

Jerusa's chin rose defensively. All he did was take from her. Why couldn't he *give* a simple thank-you? "I was only trying to save us, the same way you were!"

"Were you?" he countered, his voice still deceptively calm. "To begin a game like that and then quit halfway was far, far more dangerous."

"The way you did, spouting off your gentleman's French? You could have guessed how Hamilton would react!"

Angrily he swore beneath his breath, wishing she hadn't thrown that back in his face. If Hamilton hadn't insulted him he would have been fine. *Bastard.* He'd been called that all his life, and he thought he was long past feeling its sting. Yet because the memory of Jerusa's kiss was still so fresh, he had wanted to spare her the ugly sound of the truth, just as he'd wanted to hold on to the warmth of her respect a little longer. It was only the way he'd gone about it that was so disastrously wrong, and now it was far too late to explain why.

"*Morbleu,* Jerusa, is that all you understand?" he demanded bitterly. "Then you're no better than Hamilton yourself. Not that I should expect otherwise, should I? All you preaching, pious New Englanders are alike, all ready to play God at a moment's notice!"

"You heard him! He'd lost two sons to the French! How could he possibly feel any other way?"

"And what of the sorrow of the French widows and orphans and grieving parents left by your father's slaughter? You certainly seem proud enough of that."

She ducked her chin, struck by the appalling truth of what he'd said. All her life she'd heard how her father was a hero for what he'd done as a privateer, and she'd always accepted it without question, and without considering the consequences.

"But that's different," she began lamely. "That was—different."

"Different, *ma chère?* Because they're French, somehow their sorrow is less painful?"

"That's not what I meant!" She shook her head, wishing she could make it all clear to herself as well as to him. "Don't you understand that Hamilton would have had his men kill you if he'd known you were French?"

He drew their horses up short, wheeling around to face her. So that was it. He saved her life in the fire, and now she thought that by this bit of foolishness she'd saved his in return. He didn't want to owe her his life. He didn't want to owe her anything.

"Then why didn't you let them, Jerusa?" he demanded. "Why didn't you take the chance to add one more dead Frenchman to your family's honor?"

"Because it was *you!*" she cried. "Damn you, Michel, because it was you!"

For a moment that stretched like eternity between them, Michel only stared at her.

"Then perhaps, *ma chère,*" he said at last, "for both our sakes, you should have let them do it."

Chapter Ten

❧❦

"**W**e lost almost everything in the fire, ma'am," explained Michel sadly to the landlady of the public house. "Not that we had so much, traveling by horse, yet still my poor wife lost everything but the clothes on her back, and you've only to look at her skirts to see how near a thing it was."

"You poor creatures!" exclaimed the landlady, clicking her tongue. "Praise the Lord that guided you to my doorstep. You'll find no better lodgings between Providence and New Haven and that's the honest truth. If anyone can make you forget your travail, 'twill be myself, Catherine Cartwright, here at the Sign of the Lamb."

She beamed at them with such heartfelt sympathy that Jerusa squirmed inwardly. The woman was round faced and maternal, with a smudge of flour from the kitchen across her ruddy cheek, and clearly trusting enough that she'd never suspect a gentleman like this fine Mr. Geary of telling such out-and-out lies.

Not that what he was saying was exactly lies. She *had* lost all her clothes. They *had* been in a fire. The little scorched marks on her gown *were* from flying cinders. And they—oh, sweet Almighty, was she herself really getting to be as adept at twisting the truth as the Frenchman?

Jerusa, Jerusa, where are your wits? Better you should be listening and waiting for the chance to leave him than worrying about how many of his wicked, dishonorable ways have rubbed off onto you!

"Here now, Mrs. Geary, I'll show you to your room myself," Mrs. Cartwright was saying, already leading the way up the staircase. "'Tis your good fortune that I've the front room free, the one I generally save for gentry such as yourselves. We've not much company at present, but my, you should see the crowd we have when the court's in session!"

Only half listening, Jerusa began to follow her, then stopped when she realized that Michel had remained behind. She looked back at him, one brow cocked in silent question while Mrs. Cartwright continued discussing the last county court sessions.

"You go ahead, my dear," he said softly so as not to disturb the landlady's monologue. "I've business with some gentlemen here in the town, but be certain I'll return to you as soon as I can."

He kissed his fingers toward her, a lighthearted salute that did little to lessen the subtle warning of his words, and without answering, Jerusa hurried up the stairs after Mrs. Cartwright. She might kiss Michel Géricault a hundred times and he still wouldn't forget she was his prisoner. To him it was all some sort of strange game with rules she'd never learned, and despite the warmth of the day, she shivered. Of course he would return to her; he always did. But maybe this time, she wouldn't be there waiting.

"I hope this suits, Mrs. Geary," said the landlady as, with a flourish of her large arm, she threw open the door to the room. "Like I told you before, you'll be hard-pressed to find finer."

She marched to the bed and vigorously plumped the bolsters while Jerusa remained in the doorway. A chair, a stool, an unsteady table with a candlestick and a pitcher for washing, a black-speckled looking glass and one bed. *One* bed, thought Jerusa with dismay, which doubtless Michel would expect her to share with him to carry on this ruse of being husband and wife.

But she wouldn't do it. She couldn't. He had promised he'd never force her, and he'd kept that promise. *She* was the one who had proved faithless and untrustworthy, to Tom, her family, even her own notion of herself. With this Frenchman she didn't even seem to know right from wrong, even who she was, and she didn't want to consider what might happen between them in this room. It was almost as if he'd cast a spell over her to make her doubt every last thing about herself. One more reason—as if she needed another—for her to leave as soon as she could.

With approval Mrs. Cartwright nodded at the newly plumped bolsters and folded her arms across her wide bosom. "I'll leave you, then, to settle in, Mrs. Geary. The girls will be up directly with your bath."

"A bath?" Embarrassed, Jerusa looked down at her filthy, stained gown. She'd traveled enough with her parents to know that a bath in a private room of a public house was an unthinkable luxury. Was it obvious even to Mrs. Cartwright that her new guest had worn the same clothes for six days and nights of hard travel, so obvious that she'd suggest a bath before allowing Jerusa downstairs with her other guests?

But the landlady only smiled benevolently. "It was your husband that suggested it, Mrs. Geary. He thought you'd welcome the chance to wash away the grime of the road. A kind man, ma'am. Most husbands wouldn't be so thoughtful."

She winked broadly, her eye nearly disappearing into her round cheek. "But then, most husbands aren't nearly so comely, eh? I'll wager that's one that's a pleasure to please. No wonder he wanted you smelling sweet afore evening."

Before Jerusa could stammer an answer, two serving girls squeezed past her, struggling with an empty bathing tub that was little more than a huge sawed-off hogshead, lined with a draped sheet to spare Jerusa from splinters. Another girl followed with a bucket of hot water in each hand, which she dumped, sloshing, into the tub.

"A dozen buckets will see you ready, Mrs. Geary," said Mrs. Cartwright with satisfaction as she shooed the serving girls from the room ahead of her. "You begin to undress, ma'am, and we'll have the tub filled before you're ready. Unless, that is, you'd prefer one of the girls to stay and tend to you?"

"Oh, no, thank you, that won't be necessary," murmured Jerusa, remembering all too clearly the night she'd had to let Michel act as her lady's maid. But the lacings on the simple bodice and skirt she wore now weren't nearly as complicated as her wedding gown, and by the time the last bucket of water had been emptied into the tub, she was waiting in her shift, a ball of Mrs. Cartwright's lilac soap ready in her hand.

Jerusa sighed with pleasure as she finally sank into the tub of water. The windows to the room were open, and the warm afternoon sun slanting into the room made her welcome the cooling temperature of the water. The heady fragrance of a climbing rose outside the casement mingled with the tangy scent of the Connecticut River a half mile away, and fat-bodied bumblebees buzzed lazily from flower to flower.

Swiftly Jerusa scrubbed away at the grime and sweat of the last week, working the soap from her toes to the ends of her hair until at last she felt clean. With a sigh of blissful content-ment, she let herself sink deeper into the lilac-scented water and closed her eyes. She'd grown so accustomed to riding by night and sleeping by day that she felt drowsy here in the af-ternoon, and while she tried to force herself to plan what to do next, her sleepy, relaxed body shared no such intentions. For just these few moments, it was so easy to forget everything....

From years of habitual practice, Michel opened every door and entered every room as silently as a cat, and as he latched the door to this one behind him, Jerusa didn't stir. He smiled wryly to himself, thinking what her reaction would be if she knew he stood behind her now. She was sitting so far down in the tub that her long, wet hair hung over one side and onto the floor, and opposite that he had a charming view of her ankles and feet casually crossed and propped up over the edge of the tub. Lilac soap and a warm, wet, beautiful woman. *Morbleu,* was ever a man more sorely tempted?

He should have left the new clothes he'd bought for her with Mrs. Cartwright and gone on about his business. He still could, and Jerusa would never be the wiser. There wasn't any real reason for him to see her until supper. Lord knows, he'd seen enough of her this last week.

Though not, perhaps, as much as he was seeing right now.

She sighed and shifted in the water, dangling one hand over the edge. Her fingertips were puckered from soaking so long, dripping water like tiny diamonds in the sun, and he thought of how much he'd like to lift her from the water and carry her to the bed and—

Enough. She was his prisoner, not his mistress, and he'd be ten times a fool to think it would ever be otherwise between them. His mother had demanded to see a virgin Sparhawk bride, and by God, that was what he would bring her.

He walked silently across the room to the bed, intending to leave the new gown and go while she dozed. But as he did, her eyes suddenly flew open and she gasped and started. Automatically he turned toward her in time to see the bathwater sloshing as she tried vainly to shield herself.

"What are you doing here?" she demanded breathlessly, her face scarlet with shame. "How dare you come back to spy on me like this?"

She'd sunk down as far as she could into the soapy water, trying to hide, but there was still more of her than there was water, and though she hugged her bent knees as tightly as she could in the narrow space, her skin still glistened enticingly, pale and perfect with only the beads of water to gild it.

Yet somehow he managed to keep his face impassive as he watched her. He was, after all, a man of experience, a man of the world, and besides, he was French. Such sights shouldn't faze him. So why was it taking every scrap of self-possession to stand before her like this?

"I didn't come to spy on you, *ma chérie,*" he said as dispassionately as he could. "If I'd wished to spy, I would have stayed in the hall and peeped at you through the keyhole."

She glared at him, unconvinced. He'd tricked her again, and she was as furious with herself for letting it happen as she was at him for doing it. "Mrs. Cartwright thought you were so blessed kind, ordering me a bath, when *I* know now you did it simply for the chance to see me—to see me—like this!"

"I'm inclined to side with Mrs. Cartwright."

"Oh, aye, of course you would!" She tossed her head defiantly, scattering water across the floor. "Now, will you leave on your own, or must I scream for help?"

"Scream all you wish, *ma chérie.* Or do you forget that they believe we're man and wife?" He tossed his hat onto the bed, reminding her again that he would be expecting to share it with her. "By English law, you're mine to do with what I will, and short of murder, none can interfere."

She nearly howled with frustration. "Then must I sit here all day pickling in lilac water until you decide to leave?"

He leaned against the windowsill and smiled slowly, almost as if he were realizing for the first time that she was naked. "I'm not stopping you, Rusa, am I?"

"You've no right to call me that!" she snapped. She struck one hand on the water hard, sending a great splash of soapy water over the front of his coat and breeches.

He glanced down at what she'd done, his smile widening.

Her sweeping gesture had let him see the full, high curves of her breasts, glistening with soap as they bobbed gently in the water.

"A worthy suggestion, *ma belle,*" he said, shrugging his shoulders free of his coat and tossing it, too, onto the bed. "Perhaps I could use a bath myself. It does seem a shame to let all that water go to waste."

"No!" Frantically Jerusa looked around for something to put on. Of course she had no dressing gown, and to her chagrin she remembered that Mrs. Cartwright had taken her only clothes to wash them. At Michel's orders, no doubt; what better way to keep her here while he went about his business? All she had left was the worn sheet, draped over the back of the chair, that they'd given her to dry herself. "If you won't leave, then you must turn your back and give me your word that you won't turn around until I say so."

"My word?" He hooked a finger into his neckcloth and tugged it free. "I thought by now, *ma mie,* you'd learned how little that article would be worth from me."

"Then from common decency?" Her voice squeaked as she considered the consequences of what he was proposing. "You said you didn't want to spy on me."

His waistcoat thumped on the bed beside his coat and hat before he leaned against the windowsill long enough to pull off his boots and then his socks. "I'm still not spying. I'm taking a bath."

In a single, fluid movement he drew his shirt over his head, and she barely stifled her gasp. His shoulders seemed broader, the lean span of his waist more narrow, without the billowy linen shirt to cover them. Dark whorls of gold hair curled across his chest with fascinating symmetry before it tapered low on his belly above the waistband of his breeches. The only flaw to his perfection was a single, long scar along one arm, the kind that came from sword fighting. He looked as hard and strong as she knew he was, his muscles the obvious mark of a man who lived—and would die—physically.

Yet there was still an inborn elegance to him that showed even now, a certain grace that would always separate him from common sailors or dockworkers. In the time he'd been gone, he'd stopped at a barber, for the dark beard that had softened the line of his jaw was gone, and he looked years younger without it. The ribbon that had held his queue had been pulled off with the shirt, and his dark blond hair was as bright as the slanting sunlight that filled the room, bright as a halo for the fallen angel he must be, and, with a little catch in her breathing, she decided that she'd never seen a more beautiful man.

Michel smiled, shameless before Jerusa's scrutiny. Although her cheeks were flushed, her eyes were watching him with an eager interest that would have doubtless earned a reprimand from her mother, yet her innocent appreciation pleased him more than he'd ever expected. The worldly women in his past had purred over him like cats with fresh cream, as much, he'd guessed, because it was their trade as from any genuine admiration, and he'd always cynically dismissed their praise. But he didn't doubt that Jerusa's unpracticed response was real and true, a rare compliment for any man, and especially for him.

"Enjoying the view?" he asked lightly, his smile widening to a grin when he saw how her cheeks flushed even darker. But still, he noted, she didn't look away.

"For-forgive me," she stammered. "I didn't mean to stare."

He shrugged as he balled up the shirt and tossed it with the rest of his clothes. He shook his hair back from his face, and for once his smile reached and warmed the blue of his eyes. "Look your fill, *ma belle,* if it pleases you. Lord knows, I've done the same to you."

She didn't answer, acute embarrassment warring with her desire to do exactly as he said. In all her dalliances with Tom, he'd never gone beyond unbuttoning his waistcoat, but she'd seen her brothers without their shirts scores of times, and in the summer the sailors on her father's ships had often stripped to the waist to work, but never once had she felt the way she did now. It was more of the sensual spell only Michel seemed to cast over her, the same spell that bewildered as much as it beguiled her.

But when she saw his hands move to the fall of his breeches, reaching for the first button, her conscience abruptly jolted her back to the reality of her situation. She was sitting in a tub full of tepid water with nothing to clothe her but fading soapsuds, before a man who was going to be in much the same state in a very few moments if she didn't speak up *now*.

"Michel, don't!" she ordered, struggling to sound firm. It had been bad enough to travel alone with him across the countryside, but somehow it seemed infinitely worse—and more frightening—to be with him like this in a room upstairs in a public house. "Turn around and let me dress first, and then you may wash."

"I told you before I wasn't stopping you, sweet Jerusa." He slipped the first button free, considering how much further he'd go to tease her. "I'm still not."

"But, Michel—"

"But, Jerusa." He liked to hear her say his name, especially now that she did it so automatically.

"Michel, no!" she cried, finally panicking. He'd robbed her of so much already, and she had so little left to take. "Please don't do this to me!"

He frowned, stopped by the edge of fear in her voice. He hadn't heard that from her since the first night, and it stunned him. Only seconds before she'd been spitting fire, taunting and daring him as much as he was her. But then to have her beg like this—Lord, he'd never heard that from her before, and it made him feel low and mean.

"Whatever you please, *mademoiselle*," he said softly, and

as he turned his back to her, he caught the grateful relief in her eyes, which seemed somehow worse than the fear. He didn't want to hurt her; he'd never wanted that. But *mordieu,* what had she done to *him?*

He listened to her scramble from the tub with a great slosh of water, and he tried not to imagine how she must look with that water streaming from her lovely body only a few feet behind him. He swore beneath his breath, struggling to will his body into polite, disinterested submission. Why couldn't the favorite daughter of Gabriel Sparhawk have been walleyed, squat and pudding faced?

"It's your turn to wash now, if you still wish it," she murmured self-consciously when she was done. "I'll sit near the window while you do."

Yet when he turned to face her, he had to swallow back the groan that rose in his throat. She had wrapped the sheet around her body, tucking the ends beneath her arms and above her breasts so that she was covered from there to the floor. But if she believed she was now decent, she was woefully mistaken. The worn, thin linen clung to every damp curve of her body, accentuating the ripe flare of her hips and waist and the shapely length of her legs more than if she'd remained naked. And her breasts—*mordieu,* the water must be cooler than he realized to leave her full flesh so round and taut.

She lifted her arms to squeeze the water from her dark hair, and her breasts rose higher, the water falling across them making the sheet so transparent that the rosy circles of her puckered nipples were clearly visible. With tiny diamonds of water tangled in her lashes, she smiled shyly with the most ill-founded trust he could imagine.

Sacristi, did she have any notion of what she was doing to him? All she'd have to do was look at the front of his breeches to learn. Before she did, he stalked to the bed and tore open the package he'd left there with his saddlebag.

"Here," he said gruffly, forgetting all the genteel phrases he'd rehearsed in the dressmaker's shop. "This will suit you better than an old sheet."

He shook out the green calimanco gown he'd bought for her and flung it across the bed. A new pair of lisle stockings tumbled out onto the floor, along with a new shift and petticoat and a green silk ribbon for her hair.

She looked down at them, clearly confused. "But Mrs. Cartwright said she'd bring my other clothes directly, once they were clean."

"To hell with the other clothes," he said sharply. "For now I want you to wear these."

Swiftly her gaze rose from the clothes to him, her eyes turned wary at his tone.

He sighed with exasperation at his own want of manners. "*Sacristi, non,* that's not what I meant," he said, raking his fingers back through his loose hair. "What I did mean, Jerusa, is that I thought you'd prefer these. If you wish to wear them, that is."

Still she said nothing, and his exasperation with himself grew. The gown and other fripperies were more fashionable— and more expensive—than the things he'd given her before, but what he hoped she'd notice was that he'd chosen it all with her in mind, from the green that nearly matched her eyes to the tight-laced bodice that might actually fit her slender waist.

Given her: that was the difference. This was a gift, he realized uneasily, meant for her alone, and the first he'd ever given any woman, save his mother. He didn't know why he'd done it or why it mattered so much that she notice.

But matter it did, far more than it should. A fool's empty hope, he told himself fiercely, the gestures of a besotted simpleton who—

"Thank you, Michel," she said, her sudden smile outshining the sun and melting away all his doubts. "How ever did you guess that I favor such a particular tint of green?"

She bent gracefully to gather up the gown, and as she did, the wet sheet slipped even lower across her breasts. Hastily he looked away, but not before the heady image seared itself forever into his memory. He jerked the curtains to the bed across one side, the horn rings scraping against the metal rod.

"You can dress there," he said, not trusting himself to look back at her, "and I'll wash on the other side of the curtain. Agreed?"

"Agreed to what? You sound as if you're not sure you can trust *me!*"

"Oh, *ma chérie,*" he confessed softly, "I'm not sure of anything where you're concerned."

She stared at him, her indignation gone. "Neither am I," she whispered uncertainly. "But I thought you only did that to me, not the other way around."

He swallowed hard, feeling the shock of the current that passed between them as keenly as any lightning. No wonder she'd looked so frightened. He'd never in his life been this scared. How could a pretty girl's smile and a handful of words make his whole world lurch out of balance like this?

Desperately he racked his memory for an explanation. It must be because he'd spent so much time alone in her company, more than he'd ever passed with any other woman, or maybe it was simply lust, fueled by the stolen glimpse of her in the tub. It couldn't be her courage, or her wit, or her daring in the face of all he'd done to her, or the merry sound of her laughter.

Morbleu, it couldn't be *her.*

He shook his head, wondering how he could make her understand when he didn't understand himself. "It's not that simple, Rusa."

"Because of my family?" she asked wistfully. "Because of Tom?"

"Among others."

"You mean whoever hired you." Her pale fingers tightened around the green calimanco. "The one who's paying you to kidnap me."

Reluctantly he nodded. "Would you believe me if I told you how much I regret that?"

"No." Her smile was swift and heartbreakingly brittle. "Because if it were true, you'd let me go free, wouldn't you?"

He reached out to brush his fingertips across her cheek, and felt how she trembled beneath his touch. "It's because it *is* true that I cannot," he said sorrowfully. "I told you this isn't simple, *ma mie*. If we had only met in another time, then—"

"Then I might be the queen of England and you the king of France, and we'd be not one whit better off." She drew her face away from the light caress of his fingers, her eyes too bright with unshed tears. "You'd best wash yourself before the water's too chill."

For a long moment he held her gaze, hating himself for the coward he was, then turned away as she'd ordered, the drawn bed curtain like a wall of stone between them. No wonder his poor *Maman* had gone mad, if this was the price of caring too much!

Her heart pounding, Jerusa steadied herself against the bedpost. This must be more of the same glib foolishness calculated to break her spirit, she told herself fiercely, as meaningless as the endless stream of pretty, petty endearments that he sprinkled through his conversation. Hadn't he always known the exact teasing, taunting words to say to make her alternately wish to throttle and then to kiss him?

Yet in her heart she knew this was different. She'd seen the yearning in his eyes as clearly as if he'd shouted it from the rooftops, and heard the confusion and sorrow in his voice that mirrored her own. He couldn't have pretended that, could he? For once, had he really been telling her the truth?

And what of it, Jerusa? Why should it matter if he's told you the truth now, far too late to do any good? He's lied to you from the first word he spoke, and he hasn't a single reason to change his ways now. Remember that, Jerusa! Don't forget what he has done to you!

Don't forget simply because he's handsome as sin and his lazy smile makes your blood warm in ways it never did with Tom.

Don't forget just because he saved your life, and then you risked yours in turn for him.

Don't forget, only because in one halting moment of honesty he let himself be more naked and vulnerable than you yourself felt beneath his gaze.

Just because he cares for you, and God help you, Jerusa Sparhawk, you care for him…

The sound of the water splashing around him in the tub jerked her back to the present, and with a small flustered exclamation, she rushed to dress. He'd let her go untouched and granted her the privacy to dress when she hadn't expected it, but she'd be a fool to depend on his word—or such a promise from any man, for that matter—by dawdling about in a wet sheet.

By the time he'd finished washing and dressing and had tugged the curtain back, she, too, was dressed and sitting on the stool by the window, struggling to comb her fingers through a week's worth of knots in her damp hair. Her heart quickened when she heard him come stand behind her, but his voice when he spoke was as even as if nothing had changed between them.

"This might help, *chère*. Another trifle forgotten in our haste to leave Newport."

She lifted the heavy weight of her hair with her arm and peeked out from beneath it. In Michel's hand was a thick-toothed comb of polished horn. She smiled with relief, reaching to take it from him.

"No, *ma belle*," he said firmly as he held the comb away out of her reach. "Let me do it."

"Don't be foolish, Michel, I can—"

"I said let me do it for you, *chère*," he repeated, his voice low as he began to work the comb through her tangled hair. "You'll be toiling all night if you try to do it yourself."

Grudgingly she knew he was right, and, with a sigh, she sat straight for him with her hands in her lap. Over and over he drew the comb through her hair, each pass moving higher as he worked through the tangles.

"You've done this before, haven't you?" she asked, wishing it weren't so easy to imagine the tresses of scores of lovely, languid Frenchwomen sliding through his fingers. "Most men wouldn't begin to know how."

He chuckled softly. "I've been accused of many things, Rusa, but never of being a *coiffeur*. But you're right. I've often played that role for my mother."

"Your mother?" Jerusa smiled, intrigued by the notion. "How fortunate for her! As much as my brothers love my mother, I can't imagine them ever doing such a thing."

"Ah, well, perhaps if I'd brothers or sisters I wouldn't have done it, either. But because there was only the two of us, I never thought it strange."

She closed her eyes, relaxing beneath the rhythm of the comb through her hair. "There'd be your father, too, of course."

"Not that I can remember, no. He died before I was born."

"Oh, Michel, I'm sorry," she said softly. Her own large family had always been such a loud, boisterous presence in her life that it was hard to imagine otherwise. "How sad for your mother to be left widowed like that!"

The comb paused, the rhythm broken. "She wasn't widowed because she wasn't my father's wife."

"Oh, Michel," she murmured, her sympathy for him swelling. Though she'd heard the French were less strict than the English in such matters, any woman who let herself fall into such unfortunate circumstances was sure to be shunned by all but her closest friends. She'd heard the dire warnings often enough from her own mother. How much Michel and his mother must have suffered, how hard their life together must have been!

"But my father did intend to wed her," Michel continued, his voice growing distant. "*Maman* was sure of that, for she loved him—*loves* him—with all her heart. But he was killed before she could tell him she was carrying his child, and then, of course, it was too late."

"Was your father a soldier or a sailor?" she asked softly. Longing to see his face, she tried to twist about on the stool, but instead he gently held her head steady, beginning again to comb her hair. "You must have been born during King George's war."

"My father was a sailor, *oui,* a privateersman, a captain, the most successful of his time in the Caribbean." Michel's pride was unmistakable. "His name was Christian Saint-Juste Deveaux, and his home was more elegant and far more grand than many of the *châteaux* of France. Or it was, at least, before he was slaughtered by an Englishman and his house burned to the ground."

Slaughtered by an Englishman: no wonder he'd been so unhappy over what she'd told Dr. Hamilton. But how could she have guessed? The coincidence was eerie. Both their fathers privateers, both captains prospering, though they'd fought on opposite sides of the same war.

But maybe it wasn't a coincidence at all. "My father was a privateer captain, too," she said slowly, her uneasiness growing. "Though I expect you know that already, don't you?"

Michel didn't seem to hear her, or perhaps he simply chose not to answer. "Your oldest brother, Jonathan, or Jon, as you call him. He's twenty-six years old, isn't he?"

She hesitated, wondering why he should speak of her brother now. "Jon was twenty-six in April."

"My own age exactly. Did you know that, *ma chérie?* I, too, was born in April in 1745. But while your brother was blessed with both parents, I, alas, was not. Yours were wed on board your father's sloop, weren't they? Or rather your mother's, since by rights the *Revenge* still belonged to her, didn't it? That would be in September of 1744, in the waters off Bequia, with your grandfather there, too, to give his blessing."

"That is true," she said faintly, her uneasiness growing as he told her details of her family that no outsider should know. "But of what interest can any of this be to you?"

It was the reproach in her voice that finally stopped Michel. He hadn't meant to tell her any of this, not here, not yet, but once he'd begun he had found it impossible to end the torrent of names and dates and circumstances he'd heard repeated to him since his birth.

But maybe it was better this way. If Jerusa knew the truth as his mother had told him, then maybe she'd stop believing he was a better man than he was. She would scorn him as he deserved, and leave him free to honor his mother's wishes and his father's memory.

He wouldn't allow himself to consider the other alternative, that once she heard the truth, she might understand, and forgive. *Morbleu,* he'd never deserve that, not from her.

"Why, Michel?" she asked again, her voice unsteady. "What purpose do you have in telling me these things I already know?"

"Simply to prove the whims of fate, *ma chère,*" he said deliberately. "You've only to count the months to see that your brother, too, was conceived long before your parents wed."

"But that cannot be." Jerusa's hands twisted in her lap as she remembered again all her mother's careful warnings. Her mother could never have let herself be—well, be *ruined* like that, even by a man like Gabriel Sparhawk. But as Michel said, Jerusa had only to count the months and learn the awful truth that neither of her parents had bothered to hide.

"Two boys, Rusa, two fates," continued Michel softly as he combed the last snarl from her hair. "Consider it well. One of us destined to be the eldest son of a wealthy, respected gentleman, while the other was left a beggar and a bastard. Two boys, *ma mie,* two fates."

Because she would never know, he dared to raise one lock of her hair briefly to his lips. "And two fathers, *ma chérie,*" he said in a hoarse whisper that betrayed the emotion twisting through him. "*Our* fathers."

He knew the exact moment when she guessed the truth, for he felt her shudder as the burden of it settled onto her soul. With a little gasp she bowed her head, and gently he spread her dark hair over her shoulders like a cape before he went to the bed for his hat and coat.

He took his leave in silence, closing the door with as little sound as he'd opened it two hours before.

Silence that was alive with the mocking laughter of the ghosts of the past.

Chapter Eleven

Her father had killed Michel's father.

No, *slaughtered* was the word he'd used. Her father had slaughtered his. Her *father*.

She stared unseeing from the window, struggling to imagine Father this way. Of course she'd known he'd once been a privateer, the luckiest captain to sail out of Newport, and from childhood she'd heard the jests among her father's friends about how ruthless he'd been in a trade that was little better than legalized, profitable piracy. She remembered how, as boys, her brothers would brag to their friends about how many French and Spanish rogues Father had sent to watery graves, and how he'd laugh when he caught them playing with wooden swords and pretend pistols as they burned another imaginary French frigate.

But before now, none of that had mattered. To her, Father was gentleness itself, the endlessly tall, endlessly patient man with the bright green eyes who would always make room for her to climb onto his lap after supper and listen solemnly as she played out little games with her dolls on the table after the cloth was drawn. With her, Father never scolded if an impulsive hug left strawberry jam on the front of his white linen shirt, or refused if she begged to go down to the shipyard with him. With her, he always smiled and laughed or offered his handkerchief and his open arms when she wept, and not once had she ever doubted that he loved her as much as any father could a daughter.

And yet it didn't occur to her that Michel might have invented it all, or somehow mistaken her father for another man. In her heart she knew he'd spoken the truth. It wasn't just that Michel had been so unquestionably right about everything else to do with her family; it was the raw emotion she'd heard in his voice when he'd told her, or rather, when he *hadn't* told her. Another man would have delighted in horrifying her with the details of how Gabriel Sparhawk had killed Christian Deveaux, but not Michel. The pain he must feel had sealed all that tightly within him, and that, to her, was infinitely more terrifying than any mere bloodthirsty storytelling could ever be.

Two fates, two fathers. Fate had cast her on the winning side, while Michel had lost everything. And now, somehow he meant to even the balance.

Without any sense of how long she'd been sitting, she rose unsteadily to her feet. The shadows of the trees were long across the street below, and the smell of frying onions from the kitchen windows below told her that preparations for supper had already begun. Michel hadn't said when he'd return, but odds were he'd be back before sundown, maybe sooner.

Think, Jerusa, think! He's told you all along he wanted you, and now you know why! You can leave him now, while he believes you too distraught to act, or you can sit here like a lump of suet, waiting until he decides exactly how he'll avenge himself on your miserable self!

She took a deep breath to steady herself, and then another. In a way he'd already made her escape easier. In a seaport town such as this one, she'd have a good chance of finding someone who would know her father or brothers, and dressed as she was now, she'd have an easier time of convincing them she really was who she claimed to be.

Briskly she gathered her hair off her shoulders and tied it back with the green ribbon, trying not to remember the pleasant intimacy of having Michel comb it for her. She'd let herself be drawn into his games long enough, she told herself fiercely. It was high time she remembered she was Jerusa Sparhawk and stop playing at being this mythical Mrs. Geary.

She bent to buckle her shoes, and smiled when she noticed he'd left his saddlebag on the floor beside the bed. Though Michel might have been born poor, he certainly didn't seem to want for money now, and whenever he'd paid for things he'd taken the coins from a leather pouch inside the saddlebag. She didn't mean to rob him exactly, but after he'd kidnapped her, she couldn't see the harm in borrowing a few coins now to help ease her journey home.

Swiftly she unbuckled the straps and looked inside. The contents were the usual for a man who was traveling—three changes of shirts and stockings, a compass, an envelope of tobacco, a striker and a white clay pipe, soap and a razor, one of the pistols plus the gunpowder and balls it needed.

Gingerly she lifted the gun with both hands, considering whether to take it, too. It was heavier than the pistols her father had taught her to fire, the barrel as long as her forearm, the flintlock polished and oiled with the professional care of a man who knew his life depended on it. Reluctantly she laid the gun back into the bottom of the bag. There was no way a woman could carry a weapon like that, at least not concealed, and if she wished to slip away unobtrusively, holding a pistol in both hands before her as she walked through the town would hardly be the way to do it.

She ran her fingertips along the saddlebag's lining, searching for an opening that might hide the pouch with the money. She found a promising oval lump and eased it free. But instead of the pouch full of coins, the lump turned out to be a flat package wrapped in chamois. Curiosity made her open it, and inside lay a small portrait on ivory, framed in brass, of a black-haired young woman. Her heart-shaped face was turned winsomely toward the painter, her lips curved in a smile and her finely drawn brows arched in perennial surprise, which seemed to Jerusa very French.

Carefully she turned the portrait over, but there was no name or inscription on the back that might give her a clue of the pretty sitter's identity. Not that she really needed one. Clearly the woman must be Michel's sweetheart if he carried her picture with him. Whoever she was, she was welcome to him, decided Jerusa firmly as she wrapped the chamois back over the portrait. More than welcome, really, she thought with a sniff. So why did she feel this odd little pang of regret when she remembered how he'd smiled when he'd kissed *her?*

The rapping on the door was sharp and deliberate, startling her so much that she dropped the picture into the bag.

"Mrs. Geary, ma'am?" called the maidservant that Jerusa recognized as one of Mrs. Cartwright's daughters. "Mrs. Geary, ma'am, are you within?"

"I'll be there directly." With haste born of guilt, Jerusa shoved the picture back into the lining of the bag and rebuckled the straps to make it look the way she'd found it. Swiftly she rose to her feet, smoothing her hair as she went to open the door.

The girl bobbed as much a curtsy as she dared with a tray laden with a teapot, sugar, cream and a plate full of sliced bread and butter in her outstretched arms.

"Compliments of me mother, ma'am," she said as she squeezed past Jerusa. "Since Mr. Geary said to hold your supper for half past eight on account of him returning late, we thought in the kitchen you might get to feeling a mite peckish waiting for him."

"Mr. Geary's business can occupy considerable time,"

ventured Jerusa, praying she'd sound convincing, "but he didn't tell me he'd be so late this particular day."

"Oh, aye, he told me mother not to bother looking for him afore nightfall." Bending from the waist, the girl thumped the tray down onto the floor while she cleared away the wash pitcher and candlestick from the washstand for a makeshift tea table. "I expect he didn't tell you so you wouldn't worry over him. He's a fine, considerate gentleman, your husband is."

"He is a most rare gentleman," said Jerusa, barely containing her excitement. If he wasn't expected back until evening, then she'd have plenty of time to make her escape. "Did he say anything else before he left?"

"Nay, ma'am, save that you was to have whatever you desired." Squinting at the uneven table, the girl squared the tray on its top as best she could and then stood back, her arms stiffly at her side. She cleared her throat self-consciously. "Would you like me to pour for you, Mrs. Geary? Me mother wants me to learn gentry's ways so I can do for the gentlefolk."

"Why, yes, thank you," murmured Jerusa. "That would be most kind."

She swept into the room's only chair, gracefully fanning her skirts about her legs in her most genteel fashion for the girl's benefit. Though she didn't have the heart to tell her that, in the households of the better sort, ladies preferred to pour their own tea, regardless of how many servants they kept, she did want to hear what else the girl might be coaxed into volunteering.

The girl bit the tip of her tongue as she concentrated on pouring the tea without spilling it. "Much as me mother would wish it otherways, we don't get much custom from the gentry," she confided once the tea was safely into Jerusa's cup. "'Tis mostly sea captains and supercargos of the middling sort, tradesmen with goods bound for other towns, and military gentlemen rich enough to pay their way. Rovers and wanderers, ma'am, though me mother tries her best to sort out the rogues among 'em afore they stay."

Jerusa took the offered teacup with a nod of thanks and added a sprinkle of sugar to the tea before she poured it from the cup into the saucer to cool. "But in my experience it's always the travelers who tell the most amusing tales."

The girl snorted and rolled her eyes. "Oh, aye, ma'am, and some ripe ones I've heard, particularly when the gentlemen fall into their cups! Mermaids and serpents great as this house, oceans made of fire and land that shivers like a custard pudding beneath your feet, all of it, ma'am, the fancies of rum and whiskey."

Jerusa lowered her gaze to the saucer of tea, tracing one finger idly around the rim. "I fear that what Mr. Geary and I have heard in our travels has been much less wondrous and far more gossip. A man whose house had been struck by lightning five times, another mad with grief over the death of his sons."

She paused, daring herself to speak the last. "And, oh, yes, the bride carried off from her own wedding."

"Lud, a bride, you say?" The girl's eyes widened with fascination. "I haven't heard that one afore! Do you judge it true, or only more barkeep's claptrap?"

"Who's to say?" said Jerusa, realizing too late that the offhanded shrug of her shoulders was pure Michel. "But I wonder that you've not heard it yourself here in Seabrook. They say the lady was from one of the best families in Newport, a great beauty and much admired, and that she vanished without a word of warning from her parents' own garden, not a fortnight past."

"Nay, ma'am, then it cannot be but a yarn." The girl sighed deeply with disappointment. "If she vanished straightaway like you say, then wouldn't her bridegroom come a-seeking her? If he loved her true, then he would not rest until he'd found her again, ma'am, no matter how far he must journey. Sure but he'd come through Seabrook, wouldn't he? But we've not had a word of a sorrowful gentleman searching for his lover here, else I or me mother would've heard of it."

"But perhaps he went north, toward Boston instead," said Jerusa more wistfully than she knew. "Perhaps he didn't come south at all."

"Now I ask you, ma'am, what sort of villain would take a lady to Boston?" scoffed the girl. "Nay, he'd be bringing her south, toward the wickedness to be found in the lower colonies, and that bridegroom should've been after him hot as a hound after a hare. False-hearted he'd be otherwise, wouldn't he?"

Sadly Jerusa wondered why she was the only one who had any faith in Tom Carberry. Like the Faulks before her, this girl echoed Michel's sentiments regarding Tom, sharing suspicions that, unhappily, Jerusa had been driven to consider herself.

"But what of the poor lady's family?" she persisted. "Surely you've heard news of them? Handbills, or a reward offered for her safekeeping?"

"Nary a word nor a scrap, ma'am," declared the girl soundly. "Pretty as it may be, Mrs. Geary, I fear I warrant your tale false."

Heartsick, Jerusa wondered what she'd done to make her family abandon her like this. She thought again of the father who'd loved her so well, and of her brothers, Jon, Nick and Josh. Especially Josh. Sweet Almighty, surely Josh wouldn't have given up on her like this?

Unless Michel had sent some sort of message to them, full of lies to make them doubt. Maybe he'd told them she was already dead and beyond their help. Could he be planning to avenge his father's death by taking her life, lulling her into an ill-founded sense of trust and dependence until he decided the perfect moment to kill her? The pistol from the saddlebag that she'd held in her hand might be the very one he meant to use on her.

"If there's no other way to oblige you, Mrs. Geary, I must be back downstairs to me mother," said the girl with another stiff little curtsy. "Call for me, now, ma'am, if there's aught I can fetch for you."

"Wait!"

The girl turned, her brows raised at Jerusa's urgency. "Ma'am?"

"Another word, I beg of you, before you leave." Jerusa worked to control the shaking of her voice. "Did Mr. Geary say anything else of me to you or your mother?"

The girl studied her curiously. "Nay, ma'am, naught beyond what I've told you already. That you were to wait to take your supper for him, and that you were to have whatever else you wished brought to you. Like the bath, ma'am."

"Nothing more?"

"Nay, ma'am, but what would he say to us? Sure the man loves you dear and wishes you happy in all things. You've but to see his eyes when he watches you to know that."

Jerusa bit back her retort. It was hardly the girl's fault if she'd swallowed Michel's lies. Hadn't she been taken in by them herself?

Abruptly she stood. "I believe I shall take a short walk before my husband returns."

"But, ma'am, you've hardly touched your tea!"

"I'll take it later." She had no money and no sense of where to go in the little town, but the idea of remaining in the room alone, waiting for Michel, was now intolerable. "If Mr. Geary should return before I do, you may tell him I shall see him at supper."

Still fearing that the Cartwrights might stop her at Michel's orders, she hurried past the serving girl and down the stairs, her skirts fluttering around her. The door to the yard was propped open, and as she rushed through it, nearly running, she felt the same wild exhilaration that she had when she'd escaped from Michel that first day, from the barn. But this time would be different, for this time she would succeed.

She walked swiftly down the street, pausing at the corner

to get her bearings. Though Seabrook was new to her, the plan of its streets was similar to every other New England town that had grown around a harbor, with every street either parallel or perpendicular to the waterfront. Toward the east she'd seen the tops of masts and furled sails from her window in the inn, and she headed toward them now.

Ships were familiar to her, a welcome reminder of home, and though she briefly considered looking for the town's constable, she believed she'd be more likely to convince a seaman than some puffed-up townsman that she was a Sparhawk. Seabrook wasn't that far from Newport. Surely somewhere in this little port she'd find one sailor who knew her father, one man who'd see the family resemblance in her face and believe she was who she claimed.

But just as every street in a seaport led to the waterfront, every waterfront also tended to be the least reputable section of town, and Seabrook was no exception. Though much smaller than Newport, Seabrook had its handful of block-front warehouses and countinghouses, chandleries and outfitters, as well as taverns, rum shops and rooming houses to suit every sailor's taste and purse.

With the summer afternoon nearly done, workers from the docks and shipyard and a smattering of fishermen were beginning to trudge through the narrow streets to their homes and families. Others stayed behind to meet friends in the rum shops and bring their filled tankards to the well-worn benches outside in the fading sun.

Steadfastly Jerusa walked past them with her head high, ignoring their comments as best she could. Men had always admired her—she couldn't remember a time when they hadn't—but this kind of crude, leering invitation called after her was new. Her cheeks flaming and her heart beating faster, she wished she had at least a wide-brimmed bonnet to hide within, or, better yet, a cloak that covered her clear to her feet, and longingly she thought of the gun she'd left in Michel's saddlebag. Perhaps she should have brought it, after all. They wouldn't have dared shout at her if she'd been carrying *that*.

At last she reached the water itself, the wide, shining mouth of the Connecticut River, where it emptied into the sea. But unlike Newport, there were only three stubby wharves jutting out into the water instead of a dozen, and only four vessels of any size tied to them. She hesitated, her grand plan disintegrating in the face of reality. How was she to know which of these sloops and schooners might harbor a friendly captain who could help her? Perhaps it wasn't too late to find the constable, after all.

"Do ye be lost now, lassie?" asked a man behind her, and before Jerusa could reply, he'd seized her arm in his hand. "Lookin' for a man t'give ye proper guidance?"

"I'm not your lassie, and I'm not looking for any sort of guidance that you could offer." Jerusa wrenched her arm free, rubbing it where his fingers had dug into her skin, and glared at the man. Dressed in dirty canvas breeches and a striped shirt with a checkered waistcoat, he was young, her age or close to it, with a ruddy face that nearly matched his dark red hair and beard. "And whatever would give you the idea that I'm lost?"

The man grinned suggestively in return. "On account o' ye wanderin' about like a lamb without her mama, that's why. Or *whyever.*"

"Don't be ridiculous!"

"Oh, I've no mind to be ridiculous," he said, his grin widening. "Ye don't have no bonnet, nor bucket, nor basket, an' ye be dressed fine as for th' Sabbath. Finer, maybe."

Mentally Jerusa cursed her lack of forethought. The man had every right to judge her the way he had, and she caught herself trying to imagine what Michel would say in such a situation.

Sweet Almighty, hadn't she found trouble enough with lies and deceit? Had she forgotten what it was like to tell the truth?

The man was inching closer, his hand hovering toward hers to take it. "Yer shepherd shouldn't have let ye roam, pretty little lamb, or some great wolf might carry ye off. Or do ye be lookin' fer another shepherd?"

Uneasily she backed away. Behind this man were a half-dozen others that were his friends, each one grinning at her like the very wolf their leader had described.

And Lord help her, she'd never felt so much like that lost lamb.

"Come along now, little lamb," coaxed the red-haired man. "The lads an' I will see ye be treated right proper."

The devil take the truth. These backwater sailors wouldn't believe it anyway. She lifted her chin and squared her shoulders, drawing on every bit of her mother's training on how a lady should stand to earn the respect of others.

"I don't need your assistance, sirrah, and I never did," she said imperiously as she pointed to the vessel tied to the nearest dock. "I've business with the master of that schooner there, and I'd be obliged if you would let me pass so I don't keep the gentleman waiting."

Briefly the man glanced over his shoulder and then back to her with disbelief written over every feature. "Ye have business wit' old man Perkins? A sweet little lass such as ye wit' *him?*"

"Captain Perkins's age has no bearing on my business," she said primly as she read the schooner's name on her quarterboard. "All you need know is that I'm expected directly on board the *Hannah Barlow.*"

Crestfallen, the man shook his head as he and the others shuffled from her path. "It be beyond my reason," he muttered unhappily. "A pretty lass wit' old Perkins."

Amazed though Jerusa was that her bluff had worked, she still couldn't resist giving her skirts an extra flick as she walked past them. How Michel would have laughed to see the hangdog looks on their faces after they'd swallowed her story about this Captain Perkins!

But her triumph was short-lived as she walked along the wharf and had her first close look at the *Hannah Barlow*. The gangway was unguarded, without a single crewman in sight on the deck, and cautiously Jerusa stepped aboard. Only a piebald dog with a cropped tail growled at her halfheartedly before he lowered his head and went back to sleep in a nest of old canvas beside the mainmast.

Not good signs, she thought uneasily, and wondered if she'd traded one unfortunate situation for a second that was worse. Thanks to her father and brothers, Jerusa's knowledge of ships was far better than most women's, and what she saw of this schooner did little to reassure her. Her paint was faded and peeling, her planking stained, her lines bunched in haphazard bundles rather than the neat coils that any conscientious captain would have demanded.

"What ye gawkin' at, missy?" growled a man sitting slumped on the steps of the companionway. Hidden by the shadows, she'd missed him before, and from the meanness in his eyes she wished she'd missed him still. "Yer kind's not wanted on board here. Go along, off with ye! Take yer stinkin' trade to them who'll buy it."

"I'm not—not what you think," said Jerusa with as much dignity as she could muster. "My name is Jerusa Sparhawk, of Newport in Rhode Island."

"Oh, aye, and I'm the friggin' royal Prince o' Wales." The man took another pull of the rum bottle in his hand, his gaze insolently wandering over Jerusa. "Off with ye, ye little slut, afore I set the cur on ye."

Jerusa felt herself color at the man's language, but she stood her ground. "I'm not leaving before I see Captain Perkins."

"He ain't here." With a grunt the man pulled himself upright, swaying slightly from the rum. He was rangy and hollow eyed, his dark hair braided in a tight sailor's queue that swung between his shoulder blades as he slowly climbed to the deck to stand before her. "And he won't be back until he's so bloody guzzled that the men will have to carry him aboard on a shutter."

Jerusa sighed with impatient dismay. No wonder the other men had been so appalled that she'd call on this Captain Perkins! "Then who are you?"

"John Lovell, mate on this scow, for all it's yer business." He squinted at her closely. "Ye said yer name was Sparhawk? Of the Plantations?"

"Oh, yes, in Newport," answered Jerusa excitedly. She'd never expected her savior to be so sorry a man, but he was the first she'd met who seemed to recognize her name. "My father is Captain Gabriel Sparhawk."

The man studied her closely. "I've a mind of him. Captain Gabriel, eh? Privateerin' bloke, weren't he?"

Jerusa nodded, her excitement growing. "He sailed in both the Spanish and French wars."

"Did sharp enough to set hisself up as regular guinea-gold gentry, didn't he? I seen him once paradin' about Bridgetown, fine as a rum lord." His eyes glittered beneath their heavy lids. "Ye have the look of him, missy, right enough. But what the devil would his daughter be doin' here on her lonesome in Seabrook?"

"I was kidnapped by a Frenchman who wishes to hurt my father for—for something he did in the last war," she explained, unable to bring herself to repeat Michel's justification. "He's made me ride all across the countryside here to Seabrook, but this has been the first time he's left me alone long enough to escape."

"Hauled ye about, has he?" He smiled, looking her over again and noting her new gown. Half his teeth were broken off, and the stubs that remained were brown from tobacco. "Ye don't look like ye suffered overmuch."

"I haven't exactly," she said hurriedly, not wishing to discuss such details. "At least not in the worst ways a woman can suffer."

Lovell grunted and drank again from the bottle, and from his expression, Jerusa was sure he was busy inventing all the details she'd omitted.

"Kidnappin' should earn that Frenchman a trip to the gallows," he said. "Don't ye want to swear against him with the constable so's ye can see him dance his jig on a rope for what he done to ye?"

She could picture the scene all too easily. Michel at the gallows with his hands pinioned, his white shirt and gold hair tossing in the wind as the hangman slipped the noose over his head, her stern-faced father at the center of the crowd waiting for justice to be done, and she herself—no, she wouldn't be there. How could she bear to witness his hanging, knowing she'd killed him as surely as if she'd put a pistol to his head and fired? Once she'd wanted nothing better, but now the idea alone sickened her.

And how could it be otherwise? Unlike Michel, revenge held no charms for her. Whatever had begun with their fathers must end here, with them.

"I cannot wait the time it would take for the Frenchman to be captured and tried," she said with only half the truth. "I'm free of him now, and that's what matters most to me."

Skeptically Lovell turned his head to look at her sideways and then spat over the schooner's side. "Seems to me, missy, that ye shall lose a powerfully fine chance to rid the world of one more bloody Frenchy."

She shook her head swiftly. "Now I must return to my family and my—my friends in Newport as quickly as possible," she stammered, and fleetingly she wondered when she'd begun thinking of Tom as her friend, no more. "I was hoping to convince Captain Perkins to carry me there."

"Ye would have the old man set his course for Newport jus' because ye asked him nice? Jus' like that?"

"I'm not so great a fool that I'd believe he'd do it from

kindness alone," said Jerusa dryly. "Of course he'll be paid for his trouble."

Lovell looked at her shrewdly. "Have ye the blunt on ye then, missy?"

"I told you before, Mr. Lovell. I may need your captain's assistance, but I'm not a fool." Though she smiled sweetly, her voice crackled with irritation. "If you know my father, then you know he could buy this pitiful excuse for a deep-water vessel outright with the coins he jingles in his waistcoat pockets. Captain Perkins need have no fear on that account."

"Sharp little piece, aren't ye, for all that ye pretend to be such a fine lady. Ye musta got that from yer pa, too, that ye did." He winked broadly, then emptied the bottle and tossed it carelessly over the side. "But consider it done. Ye have my word as the first officer of the *Hannah Barlow* that we'll clear fer Newport with the next tide."

It was now her turn to be skeptical. "And what captain lets his mate decide his next port? Thank you, Mr. Lovell, but I do believe I shall wait to speak with Captain Perkins himself."

He made her a sweeping caricature of a bow. "Then come below to take yer ease in the old man's cabin, missy," he said with another sly wink. "Ye wouldn't be wantin' that wicked Frenchy to spy ye on the deck, would ye now? I'll fetch another bottle so's we two can pass the time proper between us, all companionable."

How great a fool did the man truly believe she was? She'd take her chances with a Frenchman like Michel any day before she'd go below for any reason with this rascally Englishman.

"Thank you, no, Mr. Lovell," she said more politely than his invitation deserved. "I believe I shall wait right here instead for Captain Perkins's return."

Lovell scowled and swore and scratched his belly. "Well, then, what if we go ashore together to sniff out the old bastard and fetch him back to the *Hannah Barlow?* Or is ye too genteel to be seen steppin' out with the likes of John Lovell?"

Jerusa listened warily, wondering how far, if at all, she could trust him. The sun had nearly set over the green Connecticut hills, but by the lanterns hung outside the waterfront taverns, she could see that nightfall hadn't diminished their business at all. Raucous laughter from both men and women drifted out toward the water, mingled with the giddy sound of a hurdy-gurdy. With all those people for company, how much grief could Lovell cause her? And if they really could find Captain Perkins, she would be that much closer to returning to Newport.

A little breeze rose up from the water, and absently she pushed a loose lock of hair back from her face. In the fading light she could just make out the spire of the meetinghouse that stood near to the right of Mrs. Cartwright's public house. She wondered if Michel was there now, and what he'd thought when he'd discovered her gone. Wistfully she realized that she'd probably never see him again. Would he miss her even a tiny bit, or would he only regret the satisfaction she'd stolen from him?

"Lord, how long can it take ye to know yer mind?" demanded Lovell crossly. "All I'm askin' ye to do is walk along *this* wharf until we reach *that* tavern at the end of the lane. Ye shall find the old man sittin' as near to the fire as he can without tumblin' into it, pouring the Geneva spirits and limes down his throat as fast as the wench brings it."

"Very well, Mr. Lovell," she said before she changed her mind. "We'll search for Captain Perkins. Perhaps we'll be lucky enough to find him before he's—what did you call it?— 'so bloody guzzled.'"

"Aye, aye, missy," agreed Lovell as he knuckled his forehead. "Mayhaps we will."

But as Jerusa followed him off the schooner and along the wharf, she found her uneasiness growing. He said nothing, nor did he try to take her arm like the other man had, but that in itself made her worry. He'd been interested enough earlier. His wiry frame was larger than she'd first thought, and now that he was ashore, all his initial unsteadiness from the rum seemed to vanish, making him menacing enough for other men to move from his path.

She stopped and peered into the open door of the tavern where he'd told her Perkins would be drinking. From where she stood she couldn't see any older men near the fireplace, but perhaps if—

"Quit yer gawkin'," growled Lovell. "Ye said ye would follow me, mind?"

"You told me Captain Perkins would be in here, and I—"

"Quit yammerin' and mind me!" He grabbed her wrist and yanked her along after him, around the corner into a murky alleyway. "There's another way to enter that the old man favors."

He jerked her wrist so hard that she yelped and stumbled. After the lantern's light, the darkness here swallowed everything around her. But Lovell was still here: she could hear his breathing, rapid and hoarse, smell the fetid stench of cheap rum and onions and unwashed clothes, feel the pain from the way his nails dug into the soft skin of her wrist.

Why, why had she trusted him? Why hadn't she listened to her instincts and left him when she had the chance?

With a terrified sob she tore her wrist free and stumbled again, pitching forward. As she fell she felt his hands tighten on either side of her waist, dragging her back to her feet, only to slam her hard against the wall behind her, trapping her there with the weight of his body.

"Not so proud now, are ye?" he demanded. "Every bitch looks the same in the dark, even bloody Sparhawks."

Frantically she tried to shrink away from his body, but he followed relentlessly until she could barely breathe. The bricks were rough against her back, snagging at her clothes and skin.

"Too good fer me, ye thought," said Lovell furiously, grinding his hips against hers as he dragged her skirts up around her legs. "Ye gave yerself to that Frenchy, but still ye was too good fer me. But ye shall make it up to me now, won't ye? First ye give me yer money, ye little trollop, then yer body, and then, ye high-nosed little bitch, yer precious little life."

She squeezed her eyes closed, fighting to shut out the terror of what was happening to her. Yet still she felt the cold edge of the knife as he pressed the blade against her throat, and with awful, sickening clarity she knew she was going to die.

Chapter Twelve

Instinct drew Michel to the alley behind the tavern. Instinct, and what he'd overheard from the indignant whore out front about a girl in a green gown dipping into her trade with the sailors.

As it was, he was nearly too late. Back in the shadows, her face was hidden behind the seaman's back, but at once Michel recognized her legs, forced apart on either side against the wall beneath her upturned skirts, legs that were pale and long and kicking as she fought for her virtue and her life. He would have recognized her legs anywhere; he had, after all, seen them that first night in her parents' garden long before he'd seen her face.

His Jerusa, his *bien-aimée*. And *sacristi,* he'd bought her those green ribbons not four hours past.

But he'd wasted time enough. Once again she'd left him no choice.

Michel drew his knife from the sheath at the back of his waist as he crept silently behind the sailor. Briefly he wondered who the man was, and why Jerusa had chosen him to trust. Whatever his name, he would be the one who suffered for trusting her. Another fate, another death to lay to the name of Sparhawk.

The man jerked only once as Michel's knife found its mark, his own knife falling harmlessly from Jerusa's throat to the ground with a thump. While Michel stepped away, back into the shelter of the shadows, the man swore, his voice thick and his eyes already glazing with death. As he staggered backward, he pulled the girl with him, and they fell together in a tangle of arms and legs.

Gasping for breath, she struggled frantically to free herself, still not aware that the grasp she fought belonged to a dead man. Unsteadily she tried to push herself up onto her hands and knees, and at last Michel reached down to pull her roughly to her feet.

"You see what you have done, *ma chérie?*" he demanded. "No, don't try to look away. If you had not run from me again, that man would live still."

Her eyes wild with terror, she shuddered and tried to break free. But Michel held her tight, turning her face so she was forced to see Lovell's body and the spreading dark pool of blood around it. She had to understand what she'd done. She had to know the smell and feel of death, or she'd never understand *him*.

"He—he was going to kill me, Michel," she rasped, her voice ragged from fear and the pressure of the man's knife against her throat. "He was going to rob me, and—and use me, and kill me."

"Then it was you or him, Jerusa," said Michel relentlessly. "Because of what you did, one of you would have died here tonight. Was leaving me worth your life? Think of it, *ma mie.* That could be your blood."

"It would not have been like that, Michel, I swear!"

"It couldn't have been anything else." He grabbed her hand and thrust it downward, into the warm, sticky puddle of Lovell's blood. "Did you wish to be gone from me that badly?"

She gasped and jerked her hand free, but not before her palm and fingers had been stained red. She stared at her hand in horror, her fingers spread and trembling.

"What have you done, Michel?" she whispered as the

horror of what had happened finally grew real. "God help me, Michel, what have you done?"

He smiled grimly, his pulse only now beginning to slow. "Only what you drove me to do, Jerusa," he said softly. "And God help you indeed if you ever leave me again."

"You're fine, *ma chère,*" said Michel again as he carefully sat Jerusa on the edge of the trough beside the public well. He'd gotten her away from the alley by the rum shop as quickly as he could. He'd taken care, too, that no one had seen them come here, and at this time of night, the market square was empty except for a handful of yowling, skittering cats, but still he kept to the shadows. "I swear it, Rusa. You're fine."

He smiled at her again, his face tight with forced cheerfulness. She didn't look fine now, no matter what he told her or how much he wanted to believe it. Her eyes were wide and staring, her face pale even by the moonlight, and her hands and forearms were scraped raw from where she'd been shoved against the brick wall. Though she'd stopped gasping, her breathing remained quick and shallow, and Michel still wasn't convinced she wouldn't faint. Quickly he dipped his handkerchief into the cool water and stroked it across her forehead and cheeks.

She closed her eyes and shivered, but the cool water seemed to calm her, and gently he touched the cloth to her cheeks again.

"Right as rain, *ma mie,* I swear," he said softly. "Isn't that what you English say? Though how an Englishman reared in your infernal Yankee weather could ever make rain and right equal one another is beyond reason."

Gently he took her hand and lowered it into the water, rubbing away the stains left by the dead sailor's blood until her fingers were once again white and unblemished. He had wanted to make her understand, that was all, to understand what he suffered every day of his life. But what demon had made him do it so shockingly? Not for the first time he wondered with despair if he, too, were touched by his mother's madness.

Jerusa sighed, a deep shudder that shook her body, and slowly opened her eyes. "I'm sorry," she said hoarsely. "I should never have left the inn."

"No apologies, Rusa," he murmured. "No apologies."

She shook her head. "I'm not a child. I should have known better."

"You haven't made things any easier for me, true enough." *Morbleu,* was that an understatement. By some quirk of the winds he and Jerusa had arrived in Seabrook before Gilles Rochet's sloop. Michel would have been willing to wait for him here a day or two—his confidence in Gilles was worth that—but now they would have to leave Seabrook immediately, this night if possible. With any luck the dead sailor's body wouldn't be discovered before dawn, and by then he intended to be long gone.

He took the hem of Jerusa's skirt and swept it back and forth through the water, trying to rinse away the bloodstains.

"You don't have to do that now, Michel," she said. "I'd rather go back to the inn, and Mrs. Cartwright can tend to those—those spots there."

"Not if I can help it, she won't. Right now you're the one who's in the greater danger of meeting Jack Ketch."

She looked at him uncertainly, remembering what he'd told her in the alley. "Don't be foolish, Michel. What have I done?"

"Not a thing, *ma petite,* but the constable will trust his eyes and ears more than your word," said Michel bleakly. "I had no choice but to kill the man, Jerusa. I couldn't put you at that risk, not with his knife at your throat. It had to be quick."

Briefly she closed her eyes again as her throat tightened at the memory. Michel accused her father of being a murderer, but was what he'd done himself any different? She didn't want to consider how deftly, how deliberately Michel must have thrust his knife into the other man. Yet if he hadn't, she would be the one who'd died instead. Dear God, why was it all so complicated?

"I had no choice," said Michel again, desperate that she understand. He had killed the man to save her. If he had to, he would do it again. In his world, the difference between life and death could often be measured by a second's hesitation, and tonight he had nearly been too late. "You must believe me, Jerusa."

Troubled and confused though she was, she still nodded. "Mr. Lovell—he's dead, then?"

Michel sighed. "*Sacristi,* did he know your name, too?"

"I had to tell him," she said softly, her shoulders drooping. "I didn't see the harm in it. I wanted his captain to take me back to Newport, you see."

"At least he's past telling anyone else." Michel sat back on his heels and whistled low under his breath. "All we must contend with now is that half the town knows your face."

"And because I'm a stranger in this town, and because I was the last one to be seen walking with Mr. Lovell and I've his blood on my gown, then everyone will think I killed him." She pressed her hand over her mouth, fighting to keep back her tears. "Oh, Michel!"

"They may think what they please, *chérie,*" he said softly. He took her into his arms to comfort her, even as he told himself he shouldn't. "But before they touch you, they'll have to answer to me."

Wearily she slipped her arms around his waist, holding him tight as she rested her head against his chest. This once she would forget what their fathers had done, and pray that Michel could to the same. She would forget about the bridegroom she'd left behind and about the dark-haired woman in the miniature in the saddlebag. None of it mattered, not really. But twice now Michel had saved her life, and he was promising to do it a third. She wouldn't doubt him again. If he said he would watch over her, he would.

His embrace tightened around her protectively. No one had trusted him like this before, but then, he'd never let anyone come this close, either. But with her, it somehow seemed right.

Right as rain.

Jerusa sat upright in the center of the bed and with both hands aimed the pistol at the door and whoever had knocked on the other side.

"Who is it?" she called, trying to make her voice sound properly sleepy.

"Who else could it be, Rusa?" answered Michel softly, so as not to wake Mrs. Cartwright's other guests.

Jerusa flung back the coverlet and bounded to open the door, the pistol still in her hand. "You've been gone so long," she said breathlessly as Michel slipped into the room. "I was afraid something had happened."

"Less than an hour. And what more could happen, eh?" He frowned as he noted that she was completely dressed, down to her shoes. "You were supposed to rest."

"Oh, Michel, how could I possibly sleep?" She fought back the impulse to throw her arms around his neck and hug him. Things had been different by the well. Then he'd offered his embrace as comfort, and welcomed hers in return. Now she wasn't as sure.

"I suppose sleep was too much to expect, *chère*." But she did look better, he decided, her eyes bright with excitement, and some of his worry for her slipped away. "No visitors?"

"Not a soul," she declared as she handed him the pistol, keeping to herself how she'd imagined every creak on the stairs to be the constable coming for her.

"Just as well," he said dryly as he disarmed the flintlock. There'd been a time, and not so long ago, when she would have cheerfully emptied the same gun into his back, and now she handed it to him without a thought. Progress, he supposed, though of what sort he wasn't sure. "Gather your things and we'll leave."

She didn't have much. At Michel's suggestion she had changed back into the clothes that the Cartwrights had washed and returned earlier, and she'd already packed the green gown into a neat bundle she could carry with one hand.

"Can we get the horses from the stable at this hour?" she asked. "Though I suppose there must be a boy who'll let us take them."

"The horses are gone, Rusa. I sold them this afternoon."

"Sold them?" she cried with dismay. "Even Abigail?"

He tucked the pistol into his belt and slung the saddlebag over his shoulder. "Abigail and Buck both. As charming as they were, *ma chérie,* we didn't need them any longer."

"But we can't stay in Seabrook, Michel," she said anxiously. "You said that yourself."

"And I also said we were leaving. Just not on horseback." Carefully he laid two guineas on the edge of the table where Mrs. Cartwright would be sure to find them, a more than generous settling of their account. Generous enough, he hoped, that she'd also forget Master and Mistress Geary had been her guests if the constable did come asking questions.

"By sea, then," she said uneasily, clutching her bundle to her chest in both arms. "By ship?"

"By ship." He took the single candlestick from the table and turned to face her. "But you needn't worry that I'll take you back to the *Hannah Barlow.*"

In the draft from the window the candle's flame flared and flickered, dancing shadows across the angular planes of his face, masking his expression from her.

"Or to Newport?" Reminding herself of all they'd shared together, she dared to ask, and dared more to pray he'd say yes.

For a long moment he stood before her in silence with his fingers cupped around the little flame to shield it. *Mordieu,* why had she asked this one thing of him? Her eyes were so luminous, filled with candlelight and hope he'd no choice but to destroy. If he did what Jerusa asked, he'd turn his back on his mother and his father's memory. But by granting *Maman* her wish, he was destroying the first real chance for happiness he'd ever found for himself and a future that had nothing to do with the past.

"Michel?" she asked tentatively, her voice scarce more than a whisper. Was it one more trick of the flickering candlelight, or were the pain and bitterness in his eyes really that keen?

But before she could decide, he looked away, above her head to the door and the journey beyond. "Come. I had to bribe the captain to sail early before the tide was turned, and we shouldn't keep him waiting."

She swallowed. "And where are we bound, Michel?"

"South, *ma chère,*" he said, taking care not to meet her eyes. "South, and away from Newport."

In these last shadowy hours before dawn, Seabrook was quiet and still. The slender crescent of the new moon gave little light, but still Michel walked as confidently through the unpaved streets as if he'd done it a thousand times before. For all Jerusa knew, he had, and as she hurried beside him, she realized again how little she truly did know of him.

To her relief, they headed to the opposite end of the waterfront from the *Hannah Barlow* and to another wharf where a small brig was tied. Even by the meager light of the one lantern hung at the entry port and the second by the binnacle, Jerusa could tell that this brig was better managed than the *Hannah Barlow* would ever be. The crewmen bustled about with last-minute preparations before sailing, tugging a line a bit more taut or hurrying off to obey an order. Though the ship was smaller and more provincial than anything the Sparhawks owned, she felt at least they'd be sailing with a competent captain.

"Is that you, Mr. Geary, sir?" called a man from the larboard rail as Michel and Jerusa walked up the plank. "The cap'n's below, but he asked me to welcome you aboard in his stead."

He held his hand out to Michel. "George Hay, sir, mate. We're glad to have you aboard the *Swan,* Mr. Geary, indeed we are. We don't usually carry much in the way of passengers or idlers, but as Cap'n Barker says, your company will be a change from our own dull chatter. And you, ma'am, must be Mrs. Geary."

Lifting his hat, Hay smiled and bowed neatly to Jerusa. She liked his face, broad and friendly, and because his manners and speech were so much better than most sailors', she wondered if he might be a son or nephew of the *Swan*'s owner, sent to sea to learn the trade before he took his place in the counting-house. As she smiled in return, she wondered wistfully what might have happened if earlier she'd come aboard the *Swan* seeking help instead of the *Hannah Barlow.*

She felt Michel's arm slip around her waist. She knew it was entirely proper for him to do while they were pretending to be husband and wife, yet somehow to her the possessiveness of the gesture seemed based more on jealousy than affection.

It irritated her, that arm, and she inched away from him as far as she dared. Only once had Tom Carberry presumed to act this high-handedly with her, and she'd smacked him so hard with her fan that Newport spoke of nothing else for a week. She wasn't about to make a scene like that now, not with the threat of the constable hanging over her head as long as they remained in port, but still Michel had no right to act as though he owned her.

Michel felt how she stiffened and pulled away from him. What the devil was she doing *now?*

"This is my wife's first voyage, so you must excuse her if

she seems somewhat anxious," he explained for Hay's benefit. Benefit, *mordieu*. What he wanted to do was toss the mate over the side for grinning like a shovel-faced English ape at Jerusa. "She'll be less skittish once we're under way."

Skittish, indeed, thought Jerusa irritably as she refused to let Michel catch her eye. *She'd* show him skittish!

"Your first voyage, Mrs. Geary?" said Hay with far too much interest to please Michel. "Well, now, you couldn't have chosen a pleasanter passage to make, or a sweeter vessel to sail in! Once we pick up the southerly currents, the *Swan* will be as gentle as a skiff on a pond."

"You're vastly reassuring, Mr. Hay," said Jerusa sweetly, tipping her head to one side as she smiled at him. "My husband, you see, assures me that the best way to control my fears is to keep myself as free as possible of the detail of sailing. I know you'll find it hard to countenance, Mr. Hay, being a gentleman of the sea like yourself, but I do not even know our destination, beyond that it is to the south!"

Hay scratched the back of his head beneath his hat and frowned. "What is there to fear in a place like Bridgetown?" he asked. "To be sure, some of the other islands might seem a bit untamed to a lady, but being under King George's rule, Barbados is little different from Connecticut itself."

Bridgetown! In amazement she turned to look at Michel. Her grandparents had lived on Barbados, on a hillside only a few miles from Bridgetown itself, and their sugar plantation was still run in the Sparhawk name. And her own mother and father had fallen in love there; even Michel knew that.

But could he really be doing this for her? If he truly couldn't take her home to Newport as she had asked, was he instead taking her to the next best place?

"Yes, my dear, Bridgetown," he said evenly. But his gaze never left Hay's, and to her dismay, Jerusa could feel the tension already simmering between these two, tension she'd purposefully—and foolishly—fed. "I remembered how much you've always wished to visit your cousins there."

Hay turned again toward Jerusa. "So you've family on Barbados, Mrs. Geary? I can assure you that—"

"You must have other duties to attend to, Hay," said Michel curtly. "We'll trouble you no longer. Has our dunnage been carried to our cabin?"

"Aye, aye, Mr. Geary, it has." Automatically Hay responded to the authority in Michel's voice, straightening to attention for him as he would for his captain. "You'll find your cabin aft near—"

"I shall find it, thank you." Michel's grasp around Jerusa's waist tightened again, and this time she knew better than to resist as he guided her toward the companionway and down the narrow steps.

The space between decks was low and cramped, and reflexively Jerusa ducked beneath the low beams overhead. Though they were aft, not far from the captain's cabin, the close space was filled with the smell of the cargo in the hold, the sharp, raw scent of hundreds of hewn white oak staves that would be fitted into barrels for the rum trade. Smoky oil lanterns hung from hooks in the beams, and Michel unfastened one and lowered it as he stopped to unlatch the paneled door to their cabin. With a loud creak the door swung open, and though Michel stepped inside to hang the lantern on another hook on the bulkhead, Jerusa stayed in the doorway, too appalled to move.

It was, she thought, less a cabin than a closet, and a tiny one at that. A single bunk like a wooden shelf, a lumpy mattress stuffed with wool, a row of blunt pegs along one bulkhead and an earthenware chamber pot were all the furnishings. Not that the cabin had space for more; by comparison, their room at the inn belonged in a palace. But how could the two of them possibly spend an entire voyage in such close quarters?

Michel dropped the saddlebag onto the bunk and pulled a small sea chest from beneath it. As he did, the brig suddenly lurched as her sails filled with wind, and Jerusa staggered and barely caught herself against the bulkhead. Awkwardly she braced herself against the motion of the ship, feeling stiff and clumsy without the sea legs that every male in her family claimed to have been born with.

And so, of course, had Michel, or so it seemed to her from the effortless way he'd adjusted to the brig's uneven roll. It was always that way with him, she thought grudgingly, just as he would have a sea chest waiting for him on board with only an hour's notice, just as he could magically produce horses and calimanco gowns and baths in country inns. Nothing like that surprised her anymore.

Unlocking the chest with a key from his pocket, he glanced back over his shoulder at Jerusa.

"It's a little late to turn overnice now, *ma chérie,*" he said as he began to transfer the contents of the bag into the chest. "This or the Seabrook gaol—those were your choices."

Slowly she entered, closing the door behind her. "It's only that I didn't expect anything quite this small."

"Believe me, Miss Sparhawk, there's plenty worse," he said without turning. "Or do all the berths on your papa's ships come with feather beds and looking glasses?"

She looked at his back, feeling the sting of that "Miss Sparhawk" far more than his offhanded scorn. He hadn't called her that since before the fire. Why, she wondered miserably, had he begun again?

"I'm glad we're going to Barbados," she began, hoping to set things to rights between them. "Though I'm sorry that I tricked Mr. Hay into telling me."

"The *Swan* is going to Barbados," he said curtly. "You and I are not. We'll stay in Bridgetown only until I can find us passage to St-Pierre."

"But that's Martinique," she said with dismay. "That's *French*."

"And so, Miss Sparhawk, am I."

She didn't need reminding, any more than she needed to be told she was English. Martinique was his home, not hers. She would have no friends there, no one to turn to except for Michel himself. Was this the reason he was being so cold to her? Because he no longer had to pretend otherwise?

Morbleu, why didn't she speak? Michel hated it when she fell silent like this, keeping herself away from him. But then, maybe he'd already heard enough in the way she'd said *"French"* or the fact that she hadn't bothered to hide her disappointment that they were headed for Martinique instead of Barbados. And worst of all was how she'd simpered before Hay, fluttering her lashes at the Englishman as bold as any light skirt in a tavern.

He'd let himself believe that things had changed between them, that she'd turned to him from affection, not just need. But in her blood she was still a Sparhawk, and in her eyes he would never be more than a baseborn Frenchman. It was his own fault to dream otherwise. Fool that he was, he'd come to care too much.

And *sacristi*, it hurt, more than he'd ever dreamed it would, to learn she didn't feel the same. It *hurt*.

He thumped the lid on the chest shut and turned to face her, leaning with his back against the edge of the bunk and his arms folded across his chest, studied nonchalance that was totally feigned. "Tell me, Miss Sparhawk. When you searched through my belongings at the inn, was it only from idle curiosity, or did you simply find nothing worth your time to steal?"

She gasped, shamed by what she'd done and that he'd noticed. "I didn't take a thing!"

"Then your purpose was idle amusement, not theft. How charming, *ma chère*." He didn't give a damn that she'd searched through his saddlebag. He'd certainly done worse himself. But the pain of seeing her smile for another man was making him look for ways to lash out at her, and though he hated himself for sinking so low, he couldn't help it.

"As long as we must share these quarters, *Miss* Sparhawk, I'll thank you to find other ways to entertain yourself. Just as I advise you not to look to our fair English mate for amusement, either."

"Is that what this is about, then? Your own inexplicable, unfounded, ridiculous jealousy?" She stared at him with furious disbelief. Because of the cabin's size, they stood no more than an arm's length apart, close enough that she could feel the force of their emotions roiling like a physical presence between them.

"I'd call it caution, not jealousy. I've no wish to have to kill any more men on your behalf." As if to make his point, he pulled the pistol from his belt and tossed it onto the bunk.

Jerusa gasped again, this time from outrage, not shame. "There is absolutely no reason why I should not speak with Mr. Hay if I wish to."

"Hay smiles too much, *ma mie*," said Michel softly. "He smiles too much at you."

By the shifting light of the lantern his eyes had narrowed to slits of glittering blue, and if she hadn't been so angry herself she would have seen the warning of what would come next.

"Dear Almighty, is that all?" she cried. "Because he smiles? At least *he* is a gentleman who knows how to address a lady with respect!"

"Is that what you wanted from me, Rusa? Respect and decency?"

"It's what a lady expects from any gentleman." Her heart was pounding, her whole body tensed, yet still she held her head high. She knew his quiet was deceptive. The danger was there. "Not that you would understand."

"Oh, I understand, Rusa. I know what you want better than you do yourself." He pulled her into his arms, instantly dissolving the distance between them. "And what you want, *chérie,* ah, there's nothing decent about it."

Chapter Thirteen

Michel's mouth closed down on hers before Jerusa could protest. With a smothered cry that was lost between them she struggled to break free, her hands pressing hard against his chest, but his arms were stronger and he held her fast, until he wasn't sure he could have surrendered her then even if he'd tried. This was the one way he could prove that he was worthy of her, that she needed him as much as he did her.

And God help her, she did. She couldn't help it. The more his lips moved over hers, teasing her, coaxing her, tasting her, the less she fought against him. The slow fire that had been lit between them the first time they'd kissed had had days and nights to smolder and build, until now, when they touched again, it burned white-hot, hot enough to melt away their differences and leave only what they shared.

Her palms on his chest relaxed, sliding across the hard muscles and planes of his arms and shoulders until they linked behind his neck. His hair was silky across her skin, curling around her wrists like another caress.

Confident now that she would stay, he broke away long enough to tear himself free of his coat and waistcoat and finally his shirt. In his haste a button popped off the waistcoat, rolling in a crazy circle across the deck, and Jerusa laughed, deep yet giddy, and wholly captivating. When he reached for her again, she came willingly, her eyes widening as her hands explored the different textures of his skin and the dark gold whorls of hair that patterned it. He whispered her name as his lips grazed the sensitive place behind her ear, words he'd never said to another.

Recklessly she let herself sway against him, her whole body arching with the pleasure that his kiss brought. As she moved against him she felt her breasts tighten and ache from the friction, and, as if she'd begged him, his hand slipped between them to undo the hooks on her bodice. She gasped as his fingers touched her breast, raised by the stiff whalebone stays like an opulent offering for him alone. Deftly he eased her full flesh free of the stays, teasing her nipples with his rough, callused palms until she thought she'd melt with the pleasure of it.

But it was her little moan of desire that changed everything for him. He'd never been with a woman who responded so completely to his kiss and his touch, scorching them both with her fire, and knowing he was the first to awaken such passion in her left him shuddering with the force of his own need. *He* was the one she wanted: he, Michel Géricault, who had never been wanted before by anyone, let alone a woman as blessed as Jerusa Sparhawk.

His hands slid down the length of her spine, kneading the soft curve of her hips and buttocks as he lifted her against the hot proof of his own want. His world had narrowed inexorably to the girl in his arms, and nothing in his life had ever mattered more than making her his.

Hungrily Jerusa opened her mouth as he deepened their kiss, her fingers digging into the muscles of his shoulders. She had never behaved so wantonly with Tom, but then, Michel tempted her in ways Tom never had. Marveling at how well their bodies fit together, she finally understood all that Mama had so carefully explained to her on the day of her wedding. Passion and love, declared Mama, were among the most wondrous gifts a man and woman could share, and now, here in Michel's arms, Jerusa realized exactly how wise her mother had been.

Strange that she had discovered it not with the man she was to marry but instead with the one who'd kidnapped her, and stranger still to realize, as she suddenly did now, that she loved him. *She loved him.*

She closed her eyes and smiled as he murmured to her in French, his breath warm on her skin. It didn't matter that the words meant nothing to her; it was the way he said them that touched her most. Of course he must love her as she loved him, or else how could they be discovering such unbelievable pleasure together? Hadn't Mama promised that that was the way it happened?

Yet she shivered as he lifted her onto the edge of the bunk, pushing his way between her thighs, and though still she clung to him, her heart pounding, the first flutter of apprehension rose up through her pleasure. He was shoving her skirts high over her legs, above her garters, above her knees, to let his large hands caress her white thighs with long, intoxicating strokes that left her breathless and dizzy with need.

"Ma petite amie, ma chère Jerusa," he said, his voice rough and his breathing harsh. "Are you ready for me, my own darling Jerusa?"

Impatiently his hands roamed higher, around her hips, as he pulled her closer to the edge of the bunk. She knew what would happen next, for her mother had told her that, too. But when she felt him touch her there, that most secret place between her thighs, she stiffened and instinctively tried to retreat.

"You know I won't hurt you, Rusa," he whispered, kissing her again to sway her reluctance. "Only joy, my darling, only pleasure, I swear it."

His fingers moved more gently this time, gliding over her slick, swollen flesh, and she gasped raggedly as the first ripple of bliss swept across her, as wondrous as Mama had promised.

But what of the warnings and cautions that had come before the promises? Think, Jerusa, think! Are you ready to risk the price of love and passion without marriage to bless them?

"*Ma belle Jerusa*," he whispered. "*Ma chérie*." Gently he guided her legs farther apart, lifting her knees, and she shuddered at the dizzying pleasure, her eyes squeezed shut and her head arched back.

Will you risk it all for this moment, Jerusa? Shame and disgrace, your belly swelling with a fatherless babe beneath your apron?

Will you bear a bastard child to grow in misery, to suffer as Michel, your own darling Michel, suffered even before he was born?

Think, Jerusa, think, before he decides for you!

"No, Michel, please!" Panting, she tried to twist away from him. "I can't do this!"

"Yes, you can, *ma bien-aimée*," he said, ordering more than coaxing as he began to unbutton his breeches, his fingers shaking with his urgency. "Don't say no to me now, little one."

"No, Michel, I can't!" she cried, her fear cutting through the haze of his desire. He was so much stronger, that if he wanted to take her against her will, she knew she'd be powerless to fight him. "*We* can't!"

And though his whole body ached for release, he stopped. She lay trembling before him, her eyes heavy lidded with passion and her lips swollen from his kisses, her bare breasts taut and flushed, and her legs still sprawled wantonly apart. Despite what she said, here was the proof that her body wanted his, that she craved him with the same desperation he felt for her.

Morbleu, he would give ten years of his life to be able to lose himself in her! Unable to keep away, he reached for her again, his Jerusa, his salvation—

Desperately she shook her head, her eyes wild. "For God's sake, Michel," she cried, "do you wish me to become like your mother?"

He recoiled as if he'd been struck. Could his love alone do that to her? Drive her to madness and a solitary world of black sorrow, rob her of her happiness and her good name, destroy all that was joyous and beautiful in her life? Could he do that to the woman he loved more than any other?

He wouldn't stay to be tempted and find out. She wasn't his; she never would be. Swearing under his breath, he grabbed his shirt from where he'd dropped it, and left.

Jerusa found Michel at the larboard railing, staring without seeing at the pink glow of dawn to the east. He stood with his shoulders slumped and his arms leaning on the rail, his hair whipping back untied from his face and his untucked shirt billowing around his body like the sails overhead. For a man who had spent his life striving to be inconspicuous, such an open display of his feelings was unthinkable, and Jerusa's heart wrenched to see him like this, knowing that what she'd done had left him so visibly despondent.

Carefully she felt her way across the slanting deck to stand beside him. He didn't turn to greet her, still staring steadfastly out to sea. She would have been surprised if he'd done otherwise. She wasn't sure what she was going to say to him, but she did know she wanted to be with him now, and she prayed he'd want her there, too.

She gazed out at the coming dawn, the sun still no more than a rosy feathering in the clouds on the horizon. Despite her seafaring family, this was the first time she'd been on a deep-water ship, and the high-pitched thrum of the wind in the standing riggings, the constant creaking of the ship's timbers and the rush of the waves were all new to her. After the tiny, close cabin, the wind and spray in her face felt good, helping to clear her thoughts.

Without turning, she dared to slide her hand along the rail until it touched his. "'Red sky at morning, sailors take warning.'"

"Is that a maxim on all Sparhawk ships?"

"Not on ours alone, no," she said, glad he'd answered. "You've never heard it before? 'Red sky at morning, sailors take warning, red sky at night, sailors' delight.'"

He glanced down at how their hands touched. "You English have a clever saying for everything."

"And the French don't?"

"Not nearly enough, it seems, or else I'd know what to say now." He sighed and lightly brushed his fingers across her hand. "There was no excuse for losing control as I did. It won't happen again."

"Oh, Michel, please don't!" He shouldn't blame himself like this; until the very end she'd been every bit as willing.

When at last he looked at her, she was shocked by the mixture of pain and longing she saw in his eyes. "That's exactly what you said to me earlier, *ma chère*. Thank God you did."

"But I didn't mean that we should never do—do such things again!" If only she knew the proper words to describe the intimacy of what they'd shared!

She was slanting her green eyes at him, her cheeks pink with more than the wind as she looked up at him from beneath her lashes with an unwitting blend of shyness and seduction so tempting that it tore at all his resolve and made him hard again in an instant.

"I took advantage of your trust and innocence, Jerusa. You can't deny that."

"You brought me more joy than I ever knew existed!"

His mouth tightened. "There's countless other rakes and

rogues able to do the same. It's a skill that can be learned like any other."

"I don't believe that, and neither do you! What we shared— what we *share*—is special. I may be as innocent as you say, but there are some things that even the innocent can understand." Impulsively she left the rail and held on to him instead, curling her arms around his waist.

"Jerusa, don't," he said, tensing. "You're not making this easier for either of us."

"Then think of it as more of your game, Michel. Let these sailors think Mrs. Geary is so besotted with her husband that she cannot bear to be apart from him. Better that than a public falling-out."

Sacristi, she was right. There'd be talk enough among the crew of how he'd come stumbling on deck like a drunkard. He didn't need to fuel their gossip any further by pushing his "wife" away.

"This I can do, Michel," she said softly, her lips close to his ear so he could hear her over the wind. "Because this isn't pretending. I love you, Michel Géricault, or Michael Geary, or whoever you are. I love *you.*"

"No, Rusa," he said wearily. "Don't even say it. What about Carberry, eh? I thought you loved him."

She shook her head in furious denial. "I never cared for him the way I do for you. How could I? Tom was only a girlish attachment. I see that now. Even if he still wishes to marry me, I would not have him."

Michel's smile was full of bleak amusement. "A wise decision, *ma mie.* Perhaps the best you've ever made. Now stop at that, and don't spoil it by mistaking me for your next *protecteur.*"

"You stop being so blessed *noble,* and listen to me!" Her fingers tightened in the loose folds of his shirt as she searched his face for some sign that he believed her. "I care for you,

Michel, and I love you, and nothing, *nothing* you say can change that!"

No woman had ever said such things to him before. No one had ever said she cherished him like this, or cared for him, or loved him. With every smile and jest, and even merely the graceful way she turned her head, she had become more and more dear to him, until in a handful of days she had somehow found and filled a place in his life that he'd never known was empty. For a long moment he closed his eyes, fighting the fierce joy her words brought him, joy he'd no right to claim for himself.

For in his life there was no place for love, especially not from her, and he forced himself again to think of his mother and his promise to her, of his father and how he had died. He must never forget that. That was who he *was*.

"No, Rusa," he said hoarsely. "There's too much you don't understand."

"Then tell me!" she cried with desperation. "Is it our fathers? I want to know!"

Her body was warm and soft against his side, and as he stared again out across the water again, he tried not to remember how sweet she'd been to hold in his arms.

Anything else, mordieu, *think of anything else!*

"The sun is so slow to rise or set in your Yankee waters, *ma chère.* Almost as if she knows how chilly the air will be for her, eh?" He smiled wearily. "In Martinique, the sun comes all at once. One moment the sky is blue-black with night, and the next, before you quite know how, it's day."

"I know, because Father's told me," she said eagerly. "He says the sunsets are the same way, from day to night in an instant."

"He told you that, but nothing of Christian Deveaux?"

She shook her head wistfully, brushing aside the strands of hair that the wind tossed across her face. "Perhaps he tells the boys, but not me or my sisters. He hardly speaks of the wars to us at all."

"He knew my father long before any war brought them together, *ma mie*," said Michel slowly. "They were scarce more than boys when they first clashed. Over and over they'd meet on different islands, with different ships or crews, each seeking to destroy the other. On Statia, they still speak of how the two young captains, one French, one English, nearly cut each other to ribbons at noon while every fat Dutchman in town watched in pop-eyed horror."

"You are so beautiful, my son," murmured Antoinette as she cradled Michel's face in her hands. "I look at you, and see your father again before me. He was the most handsome man I had ever seen. Not brown and swarthy, like these strutting Creole men who fancy themselves such blades, but fair like an angel, with golden hair and eyes as blue as the water in the bay."

"But the scar, Maman," *protested Michel. Young as he was, he'd heard the stories and seen how the other mothers drew their children away from him. How could he not?* "Everyone says he'd been marked by the devil."

"The devil!" She laughed bitterly. "The only devil your father knew was English, my son. A tall, green-eyed Englishman who hunted your father down without mercy. But at first he did not kill him. No, no. First he marked your father in a way that shamed him before the world."

Gently she turned Michel's face to the right in her hands. "One side belonged to the angels, a face to make the queen herself weep from longing. But may God give rest to my poor Christian's soul, not the other. The other belonged to hell itself."

Abruptly she twisted Michel's face to the right, her fingers tightening so roughly that he struggled to break free. Her eyes black with fury, she jabbed her finger into Michel's jaw and slowly dragged it up across his cheek to his forehead. "With his sword the English devil destroyed your father's face, Michel, marking him so evilly that children shrieked in fear to see him and grown men crossed themselves if he passed them

*in the street. He was never the same after that, my poor, sweet
Christian, and how could he be?"*

Lost as she was in her memories, her own face softened, so
that Michel, frightened though he was, could see how Maman,
too, had once been beautiful.

"But one day such cruelty will be rewarded," she whispered, her voice rich with the promise of vengeance. *"One day
Gabriel Sparhawk will find himself made to answer for his
cruelty. And you, my son, will do it."*

"You mean my father and yours fought with swords, before
a whole town?" asked Jerusa in disbelief, unable to imagine
such a thing. Father could be hot-tempered, to be sure, but he
was also a respectable gentleman with white streaked through
his hair who served on the council of their town and as a ves-
tryman for their church. "Just the two of them?"

"The crews of their ships were ordered not to interfere." As
soon as he'd been old enough, Michel had traveled to St. Eus-
tatius himself to stand in the square where his father had
fought, and he'd found an old man in a tavern there who remembered every thrust, every feint, every drop of blood spilled
onto the cobblestones. "Everyone knew it was between the two
men alone, not their countries. And it was far from the only
time they met, *ma chérie*."

"But why would they do such a thing? What was their
reason?"

Michel shook his head, his voice curiously distant. "I don't
know, Jerusa. Ask your father, if you wish, for I cannot ask mine."

Miserably Jerusa saw how he was shutting her out, re-
treating into himself. Whatever had caused their fathers to
hate each other so was long past any reconciliation now. It
could just as easily have been her father who had died
instead, but nothing either she or Michel could do now
would change the past. So why, then, was he so determined
to let it ruin their future?

But maybe he already had. Maybe it was already too late for them, just as it was too late for their fathers.

By now the sun had risen, the bright red circle clearing the horizon to mark a new day. But to Jerusa the wind seemed colder than it had been, her joy in the day gone, and she shivered as she eased herself away from Michel's side and back to the rail for support.

"No one has hired you to do this, have they, Michel?" she asked, already knowing the answer. "You came to Newport to kidnap me for yourself, not for anyone else."

He tried to tell himself that this was what he wanted. He'd dedicated his life to honoring his father this way, and he'd come too close to his goal to stop now. "A good guess, *chère*. But then, I never told you otherwise, did I?"

"But why, Michel?" she pleaded. "Why take me?"

When he turned toward her, his eyes were as cold and bleak as the wind. "Because you are your father's favorite child. He will go anywhere to save you, Jerusa, even Martinique. You may have thought he's abandoned you, *ma mie,* but I am certain he hasn't. He will be there in St-Pierre, waiting for us."

"And then?" But already she knew. God help them all, she knew.

"And then I will kill him."

"Ah, Mr. Geary, good morning!" boomed the man behind them. "And Mrs. Geary! I am honored, mistress, honored indeed to have you in our midst. I'm Captain Robert Barker, Mrs. Geary, your servant."

Somehow Jerusa found the words, however faint, to answer him. "Thank you, Captain Barker. I'm most happy to meet you."

"Under the weather, aren't you?" Barker peered at her from beneath his hat, flat brimmed like a parson's. He was a small, narrow man, too little for his great, thundering voice, and above his black coat his face was brown and wizened like a walnut. "Both of you look a bit peaked and green around the gills, I can see that now."

"Have we that much the look of landsmen, Captain?" asked Michel, falling in with the explanation that Barker so conveniently offered. "As I told you, this is my wife's first voyage."

"From the look of you, Geary, you've had a rough night of it, too." Taking in Michel's disheveled appearance, Barker shook his head in sympathy. "But I warrant you'll find your sea legs soon enough. If you're headed back below, I'll have the cook send you something directly to settle your bellies."

"That won't be necessary, Captain Barker," said Jerusa quickly, managing a quick smile for him alone. The thought of returning to the tiny cabin with Michel was unbearable to her now, and she desperately needed time away from him to think. "I'm feeling much better here on deck. Your sea breezes are wonderfully refreshing, aren't they?"

Cynically Michel watched as the older man seemed to preen and swell beneath the warmth of Jerusa's charm. *Mordieu,* and he knew she wasn't even trying. Delightful as the belle of Newport could be, it was the other, quieter side of her that had so devastated him.

And he'd stake his life that she didn't love him any longer.

She fluttered beside him, lightly touching his arm but carefully avoiding meeting his eyes. "But you do wish to go back to the cabin, don't you, sweetheart?" she said with a brightness that didn't fool Michel for a moment. "I know you'll feel so much more like yourself once you've slept. And I'm sure Captain Barker here will oblige me by showing me about his lovely ship, won't you, sir?"

"That I shall, Mrs. Geary, and a pleasure it will be, too!" exclaimed Barker in his thundering voice. He winked broadly at Michel. "That is, Geary, if you don't mind sharing your lady's company with an old rascal like me?"

It wasn't so much Barker that worried him as Hay, standing

within earshot at the helm. The mate had not taken his gaze from Jerusa since he'd come on deck, watching her with the same hungry admiration that she drew from all men.

But *morbleu,* was he any different himself? With the wind in her loose black hair and her skirts dancing gracefully about her long legs, she was the most desirable woman he'd ever seen, as free and wild as the ocean itself. Only when she lifted her eyes to him did he see the misery he'd brought to her soul.

"Surely you don't mind, sweetheart?" she asked again, silently begging him to agree, to set her free if only for an hour. "You know I'll be quite safe with Captain Barker."

And against all his wishes, he nodded, and left her on the arm of another man.

Listlessly Jerusa pushed the biscuit pudding around her plate with her spoon, hoping that Captain Barker wouldn't notice how little of it she'd eaten. Despite his size, Barker's appetite was as prodigious as his voice, and he was rightly proud of how the *Swan*'s cook could send out course after course to grace his table. Already she'd disappointed him by refusing the partridge and barely tasting the lobscouse, and she'd let him plop the huge, quivering slice of pudding onto her plate only to keep him from once again declaring she ate less than a wren.

Lord knows she should have been hungry. She'd spent the entire day following Barker around the *Swan,* clambering down companionways and squinting up at rigging as he'd lovingly pointed out every feature of the little brig. But though she'd oohed and aahed in all the right places, she'd hardly heard a word the captain had said. How could she, her conscience so heavy with what Michel had told her?

She dared to glance across the table at him now. He was listening intently to some interminable seafaring story of the captain's, or at least he was pretending to, just as she was. He had shaved and dressed, his hair tied back with a black ribbon. He was the model Mr. Geary again, and more handsome than any man had a right to be. How could he sit there like that, just *sit* there, after everything he'd told her?

Tears stung behind her eyes, and abruptly she shoved her chair away from the table. "Pray excuse me, gentlemen," she murmured as the three men rose in unison. "I—I find I need some air."

"Let me come with you, my dear," said Michel as he laid his napkin on the table, but without looking in his direction, she shook her head.

"There's no need, Michael," she replied, barely remembering to anglicize his name. "You continue here. I shall be quite all right on my own."

On the deck she braced herself against the mainmast with both hands, gulping at the cool night air as she struggled to make sense of her roiling emotions. She loved Michel—that hadn't changed—and in her heart she believed he cared for her, too. But though he'd shown her in a dozen ways, he'd never once told her he loved her. Instead he'd told her he had sworn to kill her father, and her blood chilled and her eyes filled again when she remembered the look on Michel's face when he'd said it. If she could only convince him to leave the past alone, that what had happened so long ago had nothing to do with them now!

"Mrs. Geary?"

With the heel of her hand she swiftly rubbed her eyes free of tears before she turned to face George Hay. He was standing self-consciously at the top of the companionway, turning his hat in his hands around and around in a three-cornered circle.

"Are you all right, ma'am?" he asked. "I've no wish to pry into your affairs, of course, but when you left the cap'n's cabin so quickly—well, I couldn't help but wonder."

Jerusa forced a smile. "I thank you for your concern, Mr.

Hay, but I'm quite well. In fact I was just on my way to return when you appeared."

She came toward the companionway, but he blocked her way. "I didn't mean just now, ma'am, but in all ways. To my mind, things don't seem to set well between you and Mr. Geary, and if there's anything amiss that I can help, well, ma'am, here I am."

She looked at him strangely, remembering Michel's warning. "Are you often in the habit of interfering between husbands and wives, Mr. Hay?"

"I'll do it if I believe the lady needs a friend, aye." He fumbled in the pocket of his coat until he found a crumpled paper. He smoothed it over his thigh before he handed it to her. "You'll forgive me if I ask you to read this, ma'am, and then tell me again that I've been meddlesome."

A handbill of some sort, she thought as she took it, for the printing was coarse and smeared, and there were holes in each corner where it had been nailed to a tree or signboard. What could it possibly have to do with her? Perhaps it was some sort of warning about coming salvation, and Hay the kind of pious busybody who worried too much for his neighbors' souls. Reluctantly she tipped it into the light of the binnacle lantern to make out the smudged type.

But what she read had nothing to do with religion. Instead it was a poster announcing the "Unfortunate disappearance of a Certain Miss Jerusa Sparhawk, a Young Lady of Newport, Aquidneck Island, lost to her grieving Friends on the Evening of 12 June." Everything was there and all of it true, from the circumstances of her wedding to a description of her person, down to the color of the garters she'd been wearing for her wedding. And finally, at the bottom, beneath her father's name and address, was the bold-faced promise of "Reward to be Given at Miss Sparhawk's Safe Return."

"Since you came aboard this morning, ma'am, I've thought

of nothing else," said the mate doggedly. "I couldn't help but remark the likeness. But you tell me, ma'am, and I'll abide by your wish. Is there anything amiss between you and Mr. Geary?"

Numbly Jerusa stared at the paper, pretending to read though the letters swam before her eyes. Dear Lord, had her prayers really come to this? All she needed to do was tell this earnest, greedy young man before her who she was, and all her troubles would be done. They would take her home. She would be returned to her family, her father would reward Mr. Hay every bit as handsomely as he expected, and her life would begin again where it had left off.

And Michel would be bound in chains by the crew of the *Swan* until they put into port and he could be given over to a constable, and the nightmare she'd envisioned of his hanging would come true.

All with a word, only a word, from her.

Carefully she refolded the paper into neat quarters. "How did you come by this, Mr. Hay?"

"It was in the mailbag, south from Boston. I've a cousin there who often sends me curiosities for amusement." He was watching her closely, ducking a bit as he tried to see her face more clearly. "Mrs. Geary, ma'am? Miss Sparhawk?"

Though her breath caught in her chest, she only smiled evenly as she returned the paper to him. Did he really believe he'd trap her with so obvious a trick? He'd have to try a good deal harder than that, for she'd been traveling and studying with a master.

"I can see why your cousin sent it to you, Mr. Hay." Did he mean to share the reward with his cousin, she wondered, or keep it all to himself? "The young lady's tale is passing sad, and I shall pray that she is returned, unharmed, to those who love her."

Still the mate blocked her path, clearly unconvinced. "I only wish to see that right is done, ma'am."

"An admirable virtue, Mr. Hay." Though she smiled at

him, her voice turned sharp. "But I'll advise you to keep your fancies to yourself, and from my husband in particular. You would not, I think, wish to find yourself in a discussion with him."

She swept by him, her head high, and down the narrow steps, into Michel's chest.

"Are you all right, *chère?*" he asked softly, taking her arm, and from the way he'd slipped back into the French, she realized how worried he'd been. "I left Barker as soon as I decently could. Where's Hay?"

She didn't answer, instead laying one finger across her lips and cocking her head toward the deck, and Hay. Understanding at once, Michel nodded and led her back toward their cabin.

Until she felt Michel's hand on her arm, she hadn't realized how much the mate had upset her. Her heart was still racing, her palms damp, and as Michel lit the lantern in the tiny cabin, she sank down on the edge of the bunk before her legs buckled beneath her.

She'd done more than refuse Hay's help. She'd chosen her loyalties, and God help her, she prayed she'd chosen well.

"Mr. Hay knows," she said hoarsely, hugging her arms around her body. "He knows who I am, and he's guessing at the rest."

Michel looked at her sharply and swore. "You told him?"

The accusation stung. "He had a handbill. My father has offered a reward. And I didn't tell him, Michel. Truly."

"You must have told him something in all that time."

"Only that I was Mrs. Geary, and that if he didn't leave me alone he'd have to answer to you."

He stood very still as he realized what she'd done. "You lied because of me?"

"I had to, Michel." She tried to smile, but after an endless day of trying she finally failed. Why, why didn't he understand? "I didn't want to go with him."

"Then take care you're not alone with George Hay again,

chérie," he said. "I've brought you this far, and I'm not about to give you up to some two-penny bounty hunter."

"Damn you, Michel, is that all?" She stared at him, her heart pounding. "After everything we've shared and done, that's all you'll let yourself say? That all I am to you is something to be kept from another man?"

Briefly he glanced down at his hands, unable to meet her eyes. She was right. She deserved more from him than he'd ever be able to give. She deserved a man who was free to love her.

Wearily he looked back at her. "I'm sorry, Rusa," he said hoarsely. "I'm sorry for everything."

For what seemed to him an eternity, she didn't answer, sitting on the edge of the bunk with her hands clutching tight to the mattress and her eyes enormous. She'd every right to be angry and hurt, but could she guess that he was frightened, more frightened than he'd ever been in his life?

Mordieu, she wasn't his and never would be. But what would become of him if he lost her now?

Then, with a sigh that rose from the depths of her heart, Jerusa came to him, slipping her hands around his waist as he folded his arms over her shoulders. Whatever her own sorrows might be, they were nothing compared to what he suffered. With her cheek against his chest, she closed her eyes and listened to the steady rhythm of his heart, and prayed that sorry would be enough.

Chapter Fourteen

Josh sat alone in the front room of the tavern, swirling the rum and lime juice in the tankard before him and considering how tired he was for having accomplished so little.

He had left his father in Bridgetown on Barbados while he had come here to Martinique. Eager to begin his search for Jerusa, he'd left the *Tiger* at dawn on Monday, only to discover that St-Pierre's citizens prided themselves on being as late to rise as Parisians, and it had been close to noon before he'd been able to meet with any of the port officials. But no matter how many coins he left on those official desks, to be discreetly slipped into official pockets, there still had been no English ships seen in the Martinique port within the last month, and certainly no tall, fair English ladies. The officials were quite sure of that.

He'd made even less headway with the letters of introduction his father had written for him. Here the Sparhawk name meant nothing. The royal governor his father had known had been recalled to France, and the man who had replaced him had been too busy to receive an English sea captain. Perhaps, suggested his officious secretary, there might be an appointment open in September, or surely in October, if Captain

Sparhawk chose to remain in St-Pierre that long. As the secretary had shrugged and sighed and shaken his fashionably powdered head, Josh in frustration had silently wished the secretary and all his kind to the devil.

His father had warned him it would be difficult, but Josh hadn't wanted to believe him. English ships and English sailors—even those from New England—were unusual in Martinique's waters, nor particularly welcome when they did appear. Though Josh had sailed in the Caribbean for years, he'd been here only once before, with his family while he was still a boy, and his single, hazy memory of the place was his oldest brother scuffling in the street with two Pierrotin boys who'd mocked his English clothes.

Not that things seemed to have changed much in the years since. As Josh had walked through the cobblestone streets, even the port's Creole prostitutes had scornfully flicked their skirts away from him. The sooner he found Jerusa and they could head back for home together, the better.

But where exactly *was* Jerusa? Wearily Josh sighed again. Now that he'd exhausted the official channels, he'd have to explore other, more risky possibilities. After supper he'd begin with the rum shops near the water, and pray he'd be more successful than his brother had been at keeping clear of fights with Pierrotins.

Through the tall, open windows of the tavern the sun hung low over the bay, and from the street came the sounds of the city rousing itself from the sleepy heat of late afternoon for the enticing promise of the evening to come: men laughing now that their day's work was done, a slave woman singing for her own pleasure, a pair of street fiddlers sawing through the latest jig. The last time Josh had heard fiddlers had been the ones hired for Jerusa's wedding....

"Monsieur? Pardon?" said the serving girl. *"S'il vous plaît, monsieur?"*

"Forgive me, lass, my thoughts were elsewhere." But the girl only stared blankly, and Josh groped for the foreign words to say the same thing. These last days his limited sailor's French had been sorely tried, and having the girl waiting before him with a tray tucked beneath her arm wasn't helping him concentrate. *"Ah, plaît-il, mademoiselle?"*

"Oui, monsieur, avec plaisir." Like most of the women on the island, she was small and dark, her skin dusted gold and her cheeks full and blushed like peaches. But unlike all the other women, she didn't scorn him but smiled instead, and enchanted, Josh grinned in return.

"What's your na—oh, hang it, lass, I've forgotten myself again," he said, but the girl only giggled behind her fingers, her black eyes sparkling with merriment. Though her striped bodice and skirts beneath her apron were cut modestly enough, there was still something charmingly, innocently flirtatious about her that no English serving girl could ever hope to copy.

"You're *anglais,* aren't you, *monsieur?*" she asked, cocking her head to one side like a small, bright-eyed bird.

"And you speak English," said Josh with both delight and relief.

She raised one arched brow impishly. "It's good for business. *Papa* has taught me English, Spanish and Dutch so I can sell his rum to any sailor who stumbles through his door."

"So that's how I seem to you?" asked Josh with a great show of forlorn self-pity. "One more stumbling, blind-drunk sailor?"

"Peut-être." The girl tossed her black curls as she smacked his arm with her tray. "But how much rum would you buy from me if I told you that, eh?"

"Not a blessed drop," he agreed. "But I might buy a whole cask if you told me your name."

"Cecilie Marie-Rose Noire. You may call me Ceci. Most everyone else does, so I will not charge you for the cask of rum."

"Generous *and* beautiful!" She couldn't guess how much

her teasing, good-natured banter meant to him after the disappointment of these last days. "My name is Joshua Sparhawk, captain of the sloop *Tiger* of Newport, Rhode Island, and you, Miss Ceci, may call me whatever you choose. Josh would suit me just fine."

"A captain!" Her eyes widened. "But you are so young!"

Flattered, he considered briefly pretending he'd earned his place on the *Tiger* entirely on his own merit. Lord knows he'd let other pretty girls believe it before this. But somehow, with Ceci, he didn't want to.

"I'm the captain, aye, and the *Tiger*'s been mine since I was nineteen." He smiled sheepishly. "I've had the good fortune, y'see, to have my father as her owner."

"Then you should be doubly proud, *monsieur!*" declared Ceci warmly. "Who expects more than a father? If you proved yourself worthy to him, then you must be a grand, fine sailor!"

"I do well enough." He shifted his shoulders self-consciously, torn between relishing her praise and being shamed by it. He *was* proud of his skills as a sailor, but in his family such accomplishments were taken for granted, even expected. He knew that no matter what he did, he'd never come close to equaling his father or older brothers. But for little Ceci, he was the only Sparhawk that mattered. No, better than that: he was the only Sparhawk.

Swiftly he glanced around the room. It was still early for supper, and earlier still for the serious drinkers who would later fill every chair and bench and the spaces in between. For now, at least, he was the only patron.

"Could you join me, Ceci?" he asked. He rose to his feet to bow toward her, and saw how her eyes widened at his size. Well, so be it; beside these Frenchmen, the Sparhawks might be the lost race of giants. "I'd be honored by your company, and you're the first soul I've met on this island I'd say that to."

"Oh, *monsieur,* what you ask!" she demurred. "I'm a good

girl, *monsieur,* a respectable girl. *Papa* would never allow such a thing."

Yet from the way she blushed again and fidgeted with her apron as she peeked up at him from beneath her lashes, Josh was sure the invitation pleased her.

"What harm could come from it?" he asked, warming her with a smile made to break hearts. "There's not another person in the place. Please, Ceci. Please."

She shook her head, her black curls bobbing above the tiny silver rings in her ears.

"I swear I'm a good boy, too, Ceci. Respectable enough for any papa."

Though she tried not to laugh, her dimples betrayed her, twitching in her cheeks as her mouth curled. "Handsome, green-eyed boys are never respectable," she scolded, "especially *les Anglais.* But if you dine from our kitchen, I will come back. Tonight there is a fine *fricassé* of chicken and red crayfish with onions, and our *blancmanger*—you would call it a pudding, no?—is fresh coconut with nutmeg, and—"

"You choose, Ceci," he said softly. "Whatever brings you back here the quickest."

She made a dismissive sound deep in her throat and tossed her head one last time as she headed to the kitchen, but it seemed to Josh that she was back again before he'd scarce begun to miss her.

"*Papa* has seen your sloop in the harbor," she said as she carefully set a steaming bowl of pumpkin soup before him on the worn, bare table. "He says it is a very fine ship, and he wishes to know if you will be regularly trading in St-Pierre."

Josh smiled wryly. Whether in Newport or St-Pierre, fathers with marriageable daughters all asked the same questions.

"I'm not in St-Pierre to trade, lass," he said softly. "I'm here to find my sister."

Briefly he told her how Jerusa had disappeared, and that he

hoped to find her here on Martinique. While he spoke, Ceci slipped into the chair beside him, her little hands clasped on the table before her and her lips parted as she listened.

"That is so terrible!" she cried when he was done. "For your family, your sister, for you, *monsieur!* Whoever would steal a lady on her wedding night is a monster!"

"You'll find no quarrel from me there." He dipped his spoon into the soup, hot and spicy with flavors he couldn't quite identify. Until he'd begun to eat, he hadn't realized how hungry he was. "My father believes it is the work of Frenchmen connected to a long-dead pirate from this island named Christian Deveaux."

From his pocket he pulled out a copy of the black *fleur de lis* found with Jerusa's jewelry and smoothed the sheet on the table. "Though it's been nearly thirty years since Deveaux sailed from Martinique, Father believes that some of his men must still be alive and acting in his name against our family."

"I understand, *monsieur.*" Ceci nodded solemnly. "I do not know how it is among the men of your country, but here in mine, thirty years would be as nothing when a gentleman's honor must be avenged."

"For God's sake, Ceci, we're talking about pirates, not gentlemen!"

"Even the worst rogues have honor, *monsieur.*" She frowned, touching the paper on the table between them. "I thought that I knew every name on our island, but this Deveaux—why, I wonder, have I not heard of him?"

Josh sighed and pushed the empty soup bowl away from him, resting his chin in his hand as he leaned his elbow on the table. "It was long before either of us were born, lass."

"But not before my father's time." She stood and leaned forward to take the empty bowl, and Josh caught the scent of her skin, spicy with the same fragrance as the soup. "He could remember pirates back to Captain Morgan! I'll go ask him, and return with your *fricassé.*"

Josh watched her hurry across the room, her small, slim figure weaving gracefully between the tables. There were other patrons in the tavern now, calling her by name as they ordered their wine or rum, and with regret Josh realized he'd no longer have her company to himself. But maybe later, when she was done working for the night and he'd made the first round of the rum shops, he could return.

Smiling to himself, he looked back out the window to where the sun had dropped below the horizon and the first stars were beginning to glimmer in the evening sky. Jerusa would like Ceci; they were two of a kind, both beautiful and outspoken, and Josh suspected that somehow Ceci, for all her claims to being a good girl, was every bit as accustomed as his sister was to getting her own way.

"You, *monsieur?*" demanded the heavyset Frenchman with a barkeep's canvas apron. "You are the English sea captain, *non?*"

"Aye," said Josh warily. Ceci's father: the man could be no one else. But why should the Frenchman be so all-fired angry with him? All he'd done was talk to the girl. "Is there a problem, Mr.—uh, *Monsieur* Noire?"

"*Oui, oui,* there is a problem, Sparhawk, and *mordieu,* it is you!" Noire grabbed the tankard from Josh's fingers, slammed it on the table and pointed dramatically at the door. "This is a decent house, and I won't have your kind here! You go, now, and do not come back ever again!"

Conscious of every face in the room turned toward him, Josh rose slowly to his feet. He knew he didn't have much choice but to leave as the tavern keeper requested, but he hated the feeling of slinking away for something he hadn't done. It had a low, cowardly feel to it, and Sparhawks were never cowards.

"Of course, *monsieur,* I'd ask your forgiveness if I'd offended your daughter," he said, intensely aware of being the one Englishman among so many French. "But by my lights, I've done nothing to shame or dishonor her. You can ask her yourself."

"Nothing, eh?" The Frenchman smacked his palm down hard on the table. "I'll give you your nothing! For twenty-seven years no one has dared defile this house by speaking the name of Christian Deveaux, and now you come in here and speak of him to my daughter, my sweet little Cecilie, and then claim you've done *nothing!*"

"You know of the man, then?" asked Josh excitedly. "You remember him and—"

"I can never forget the black-hearted bastard of the devil, and for that reason alone you will never be welcome again in this house." Noire spat contemptuously on the floor beside Josh. "Now get out, before my friends here toss you into the gutter where you belong."

Instinctively Josh's hands tightened to fists at his sides as his gaze shifted from Noire to the men who had come to stand behind him, fishermen and other mariners, some already with long-bladed knives in their hands and all of them spoiling for a fight.

Young though he was, Josh knew well enough that the line between being a hero and a fool could often be as fine as a hair. To walk away now went against every fiber of his being, but what good could he do for Jerusa if he let himself be carved to bits by a pack of ravening Frenchmen for the sake of his pride?

But if he had to leave, he could at least do it on his terms, not theirs. Measuring his motions so as not to startle them, Josh reached for the tankard and emptied it. Slowly, he reached into his pocket for a handful of *sous* to pay for what little he'd had the chance to drink and eat, and dropped the coins rattling onto the table. With all the bravado he could muster, he then walked directly through the little crowd of Frenchmen to the door. His head high, he did not deign to watch his own back, nor did he threaten or scowl at the men who were driving him away, and when he finally stepped out into the street unharmed, he managed to keep his sigh of relief to himself.

But when on an impulse Josh couldn't explain he turned at

the corner of the street to look back at the tavern, it was Ceci he saw in the second-floor window, her face small and sorrowful as she peeked from behind the louvered blue shutter.

And despite her father's threats, he knew he would return.

"Shove off, Dayton," roared the *Tiger*'s bosun. "Shove off *now!* That is if ye still bloody well can without topplin' on yer pickled arse!"

Sitting in the boat's stern sheets, Josh bit back his own reprimand and tried instead to look grimly above such tomfoolery, the way a captain should. No matter how many insults were bellowed at Dayton, the man was still so blissfully drunk on cheap Martinique rum that it was a wonder he could stand at all, let alone push the boat free of the shallows and into the deeper water.

And Dayton had supposedly been with the boat the whole evening; God only knew in what condition Josh would find the men he'd granted shore leave. He'd chosen his crew for this voyage carefully, looking for men with a reputation for sobriety, but St-Pierre was the kind of overripe, indolent place that could tempt a Quaker, let alone an idle seaman. Josh shook his head and felt in his coat pocket for his pipe and tobacco. One more reason to find his sister as soon as he could, before every last man became a hopeless sot.

The boat lurched free at last, somehow Dayton managed to climb aboard, and Josh settled back glumly with his pipe for the short row back to the *Tiger*. If only he'd had more success in his inquiries tonight, then perhaps he'd be in a better humor. For a man who'd been as notorious as his father claimed, Christian Deveaux seemed now to inspire nothing but uneasy silence.

If only the evening had continued as pleasantly as it had begun, when he'd met little Ceci Noire. If only...

"*Capitaine Sparhawk! Capitaine,* wait, I beg you!"

He turned and saw the flicker of white petticoats and a

handkerchief waving from the beach. She wore a dark shawl draped over her head that shadowed her face, but even across the water there was no mistaking Ceci's voice.

"'Vast there," he ordered quickly. "Haul for shore. Handsomely now, lads, handsomely!"

He didn't miss the amused, knowing glances the men exchanged among themselves as they turned the boat short round, but this time he didn't care. They could gossip all they wanted between decks. He was simply going to talk to the girl, apologize if she expected it and listen to what she had to say. Where was the harm or the scandal in that?

She came skipping along the beach right to the water's edge, heedless of the damp sand that clung to her shoes and hem. *"Grâce à Dieu!"* she cried as Josh climbed from the boat. "I feared I was too late, that I'd never see you again to explain!"

Without thinking, Josh reached for her hand and felt her fingers tremble against his. "You shouldn't be prowling around the waterfront alone like this, lass, not at this hour. Must be three o'clock in the morning at the least."

"I had no choice, *monsieur.*" She shoved the shawl back from her face, and in the moonlight her dark eyes shone bright with excitement. "I couldn't leave until *Papa* had closed the shutters and gone to sleep. But I'm safe enough. You forget my living depends on drunken rogues, and I know how to take care of myself."

Josh could only shake his head, remembering how Jerusa had always claimed she, too, would be safe in Newport. "You could have waited until morning."

"Mordieu, and let you go to your bed believing the worst of me?" She squeezed her fingers around his. "What you must believe instead is this—that until this night my father had never spoken that evil man's name in my hearing! Not a word, no, not once, not even after what Deveaux did!"

"Then your father did know Deveaux?"

"*Dieu merci,* they never met. Deveaux was too clever, too grand for that. But *Papa* and *ma chère Maman,* may she rest in heaven by the side of the Blessed Virgin, how they suffered at his hands!"

She quivered now with the same righteous fury as her father's, her face with its small, plump chin every bit as fierce. "Deveaux was born a gentleman, *monsieur,* and *Papa* says he was handsome enough to melt the sun from the sky, else Antoinette would never have done what she did."

"Antoinette?" asked Josh.

"My mother's sister, my aunt." She was speaking so swiftly, driven by the shame to her family, that she was almost breathless with outrage. "Antoinette, too, worked in our *petite auberge,* and *Papa* says there was not a man in St-Pierre who did not worship her. But the only one she listened to was Deveaux. My mother's tears, my father's pleas, were nothing against his false promises and candied words. Nothing!"

Sadly Josh could guess the rest. Who couldn't? "He seduced her?"

Ceci nodded, shaking her little fist at Deveaux's ghost. "He seduced her, *monsieur,* and took her from those who loved her to his grand house, built with the blood and tears of those he had robbed and murdered. And it was there she perished by his side, in the fire that God sent in his fury to destroy that evil place and Deveaux with it!"

She wove her fingers into his to draw him closer. "You can understand it all now, *monsieur,* can't you?" she said, almost pleading. "Why my father said what he did to you? It was because he loves me, *monsieur,* because he would not see me come to the same sorrow as poor Antoinette."

"He believes I would do that to you?" demanded Josh incredulously. "Just because I mentioned Deveaux's name?"

Ceci shook her head helplessly. "He said you would not

seek out those left of Deveaux's men unless you wished to join them yourself. He said—"

"He can damn well listen to what I have to say!" said Josh hotly. What right did some little hotheaded French barkeep have to insult him like this? "I'm sorry about his sister-in-law, sorry as can be. But it's my sister that concerns me now, and if asking about Deveaux is going to bring me any closer to finding her, then I mean to ask you or him or anyone else I please until I find her."

"But *Papa* said—"

"I'm not done yet, Ceci!" Struggling to keep his temper, Josh forced himself to lower his voice. "Your father's got it all wrong, mind? I don't know what happened to Antoinette, but Deveaux didn't die in that fire. I know because he lived long enough to try to kill my parents. Instead my father wounded him so gravely he decided to take his own life, there with my own mother as witness."

Now Ceci's eyes were round as the moon above. "Your father killed Deveaux?"

"My father wouldn't lie about a thing like that," he said sharply. "Why else would Deveaux's men decide to kidnap my sister now?"

"Revenge," she whispered. "Oh, Monsieur Sparhawk, forgive me!"

"You're not the one who needs forgiving." Suddenly weary of the whole misunderstanding, he freed his fingers from hers and stuffed his hands into his coat pockets. "You tell your old papa that we're on the same side. My sister Jerusa, his sister-in-law Antoinette—it all amounts to the same thing, doesn't it? You tell him that, Ceci. And if he's got any notion of justice and wants to help, he can find me easy enough on the *Tiger.*"

He turned and began to walk toward the boat, his shoes silent on the packed sand.

"Wait, please, I beg you!"

He stopped and looked back over his shoulder. She was standing with her fists clenched at her sides and her chin lifted high, the black shawl trailing like a ragged pennant from her shoulders.

"He will help you, *monsieur*," she said slowly. "If he has any hope of finding peace in this world or the next, he will help you."

Chapter Fifteen

Michel lay in the hammock, cleaning one of his pistols and listening to the doleful ballad of lost loves and thwarted dreams sung by one of the *Swan*'s crewmen on the deck above. Michel sighed. He could sympathize all too well with whoever had written that ballad. His own love wasn't exactly lost—she was lying soundly asleep in the bunk not three feet away from him, her hair tousled about her face and one arm thrown back enticingly behind her head—but she wasn't exactly his, either.

This last week together with Jerusa had been both the best and the worst of his life. She had rarely left his sight, day or night, and with so much time together, he'd come to appreciate her as a companion as well as a woman. Which was, he thought wryly, just as well, since companionship was all he and Jerusa were destined to share.

Idly he kicked his foot against the bulkhead, rocking the hammock in time with the song. The hammock was one of the precautions he'd taken against being tempted again, and, even so, he'd been sorely tried by being able to hear Jerusa's soft little sighs as she slept in the bunk across from him. *Sacristi*, he wanted her more than he'd ever wanted any woman, but to give in to his desires would be the worst possible thing he could do for them both.

And she knew it, too. After that first night aboard the brig, she'd been as careful as he had. There had been no more kisses, no more embraces and certainly no more of what they'd done so pleasurably that one time on the bunk. They slept in their clothes the way they had while traveling, and they made elaborate, self-conscious excuses whenever one or the other finally wished to change and needed the cabin's privacy. The entire contrived arrangement, thought Michel with another sigh, would have been worthy of the great Molière himself.

But this wasn't the only truce they'd uneasily, silently declared between themselves. Since that first night, neither of them had spoken of their families or fathers, or of the circumstances that had brought them together aboard the *Swan*.

And not once since then had she told him again that she loved him. He wasn't surprised—what decent woman would profess to love a man who'd sworn to kill her father?—but he did feel more regret, more longing, than he'd ever admit to anyone, especially to Jerusa. No, he could not blame her. But what would she have said if he'd blurted out the truth, that he loved her, as well?

His hands stilled as he thought again of how close he'd come. He'd realized since then that when she'd cried out to stop in his mother's name, she'd been afraid of conceiving a child, not of his mother's madness. His conscience had been the one to hear that. But however the warning had come, he'd listened. He did love Jerusa, more than he'd ever dreamed possible. But because he loved her, he refused to risk condemning her to the same terrifying half existence that his father had done to his mother.

What would happen once they reached Martinique—especially since he expected Gabriel to have arrived first—was still to be seen, and how his mother would respond to Jerusa, he could only guess. But for now this journey was a no-man's-land, a few brief, precious days when their lives really were as uncomplicated as those of the dull, respectable Mr. and Mrs. Geary.

Deftly Michel pulled the flannel cleaning cloth, dipped in rosin, through the pistol's barrel. In the damp air at sea he cleaned his guns daily. Another precaution, though this one was aimed at George Hay. The mate had said nothing else about Jerusa's identity, but Michel believed in being careful. He had to. Even when she was at Michel's side, Hay's gaze seldom left Jerusa, and whether the man was interested in her solely for the reward her father had offered or for her beauty, as well, Michel wasn't taking any chances. Wherever he was on the little brig, he kept one of the pistols hidden beneath his coat, and his long knife, too, was always within easy reach at the back of his belt. If George Hay was lucky, he'd never learn precisely how far Mr. Geary would go to protect his pretty wife's virtue.

Michel heard the shouted order to haul aback, and with an oath of disgust he stuffed the cleaning rag back into its bag and wiped his hands clean. For a vessel as fast and well-handled as the *Swan* was, she was making a wretchedly slow passage because her captain was the most sociable old man Michel had ever known. Barker spoke every other ship the *Swan*'s lookout spotted, sometimes even changing his course to pursue a particularly interesting sail on the horizon, and at every invitation he'd drop his boat to go a-visiting like some eager spinster racing off to have tea with a new curate.

Jerusa rolled over slowly, clutching the coverlet as she yawned. "Whyever are we stopping now?" she grumbled. "It must be the middle of the night."

"Eight bells, *chérie*. The sun's high in the sky." Even if he didn't share her bed, Michel liked being able to see her when she woke in the morning, her face plump and flushed and her eyes heavy lidded with sleep. "If we're truly fortunate, our dear captain will have found us yet more company for the breakfast table."

Jerusa groaned as she pushed herself up onto one elbow. She'd never been one for early rising, and Michel could be appallingly cheerful. "Nothing could be worse than that captain from the Portuguese whaler at supper two nights ago! I've never met a man who talked so much or smelled so bad!"

"Oh, it could have been worse, Rusa. We could have had to dine with him on empty stomachs at breakfast."

Jerusa groaned again and dropped back down onto the pillow. It was strange how they'd fallen back into this pattern of teasing banter with each other, the same kind of jests and nonsense she'd always shared with Josh. She enjoyed it, true, but it also put her on her guard. For all that they might be brother and sister, she knew better. Nothing with Michel was ever less than complicated, and nothing was what it seemed.

But as she watched Michel swing out of his hammock in one fluid motion, she wasn't thinking sisterly thoughts. Far from it. He moved with the ease of a cat, his movements both purposefully spare and graceful in the narrow space. They'd sailed far enough south that the cabin was warm, especially at this hour, and he was dressed in only his breeches and shirt, the full sleeves rolled up high over his muscled arms to keep the linen clean as he worked with his guns. He crouched down to pull his sea chest from beneath the bunk to stow the cleaning rags back inside, and Jerusa raised her head and leaned forward, the better to see how his shirt pulled across his back and the way his breeches stretched taut.

He snapped the lid of the chest shut, and hurriedly she dropped back down onto the pillow before he caught her ogling him. She closed her eyes, pretending she was dozing, but the image of him remained to tantalize her. She'd been the one who'd stopped their lovemaking, not him, so why did he seem to be so much better able to cope with the intimacy of their shared quarters? She was the one who awoke in the night with her pulse racing and her heart pounding from dreams that were little more than memories of what they'd done that first night, in this very bunk, while Michel seemed to sleep as easily as he did everything else.

Perhaps it was because everything had been so new to her. She'd been kissed before, true, but Michel was so different from Tom and the others that kissing him seemed like something new, heady and breathtakingly sensual. And as for the rest, while he had seen and caressed a great deal of her, she'd been too inexperienced to explore him in return, and over and over again her thoughts struggled to try to fill in what she still didn't know.

Didn't know and now wouldn't learn, at least not with Michel, and the wave of sorrow that washed over her immediately doused her desire. She still loved him. If anything, the voyage had drawn them closer, not further apart.

But she hadn't been foolish enough to tell him again how she loved him. No matter how much she guessed at the depth of his feelings, he'd made it painfully clear that they didn't include love, at least not for her. She thought one more time of the miniature she'd found in his saddlebag, and wondered unhappily if his heart was already promised to the black-haired Frenchwoman.

The other possible reason was one Jerusa liked even less. Because her name was Sparhawk, she remained Michel's enemy. An enemy he'd kiss and tease and protect if it suited him to do so, but an enemy nonetheless. The way he spoke of her father proved that.

With her eyes still closed, she listened to the sounds of Michel shaving, the little drip as he dipped his wet razor into the cup of seawater, the muted scrape as the blade crossed his jaw. The only other man she'd watched shave was her father, and her fingers bunched into fists beneath the coverlet as she imagined what would happen when these two men she loved finally met.

She did not want either of them to die; she didn't want them to fight at all. But the more she tried to find an answer, the more complicated the question became. The best idea she'd found so far was to find Michel's mother on Martinique and beg her to intervene. Though Michel seldom spoke of her, she apparently still lived. Surely no mother would want to see her only son commit such an awful sin. Surely for the sake of the man she'd once loved, Michel's mother would help her try to end this feud before it claimed another life.

"Will you come topside with me, *ma mie,* or shall you spend the day where you are?" He had braided his hair in a sailor's queue, cooler in the hot sun, and now stood tucking the long tails of his shirt more neatly into his breeches before he shrugged into his coat. "From the *cacophonie* on deck I should think you'd be a little curious as to exactly what our captain has drawn to our side this time."

Jerusa opened her eyes and frowned, not sure she liked the idea of such cacophony on the deck over her head. Whatever its source, she'd never heard such a racket of screams and squawks, and she didn't need another of Michel's fancy French words to tell her she'd have no more sleep this morning.

Braiding her own hair much like his and daring to leave her stockings and shoes below, Jerusa followed Michel to the deck. After the twilight of their cabin, the sun was blindingly bright as it glanced off the water, and squinting, she shaded her eyes with the back of her hand.

The tropical summer sun was as hot as it was bright. The smooth, worn planks of the deck were warm beneath her bare feet, and despite the wind that filled the brig's sails, Jerusa felt the prickle of perspiration trickling down between her shoulder blades, under her layers of ladylike clothing. No wonder the men working in the rigging had stripped down to canvas trousers and little else besides hats to shade their faces.

"Ahoy, Mr. and Mrs. Geary! You're just in time to settle a question for me!" Captain Barker waved to them from the larboard entryway. Behind him the single mast of a small boat was just visible, bobbing alongside the *Swan*.

"Look here," Barker said as they joined him and his cook, still in his apron and a knitted wool cap. "I must decide which of this fellow's wares to buy for our breakfast. If you were at market, Mrs. Geary, which would take your fancy, eh?"

Jerusa peered over the *Swan*'s side to the little fishing boat below, floating on the transparent Caribbean water as if hanging in air. Her master, a black-skinned man in white trousers and an open red waistcoat, waited patiently with the pride of his catch spread out on his deck for the Englishman to make his decision. Swinging from a bracket on the mast was a large cage of woven reeds, full of small, brightly colored birds—scarlet, yellow, emerald and turquoise—and it was their shrieks and whistles and chattering that Jerusa and Michel had heard from their cabin.

Jerusa shook her head. "I really can't say, Captain. There's not a fish I'd recognize from home."

The fisherman waved his arm grandly toward the cage of birds and said something to Jerusa in a language halfway between French and Spanish.

"He says he hopes the lovely English lady will buy one of his pretty birds," explained Michel at her side. "All ladies like them, he says. But I wouldn't advise it, *chère*. Away from their companions, the little creatures fall silent and pine away. They also bite, and odds are, beneath those pretty feathers, they're covered with pests."

"How charming," said Jerusa as she smiled and shook her head at the fisherman. "But I'd wager he'd still likely do a wonderful trade in the market house at home."

Barker conferred one last time with his cook, then tossed a handful of coins to the fisherman. "Shark and cod, and a brace of those handsome *langoustes*," he said with relish as the fish and lobsters were handed up in a basket. "Oh, we'll have a fine breakfast, won't we?"

Less than an hour later, Jerusa, Michel and Captain Barker were sitting on the quarterdeck beneath an awning rigged to shade them from the worst of the sun. The dining table brought from the captain's cabin was graced by fillets of the fish he'd bought earlier, now cooked and sauced, as well as biscuits and a pot of incongruous, glittering beach plum jam from some distant Connecticut kitchen. For Jerusa the biscuits and tea were breakfast enough, but Michel and the captain argued happily over the different merits of the shark versus the cod as they ate more than enough to make their decisions.

Only half listening, Jerusa sat back in her chair, lazily sipping her tea. On a morning like this, with the bright blue sea and a cloudless sky all around her, it was easy to forget her troubles, or at least to put them temporarily aside. Not even the sight of Hay, glowering from the helm at the little breakfast party to which he'd not been invited, could dampen her spirits. He'd barely spoken to her once she'd assured him she wasn't worth a grand reward. Not that she cared. She had enough on her platter without adding a disgruntled fortune hunter. Besides, after tomorrow, when Captain Barker said they'd reach Bridgetown, she'd never see Mr. Hay again, and he'd be free to go search for some other missing lady with a wealthy father.

She stifled yet another yawn and set her teacup onto the table. "I'll leave you two to settle the state of the fishy world," she said as she rose. "I'm going back below."

Swiftly Michel looked at her with such concern that, without thinking, she rested her hand on his shoulder. "Don't worry, Mr. Geary," she said lightly. "I'm merely going back to sleep."

He glanced down at her hand, then back at her face, and smiled so warmly she felt the day grow another ten degrees hotter. "Take care, my dear," he said, his eyes as bright as the sea as he watched her. "I'll come to you soon."

Quickly she drew back her hand and fled before Captain Barker would notice how she blushed. Dear Almighty, why did it take so little from Michel to affect her so much? Yet as she drifted back to sleep, she prayed her dreams would be of him; for dreams, for now, were all she had.

She had just rebraided her hair when the door to the cabin opened behind her, and she turned eagerly. "Michel, I was just coming—"

But she broke off when she saw him, unsteadily supporting himself in the doorway. He was pale and sweating, with deep circles beneath his eyes. "Rusa, *chérie,*" he said, his words slurring and his smile weak. "Help me."

The brig heeled on a new tack, and Michel pitched forward. Jerusa grabbed him beneath his arms and nearly tumbled over herself beneath his weight. Her first thought had been that after breakfast he and Captain Barker had turned to rum. But she'd yet to see Michel drink more than he could hold, certainly not to this state, and as she tried to haul him back to his feet and toward the bunk, she felt how his body was warm with fever.

"Here we are, Michel," she said as they reached the edge of the bunk. With a groan he fell back onto the bunk and curled on his side with his eyes closed. She eased his arms free from his coat and tossed it aside, and then carefully pulled the pistol from his belt before she drew the coverlet over him.

"Th' damned Creole's fish," he muttered thickly. "Should—should have known better."

Gently she smoothed his hair back from his forehead. She remembered the fish spread out on the deck in the hot sun. If it had been fresh caught, then there should have been no danger, but in this climate, perhaps food turned faster. "Can I get you anything, Michel?"

"Should—should be better soon. Th' fish an' I parted company at th' rail." His smile was ghastly. *"Très dramatique, ma mie."*

"Oh, Michel." She knew he was right. If he'd already been sick to his stomach, then he should be well enough in a few hours. But that didn't ease his misery right now, and she thought of what she could do to make him more comfortable. A damp cloth for his forehead, water to sip, perhaps some broth and biscuits for when he felt better. "I'm going to the galley for a few things, but I'll be back directly."

She wasn't sure he'd heard her, for he looked as if he'd already fallen asleep. That was good; he needed the rest. In this heat, the worst danger would be from letting him go too long without water. She retrieved her shoes from beneath the bunk and opened the door. As she did, he turned his head slightly toward her without opening his eyes.

"Th' gun, Rusa," he said hoarsely. "Take th' gun."

She hesitated, wondering if he was insisting for a reason or if this were only some feverish whim. There'd be no way she could hide one of his long-barreled pistols beneath her clothing the way he did, and she'd feel downright foolish to appear in the *Swan*'s galley before the cook brandishing a gun like some sort of pirate's lady.

"Take it, Rusa," he rasped again, fumbling beneath the coverlet for the gun. "You must, *chère.*"

"Rest now, Michel, and stop worrying about me," she said softly, but he had finally drifted off to sleep, and she quickly left before he woke.

She had been aft to the galley several times with Michel, and it was easy enough to find by the fragrances from the cooking pots. But this time the kettles were empty and the fire burned low, and the only person in the galley was the towheaded ship's boy, Israel, at the table peeling potatoes with little interest or aptitude.

"Where's the cook?" asked Jerusa as she went to fill a battered pewter pitcher from the water barrel. "Mr. Geary's unwell, and I wished to bring him some broth, if the cook has any, and some dry biscuits to try to settle his stomach."

"Cook's taken sick, ma'am," said the boy laconically. "Him an' his mate both, same as th' cap'n hisself. But I warrant you can have what you pleases."

Jerusa looked at him sharply. "Did they all eat the same fish that Captain Barker bought this morning?"

"Aye, aye, ma'am, that they did." He jabbed his knife into another potato. "Cook an' his mate an' th' cap'n. An' now yer man, too, I warrant."

"Then who is in charge of the ship?"

"Why, Mr. Hay, o' course," answered the boy promptly.

"Of course," echoed Jerusa uneasily. Perhaps this was the reason that Michel had wanted her to take his pistol. Swiftly she gathered the pitcher and the basket with the other food. "Please tell the cook when you see him that I shall pray for his recovery."

She hurried back toward their cabin, the heavy pitcher balanced carefully before her. She should be thankful that Mr. Hay was aboard and well. From what she'd seen he was a competent sailor, and so near were they to their destination, he could surely see them to Bridgetown safely, and that was what mattered most.

But when she climbed down the last steps to their cabin, she was stunned to see Hay himself waiting outside the door.

"So there you are, Mrs. Geary," he said cheerfully with a bow. "I'd wondered where you were about. I'd heard your husband had been stricken, too, and I came to see how he was faring."

"He's resting now, or was before I went to the galley." She tried to squeeze past him to her door, but stubbornly he blocked her way. "Now if you'll excuse me, Mr. Hay, I'll be able to see his condition myself."

"Asleep, you say?" he said, still not moving. "I could have wagered I heard him answer himself when I knocked on the door not five minutes past."

"Then perhaps my husband is awake," she said uneasily, wondering why he insisted on staying. If he was the *Swan*'s master, didn't he have more important things to do than to linger here, provoking her? "He's been quite restless. Or perhaps you woke him."

Though he shook his head, his smile remained. "Well, now, I'd be sorry if I'd done that. But the strangest part is this, Mrs. Geary. When I knocked on your door, do you know how your husband answered?"

"Mr. Hay, my husband isn't well, and I—"

"He asked if I were Jerusa," declared Hay, continuing as if she hadn't spoken. "Jerusa! Can you fathom that? Calling me after a woman's name, and the name of that missing Newport lady in the bargain."

"Oh, Mr. Hay!" she scoffed. She would bluff; she had to. "Whyever would my husband do such a thing? I'd say you've been reading that handbill of yours a bit too far into the dogwatch and dreaming of yourself chasing after wealthy young ladies."

"I'm not dreaming now, am I, *Mrs.* Geary?" He leaned closer, his smile becoming more of a leer, and Jerusa's thoughts fearfully jumped back to what had happened with Lovell in the alley.

"Not dreaming, no," she said as tartly as she could. She would not let herself be afraid or he would know, and everything would be over. "But from your unseasonable actions, Mr. Hay, I can only conclude that you are ill as well as the others. Now if you would let me pass—"

"Nay, *Mrs.* Geary, not quite so fast. I've yet to tell you what else I've heard your husband say. He speaks in French, Mrs. Geary. Did you know that? Prattles on as if he'd learned it in the cradle."

"Perhaps, Mr. Hay, that is because my husband's mother is French, and mothers are generally the ones to rock cradles. Not that any of this is your affair in the least."

"I'm the captain now, *Mrs.* Geary," he said, his smile fading, "and it's most definitely my affair if we're harboring a Frenchman on board a decent Yankee vessel."

He edged closer, and Jerusa decided she'd had enough of bluffing. She swung the heavy pewter pitcher as hard as she could, catching him in the jaw and drenching him with water. He swore and stumbled back, and as he did, she wrenched open the latch and threw open the door to the cabin. But she was only halfway inside before Hay grabbed her arm to pull her back.

"Let me go at once!" she cried, struggling to hang on to the door and fight her way free of his grasp. "Let me go *now!*"

The basket flew from her arm, scattering biscuits in the air, and when she tried to strike him again with the pitcher, he twisted it from her fingers and tossed it down the companionway with a ringing clatter. But as he turned, she was able to jerk her arm free, and swiftly she whirled into the cabin.

"Come back here, you lying little bitch!" growled Hay as he grabbed for her again, slamming his shoulder against the door to keep it open. With a yelp, Jerusa tumbled back onto the deck as the door flew open with Hay behind it. With another oath he swept down to yank her to her feet, and as he did he caught the glint of metal from the corner of his eye, realizing a fraction too late that it was the barrel of Michel's gun.

"You lying French thief," he said, panting, as he slowly rose to his feet. "I should throw you and your little whore over the side where you belong."

"Foolish words from a man in your position, Hay," said Michel. His hair and face were slick with sweat, but as he sat against the pillows his eyes were ice-cold and his hand holding the pistol didn't waver a fraction. "Are you unharmed, *chère?*"

"I'm fine, Michel," said Jerusa breathlessly as she scrambled up from the deck. "But you—"

"I warned you, *ma mie*. You should have taken the gun," he said, his gaze never leaving Hay's face. "This ship is remarkably overrun with vermin."

"Speak for yourself, Geary," snarled Hay. "You're the worst of the lot, a yellow-bellied Frenchman hiding in some chit's bedclothes. Why, I'd wager that gun isn't even loaded, you cowardly little French bastard!"

Jerusa gasped, seeing the change in Michel's face. Better than Hay, she knew all too well exactly what Michel was capable of doing, and loading the pistol was the least of it.

"And you, Hay, you doubtless believe yourself to be a brave man for speaking to me like that," he said, his musing tone deceptive. "Would you care to test yourself against me, Hay? At this range a blind man could hit you, but if you truly believe that this pistol is only a prop, then come, I invite you to take it from me."

Jerusa flattened herself against the bulkhead and squeezed her eyes shut, terrified of what she'd see.

If he killed George Hay now, would it be her fault, too? Another death, as Michel said, another man who would live still except for her? And would it be like this when he met her father, too, insults and dares and then coldhearted death?

"It's your choice, Hay," Michel was saying. "You leave, and you agree never to insult this lady again, or you gamble your life on whether I'm the coward. Your choice, *mon ami*. Your choice."

God in heaven, she could not look....

Chapter Sixteen

"Damn you, Geary," sputtered Hay. "You wouldn't shoot an unarmed man, would you?"

Michel shrugged. "I'm French. You're English. Can you be sure what I'll do, eh? And you have a knife, don't you? If my gun's but a bluff, *mon ami,* then you can use your blade on me. Not even an English court would find you guilty."

He watched and waited as Hay decided. *Sacristi,* the mate's bland English face was so open he could read the fool's thoughts as if they were written on his forehead. He himself had played this game so many times that it held neither risk nor excitement for him any longer. Spaniards could still surprise him on occasion, but Englishmen like this one, quivering before him, always backed down because they cared too much for their own skins.

Mordieu, but he was tired, and his head throbbed and burned like the crater of Montagne Pelée, the old volcano beyond St-Pierre. It was taking every last bit of his concentration to hold the pistol steady. Hay must be hesitating because of Jerusa. Not even an *Anglais* wished to be thought a coward with a woman watching.

But to Michel's surprise, she wasn't watching. Instead she'd

202

pressed herself as flat as she could against the bulkhead, as if she hoped she'd somehow squeeze through the cracks to another, happier place. Her face was pale and her eyes were closed, and Michel frowned with concern, wondering if she, too, was ill. Then he remembered the alley in Seabrook, and what in his fury he'd done to her there. Poor Rusa, no wonder she was terrified! Remorse swept over him as he saw she was trembling, and he longed to be able to tell her this would not end that way.

But his own hands were beginning to shake, too, and his shirt was plastered to his chest with sweat. That way, this way: he didn't care which ending Hay chose, as long as he did it soon.

And to Michel's relief, the Englishman did. "Very well, Geary, have it your way," he said abruptly, his face red enough to be on the verge of apoplexy. "I've a vessel to command. I can't tarry here until you come to your senses."

"A wise decision," said Michel blandly. He waved the pistol's barrel from Hay toward Jerusa, and contemptuously he noted how that slight gesture was enough to make the mate's eyes grow round and owlish. "Now your regrets to the lady, *s'il vous plaît.*"

Hay sighed with irritation as he turned to bow curtly in Jerusa's direction. "Forgive me, ma'am, if I have offered any insult to you or your person," he said. He glared back over his shoulder at Michel. "Does that satisfy you, Geary? Or must I bend my knee and kiss the chit's hem?"

Michel clicked his tongue, scolding. "You can begin by not calling her a 'chit' or any of your other charming little endearments again in my hearing. 'Mrs. Geary' will be sufficient." He leaned back against the pillows and lifted the pistol's barrel to tap it gently once, twice across his lips. "If I hear otherwise, you will answer to me. And next time, Mr. Hay, I shall not be as understanding. *Bonjour, monsieur.*"

His eyes had already begun to close as the Englishman

slammed the cabin's door. He felt the gun slide from his fingers onto his chest, and though he vaguely thought he should stop it, he didn't seem able to make his hand cooperate. He didn't seem able to do much at all except slip further into the heat and the darkness that were drawing him down, pulling him under like velvet waves, so warm and soft and black....

"Michel?" asked Jerusa anxiously. "Michel, love, are you all right? Can you look at me, Michel? Please? It's Jerusa, and I want to know if you're all right."

But if he heard her he made no sign that he did. His skin burned with fever, and he'd gone limp as a doll made of old rags. This wasn't right, she thought frantically. How could he have been so lucid—and so menacing—only minutes before, and now be unconscious?

"Oh, please, Michel, can you hear me at all?" She brushed her fingertips across his brow, smoothing aside his hair. His forehead was dry and hot, too hot. Belatedly she thought of the water pitcher she'd thrown at Hay and knew she'd have to go back to the galley for more.

With a sigh she looked down at the pistol on the coverlet, where it had slipped from Michel's fingers. Lord, he'd left it cocked, and with a little grimace she picked the gun up and latched the flintlock before she cradled it in the crook of her arm. She didn't want to take the thing with her at all, but she didn't trust the mate to keep his word, especially not with Michel ill, and with one last look at Michel, she headed back toward the galley.

The boy Israel had finished peeling the potatoes and had moved on to a wooden trencher filled with onions. With tears streaming from his eyes, he barely looked up when Jerusa returned.

"Cook's no better, ma'am," he said, flicking off the onion's thick yellow skin. "Nor is th' cap'n, they say."

"I'm sorry to hear that," murmured Jerusa as she refilled the pitcher she'd retrieved rattling around the mainmast between the decks. "I hope they'll all feel better soon."

Israel tossed the peeled onion into a battered iron kettle. "Either they will or they won't, ma'am," he said philosophically. "Hopes an' wishes got nothin' to do wit' it."

Unhappily Jerusa thought of Michel. "But surely our prayers will help."

"If'n you say so, ma'am." He glanced up at the tin lantern that hung from the beam overhead. The motion of the ship had increased, and the lantern was swinging back and forth so that their shadows danced first large, then tiny, along the bulkhead. "No cookin' tonight, anyways, ma'am. I warrant th' order will come down most any minute t' douse th' cook fires. We're in for a blow, no mistake."

No mistake, indeed, thought Jerusa uneasily as she made her way, stumbling aft to the cabin. She could hear how the wind had changed from the higher-pitched sound that shrieked through the rigging above her, and beneath her feet the deck seemed to have a new life of its own, plunging up one moment and then down the next with such unpredictable violence that before she reached the cabin she nearly spilled this second pitcher full of water, too.

In the bunk Michel hadn't moved at all. She dipped a handkerchief into the water and wiped it across his face, and then, feeling greatly daring, she lifted back the coverlet and his shirt to draw the damp cloth across his chest and arms. He was still warm, far too warm, but there was nothing else she could do for him now, and with a sigh she rinsed the cloth one last time and laid it across his forehead. She tucked the coverlet firmly around him and beneath the mattress, hoping to keep him from rolling into the high sides of the bunk.

The deck lurched again at yet another new angle, slamming Jerusa into the bulkhead. She had thought she'd found her sea legs by now, but she wasn't prepared for *this*, and, rubbing her elbow where she'd hit the latch, she decided the deck itself would be the safest place. She sat beside the bunk with her head level with Michel's, her feet braced against his trunk, her back against the bulkhead and the pistol resting in her lap, and prepared to ride out the storm and his fever both.

She didn't know which frightened her more. As the minutes stretched into hours, the depth of Michel's illness terrified her. Only rarely did he shift or stir, and though she tried to cool his fever as best she could, it seemed to her that his skin only grew warmer to the touch. She could feel him slipping further and further away from her, and there wasn't a blessed thing she could do to draw him back. She knew from her brothers' stories that illnesses here in the Caribbean were different from those at home. Here the heat made wounds turn putrid in an hour's time, and a single fever could kill the three hundred men of a frigate's crew in a week.

But Michel wasn't going to die, she told herself fiercely. He'd only eaten some fish that had turned in the sun. Surely even in the Caribbean people didn't die from such a thing. Besides, they were less than a day from Bridgetown, and there, if he still were ill, she'd find all manner of physicians and surgeons.

Gently she traced the line of his jaw with one finger, feeling the bristles of his beard. He was a strong man, a man too proud to die like this without a fight. Any minute now his fever would break, he would roll over and smile and call her his dear Rusa, and he would be fine.

He *would* be fine. Right as rain.

"I love you, Michel," she whispered sadly. "Whatever else happens, I want you to know that. I love you."

But her words were lost in the earsplitting crack that came from the deck, like a tree splintered by lightning. The mainmast, thought Jerusa with horror, for the sound had come from midships. As wild as the brig's movements had been before this, her motion took on a new unevenness without the largest sail and mast to steady her.

Over the roar of the wind she could hear the faint voices of the crew, shouting orders to one another, and she could picture the men working frantically against the storm to free the *Swan* of the wreckage of her broken mast. She'd heard stories enough of what damage that wreckage could do, trailing over the side of a ship and pulling her sideways into the deep trough of a wave until she broached to and capsized.

She was straining her ears so hard to hear the storm that she hadn't noticed when Michel had begun to mutter, his head tossing uneasily against the pillow. Eagerly she put her ear near his lips, but all he said was fragmented and jumbled, and in French, as well. And her name: dear Lord, had she really heard it? Again he murmured it, this time clear enough for her to know she hadn't dreamed it. Maybe somehow he knew she was here, knew she was trying to help him.

Oh, Michel, how much I love you!

Grinning foolishly with no one to see her, she tugged him up higher onto the pillow and trickled water between his lips. The fever still held him in its grip, but to her, even the garbled words were so much better than the awful stillness.

More shouts, more wind, the ringing thump of axes as the lines were hacked away. But the shouts seemed closer now, and she could hear heavy footsteps racing up and down the companionway beyond their cabin. Somehow the waves seemed louder over the creaks and groans of the ship's timbers. Was she imagining it, or was the brig riding lower in the water now, far enough down that only the pine bulkheads and the oak timbers behind them separated her from the sea itself?

Someone ran directly past their door. Sweet Almighty, she had to know what was happening! Bracing herself in the doorway, she pulled the door open and gazed down the narrow passage to the steps. Seawater splashed over her feet and skirts, and she realized the whole deck was awash. The lantern that usually lit the passage was gone, but an eerie, otherworldly light filtered down the steps, bathing the figure of the man coming toward her now with a strange glow that she realized must be dawn.

"Please, can you tell me what is happening?" she shouted at the man. "No one has told us anything!"

The seaman shook his head with exhaustion as he peered at her. "Cap'n's dead, ma'am," he shouted back hoarsely to her. "Dead from th' sickness. We've lost th' mainmast whole an' half th' mizzen with it, an' we're takin' water something awful. We're workin' every man at the pumps, ma'am. Every man."

Before she could ask more, he staggered off, bound for the pumps himself. Her terror mounting by the second, Jerusa forced the door closed again and went to crouch beside Michel. She had thought he was improved, but Captain Barker had died. But not Michel; please, God, not Michel, too! She threaded her fingers through his as much to comfort herself as him, and was rewarded by him turning his face toward hers, the merest hint of a smile on his lips.

She listened to the sounds of the storm, her fingers tight around Michel's. The night before her father or any of her brothers sailed, Mama had always made a ritual of saying special prayers for them at the supper table before grace, and the unspoken belief in the family was that that alone was the reason none of the Sparhawk men had ever been lost at sea. But what if she were the one who was drowned instead, if she were the one who never returned home, whose grave in the churchyard was empty beneath the headstone?

Accustomed as she'd become to the shrieking of the wind and sea, she still jumped and gasped when she heard the pounding on the cabin door.

"Open up, Mrs. Geary! It's me, George Hay!" shouted the

mate, his voice ragged from struggling to make his orders heard over the wind. "Open up now!"

She seized the pistol from where she'd left it on the bunk and stood close to the door. Storm or no, she wasn't going to make the same mistake twice. "What is it you want, Mr. Hay?"

"Damnation, woman, I want to talk to you!" he roared. "Now will you open the door, or must I break the bloody thing down?"

She took a deep breath and opened the door, and immediately Hay lunged for her. But this time she darted backward, away from him. With her legs spread wide against the ship's pitching and her back against the bunk for support, she held the pistol level with both hands and aimed it squarely at his chest.

"For God's sake, put that down!" he ordered. "Haven't we trouble enough without you waving a gun in my face?"

She raised her chin, shouting herself. "You tell me, Mr. Hay."

Hay raised his hand toward her, but she shook her head vehemently and held her aim. His hat was gone, his clothes as wet as if he'd worn them swimming, his hair without its ribbon hanging lankly to his shoulders. He swore, wearily wiping his face with the soaked sleeve of his coat, and if he hadn't threatened her earlier she would have pitied him.

"You're coming with us, Jerusa Sparhawk. In the boat, with me. Now."

Still she shook her head, refusing to believe him.

"Look, the *Swan*'s going down," he explained heavily. "There's nothing we can do to save her. We've ordered the boats, and we're shoving off, and you're coming with me."

"No!" Wildly she glanced over her shoulder at Michel. "I'm not going anywhere with you, especially not without Michel!"

"For God's sake, woman, if he's not dead now, he will be soon. Barker went hours ago. You'll die yourself if you stay here."

"I don't care!" cried Jerusa. "I'm not leaving Michel!"

"You bloody little fool," growled Hay. "I'm not going to leave a fortune like you behind to go to the fishes."

He reached to take the gun away from her and instead she jabbed the barrel against his chest.

"Once before, Mr. Hay, you had to guess whether this gun was loaded and primed or not," she said, her raised voice almost giddy. "You can guess again if it pleases you, or you can leave again. But remember that either way I have nothing to lose."

He stared down at the gun, then at her, before he backed away. "Then damn you to hell, Miss Sparhawk. You and the Frenchman both!"

This time he didn't bother to slam the door when he left, and Jerusa had to put all her weight behind her shoulder to force it closed against the wind and spray that were sweeping down the passage.

"Rusa, *chère.*"

Jerusa whipped around. Michel was sitting up in the bunk, watching her.

She ran to him, the pistol swinging clumsily in her hand as she threw her arms around his neck. "Oh, Michel, you're alive! Thank God you didn't die, and, oh, Michel, how much I love you!"

"Then put down the pistol before you kill me." He smiled weakly as she pulled away to drop the gun onto the bed. "Now, what is happening, *ma mie?* What did Hay want now?"

"He wanted me to come with him in the boat," she explained breathlessly. "He said the *Swan* is sinking, and he wanted me to leave you behind and go with him."

His smile vanished, his face drawn and serious as he listened to the groans of the dying ship. "Then go to him now, *ma bien-aimée.* Hurry, before it's too late." Briefly he lifted her fingers to his lips before he returned his hand to her, gently pushing her away. "I would not have you die because of me. *Au revoir, ma mie.*"

"No, Michel, I won't do it!" she cried, her eyes filling. "He couldn't make me leave without you, and neither can you. Why do you think I had your gun?"

He stared at her with disbelief. "*You* threatened him?"

She grinned through her tears. "I did the same thing you did. If he'd challenged me and the pistol hadn't fired, I suppose he could have hauled me off with him the way he wished, but otherwise—well, he didn't choose to trust me, either."

"Oh, Rusa." His smile was tight, and if she hadn't known better she would have thought that he, too, was close to tears. "Perhaps we truly do deserve each other."

"Then maybe there's a place in that boat for us both." Now that he was back with her, the storm seemed less frightening. If he wasn't ready to die, then she wasn't, either, and together they would find a way to safety. "Do you think you can walk?"

"As well as anyone can on board a sinking ship, *chère*." He shoved back the coverlet and swung his legs over the edge of the bunk. With Jerusa's help he was able to reach the steps, and by the time they had fought their way against the wind to the deck itself, by will alone he was supporting her as much as she was him as they huddled in the companionway, shielding themselves from the full force of the wind.

As much as Jerusa had guessed at the havoc the storm had caused during the long afternoon and night, she still was unprepared for the sight of the wreck that the *Swan* had become. The shattered stump was all that remained of the mainmast, and along with the mast itself and all the sails and lines, the starboard rail had also gone over the side. The brig had settled low into the water and the waves broke and washed freely across her now, sweeping everything else away and leaving the deck oddly empty.

Empty of lines and rope, buckets and hatch covers, and empty, too, of any other people except for them. The davits that lowered the boats to the water were empty, also, and with a desperate disappointment, Jerusa realized that George Hay had kept his word and abandoned her and Michel to die together aboard the sinking brig.

But Michel was pointing in the other direction, over the bow. Through the blowing rain and spray Jerusa could just make out a long, shadowy shape on the horizon, land that seemed to be creeping closer every second. No, they were *racing* toward it, decided Jerusa, and abruptly they stopped. With an impact that tossed them both back down the steps, the *Swan* was hurled against an outcrop of rocks so large that it was almost an island, and then stayed there, her hull wedged awkwardly between the two largest rocks.

"Hurry, Rusa," shouted Michel urgently as they climbed back to the deck. "There's no guessing how long she'll hold."

Hand in hand they ran across the deck, now strangely still beneath their feet, forward to the bow. The island Michel had first spotted remained a tantalizing distance across the water, though exactly how far—a hundred yards, two hundred?— Jerusa couldn't guess. He drew her to the very edge of the deck, where the rail had been before it had been washed away. Below them the bow hung free over open water, beyond the rocks that trapped the hull.

Michel cupped his hand around Jerusa's ear so she could hear him. "If we stay on board the *Swan*, she'll only break up around us, *ma chérie*. But if we can reach the island, we'll have a chance of it."

His eyes were bright with excitement, his whole body so alive with the challenge of what lay before them that she couldn't believe she'd feared he would die. Not Michel, she thought with boundless happiness, not today.

"I love you, Michel Géricault!" she shouted, as much for the world to hear as for him.

He grinned back at her, his hand tight around hers and the

wild daring in his eyes that she'd come to know as his. "And I love you, Jerusa Sparhawk!" he shouted back. "Now jump!"

And with a wild, joyous whoop, she did.

Chapter Seventeen

"Jerusa?"

Michel rolled over on the sand, automatically reaching for the pistol at his waist that wasn't there. But Jerusa wasn't there, either. All that was left were the prints from her bare feet and the sweeping marks where her skirts had dragged across the sand. But *mordieu,* where could she have gone? She had been there beside him when they'd finally crawled from the surf, and she'd been curled beneath his arm after they'd collapsed here, high up on the beach where the palms would shelter them.

"Jerusa!" Unsteadily he rose first to his knees, then his feet, using the palm for support as his gaze swept up and down the empty beach. His gun was gone but his knife had somehow remained in its salt-stiffened sheath, and he drew it now, straining his ears for sound. He was light-headed from hunger and swallowing too much seawater and the lingering weakness of the fever, and the last thing he wished to do was to track her down, wherever she'd wandered off to.

Unless she hadn't wandered off at all. Unless the beach wasn't as uninhabited as it first had seemed, and while he'd been asleep like some great useless slug, some other man had come along to claim her. Unless...

"Oh, good, Michel, you're awake!" She came bounding toward him through the tall grass at the edge of the heavier forest, her bedraggled skirts looped up over her long legs and a small bunch of yellow-green bananas, still attached to their stem, tucked under her arm. "Look what I've found!"

"You shouldn't have gone off on your own like that, *ma mie*," he cautioned. He might feel like the wrong end of a sailor's leave, but she certainly didn't. "You don't know who or what you might have found."

"Oh, fah, Michel, don't be an old woman about it," she scoffed, shoving her tangled hair back from her face, and she looked so pointedly at the knife in his hand that he finally tucked it back in its sheath. "I've told you before I grew up on an island, and I can take care of myself, too."

He waved one arm through the air, encompassing the long empty beach, the wild, bright green forest and the vast turquoise sea. "This is hardly a proper little island in Narragansett Bay."

"No, and we're not proper little islanders, either, are we?" She grinned mischievously. "Have you any notion of where we *are?*"

He sighed, wishing he felt as cheerful as she did. "Somewhere off Dominica, perhaps, or maybe the Iles de la Petite Terre. Near enough that Mr. Hay and his friends should have kept to the *Swan* instead of scurrying off in their boats."

She followed his gaze to where the brig lay wedged between the rocks, held in place as neatly as if she'd been set there for display. In the bright, warm sunlight it was easy to forget yesterday's storm and how close they'd come to disaster.

"Do you think they reached land?" she asked. "I haven't seen any sign of them in this cove, have you?"

"No," said Michel, letting the single word answer both her questions with chilling directness. "Later, as soon as the tide falls, we'll want to go back aboard. There's things I'd rather not leave for the wreckers to find."

"Wreckers?"

"Of course, *ma chérie,*" he said, surprised by her naïveté. Did she really believe they'd been cast away on some storybook desert island? There had been French, Spanish and English prowling about these waters for the last three hundred years, and Indians before that, and the odds of finding a truly deserted island anywhere in the Caribbean would be slim indeed.

"A prize like that brig won't go unnoticed for long," he explained. "And since she was abandoned by her crew, the salvage laws will let her be claimed by whoever wants her. Not that the wreckers will wait for the niceties of the law. I'll wager that the first boats will be here by noon tomorrow, and then we'll be on our way to St-Pierre."

"Oh," she said so forlornly it was more of a sigh, as she dropped onto the sand, the bananas in her lap. "I didn't realize we'd be rescued quite so soon."

Morbleu, she *had* believed they'd been stranded here for eternity! But as foolish as such an idea was, it did remain a pretty, tantalizing fantasy, and he could understand all too well why she'd wished for it. Waiting in Martinique with bleak certainty would be his mother and, quite likely by now, her father, and what would happen there was now more than he could guess.

But here on this island the world narrowed to the two of them, a world that existed without the grim entanglements of loyalty and honor and revenge. Here none of that mattered. He and Jerusa had survived the storm unharmed and they had each other, and he couldn't blame her at all for wanting life to stay that uncomplicated. *Sacristi,* what he'd give to keep it that way, too!

With a sigh he sat beside her, taking her hand gently in his. "Whatever else happens, *chérie,* remember that I love you."

She smiled wistfully. "And I love you, Michel." She looked down at how neatly their fingers intertwined and wished their lives could do the same. He loved her and she loved him, but she wasn't foolish enough to believe that what they shared could survive whatever lay ahead in Martinique.

With infinite care she slipped her fingers free. "I thought you would be hungry," she said, lifting the bananas from her lap. "I'm not certain, but I thought this must be some sort of fruit."

"Bananas, *ma petite*. Something else that you won't find on your Narragansett island." He took the bunch from her, snapped the ripest banana free and peeled back the skin. Breaking off a piece, he held it before her until she opened her mouth to take it from his fingers. "They're everywhere in the islands."

She chewed it slowly, relishing the sweet, unfamiliar flavor before she finally smiled. "That's very good," she said, taking the rest of it from him to finish herself. "But surely you would like one, too?"

He shook his head. "Before I eat anything, Rusa, we must find fresh water."

"Oh, I found that already." Quickly she stood, thankful for something to do. "Near the bananas."

The path through the forest was wide and clear, so easy to follow from the beach that Michel was certain it was used by ships refilling their water barrels after long voyages. But he'd expected a utilitarian stream or river, not the exquisite clearing that Jerusa now led him to, and familiar though he was with the beauty of the islands, this took his breath away.

Twenty feet above their heads, a narrow stream of fresh water rushed down from the island's higher ground over smooth black rock before it fell, glittering like diamonds in the dappled sunlight, into a wide, clear pool. Tall, feathery ferns and trees shaded the pond, and yellow and lavender orchids punctuated the shadows with bright spots of bobbing color. The air around them was alive with the sound of falling water and the cries of the forest thrushes.

And yet as beautiful as the place was, for Michel the loveliest part of it was Jerusa as she stood on one of the smooth, flat rocks that hung over the water, just within reach of the cascade. She held her arms slightly bent, her fingers spread and her shoulders raised as she let the cool drops of water sprinkle over her, and her smile was so full of unfeigned, open pleasure that Michel knew he'd never forget it.

She laughed when she caught his eye, shaking her hair back over her shoulders and scattering a new shower of droplets into the air.

"I'll say it before you will," she called over the sound of the water. "No, there is no place like this on any island in Narragansett Bay, nor any other place in all of Rhode Island, either."

He laughed with her as he came to kneel on another rock near hers, reaching down to scoop up the cool, clear water. No wine or brandy had ever tasted so fine to him, and he drank deeply, letting the water take away the parched heat from his throat. When he was done, he sat back on his heels to watch Jerusa.

She'd inched closer into the waterfall itself, and she stood with her head arched back, her eyes closed, and the same blissful smile on her face as the water streamed over her body. Her tattered green gown was soaked, clinging to her body in a way that reminded him of the tub at the inn in Seabrook.

"You are very hard on your gowns, *chère*," he called. "I pity your husband."

She opened her eyes and grinned wickedly. "What, because you think I'll be hard on him, too?"

"I hadn't intended it that way, *ma petite* Rusa, but now that you say it, I shall consider the possibilities."

He liked seeing her laugh as she did now, and with regret he realized how rarely she'd smiled or laughed since he had come into her life. And yet, in reverse, how often she had brought joy to him, a man who'd always before found little in the world to amuse him!

"You may consider them, but that is all," she said with mock solemnity. "The possibilities themselves shall remain private between my husband and myself."

"Oh, I wouldn't dream of intruding. Unless, of course, you'd wed Carberry."

"You've no right to say that!" she scolded, trying to look as indignant as she could while soaking wet. "Tom and I simply didn't suit one another, that was all."

"All, and everything, *ma mie.*" Watching her in the water reminded him not only of the Seabrook inn but of how gritty and hot he felt himself, covered with sand and sticky with salt from the sea. He glanced from her to the water and back again, his lazy smile of suggestion widening. What was he waiting for, anyway?

"Whatever are you doing, Michel?" asked Jerusa as he pulled his shirt over his head and dropped it onto the rock beside him. He unbuckled his breeches at the knees and then stood to unbutton the fall at his waist. *"Michel!"*

His smile was his only answer, and swiftly she turned her back to him, staring into the wet black stone of the waterfall rather than see him naked. She heard the splash as he dived into the water, and next his shouted exclamation as he discovered how cool the water was. It was easy to imagine him behind her in the pond, and easier still to picture him without his clothing, no matter how much her conscience ordered her to do otherwise.

"Come join me, *chérie!*" he called. "You will, I promise, feel much refreshed!"

"I would feel most indecent, thank you," she answered, sounding impossibly prim even to her own ears. But his words had done their work. Despite the waterfall, she still could feel the sand that had been washed under her clothes by the waves, bits of grit trapped between her shift and her skin. The water would be so deliciously cool, and it would be wonderful to feel clean again.

"Jerusa, Jerusa," he chided mockingly. "Why deprive yourself? It would be, after all, nothing I haven't seen already. If you'll but recall that afternoon in Seabrook—"

"I remember!" she snapped, and with a deep breath she spun around. Though he was in the water and his clothes remained on the rock, he was not exactly indecent; the ripples in the water around him hid all but his shoulders and arms. He flung his wet hair back from his face and slowly smiled, as blatant an invitation as any she'd ever had.

What *was* she waiting for, anyway?

Before she could change her mind she unhooked her bodice and tossed it onto the next rock. Her skirts, petticoats and stays followed, until all that was left was her shift. She looked down and saw the rapt look of anticipation on Michel's face, and before he could ogle her any longer, she whipped the shift over her head and leapt into the water.

She gasped with surprise as her head broke the water's surface, and Michel laughed.

"It's not so bad after a minute or two," he said. "Truly."

"Not so bad if you're accustomed to swimming in December!" she said, still gasping.

But as he'd predicted, the longer she was in the water, the less chilly it seemed to be. The pond was deeper than she'd realized, too, well beyond her depth, and automatically she began to tread water to keep afloat. Like loading and firing guns, her father had insisted she learn how to swim alongside her brothers, too, and as she paddled in the cool water now she was thankful he had.

"Are you all right?" he asked with amusement. "Would you rather stand, *chère?* The water's not as deep here, by me."

"I don't need to stand, near you or otherwise." To prove it, she swam away from him, enjoying the feel of the cool water against her skin and how her body warmed from the swimming.

Or maybe it wasn't the swimming alone. She turned and glided back toward Michel, taking care to keep from getting too near.

Too near for what, Jerusa? What could possibly happen in a pond?

He sank deeper into the water until the surface was just level with his eyes, eyes that seemed very blue against all the shining black stone and green leaves. Silently he began to swim toward her, his strokes barely ruffling the water's surface as his long blond hair streamed out behind him. Even though she knew it was no more than another of his endless games, she felt her heart quicken. There was something about the way he was watching her that was decidedly predatory, and she was his prey.

She narrowed her eyes and slammed her palm down on the water with a great splash, a ploy she'd learned from her brothers, but still Michel came closer. She twisted about in the water and plunged beneath the surface to get away from him, and instantly regretted it. Or at least her conscience did; the rest of her didn't mind at all. There, before her in the water, was everything his breeches ordinarily hid, the last important detail her imagination hadn't been able to supply, and Lord, he was a beautiful man.

He grabbed her ankle and jerked her up to the surface, sputtering. "Let me go, Michel!" she cried, blushing furiously as she tried to thrash free.

"Why should I, Rusa?" he teased. "All you've done is try to swim away from me."

"Please, Michel!" It was nearly impossible to keep her body decently underwater while he insisted on dragging her foot into the air. He was going to upend her completely if he wasn't careful.

"I'll release your ankle if you give me your hand," he bargained, and with little choice she reluctantly agreed, offering her hand as he let her foot glide back down through the water. "Now trust me, *ma mie*. Relax, and let yourself float."

"Michel, I—"

"Shh, Rusa. You must trust me," he ordered softly. "Remember that I love you, and trust me."

Her gaze locked with his, gradually she did what he asked,

letting her legs and body float upward behind her. Instinctively she extended her other arm to keep her head above the water, and Michel took that hand, too. Inch by inch she relaxed, the roar of the falling water filling her ears until she felt as if she were floating, weightless, not just in water but above it. Slowly he glided her closer to him, drawing her arms against him until their faces were only inches apart.

"Ma belle Jerusa," he murmured, *"ma bien-aimée."*

It seemed right for her to cross that last distance until their lips met. He kissed her gently at first, teasing her, their lips grazing together and then separating as he let her drift away, breathless with desire for more.

"Who's running away now?" she whispered, her voice husky with frustration.

His smile was knowing, his eyes hooded. "Not I, *ma mie.*"

At last he pulled her close, releasing her hands so she could circle them around his neck as his mouth slanted over hers. Hungrily she parted her lips for him, needing to taste him, and she felt the first shimmer of pleasure ripple through her. She brought her body through the water to nestle close to his, her arms tightening around his shoulders to steady herself. His hands eased along her body, from the narrowing curve of her waist upward until, with a shudder, she felt him cup her breasts in his palms, his thumbs stroking the tips into hard, tight peaks of response that made her cry out.

She slid her hands along the length of his back, exploring the feel of him, learning how the hard muscles of his back narrowed and lengthened at his waist. She brushed across the small pebble of his nipple, nearly hidden in the hair, and learned from the sharp break in his breathing that he, too, found pleasure there.

She felt his hands slide lower, over her hips, cradling her as he guided her closer to him, and instinctively her legs parted and curled around his waist. Too late she realized the intimacy of what she'd unwittingly done, and with a startled splash she pulled back.

"Trust me, Rusa," he said, his voice dark with promise as he held her. "This isn't Martinique and it's not Newport. This is here, and it's only for us."

She drew back to see his face, her throat tight from longing as she gave him a shaky smile. She loved him so much, and she wanted this to be *right* for them both. With infinite care and curiosity she let her body slide back down against his, aware of his eyes on her as he waited for her response. She lifted her legs around his hips again and drew herself closer until their bodies touched. She could feel his heat where they touched, the hard length of him pressed between her open legs, and she thought of how much he'd changed since she'd first glimpsed him beneath the water.

Tentatively she moved against him, startled by the sensations that swept through her. It had been like this in the cabin when he'd touched her, but this was better, far, far better. She pulled herself upward along his body, delighting in how the rough hair of his chest dragged across her sensitized breasts, then she eased down again along his length.

Her breath caught at the languorous pleasure of it, and she tightened her legs around him, instinctively offering more of herself as she raised herself upward again. This time her motions weren't quite as measured, her body eager for more as the cool water splashed and sluiced over them.

His fingers dug deep into her hips, lifting her against him, increasing the pressure of her sliding caress, and this time she cried out, feeling his touch in every nerve. He groaned in response, his breath hot in her ear.

"Enough of this, *chère,*" he said raggedly as he moved to swing one arm beneath her knees. "I don't want to drown."

He lifted her dripping from the water to the bank beyond the rocks, and she welcomed him, her wet, glistening body feverish in her need. With her black hair curling damply around her full, pale breasts, her nipples and her mouth red and swollen from his kisses, she looked like a mermaid from a sailor's dream, wanton and eager for him alone.

He tried to tell himself to go slowly, that she was still a maid, and he'd no wish to frighten her again as he had before. But the idea that he would be the first man to have her was wildly intoxicating, adding more fire to a desire that was already hotter than anything he could remember. He kissed her again as he eased her legs apart, and when he touched her sweet, hot flesh, she moaned and moved shamelessly against him, and he knew they'd both waited long enough.

Her eyes widened as he entered her, and she gasped at the new sensation of joining with him this way and giving so much of herself. Yet when he began to move within her, she gasped again and cried out his name, as with each thrust, each stroke, he drove the pleasure higher, hotter than she ever could have imagined. Now when she curled her legs around his waist she understood, drawing him deeper within her and rocking her hips to meet him.

Now she understood about love and passion, and the white-hot need that Michel had raised in her soul and her body, and when at last she thought she could bear no more, he gave her the last and best secret of all. With a wild cry that rose above the waterfall she found her release.

Her cry reached to every corner of his heart, and in response he plunged more deeply into her, frantic in his need to lose himself within her, and when it came, the end left him shuddering and complete. Yet even then he did not want to let her go. With her he had discovered more than love; he had found the rare contentment and joy that only she could give, his Jerusa, his love.

"I love you, Michel," she whispered drowsily afterward as she lay with her head pillowed against his chest. "Oh, how I love you."

"Je t'aime, ma chère," he said softly, marveling at the words he thought he'd never hear or speak. *"Je t'aime tant, ma petite Rusa."*

But even as he still held her safe in his arms, the warmth was fading and his eyes were bleak, and though he'd give half his life for it to be otherwise, he knew that, for them, love alone would not be enough.

Chapter Eighteen

When the tide was low late that afternoon, Michel and Jerusa found they could wade to the rocks where the *Swan* had been wrecked. Despite Michel's predictions, no one else had discovered the abandoned ship yet, and after they climbed up her slanted, broken side they found everything on board exactly as it had been left. While he retrieved the chest with his belongings from their cabin, she went one last time to the galley for a few things—a cooking pot, forks and spoons, sugar and tea—that would be useful to them on the island. But she didn't linger, eager to return to Michel's side and the cheerfulness of the sunny afternoon.

"It's almost as if it's haunted," she said in a whisper when her hand was once again firmly in Michel's. Even in the bright sun, to her the strange stillness of the wreck was more disturbing now than during the height of the storm.

"Perhaps it is, *chérie*." Michel ran his hand lightly along the shattered remains of the mainmast. "If Captain Barker had lived, I doubt he would have let things come to this sorry pass."

Jerusa shivered, remembering that the bodies of Barker and the other men who'd died early during the storm were most likely still on board. As for Hay and the others who'd abandoned the brig, there was no guessing if they'd survived the storm's fury in the open boats. Strange to think of all the people who'd been aboard the *Swan* two days ago, congratulating themselves on such an easy passage with their destination so near, and now she and Michel were all that remained. Impulsively she slipped her arm around Michel's waist and stretched up to kiss his cheek.

He glanced down at her and smiled fondly, brushing his fingers across her cheek. "Now what was the reason for that, eh?"

"Because I love you," she said, strangely close to tears. "Because I can't believe how lucky I am to have you in my life."

"I'm the lucky one, Rusa," he said softly, and as he kissed her, he, too, thought of how fragile life—and love—could be.

They decided they needed to wash the salt from their skin again, and with that excuse they returned to the pond and the soft bank of ferns and moss beside it. Afterward, for supper, they ate ham and biscuits with beach plum jam that had come from the *Swan,* and *carambolas,* a sweet, star-shaped fruit like apples that Michel found growing not far from the waterfall. They lay on the sand and counted the stars overhead until the fire they'd built burned low and Jerusa drowsed contentedly in Michel's arms.

"I wish we could stay here forever," she said sleepily, her eyes closed with contentment.

"So do I, *ma mie,*" he said, his voice filled with inexpressible sadness. "But as much as we wish it, we won't have this beach to ourselves much longer. Look."

Reluctantly she opened her eyes to look where he pointed. On the far edge of the horizon rode the pale triangle of a sail in the moonlight, and in silence they watched as it glided past them, finally to disappear.

With a sigh Jerusa moved closer to Michel. "There, they won't bother us now."

"They'll be back," said Michel. "Or others like them." Gently he kissed her forehead, then eased himself free of her. He'd needed a reminder like that sail. Because he'd found such peace with her, he'd let himself be uncharacteristically lax about their safety. There were no guarantees that whoever finally rescued them would do so from kindness alone; in this part of the world, in fact, that would be the exception, not the rule.

And there was more than that, too, for soon they'd be in St-Pierre....

While she watched, he brought his sea chest into the fading circle of light from the fire. He pulled out the bag that held his money, a motley treasury of gold and silver coins stamped with the heads of English, Spanish, French and Dutch monarchs, counted out half and tied it into a bundle in a handkerchief.

"Take this, *chérie*," he said brusquely as he handed it to her. "You may need it."

Bewildered, she shook her head. "Whyever would I need that?"

"You may, that is all." When she still didn't take it, he set it beside her in the sand. "I'll give you one of the pistols, too."

"I don't understand, Michel," she said, searching his face for an answer. Was she imagining it, or did he seem suddenly colder, more distant? "The money, the pistol. Why would I need them when you're with me?"

"Because I may not always be there," he said, looking down at the pistol in his hand to avoid the fear in her eyes. "There's always the chance that whoever finds us will want to take you with them, not me. Look at what happened on board the *Swan*, Rusa. You chose to stay with me, but what would have become of you if I'd died, or if the ship had sunk outright? No, *ma chère*. I want to know you'll be safe, and this will help."

"Michel, that makes no sense, no sense at all!" She sat up abruptly and shoved the handkerchief with the coins back toward him. "For weeks you've scarcely let me from your sight. You've always been there to protect me, whether I wanted you to or not. You gave me a new name, new clothes, a whole new life where who I'd been didn't matter so much as who I *am*. But now that you've made love to me, you believe you can send me on my way with a handful of coins?"

He sat back on his heels, his palms on his thighs, and frowned at her, stunned that she would misunderstand so completely. "Jerusa, no. It's *because* I love you that I care what becomes of you. These waters are still a haven for pirates, *guardacostas,* runaway slaves and navy deserters, rogues of every sort, and—"

"That has never bothered you before in the least!" she snapped. His callousness wounded her so deeply that she couldn't accept it, and fought back instead, striving to hurt him with words the same way he was doing to her. "Or is it because you're one of those selfsame rogues that you can know so well what they'll do?"

He hadn't expected that from her. He'd never tried to hide his history, but then, he'd never expected her to toss it back into his face like that, especially not after they'd spent most of the day making love.

"Things are different in these islands, Rusa," he said carefully, trying to explain. "Your waters to the north are less dangerous."

"Then why didn't you simply leave me there in the first place?" She wrapped her arms around her body, an empty imitation of the embrace she suddenly feared she'd never feel again. "Why didn't you leave just me where I was?"

"I couldn't, *ma chère,*" he said softly. "I had to steal you. In Martinique—"

"Damn your Martinique!" she cried, anger and anguish melding to tear at his heart. "I know what you're going to tell me. That my father will be there, and that you still intend to try to kill him, and you'd rather not have me there to be in your way. But what if he kills *you*, Michel? Have you considered that possibility? Have you considered what that would do to *me*, to lose you just as your mother lost your father?"

He closed his eyes, his head bowed. "I won't fail, Rusa," he said hoarsely. "*Mordieu*, I cannot."

And for the first time she knew with chilling certainty that he was right.

"You're going to kill my father," she whispered, her hands tightening around her arms. "You'll kill him because he came for me."

"I have no choice, *ma mie*. No choice at all." When he lifted his face, his eyes were haunted and empty. "But I love you, Jerusa."

She was trembling and she could not stop. He could talk all he wished of choices: had she chosen to love him as much as she did? "How can you say you love me when you've sworn to do such a thing to my family?"

He shook his head, his blond hair glinting in the firelight. He was trying so hard to smile for her sake, but all that showed on his face was the misery in his soul.

"I love you, Jerusa," he said, his voice thick with emotion. "*Je t'aime tant!* Did you know I've never said that to anyone else? I've never loved anyone but you, Jerusa. Never. Perhaps that's why I can't explain this now. I don't know the words. *Sacristi*, how can I say it so you'll understand?"

He plunged his hand deep inside the sea chest and pulled out the a small, flat package wrapped in chamois, and as he unwrapped it, Jerusa's heart plummeted. The black-haired beauty with the laughing eyes.

Was this, then, why he'd insisted on returning to the Swan *this afternoon, to save this woman's portrait from the looters? Was she Jerusa's rival, one more reason why he would not want her in Martinique?*

"Here, *ma chère*, look." Michel thrust the little portrait out for her to see, his hand shaking. "Look at her, my blessing and my curse!"

"She—she is very beautiful," said Jerusa haltingly. What else could she say?

He studied the portrait himself, cradling the brass frame in the palm of his hand. "She was beautiful once. I can remember her that way if I try very hard, and look at this. Perhaps that is why she would never sell this, no matter that there was no food on the table and my belly was empty. For *Maman,* pride was enough."

"She's your mother?" asked Jerusa, struggling to make sense of all he said.

He nodded, absently tracing his finger around and around the oval brass frame. "Antoinette Géricault. She was only seventeen when my father loved her, *ma mie,* only seventeen when he died and when I was born."

When he was a child, the two portraits had always hung near his mother's bed, low on the wall so Maman *could see them as soon as she woke in the morning. The beautiful lady with the charming smile, the handsome gentleman turned in profile as if to admire her. It wasn't until he was older that he'd learned the beautiful lady and the handsome gentleman were his parents, and heard the story of how* Maman *had saved the portraits, one in each pocket, as she'd run down the stairs the night of the fire that had destroyed everything else.*

The fire that had been set by Gabriel Sparhawk and his men....

"Then she was the most beautiful girl in St-Pierre, and men would beg for her smiles. Christian Deveaux fell in love with her the moment he saw her, as she walked one morning from the market with a basket of white lilies." Michel smiled, remembering how his mother would bend her arm as she told the story, showing him how the basket had rested against her hip, just so. "But that was long ago, before the sorrows claimed her beauty and her smile."

The sorrows, and the Sparhawks.

That was how it had begun for him: every misfortune, every injustice was blamed on the Englishman Gabriel Sparhawk. He had murdered Christian Deveaux. He had destroyed poor Christian's name and honor. He had robbed them of the fortune and position that should by rights be theirs. And worst of all for Michel, he had drained every bit of love from his poor Maman's heart, and left it filled with the poison of hate.

No wonder he had no memory of Maman's smile beyond the one that was painted on the ivory oval.

Quietly Jerusa came to stand behind him, drawn by the need to comfort him however she could. She rested her hands on his shoulders, her cheek against his, watching as he circled the frame and his mother's face with his fingers.

"I should like to meet your mother when we're in St-Pierre," she said softly. "If she's your mother, Michel, I know I shall like her."

She felt how he tensed beneath her fingers. "She isn't well," he said, so carefully that she knew there was more that he wouldn't tell her. "She seldom sees anyone, *ma chère.* She is unsettled in her thoughts, and company distresses her."

Like the matching portraits on the wall, her madness had always been there. When he was young, he was terrified that some demon had come to claim his mother and make her wild as an animal in the forest, and that it was somehow his fault if she hurt him. She wouldn't do it unless he deserved it, not his Maman. But he was so often disobedient, and when she was forced to beat him he wept, not from pain but because of the sorrow his wickedness brought to her.

If his father had lived, it would not have been like this. Maman would have laughed like other mothers, and there would have been food and clothes and a fine place to live, all if Gabriel Sparhawk had not murdered his father!

"I still should like to see her, Michel," she said softly, "if only for a few minutes. It couldn't hurt her to talk, would it? Most likely she'd enjoy it."

"Don't make the mistake of believing she's like other mothers," he said sharply. "She's not some happy, round-cheeked lady like your own Mariah who will offer you tea and jam cakes and coo over your gown."

"Michel, I didn't mean—"

"*Sacristi,* Jerusa, she's all I have!" He pulled free of her arms, his eyes tortured as he faced her. "When I was a child, she did everything she could for me. Can you understand that, Jerusa, you with your brothers and sisters and father and mother? She did everything for me. How could I not do the same for her?"

"But that's the way of every mother and her child," said Jerusa, reaching out her hand to calm him. "What son or daughter doesn't strive to please?"

He shook his head and stepped back beyond her reach, the portrait still clutched in his hand. "Like every mother? *Grâce à Dieu, non!*"

He laughed, a harsh, bitter sound as he tossed the little portrait into the open chest. "Does every mother wish her son to be so much like his father that she will sell him to a drunken shipmaster when he's but nine years old, set to learn the honorable trade of privateering? Does every mother rejoice when her son learns to kill, delighting in every lethal refinement or new skill he acquires in the name of death and justice, revenge and honor?"

"But in her way she loves you, Michel," said Jerusa urgently. "She must! That is why I must speak with her. If she loves you, she'll be as unwilling as I am to see you risk your life for the sake of an empty feud nearly thirty years old."

"Oh, *ma bien-aimée,* my poor, innocent Jerusa," he said softly, too softly for the pain that etched his face. "You still haven't guessed, have you? It was my mother who made me swear to kill your father. And it was my mother's idea, *ma chère,* to kidnap you."

Chapter Nineteen

Gabriel thumped the empty tumbler down on the table and rose to his feet. Angry as he was, he seemed to fill the small captain's cabin of the *Tiger,* the way, thought Josh glumly, his father did every space he'd ever entered.

"Do you mean to tell me that after a week in this place, all you have done is dawdled with some *barmaid?*" demanded Gabriel furiously. "Your sister's life is in danger, and you're chasing after some Creole baggage?"

"It's not like that, Father," said Josh, wishing his father wouldn't immediately thrust whatever he did or said into the worst possible light. And it wasn't as if Gabriel had had such great success himself on Barbados. He'd found no trace of Jerusa, and though he'd dined with the rear admiral from the fleet stationed there, no promises had been made and nothing accomplished. "I told you before. I might as well have been shouting at the moon for all the good the governor and his lot have done for me."

"But damnation, Josh, didn't you give them the letters of introduction?"

"I did, and they could scarce be bothered to break the seals." He stood with his hands clasped behind his back so his father couldn't see how he clenched and unclenched his fingers through the conversation. "None of the men you knew, or who knew you, are still here. The old governor was recalled to Paris five years ago, and the new one doesn't know a Sparhawk from a sea gull."

"More's the pity for him," grumbled Gabriel, but at least he'd sat back down into his chair.

Josh stepped forward to refill his father's tumbler. All the stern windows across the cabin's length were open to whatever breeze might rise from the water, but at midday the cabin was still stifling, and both men had shed their coats and waistcoats.

"When the officials turned their backs on me, I went to the rum shops and taverns. If any of Deveaux's men were still alive, I figured they'd be there, not on their knees telling their beads in the churches."

"True enough." Gabriel took the tumbler, holding it critically up to the sunlight to see the pale gold color of the rum. At least he couldn't question that; Josh had been careful to ship rum from the family's firm in Newport, even though Martinique must have a score of distilleries of her own. "Though if there's any justice in this life, the rogues that sailed with Deveaux have all gone to the devil with their master by now."

"That's what Ceci believed, too, until—"

"Ceci?" Gabriel frowned. "Who's Ceci?"

"Mademoiselle Cecilie Marie-Rose Noire. Ceci. Her father owns the tavern where we met."

"Ah, the barkeep's daughter." With a cynical sigh, Gabriel tapped his fingers on the edge of the table. "So, is she all the things a woman should be, Josh? Fair, charming, willing?"

Josh bit back his retort, but warmth still crept into his words. "She is both fair and charming, Father, but though she is the barkeep's daughter, she's not the slattern you seem determined to believe she is."

"Then my sympathies to you, lad," said Gabriel dryly. "If

you've wasted your days with this girl instead of finding Jerusa, then at least you should have had her warming your bed during the night."

And at last Josh's temper spilled over. "Damn and blast, Father!" he exploded. "Is that all you can say about a woman? Will she warm my bed?"

But to Josh's surprise, his father merely leaned back in his chair, rocking the tumbler gently in his hand.

"I haven't thought that way about a woman since I met your mother," he said slowly. "But you, lad. I've never heard otherwise from you. Not that at your age there's anything wrong with seeing what the ladies have to offer, but this French girl—Ceci, was it?—must be a rare little bird to have clipped your wings so soon."

Josh's face went expressionless. Were his feelings that obvious, then, that even his father could read them? "She hasn't 'clipped' my wings, Father," he said stiffly. "I've known her but a week."

Gabriel looked up at him from beneath his brows. "I didn't say I was posting the banns yet, Josh."

"A good thing, too." Self-consciously Josh toyed with the cork from the bottle of rum. "That is, I like Ceci. I like her just fine. She's clever and amusing and pretty and all that, but she was also the only person on this blessed island worth talking to."

"Then I'd say in a week she's made more headway than poor Polly Redmond has been able to make with you in Newport in the last two years."

"Oh, hang Polly Redmond, Father!" Impatiently Josh jammed the cork back into the neck of the bottle. "Ceci's special, aye, I won't deny it. But what's most important now is that she and her father are using all their connections in St-Pierre and beyond to help find any of Deveaux's men, and Rusa with them."

Eagerly Gabriel leaned forward, his eyes gleaming with the

excitement of a hunt finally begun. "So you have found something, eh, Josh? Are we any closer to bringing my Rusa back home? What kind of news did your barkeep and his daughter bring you?"

"The best in the world," said Josh. "Monsieur Noire isn't just any barkeep, Father. He lays the blame for his sister-in-law's ruin and death at Deveaux's door. And because of that, tomorrow, through him, I'm meeting the one man on this island who still admits to having sailed for Christian Deveaux. If anyone can make heads or tails of your black *fleur de lis,* then he can."

"And we'll be that much closer to the bastards that took your sister." Gabriel's green eyes were bright with ruthless anticipation. "You've done well, lad. And you tell that lady of yours from me that she's a rare bird indeed."

"We must be almost there, Josh," called Ceci as she leaned over the side of the boat to see beyond the sweep of their single sail. "*Papa* said to look for a little house with red tiles on the roof that was nearly hidden by palms on the far side of Anse Couleuvre."

"*Anse* means cove, doesn't it?" said Josh, his arm resting lightly on the tiller as he squinted into the sun. It had been a long time since he'd sailed a boat this small, and he was enjoying responding to the feel of the wind and sea in a way he seldom could on a vessel as large as the *Tiger.* He was glad Ceci had trusted him enough to sail the boat alone, much preferring to have her company to himself than to share it with some gloomy Creole fisherman as a chaperon.

Unlike so many women, she was fearless in the little boat, hopping back and forth from one side to the other until he finally had to tell her to sit still or risk capsizing them. Not that he'd put any damper on her eagerness; still she leaned over the side to point out landmarks to him or jumped to her feet to help him set the sail on another tack. She'd looped the sides of her skirts up through her pockets so they didn't flap in the wind, and she didn't particularly seem to care that the makeshift style offered him frequent views of her charmingly plump knees as she clambered about the boat.

They'd been fortunate in their weather, too, after two days of storms that had closed the port. But this was a cloudless day that made the water so translucent and smooth that the little boat flew like the wind itself. The bright, lush green of the tropical trees and plants flowed down the hills almost to the water, and today even the misty clouds that always hung about the crest of Montagne Pelée, the tall, barren mountain that dominated Martinique's skyline, were a light pink haze.

"So if the *anse* in Anse Couleuvre stands for cove, what's the *couleuvre?*" he asked as she came to sit beside him. He had yet to kiss her, and he wondered what she'd do if he leaned across the tiller right now. Strange to think that he'd known her less than a fortnight. It seemed more like a lifetime. "Covered? Colorful?"

"Non, non, Josh! It means snake, of course!" She laughed merrily and clapped her hands so that he didn't mind in the slightest that she'd corrected him. "Snake Cove. For the *fer de lance.*"

Josh sighed pitifully. "I'm afraid I don't know that one, either, sweetheart."

"Oh, but you would if one bit you!" Ceci's eyes widened dramatically beneath the yellow-striped scarf she'd used to tie back her hair. "The *fer de lance* is a most evil snake—as long as your arm, *mon cher!*—who lies in the forest and waits to pounce on poor travelers, who die within hours from its bite if the *panseur* does not arrive in time to cut away the poison. And only on this island, only on Martinique. These snakes are to be found nowhere else."

She cupped her fingers like the head of a snake with her thumb as the jaw as she moved them together. "Snap, snap, snap, and goodbye to you, my poor Josh!"

"Well, pleasant sailing and goodbye to you, too, Ceci," he said, laughing. "I do believe I'll keep to the beach."

"That is wisest, true," said Ceci, letting her snake become demurely clasped hands in her lap once again. "Though I would be surprised if this Jean Meunier will be any more gracious to us than the *fer de lance* himself. *Papa* had to give three kegs of rum to Claude Boulanger simply to learn where the man keeps himself, but if any man on Martinique can help you find your sister, it is he."

"Jean Meunier," repeated Josh carefully, practicing the name. Thanks to Ceci, his French was much improved, but still he didn't want to take chances with mangling the man's name. Too much depended on it.

"Oui, c'est bon." She leaned back against the stern to trail her fingers in the wake. "But I suppose since you are English, you could call him by his English name, too—John Miller."

Josh looked at her sharply. "How can he be English? The man sailed with Deveaux during two wars against the English. How could he fight against his own countrymen?"

"I'm only telling you what I know, *mon cher,* not why it is. *Papa* says Deveaux chose his men for their wickedness and greed, not for their loyalties. They fought for him, and for gold."

Josh thought of his own father and suspected the same could have been said of Gabriel's crews during the same wars. Why, he wondered, had this John Miller decided to sail for one captain and his flag over another? Though his father had told him a few more of his privateering stories on the voyage south, Josh sensed that Gabriel wanted to keep the past as firmly behind him as he could, and that having Christian Deveaux so tangled in Jerusa's disappearance had made it doubly painful to him. Did her kidnappers know that about him, as well?

Ceci was the first to spot the red-roofed house, and Josh pulled their boat up onto the black sand beach beside another boat that must belong to Miller. The place hardly had the look of a pirate's stronghold. In addition to the cheerful red roof tiles, a vine with crimson flowers had been trained to grow over the wall in front of the house, and someone had carefully outlined the walk of black sand with white shells.

But as soon as Ceci began up the path, a single musket's blast rang out across the water. Josh grabbed her, shielding her with his body as he pulled her to the ground, while scores of parrots and other birds raced shrieking into the sky from the gunshot.

"What are you doing, Josh?" Ceci demanded indignantly as she wriggled free. "What will this man think, to see you treat me like this on his walk?"

She tried to stand and Josh jerked her back down, pulling her along with him behind the trunk of a short, fat palm.

"What the hell do you think I'm doing?" he said. "Some fool just emptied his musket at us, and I'd rather not give him another chance to improve his aim."

"C'est ridicule!" she huffed. "This man has had word that we would come."

Josh sighed with exasperation. "I'd say he has."

"You are being too foolish." Before he could stop her she darted forward to stand squarely in the path, her arms folded defiantly across her chest and her yellow scarf bobbing with impatience.

"Monsieur Meunier!" she called. "I am Mademoiselle Cecilie Noire, and I have come with my friend to speak with you. Do not dare to fire at us again, or I shall tell everything to your friend Claude Boulanger!"

"As if Boulanger would give a shake about what I do!" Miller had come out onto his porch, the musket still in his hands. Cowering behind him was a very young black woman with her apron pressed to her mouth in fear and two small mulatto children shrinking behind her skirts. "Who's the man what came with you, Miss Cecilie?"

From the man's voice Josh guessed he was not only

English but from New England, as well, and he wondered again how he'd come to serve under Deveaux. But English or not, Miller kept the musket raised to his eye, and obscuring his face, and with a prayer that his next step wouldn't be his last, Joshua stepped from behind the palm's shelter to stand beside Ceci.

"I'm Captain Joshua Sparhawk of the sloop *Tiger*, Newport, Rhode Island," he called, "and I've come here to ask for your help."

"Damn your eyes!" the man shouted back. "Why the hell would the son of Gabriel Sparhawk need help from me?"

"If you know my father, then you know I wouldn't ask if I didn't need it." He'd also know better than to keep a Sparhawk waiting, thought Joshua as his temper simmered. "But I'm not going to say another blasted word until you put down that gun and stop roaring at us like some penny-poor bosun's mate!"

With an oath, Miller set the butt of the musket down on the porch with a thump. "Then come aboard, Cap'n, and we'll talk."

Ten minutes later they were seated in reed chairs on the porch as Cyrillia, Miller's wife, served them *mabiyage,* white rum mixed with root beer. Josh's guess had been right: Miller had been born on the Kennebec River some sixty years before, and patiently Josh first answered all his questions about politics in Boston and Portsmouth before he finally told him why he and Ceci had come.

"Took your sister, did they?" said Miller, shaking his head. He was nearly bald, compensating with a gray-streaked beard that hung nearly to his waist. "That's bad, Cap'n, very bad indeed. But I don't think it's the work of Deveaux's people."

He draped his beard over his left shoulder and pulled up his shirt to point to a faded black *fleur de lis* branded into his chest.

"Look close at that, Cap'n, for it's the only one you'll see in this life," he said proudly. "I'm the last of the *Chasseur*'s crew, and that's a cold, hard fact. Them that didn't drown when the *Chasseur* went down was strung up at Bridgetown. Your pa saw to that, Cap'n, swore his word against every last man."

He winked broadly. "Well, now, not quite every last man, or I wouldn't be here now, would I?"

"You were not guilty, *monsieur?*" asked Ceci innocently, bouncing one of the little boys on her knee.

"Nay, lass, let's just say I found another berth before the trial," he said, and winked again before he turned back to Josh. "But this business about your sister, Cap'n. I can't find the sense to it. You know I'm not behind it. There's a score of fellows in St-Pierre who'll swear I haven't left this island in twenty years."

Josh sighed, believing him. Whatever wickedness Miller had done in his youth, he clearly wasn't inclined that way now. "Can you think of anyone else who might have worked for Deveaux? On his lands or in his house?"

Miller thought for a moment, then shook his head. "Nay, you'll find nothing there. Cap'n Deveaux liked slaves on account of not having to pay them wages. He weren't particular. Africans or white folks he'd captured, 'twas all the same to him. But you won't find none of them now, leastways not coming clear up to Newport to steal your sister."

Josh sighed again, his frustration growing. The last thing he wanted was to return to his father empty-handed. Miller was his last hope. But where the devil could Rusa be?

"Is there no one else, Miller?" he asked. "A sister or brother, a widow or mistress?"

From the corner of his eye he saw how Ceci stiffened, and he promised himself to apologize to her later. He wouldn't have asked the question before her if he hadn't been so desperate.

"Mistresses? Cap'n Deveaux?" Miller laughed uneasily, glancing at Ceci and his wife. "Ah, Cap'n, surely you've heard about him and the women. He was as fine a sailor as any afloat, and the coolest man you've ever seen in a fight, but with women things were never right, if you con my meaning."

But Josh wasn't sure he did. "There were that many?"

"Nay, Cap'n, it weren't the numbers of ladies, though there were a sight more'n I ever had in my bed, to be sure. It was how he treated them that wasn't decent. He had strange ways of taking his pleasure, Cap'n, and—well, there were plenty of stories that don't bear repeating now. But there weren't no love in it, and no kindness, neither. I wouldn't guess there's any of them ladies now who'd think too kind of that Frenchman's memory."

"But that could be reason enough for them to act in his name," said Josh slowly. "Can you recall any of their names, and if they still live on the island?"

Miller chuckled nervously. "Oh, Cap'n, it's been almost thirty years now, and most of them ladies never was with him long enough for us to learn their names. I expect most of them are dead now, too, or wish they were. One of the last was like that, a pretty little thing when he first brung her to the house, but mad as a hare by the time he'd tired of her, right before the end."

Josh saw how Ceci was sitting on the very edge of her chair, her hand twisting anxiously in her lap and her eyes enormous, and he wished now he'd spoken to Miller alone.

"*S'il vous plaît, monsieur,*" she said in a tiny, nervous voice. "If you please, do you recall that lady's name?"

"Oh, aye, that one I do, on account of having her pointed out to me in her carriage. We thought she'd died in the fire, but up she popped years later, living grand in a house her son bought her. Still mad as they come, she is, and the son's too much like his pa for comfort, but then, there's all sorts in this world and likely the next, as well."

"Her name, *monsieur?*" begged Ceci again. "The lady's name?"

"Antoinette Géricault," Miller said promptly. "Lives in a house in the Rue Roseau."

Ceci leapt to her feet, her eyes shining. "*Merci, monsieur,* a thousand thanks!" she cried as she turned to Josh. "Is this not wonderful news, *mon cher?* My aunt still lives, and I have a cousin, too!"

"It may be more wonderful still, if you can wait a moment longer." Lightly he rested a restraining hand across her shoulders. "You said the lady's son is too much like the father. Do you know the man?"

"I thought I'd made that clear enough." Miller looked sheepish. "He's Deveaux's bastard, of course. Michel Géricault. You've only to look him in the face to see it, and to hear the gossip, too."

Michel Géricault. Josh nodded, certain this was one name he wouldn't forget. He'd stake his life that Géricault was the man who had his sister. No, more than that: he was staking Jerusa's life, too.

And he'd pray to God he was right.

"Such wonderful news!" sighed Ceci happily yet again as they left the boat at the wharf. "Such wonderful news for us both, Josh!"

More realistic, Josh merely patted her hand. As useful as it was, learning Géricault's name was only the beginning of what he and his father must still do to find Jerusa.

"And consider, Josh, how proud your father will be of you!" She sighed blissfully, looping her arm through his, and he thought of how impossibly dear her little face had become to him.

"Then will you come with me when I tell him?" he asked, and as soon as he'd said it the idea seemed perfect. "Come with me now, Ceci, back to the *Tiger.* Father wants to meet you, and this would be as good a time as any."

Her eyes widened and she stopped walking. "To meet your father?" she squeaked. "Now? Oh, Josh, I am not ready for that! Look at me, my clothes, my hair—"

"You look beautiful," he said warmly, and he meant it. Gently he guided her into an arched doorway, out of the street. "Come with me now, Ceci. Please."

"Oh, Josh," she murmured as she searched his face. "I do not know."

But when he kissed her, he knew everything. He knew that he loved her, and that somehow, miraculously, she loved him in return, and that when he sailed from St-Pierre, she would be with him in the captain's cabin of the *Tiger,* and that Newport would never be quite the same dull place once she was there with him.

"I love you, Ceci," he said softly, his voice rough with emotion as he cradled her face in his hands. "I love you, *mon chère.*"

Her cheeks were pink and her eyes now were wide with wonder and joy. "It's *ma chère,* Josh, not *mon,*" she whispered. "But, oh, I did not dare to dream!"

"Then don't." Gently he pulled away her scarf so he could tangle his fingers in her soft curls. "Just say you love me."

"Oh, Josh, I do, oh, so much!" She reached up to slip her arms around his neck and pulled him lower to kiss him herself.

"Then say you'll come back to Newport with me, Ceci. Say you'll marry me."

She gasped, stunned. "But this is so rapid, Josh, I do not know what to say!"

"Say yes." He chuckled, delighted that he'd surprised her this way. Hell, he'd surprised *himself.*

"But that a man like you should wish to marry Ceci Noire, la! You are an English shipmaster, a fine gentleman, and so very handsome and clever!"

And not a word about being a Sparhawk, he thought happily. Lord, she loved him for who he was, not his father's name, and he loved her all the more for it.

"It doesn't matter who or what I am, Ceci," he said softly,

"except that I'm someone who loves you dearly and will do his best to make you happy."

"Oh, Josh, how could you not?" With a little sigh of contentment, she wriggled closer into his arms.

"Then you'll say yes?"

She tipped her head, suddenly prim. "My answer's in my heart, and you know it already. But before I can tell you, you must speak to *Papa*."

"Hang it all, Ceci, I'll speak to a hundred papas—a thousand!—if it means I'll have you!"

"One is quite enough," she said mischievously. "I don't want to wait the time it would take you to ask all those others."

"Then you will come with me to meet my father?"

"I cannot, Josh, not now," she said sadly. "Oh, I know your news is most grand, but mine is very wonderful, too. Think what my father will say when I tell him my aunt still lives!"

"She lives, true enough, but you heard what Miller said," he cautioned gently. "She's a madwoman, Ceci, kept by her son in a house away from town. Surely they know where you and your father live. If they had wished to find you, don't you think they would have done so before this?"

Ceci hesitated, reluctant to abandon her dream. "If my aunt is unwell, she may have forgotten. Or she may have believed my parents would not forgive her shame."

"She may still feel that way."

She shook her head fiercely. "But you don't understand, Josh! Antoinette is my dear *maman*'s only sister. Whether she is ill or not, that does not change. *Maman* loved her, I know, and now I will, too."

"But, Ceci—"

"*Non,* Josh, you shall see that I'm right!" She kissed him again, and slipped free of his embrace, dancing away from him in the street. "I will come meet your papa tomorrow, I swear to it! And I love you, Josh Sparhawk! I love you!"

* * *

Antoinette sat in the chair by the window, laying out the silk threads she would need this day for her embroidery. At first the doctor had forbidden it. The needles were a danger, he said, and because of him they had taken away her beautiful colored threads and her hoops and her needles, and she had wept with frustration and shame.

But Michel had made them give them back, because Michel remembered. In all the years when she had worked for the dressmakers, those years when they had been so poor after Christian was murdered and her family, her sister and her husband, had refused to help her from the shame she'd brought to them. In all those years, she had never once pricked her finger and spoiled a length of silk or linen.

Never once, never once... Mother of God, where did the words go? She pressed her hands to her forehead, scrubbing away at the skin, as if she could wash away the blackness, too.

A length of silk or linen. She took a deep, shuddering breath before she opened her eyes. For now the blackness had receded like the tide, and the words were hers again.

Her fingers still trembled as she held the needle up to the light to thread it. Danger, fah! How could a woman be dangerous with only a needle for a weapon?

But then, she had Michel.

Her handsome son was her weapon, and she thought with grim satisfaction of how the doctors and the others grew pale whenever Michel came to see her. He terrified them all, her gold-haired hero of a son who was so much like his father. A word from him, and they had taken away the chains from her bed. A frown, another word, and she was freed from the dark attic room they'd tried to make her prison. He made certain that she was treated with respect, as both a lady and the mistress of this house.

Her gaze drifted to the little portrait over the bed. Her Christian would have done the same for her; he would have done anything she wished, for he'd loved her that much. Hadn't he even sworn it to her, his fingers on the jeweled cross of his sword? He'd been so certain of it that he would punish her if she forgot herself and did something, anything, that he claimed a true lover wouldn't.

Her needle paused over the linen as she remembered. She had not liked Christian's punishments. She carried the scars still, on her back and her legs and breasts. But his reasons had been as pure as his love, noble and fine, like the gentleman he was. He had done what he had because he loved her, and she bowed before his punishments because she loved him so much and wished to be worthy of him.

No more, oh, please, no more!

She gasped as her fingers flew to her forehead again, the needlework in her hand falling to the carpet. She would fight back. She would not let the blackness take her again.

Dear holy Mother, if only Christian had lived, spared to become her husband and with his love guide her through the perils of life! The time they'd had together had been so short, and then he had been torn away from her and murdered. God rest his precious soul, he had not even been able to say farewell to her. The Englishman had come, and then it was too late.

The Englishman, the Englishman! She jabbed her needle furiously through the linen, remembering all that the man had stolen from her. Her darling Christian, her life, her love, all destroyed by his cruelty. She had seen Gabriel Sparhawk only twice—once when he'd been Christian's prisoner, and years later, with his little whore of a wife and their litter of brats—but she'd never forgotten his arrogance and his bragging self-confidence, the marks of a man who thought he was invincible.

But soon that would change. She would never forgive what he had done to her, and soon he would never forget the pain she would bring to him in return. Soon he would meet her Michel, and justice, at last, would be served.

"Excuse me, ma'am, there is a lady to see you. She said it was most urgent."

Antoinette frowned. This serving girl was the stupid one. Ladies did not receive at this hour. Christian had always been most strict about that.

"The lady, ma'am? Should I show her in or send her away?"

Antoinette nodded and set aside the neat piles of silk threads. Even Christian would forgive her if the matter were truly urgent.

"Oh, *madame,*" cried the girl as she rushed into the room. "I have waited so long for this moment!"

She was no one that Antoinette recognized. She was small and young and pretty and there were gold hoops in her ears and tears on her cheeks, and when she held her hands out to Antoinette, Antoinette took them. What else could she do?

The girl was kneeling on the carpet before her, her black curls quivering as she wept. "Oh, *madame,*" she said. "You can never know what it means to be here finally with you! You must forgive my father's silence over all these years. He—we never meant to be cruel. But how could I know you still lived?"

Forgiveness? Antoinette frowned. Her father's silence? What did any of it mean to her?

Unless, of course, she was Jerusa Sparhawk.

Magically her frown vanished. Yes, of course, the Sparhawk bride. *That* was who she was. The black curls, the small, lovely face. She had only seen the girl once before, with her parents, but Antoinette could still remember Gabriel's little daughter, the favorite of all his children, here now to do with what she pleased.

Once she had been like this, too, full of hope and love and joy for her future. Once her cheeks had been this rosy and her eyes bright. But now this girl would learn sorrow and pain, grief and suffering, just as her father had taught them to Antoinette.

Oh, Michel was such a good son to remember his promise!

Antoinette stood, and the girl stood with her. "Oh, *madame,* you cannot know how I feel!"

"Then you shall tell me. We'll have such a splendid time together, won't we?" There was the little room upstairs with the tiny windows and the lock on the outside of the door. No one would find them there, because no one would think to look.

Slowly, though she thought she had forgotten how, Antoinette smiled. "Come, little one. I myself will show you to a place where at last we can be alone."

Chapter Twenty

⧼⧼⧼⧼⧼⧼⧼⧸⧸⧸⧸⧸⧸⧸

The sun was high in the afternoon sky when the little fishing boat made its way into the curving arms of the bay of St-Pierre.

Despite Michel's fears, these fishermen who had been the first to spot their fire on the beach were both friendly and honest. For a single gold piece they'd put aside their nets for the day and brought the two castaways directly here to St-Pierre.

Alone at the rail, Jerusa stood in the shade of the boat's sail and tried to make herself look at the city before her. It was pretty enough as cities went, nestled on the side of the green-covered mountain with all the houses painted yellow and blue beneath red-tiled roofs, the largest city in all the islands. Prettier than Newport, really, with the winding cobbled streets and immense nodding palms dropped in among the houses like radish stems in a garden. But lovely as it was, St-Pierre alone wasn't enough to make Jerusa forget the weight that hung like iron from her heart.

She had loved Michel, and it wasn't enough. She had given him everything she had to give, from her love to her body to her very soul, and it still wasn't enough to save him.

"Welcome to my home, *ma chère,*" he said, coming to stand

beside her. "I can't promise you waterfalls here on Martinique, but you shall find a vast improvement in the food and lodgings."

"Indeed." She looked down at her fingers on the rough wooden rail, away from the city and away from him. She didn't need to see Michel's face to picture the way his blue eyes were narrowed in the sun, how his hair was blowing back like a golden pennant, how his smile was charmingly crooked, admitting openly that what he'd said was the kind of empty advertisement favored by innkeepers. "I'd rather enjoyed what we shared these last two days."

His pause as he remembered, too, said more than any words could. "I didn't say it would end, Rusa," he said softly, sliding his hand along the rail to cover hers. "I meant only that it would be different."

She wished she were strong enough to pull her hand away, but miserably she knew she wasn't. She hadn't been able to turn away from him last night when they'd made love on the beach beneath the stars. Why did she think she could now?

"Oh, Michel," she said sorrowfully. "Whatever will become of us?"

Again the long pause, the hesitation that said so much from a man who was ordinarily so glib. "I don't know any more than you do, *chérie,*" he said with a longing that equaled her own. "I wish to God I did."

"Will we stay with your mother?" Perhaps if she kept to the practical, this conversation wouldn't hurt as much as it did now.

"Her health is too fragile to bear visitors," he said with sympathy that didn't fool her at all. "I seldom stay with her myself."

Jerusa raised her chin stubbornly. If his mother had declared herself the enemy, then she wanted to begin the battle as soon as possible. "I thought she was in such a dreadful rush to meet me."

"Later, *ma mie,* later," he said evasively. He'd said no more to her about his mother, and clearly he wasn't going to now, either. "But there's an inn I favor with a splendid view of the harbor and a cook trained in Paris."

An inn with a view and a cook and doubtless a single large bed like the one in Seabrook, only this bed was one she'd be all too willing to share with Michel. She smiled wistfully. "Shall we be Mr. and Mrs. Geary again?"

"*Monsieur et Madame,* this time, I think."

She studied his hand, a hand she'd come to know so well, broad and brown as a working man's and covered with old scars and new scratches. "How can I be a *madame* when I don't speak French?"

"But I do, *ma bonne femme.* You can be my English wife. Though this innkeeper knows me as well as his own son, he'll accept whatever I say."

She had posed as his wife since the beginning. So why, then, did it hurt so much now to hear how casually he could continue to pretend what, in so many ways, was already real?

"I'll take you there and see you settled," he continued, "and then I must go to my mother. But I shall be back for supper, *chérie,* if you'll wait for me."

"The way I did in Seabrook?" Mutinous, she couldn't resist glancing up to see his reaction.

But though she'd hoped to crack the veneer of civility that he'd assumed ever since they'd been picked up by the fishing boat, his expression didn't change. The heartbreaking openness he'd let her see on the beach was only a memory, and one he wasn't going to share again. Now he wasn't even looking at her, but gazed instead at the city.

"No surprises this time, Rusa, I beg you," he said evenly. "You'll find the waterfront here is a good deal more, shall we say, *challenging* than Seabrook's."

His smile was warm and cheerfully empty, and if she needed one more reminder that Mr. Geary—or Monsieur Geary—had joined her again, Michel critically studied the tatters of her green gown and shook his head. "I'll arrange for a mantua maker to call on you with a selection of gowns. If you must surprise me, *chérie,* do it that way."

Before she could answer, the boat's captain called to Michel in his lilting Pierrotin dialect. Michel turned toward the man with an eagerness that wounded Jerusa all the more.

"Excuse me, *ma mie,*" he said, already halfway across the little deck, "but I must go see what that rascal wants before he somehow contrives to toss us all in the bay."

But suddenly she forgot the gowns and the mantua maker, and even Michel.

There were a half-dozen deep-water vessels in the harbor, but it was the sloop tied far to the west that riveted her attention. She'd recognize the rake of that mast anywhere, and even if she hadn't, there was the bright orange figurehead of a charging tiger tucked under the sloop's bowsprit.

Sweet Almighty, Josh was *here,* here in St-Pierre! She felt a great wave of homesickness sweep over her as she stared longingly at the painted tiger and tried to make out familiar faces among the tiny moving figures on the sloop's deck. Hundreds of miles from home, and here her twin brother was so near she could almost shout his name.

But she wouldn't. Swiftly she glanced over her shoulder to where Michel still stood talking and jesting with the fishermen, his back to her and the sloop across the bay. He hadn't noticed the *Tiger,* and she prayed he wouldn't, at least not yet.

For if Josh had followed her here to St-Pierre, then Father would have, too. Later, while Michel was with his mother, she must find a way to get a message to Josh. Her father could be a hot-tempered man, and if he and Michel's father had fought each other through two wars all across the Caribbean, then he'd likely jump at the chance to meet Michel, too. She shuddered to think of the consequences to them both. If only she and Josh could somehow find a way to stop their fighting before it started!

The fishing captain changed his boat's tack, and the *Tiger* was once again obscured by a larger ship. All that Jerusa could see of her now was the scarlet pennant fluttering from the top-gallant mast, the house flag of Sparhawk and Sons, and she stared at the little strip of red until she could see it no more.

Sparhawk and Sons, she thought forlornly, Sparhawk and Sons, and one lost, desperate daughter....

Michel stood at the window of his mother's sitting room, pretending to look at the garden below as he waited for her to join him. Like all the houses in St-Pierre, there were no glass panes to impede the breezes from the water, only shutters to keep out the rare rain and narrow iron bars to keep thieves out. Or, in his mother's case, to keep her within.

He sighed, absently tapping his fingers against the window-sill. Before he'd come he had washed and shaved and dressed like the gentleman she believed him to be, but even as he heard her footsteps on the stairs, he still hadn't decided what he was going to tell her about Jerusa.

"Michel, my own son!" she cried happily as she swept across the room to greet him. "I did not expect you for another week at least!"

He bent to kiss each of her cheeks in turn, finally raising her hand to his lips with the show of gallantry she adored. "You're looking very well, *Maman*. Perhaps I should always surprise you."

But he was the one, really, who was surprised. Only two months had passed since he'd last said farewell, but the difference in Antoinette was staggering. It wasn't just that today she was dressed as correctly as any woman in St-Pierre, instead of in the nightgowns she usually favored. Her hair was combed and dressed, her stockings tied with garters, and shoes, not slippers, were on her feet, and when she'd walked to him there'd been no trace of her past halting, hesitant walk. Her eyes seemed clear and her greeting genuine, and immediately Michel was on his guard.

She sat in an armchair near the window, waving at the chair beside her for Michel to sit. He didn't; whatever was happening, he'd do better not to let himself become too comfortable.

"You seem very well, *Maman*," he began cautiously. "What has Dr. Benoit to say?"

"I haven't seen Dr. Benoit in a fortnight," she said in the breathy, little-girl voice she'd never outgrown. "He came, but I sent him away, so you should be sure that he doesn't ask for a fee for the visit."

"Thank you." Cynically he wondered if she'd somehow contrived to find a lover. Was his father's picture still hanging over her bed, or had Christian Deveaux at last been replaced by another?

He looked past her, out the window again, and prayed that the right words would come to him. "Do you recall the purpose of my last journey, *Maman?* Where I have been?"

"Of course I do, Michel! How could I possibly forget?" Languidly she leaned back in her chair, crossing her ankles on the footstool before her. "At last, after so many years, you've begun to answer my dearest prayers."

Her reproach was slight but unmistakable, just enough of a flick to Michel's conscience to make him inwardly flinch. "We agreed long ago, *Maman,* that the time had to be right. Gabriel Sparhawk is not some backcountry plantation wastrel who can be disposed of with a knife in his back."

She tipped her head against the back of the chair, her eyelids heavy. "There's no need for excuses, my dear Michel. I am only your mother, after all. I understand completely."

Oh, she understood, all right, thought Michel grimly, and so did he. "Then you'll recall, *Maman,* that it was your idea to draw Sparhawk away from his home. You wanted him to die on Martinique, not in Rhode Island. You wanted it that way, for Father's sake."

"Of course I remember, my dear. I remember it all better, perhaps, than you do yourself. But then, how could you, without knowing your father?"

She made a graceful little tent of her fingers, and as the white lawn cuffs of her sleeves slipped back, Michel could see the pale scars that had always marked her wrists like bracelets. She had never told him what they were from, and he had never wanted to ask, leaving the scars to be one more mystery among the many.

"What I know is that I have always tried to honor my father's memory by obeying your wishes," he said slowly. "And now, soon, you'll have all that you've ever wanted."

"You've done very well, Michel." She almost purred her satisfaction. "Why else would I have prospered so since you left, eh? Knowing that at last justice will be done has cleared my head wonderfully. You've gone to Rhode Island, and you've captured Sparhawk's daughter right from under his nose. Of course he will follow, just as we planned."

Michel frowned, startled. How could she have learned already about Jerusa? He'd left her in their room at the inn not two hours before, the center of a mass of ribbons and swatches as a dressmaker and her assistants flew to answer Madame Geary's whims. "You know about Miss Sparhawk?"

"I know that you have done precisely what I asked of you, Michel. I'm most grateful, too, and proud, the same as your dear father would have been."

Michel shifted his shoulders uneasily. For the first time in his life he found he didn't want her approval, at least not for this.

"I've done what you've asked, *Maman,* true enough," he began, choosing his words with infinite care. "But I would like to speak to you of your plans for Miss Sparhawk. Things have changed since I was here with you last."

"Oh, yes, they have, haven't they?" Her dark eyes were almost merry, glittering against the dustiness of her powdered cheeks. "The little bitch will never see Newport again. She will never be any man's wife now, and she will go to her grave knowing she brought about her father's death."

"No, *Maman*," he said softly. He'd never once denied her anything, but this at last was more than he would give. "It will not happen like that."

"Fah, and why not? Sparhawk won't get her back now, nor will he want her, when I've done!"

He stared at her, appalled by her glee. So this was the strain her madness had taken now, made all the more disturbing by her new well-mannered appearance. With terrifying clarity he remembered the countless beatings and punishments he'd endured as a child, the endless ways she'd known how to make him suffer whenever he'd erred, all the tears of loneliness and failure, so much worse than the pain itself, that he'd tried to hide from her.

God help him, how had he ever agreed to such a fate for Jerusa? Why hadn't he understood what his mother wanted to do before this?

"Listen to me, *Maman*," he said urgently. "Whatever happens between Sparhawk and me, I'm keeping the girl out of it."

She rolled her gaze toward the ceiling and shrugged. "Such concern for the little chit, Michel, such concern for a deed that is already done! You with your 'Remember this, *Maman*' and 'You don't recall that, *Maman*.' Have you forgotten you yourself sent the girl to me this very morning?"

"This morning?" he repeated, baffled. This morning he and Jerusa had still been on their way from the other island, and this afternoon, now, he knew she was safe at the inn.

"Yes, yes, yes, and a pretty show she made of it, too, kneeling on the carpet to beg my forgiveness for her family's sins." She put her forefinger to her mouth, gnawing delicately at the tip. "You would have delighted in it, Michel. She's a small little thing, to be sure, scarce worth the effort she'll take from me if her name weren't Sparhawk."

So she hadn't changed, after all, he thought with a strange mixture of relief and regret. The clothes, the hair, the eyes that had seemed so clear, all were meaningless compared to the illness that poisoned her mind and her soul. He would call the doctor to come first thing in the morning and insist that she see him.

"She is pretty, true, but obstinate, Michel," continued Antoinette. "Even though I have your word that you've brought her, after her first confession she changed her song and denied it all. As if such lies would make me pity her!"

Gently Michel took her hand. He should never have left her so long. He had always tried so hard to be the son she wanted, but even now, when he'd done the one thing she'd wanted most, he'd failed and fallen in love with his enemy's daughter.

"She'll listen, *Maman*," he said gently. He knew from long experience that she'd do better if he agreed with the fantasies; she'd only suffer more if he tried to convince her of the truth. "If anyone can tame her, it will be you. But you be sure to rest now. I don't want you tiring yourself over this silly girl."

"You're a good son, Michel, so much like your father." She lifted his hand to her cheek, rubbing her face like a cat across the backs of his fingers. "And you'll always love me, won't you, Michel?"

Before he could answer, her voice sank low and her gaze faded as her thoughts turned inward. "Just like you, Christian," she murmured, "your son will always love me."

Jerusa's footsteps echoed against the walls of the houses on either side of the narrow street. She was nearly running, her shoes ringing on the stone sidewalks, determined to reach the wharves before nightfall. She'd seen enough of the waterfront and the men there when she'd been at Michel's side to realize he'd been right about his warnings, and she'd no wish to be caught there alone after dark. But she had to reach the *Tiger* and Josh before Michel returned and found her missing. Oh, if only that infernal dressmaker and her dithering assistants hadn't kept her so long, clucking and chattering about her like a pack of hens!

She crossed to the next sidewalk, hopping over the open gutter that ran like a stream down the center of every street in Martinique. The houses that from the water had seemed so cheerful with their red roofs and blue shutters struck her now as dark and oppressive, their thick stone walls blocking the sun so late in the day and casting most of the street into shadow. But at the end of the street glowed the bright blue of the harbor, her goal, and she ran toward it, her heart pounding with excitement and her skirts sweeping against her legs.

But the closer she came to the waterfront, the more crowded the street became, and impatiently she dodged and skipped around anyone who walked too slowly. At one corner she was forced to stop and wait while a wagon drawn by four mules slowly made its way through the intersection, and while she waited, sighing with frustration, she glanced up and down the cross street for another path.

And just as she'd first seen the *Tiger*'s mast in the bay among the other ships, she now saw a three-cornered hat of gray felt on coal black hair above unmistakably broad shoulders, and far above, too, every other man or woman in the street.

"Josh!" she shrieked, running toward him with her arms outstretched. "Oh, Josh, wait!"

He turned with surprise at the sound of her voice, barely in time to catch her as she threw herself into his arms. "Jerusa, by all that's holy! What in blazes are you doing?"

"I'm hugging you, you great oaf!" She held him tight around his waist, her head pressed to his chest as she fought back the tears of joy at finding him again. "Oh, Josh, there have been so many times these last weeks that I thought I'd never see you or any of the others ever again!"

"You've given us our share of fright, too, Rusa," he said as he patted her on the back. "But where have you been, you foolish hussy? Do you know what a trial Father and I have had to chase after you?"

She pushed away from his chest. "Don't you call me a hussy, Josh," she said indignantly. "I was kidnapped, right out of Mama's rose garden the night I was going to marry Tom!"

Josh's face grew serious, and gently he led her away from the main street and into a smaller, quieter one where their words wouldn't be drowned out. "I wish I'd better news for you there, lass. When you disappeared, Tom bolted, and decided you were too lively a creature for him to take to wife. Or rather, he tried to tell Father, and Father told him that your match was broken then and there. I'm sorry, Rusa, but that's the truth."

"Tom's run? Really?" She couldn't help laughing. "Oh, Josh, that's too perfect! You see, while I've been gone I've fallen in love, really in love, with someone else, and I would have—"

"Hold now, tell me first about how you've gotten yourself free from the rogues that kidnapped you."

She hesitated, at a loss for how to explain. "Well, to begin with, it was only the one rogue, and I haven't really gotten myself free from him. You see, he's the one I'm in love with now."

"Have you lost your wits?" Thunderstruck, Josh stared. "If it's this man Géricault that Father and I have been tracking—"

She nodded. "Michel, you mean."

"'Michel,' for all love! Now I know you are mad as a hare! Jerusa, the man is a monster. Once you hear everything his father did to our parents, you'll never want to speak to him again."

"But I do know it all, Josh, because Michel has told me himself." She took her brother's hands in hers, searching his face as she tried to make him understand. "Can't you see that's all old history, things that happened far before any of us were born? Michel isn't his father, and he hasn't done any of the same things. Do you think I would have fallen in love with him if he were otherwise?"

"I don't know what you'd do, Rusa, not after this." He shook his head, and she noticed the lines of strain around his eyes and mouth that she didn't remember being there. "And Géricault has sinned against us. There's a girl here in St-Pierre that I've asked to marry me and—"

"Josh!" She grinned up at him with delight. "Oh, Josh, that's wonderful! The way you've always let my friends chase after you, I thought you'd never find a wife!"

"Hold there now, Rusa. I said I'd asked her, true, but before she'd had the chance to give me her answer, this bastard Géricault stole her away same as he took you. That's where I was bound now, to his house."

"That's ridiculous!" Jerusa gasped indignantly. "There's simply no way that Michel could have done such a thing!"

Behind them came the scraping sweep of a sword being drawn, the sound echoing over and over against the stone houses.

"You are quite right, *ma chére*," said Michel. "I don't believe I'd ever stoop to stealing some poor woman I didn't know off the streets. But then, I didn't believe you would run from me to your brother, either."

"Géricault, isn't it?" demanded Josh. "My God, how I've looked forward to this!"

To Jerusa's horror, Josh drew a cutlass from the belt at his waist, the blade mirror-bright in the fading sun. Sweet Almighty, since when had her brother begun to wear a sword? He'd know something of how to use it—all her brothers would, thanks to her father—but he was too young to have served in any war aboard a privateer or anywhere else for real experience, while Michel had done nothing else. He'd told her that himself, and one look at the confident, relaxed way he stood and held his sword only confirmed it. He could kill Josh before her brother had a chance to think.

And, oh, please, God, let Michel have come too late to have heard Josh call him a bastard….

"So you, *mon ami,* must be Joshua," said Michel easily, as if they'd just met in a drawing room instead of a shadowy street with drawn swords. "But then, how could you be anyone else? Look at you, as alike as a pair of chimneypiece cats! A pity it will be to break up the set, eh?"

Jerusa clung to Josh's arm, holding him back. "Michel, don't! Your quarrel's not with him!"

"Your father, your brother, it makes no difference to me." The hint of a smile that played about his lips chilled her more than the deceptively bored look in his eyes. She remembered how easily, how efficiently he'd killed the sailor Lovell, and how, even when he'd been ill, he threatened George Hay with such chilling menace that the other man had had no choice but to back down. But Josh wouldn't back down, any more than her father would. She knew that all too well.

"Michel, please," she begged. "He's my brother, my twin!"

Josh pushed her aside. "Clear off, Jerusa. I don't need you to fight my fights."

"But you do want her back, don't you?" asked Michel. "Even after she's spent every night since she left Newport lying by my side?"

"Damn you, Géricault, if you've laid even a breath on my sister—"

"No, Josh, no!" Jerusa grabbed his arm again, struggling to hold him back. "Michel kidnapped me, true, but he never forced me to do anything against my will. Listen to me, Josh! He never hurt me or used me ill, not once! Not *once!*"

"Yet still you left," said Michel softly. "I loved you and trusted you to stay, but you ran to your family the first chance you had."

"Damned right she did," growled Josh, but swiftly Jerusa

reached up and put her hand over his mouth with the proprietary assurance she'd had since they were children.

"Hush, Josh," she said breathlessly, her whole body attuned to Michel. "Just you hush."

Michel's smile was bleak, for her alone. "So you might speak, or listen?"

She wanted to listen. The sorrow in his voice spoke with a poignancy meant for her alone, and she was filled with passion and yearning so deep that, instead of merely hearing it, she felt it deep within her, her heart crying out in eager response.

Her hand slipped away from her brother's mouth as she took one step toward Michel, her arms outstretched in silent pleading. "Don't you know by now how much I love you, Michel?"

Yet he made no move toward her, remaining at once determinedly alone and yet unbearably lonely. "Is this how you show it, then, *ma mie?* If your brother had come to the inn to claim you, I would have understood, but instead you left on your own." His smile was full of infinite regret. "Would it have cost you so very much to have said farewell?"

"Michel, no, it was not like that!" she cried frantically. "I didn't say goodbye because I wasn't leaving. I meant to go to Josh so he could speak to Father and try to stop this dreadful fight before it's begun. Can you understand that? I no more wish you to die by his hand than I want you to kill him."

He looked away from her and instead to the sword in his hand, almost as if he were surprised to find it there. Gently he turned his wrist, circling the blade elegantly through the air.

"I have given more for you than you'll ever know, *ma chère*," he said quietly. "Now it's your turn to choose. Your family or me, for you cannot have both."

She thought of her brothers and sisters, her mama and father, a family that would do anything for one another. She pictured them surrounding the dining table at Crescent Hill, three children on either side with her parents grand as a king and queen in the tall-backed armchairs at either end, and she remembered the laughter and love that had always filled the big house and supported her every day of her life.

And then she thought of Michel Géricault. A man who'd been cursed since his birth as the illegitimate son of her father's oldest enemy, a man with a past of sorrow and violence and a future he couldn't predict. A handsome, reckless Frenchman who had burst into her life uninvited and unwelcome, yet had somehow magically become the center of it, filling her days and her soul with passion and laughter and joy and tenderness beyond all her dreams. The man who stood before her now, waiting, with nothing to offer beyond his heart and his love.

"Oh, Michel," she said softly, though her own heart already knew the answer. "Do you know how much you ask of me?"

He nodded and at last raised his gaze to meet hers, one last ray of the setting sun slanting between the houses to fall across his face.

"I know I've no decent reason under heaven to ask you anything, Rusa," he said slowly. "None at all, *chère,* and yet I cannot help it. Will you choose me, love, and be my wife?"

Chapter Twenty-One

He was going to lose her. Here, now, she was going to turn and walk away, and his life would be done as surely as if Josh Sparhawk had driven the sword into his heart as he so clearly wished to do. His Rusa, his dearest. She would go, and she would take the only happiness he'd ever known and the only hope he'd ever had for a life built on love, not hate. He would lose her, and he would have no one to blame but himself and then—

"Are you asking me to marry you, Michel?" asked Jerusa, her eyes wide with wonder. "Do you truly love me enough to wish me to be your wife?"

"Enough and more, *ma chère,*" he said, daring to hope. "More than I could ever begin to tell."

And then she was running toward him, and he let the sword drop to the paving stones as he gathered her up into his arms.

"Oh, yes, Michel, I will!" she cried, laughing with joy even though her eyes filled with tears. "Yes, yes, yes!"

He pressed his face into the warmth of her hair, still afraid to believe she'd really accepted him. *"Je t'aime tant,"* he murmured. *"Ma chère Jerusa, ma bien-aimée, ma chère épouse—"*

"Now hold a moment, Jerusa," demanded Josh. "You can't go swearing you'll wed this rogue! You'll have to get Father's permission, and I'll warrant he'll have a fine word or two before he'll let you marry the son of Christian Deveaux!"

"I'll do what I wish, Joshua," she said defiantly as she turned in Michel's embrace, her arms still linked around his neck. "I'm of age, and I can marry whomever I please, or rather, whoever pleases me. And that's Michel."

Grimly Josh shook his head as he thrust his cutlass back into the scabbard with a scrape of steel. "You won't get a shilling if you do."

"Do you think I care, *mon ami?*" asked Michel. "I would take your sister with nothing more than her smile."

With his arm around Jerusa's waist he bent swiftly to retrieve the sword that he'd dropped. Josh might wish to believe they were past fighting, but from hard-won experience he wasn't quite as quick to trust.

"He means it, Josh." She couldn't resist a little grin. "After all, he did it once already."

But Josh didn't smile in return. "Then you can come along with me back to the *Tiger* and tell Father yourself." His scowl deepened as he included Michel. "Both of you."

"Not quite yet, *monsieur,*" said Michel. "There are still other things that remain to be settled among us."

He spoke with a quiet that tore through Jerusa's new happiness, and she twisted about in his embrace to see his face.

God help her, he still meant to kill her father. Even though she'd agreed to marry him, he hadn't changed his mind or purpose.

"Michel, love, please," she began, but Josh cut her off.

"You're damned right there're things to be settled, Géricault," he said sharply. "First being what you've done with your cousin."

Michel shrugged. "You're mistaken. How can I be responsible for a cousin I don't have?"

Josh cleared his throat, making it obvious he didn't believe

Michel. "Miss Cecilie Noire. Your mother's name's Géricault, isn't it? Well, so was Ceci's mother's. Sisters, they were, meaning you and Ceci are cousins. Understand now?"

"But *Maman*—" Michel broke off, his thoughts spinning. His mother had always claimed they were alone, the two of them together without another living relative. The idea of an aunt and a cousin he'd never known living here in St-Pierre was impossible. Yet what reason would Josh Sparhawk have to invent this cousin?

"I don't care what in blazes your mother's told you or not, Géricault," said Josh. "You and Ceci are cousins. She just learned it herself. Maybe that doesn't mean much to you, but she was so all-fired bent on meeting your mother that she went off this morning to find her house, and no one's seen her since."

And with hideous, sickening clarity, Michel knew what had happened. "Is this Ceci a small woman with black hair and fair skin?"

"Aye, though that's but the half of it," declared Josh. "She's the prettiest girl in St-Pierre, and I mean to marry her."

"Then come, *mon frère,* and hurry," said Michel as at last he put away his sword. "And pray we're not too late."

The Creole serving girl twisted her hands in her apron. "I am sorry, Monsieur Géricault," she whispered miserably in her island French. "But *madame* has been so much better these last weeks that I saw not the harm."

"With my mother, you don't see the harm until it's too late." He sighed, struggling to control his temper. "How long ago did she leave the house?"

Anxiously the girl pulled at her turban. "Soon after the last bells, *monsieur.*"

Michel glanced swiftly at the tall clock in the hallway. "Half an hour ago, then. Have you any notion of where she went? To walk in the park? To a shop?"

"Oh, no, *monsieur, madame* didn't walk," said the girl, eager to make amends. "*Madame* called for a carriage and asked the driver to take her out to the north road. I heard it plain as can be, *monsieur.*"

The north road led to the grand houses of some of the wealthiest families on Martinique, houses that were surrounded by vast sugar plantations that had been cultivated for generations. When thirty-five years ago Capitaine Christian Deveaux had chosen to create a house with his spoils to rival the greatest châteaus of old France, he had naturally followed the north road to build on the high land overlooking the sea. Where else, really, would Antoinette go?

"But *madame* did not go alone, *monsieur,*" the girl was saying. "She took another lady, too. I think it was the pretty little one who came to call this morning, but since she wore one of *madame*'s cloaks—the black one, *monsieur*—the hood drawn across her face, I cannot say for certain. She and *madame* went together."

Michel swore. It had to be Ceci Noire. Of course his mother would take her there if she believed her to be Jerusa. What better place for the final punishment of Gabriel Sparhawk's daughter?

"What the devil is the girl saying, Géricault?" demanded Josh impatiently in English. "Does she know where Ceci and your mother have gone? I want to send word to Father to come meet us."

Already Michel was on his way out the door, pulling Jerusa along with him. "Then tell him to join us at my father's house," he said. "He will, I think, remember the way."

The trees were taller than Antoinette remembered, and the road that once had been white like snow with raked, crushed shells was now grown over with ferns and vines. The lantern that had seemed so bright when they had left the carriage at the north road now seemed as faint as a single candle, barely able to penetrate the velvet darkness of the forest around them. But they were not far from the house now; some things she would never forget.

The girl stumbled again, this time falling to her knees in the black soil and refusing to rise. She was crying again, too, wretched little mewling noises that were smothered by the scarf tied across her mouth. Furiously Antoinette jerked on the rope that ran like a leash to the bindings around the girl's wrists, trying to pull her to her feet again.

"Clumsy, awkward creature!" she snapped. "Enough of your laziness! Who would have thought one so small could be so obstinate?"

The girl looked up at her, pleading as the tears trickled from her red-rimmed eyes, and tried to speak against the gag. Her temple was bruised purple from her attempt to fight Antoinette earlier, and the gag had cut into the corners of her mouth. Her gown was torn and filthy, the borrowed cloak left in the carriage, and twigs and bits of grass clung to her tangled black hair. Still obstinate, perhaps, thought Antoinette with satisfaction, but no longer proud. What bridegroom would want her now, even with the name of Sparhawk?

She jerked again on the rope, and finally the girl staggered to her feet with a moan.

"Come along, *Miss* Sparhawk," ordered Antoinette curtly. "We haven't far to go."

And a good thing, too, thought Antoinette. She was a lady now, unaccustomed to walking, and carrying the heavy lantern while she pulled the useless Sparhawk bitch was harder than she'd expected. With each step the pistol in her pocket thumped against her thigh, and if she hadn't feared she'd need it she would have tossed it into the bushes.

Still, it pleased her to think of how readily the driver of the hired coach had given the gun to her in return for the gold louis, just as earlier the gold piece had bought his silence and his blindness, too, when he'd hauled this wretched girl, bound and gagged, into his carriage. How amusing it had been to tell him that the girl was mad, and to feel for once the smug superiority of the keeper over the kept!

At last they reached the clearings that thirty years before were the lawns surrounding the house like another emerald sea. Ghostly pale in the moonlight stood the house itself, or what remained of it. The tall limestone walls had not burned, though the black streaks from the flames still marked the empty windows, and the brick chimneys on either end, crumbled by time, still towered above the palms and white gum trees that had sprouted up in the ruin's empty shell. The four pillars that had once supported the roof, and the balcony that had overlooked the ships moored in the cove remained, too, like leafless trees turned to stone.

"Ah, Christian, to see what Sparhawk did to your home!" said Antoinette sadly as they drew closer to the house. "But he shall be made to pay, my darling. Soon, so soon, and your death shall be avenged."

Ruined though the house was, it was still so easy for her to look at the sweeping white stone stairs and imagine Christian standing in the doorway at the top, beautifully dressed in royal blue and gold, and beckoning her to join him one more time for supper.

"I'm coming, Christian," she called, breathing hard as she struggled to run across the lawn to him. "Oh, Christian, please wait for me!"

It was the girl who was holding her back, dragging her heels purposefully to make Antoinette late. Christian hated to be kept waiting, and the sly little bitch must know that Antoinette would be the one to suffer if she were not in her silk-covered chair when the first dish was brought to the table.

They were almost to the first step when the girl fell again, and furiously Antoinette lashed out at her, slapping her hard across the cheek. "Wait until Christian hears of this!" she shouted. "Christian will he happy to instruct even a stubborn Sparhawk slut in her manners!"

"Maman!"

Antoinette's head jerked up and her gaze swept across the lawn. Christian must be more generous with the torches after dark. Who knew what manner of rogues and thieves could creep to the house in darkness like this?

"Maman, don't!"

Nervously she felt for the pistol in her pocket. Who would mock her by calling to her this way? She was too young to be a mother, scarcely more than a girl herself.

"Maman, stop! Let her go!"

"Michel?" She stared at him, confused, as he stepped into the ring of the lantern's light. How could Michel be here to dine with Christian?

"Maman, it's Michel." Slowly he held out his hand to her, trying to win her trust as if she were a wild animal. In a way she was. Her movements were quick and jerky and her eyes were wary, and he never knew what to expect if he startled her. He noticed how she'd felt for her pocket. Was it only a random gesture, or did she have something hidden there, a large stone or even a knife? He couldn't risk that now, not with poor Ceci Noire cowering at her feet. Dear Lord, what had his mother done to her?

Behind him, in the shadows, the lantern they'd brought covered, he heard Josh swear in anger and shock as he, too, saw Ceci, and Michel tensed, praying the other man wouldn't try to play the hero just yet.

"Christian?" Antoinette's voice quavered as she reached out her hand toward his, her lantern dangling clumsily from her wrist. "Ah, Christian, how handsome you are tonight!"

"And you look lovely, too, *Maman,*" he murmured. The gap between them was closing, and slowly he reached his other hand out to take from her the rope that held Ceci.

But suddenly she darted back to the steps, dragging Ceci with her. "You won't take her back, Michel!" she said, recognizing him at last. "You gave me the Sparhawk bride, and she's mine!"

"But you're wrong, *Maman*," he said softly. "That girl isn't the Sparhawk bride. She isn't even a Sparhawk. She's your niece, *Maman*, the daughter of your sister, Jeanne."

"Jeanne?" Antoinette's lip trembled and her eyes filled with long-past sorrow as she stared down at Ceci. "I have not seen my sister since her husband turned me away from their door. He said I was no better than a whore, that I had brought dishonor and shame to my sister. He said it would have been better had I died in the fire, for to them I was already dead. All I had left was you, Michel. Only you."

"Oh, *Maman*," said Michel, understanding everything. "My poor *Maman*."

But Antoinette had already forgotten her sister. "Where is the bride, then, Michel?" she asked plaintively. "You promised you'd bring me Gabriel Sparhawk's daughter. Where is she?"

"I'm here." To Michel's horrified surprise Jerusa herself stepped into the light, closer to his mother than he'd have ever wished. "Look at me, *madame*. If you remember Gabriel Sparhawk, then you've only to look at my face to know I'm his daughter."

"Sweet Mary in heaven, you are," breathed Antoinette as she stared at Jerusa. Automatically she had switched from French to English to answer Jerusa, somehow remembering the language she'd learned so long ago when she'd worked in the Noires' bistro. "*You* are Jerusa Sparhawk!"

The rope slipped forgotten from her fingers, and with a strangled cry, Ceci staggered free. Michel watched her long enough to see her collapse, weeping, into Josh's arms, to see how he cut away the cruel ropes and gag from her mouth, and how they clung together as if they'd never part.

Now all that he had to do was reach his mother without her using whatever was in her pocket.

"You asked Michel to bring me here, and he did," Jerusa was saying, her voice low and soothing. "He obeyed you exactly as you wished, didn't he?"

Michel looked at her, standing there as calm and beautiful as an angel to comfort his poor, bewildered mother, and he felt his love well up inside him all over again. What had he ever done to deserve a woman this kind and compassionate?

"She's right, *Maman,*" he said, looking at Jerusa. "I sailed to Newport and I watched and waited until the night of her wedding. Then I stole her away from her family and her bridegroom, and left them nothing but a rose and the black mark of Christian Deveaux. I made them suffer, *Maman,* just as you wished, and then I brought her here to Martinique."

Jerusa turned her face toward him, her eyes luminous and full of love. For him, he marveled. For *him.*

"I brought her here, *Maman,* exactly as you asked," he said softly. "Everything was as we'd planned. Except for one thing. I fell in love with her."

"Love?" repeated Antoinette, gasping with horror. "You love *her?* The daughter of Gabriel Sparhawk?"

Michel nodded, his eyes never leaving Jerusa. "Yes, *Maman.* I love her, and she loves me, and she has done me the inestimable honor of accepting my offer of marriage."

"No!" screamed Antoinette, and before Michel had realized what was happening, she grabbed Jerusa and yanked her toward the stairs at the same time that she pulled the little pistol from her pocket and thrust it against the side of Jerusa's head. Automatically he lunged forward to grab the gun, but Antoinette screamed again, dragging Jerusa in front of her.

"I'll kill her now, Michel, just as you've killed my heart," she said wildly. The lantern on her wrist swung back and forth, black shadows and bursts of light dancing across her face like an ever changing mask. "Do you want to see that, my darling son? The blood of your dear little Sparhawk whore scattered like dew across the steps of your father's house?"

Michel froze, knowing too well that his mother could do it. Where in God's name had she gotten the gun? From here he couldn't tell if it was cocked or even loaded, but he couldn't gamble with Jerusa's life. In the swinging light her face was pale with fear, her eyes silently beseeching him.

"Let her go, *Maman,* please, for me," he said softly. "She has never done anything to you."

"She has made you betray *me!*" she cried bitterly. "Isn't that sin enough, Michel, even for you?"

She was smaller than Jerusa, but the gun pressed to the younger woman's cheek changed everything, and when Antoinette began to climb the stairs, Jerusa had no choice but to follow, their skirts dragging across the white stone as they slowly, awkwardly backed to the top.

Her heart pounding, Jerusa stopped at the top of the stairs. Antoinette's fingers dug deeply into her wrist, and the barrel of the gun was cool against her cheek as she forced Jerusa to turn and look down. Before them the stairs fell off into nothingness, a drop of twenty feet from what had been the house's second floor to the blackness of the cellar, the lantern's light only hinting at the overgrown wreckage far below.

"Once this was the grandest house in all the Indies," said Antoinette fiercely. "My chamber was there, to the east, with rose silk hangings on my bed and a gilt-framed looking glass on every wall. There Christian loved me. There I conceived his child, the son you have stolen from me!"

She tried to push Jerusa forward, but with a little cry Jerusa pulled back, barely keeping her balance over the yawning emptiness. If there were only something to hang on to, something to give her purchase!

"Think of what you are doing, *madame,*" she begged frantically. "If not for me, then for the son who loves you so well!"

But Antoinette wasn't listening, staring instead into the shadows of the ruined house and the blacker world of her past. "Once this was a place of beauty and happiness for me," she whispered in French. "Do you remember, Christian? Do you remember how you carried me up the stairs and then loved me here, on this landing? Before the Sparhawks came and burned it, do you remember how you loved me?"

She inched closer to the edge, pulling Jerusa with her, their skirts fluttering gently over the emptiness.

"No, *madame,* no!" cried Jerusa, struggling to twist away until she heard the little click of the flintlock being squeezed back.

God help her, she was going to die, here at the hands of a madwoman determined either to shoot her or shove her to her death. She would never marry Michel, never feel his arms around her or taste the passion of his kiss again. But at least she could tell him one last time...

"I love you, Michel!" she shouted, her voice breaking as she prayed that he would hear her. "I love you!"

"Damnation, let her go!" thundered Gabriel Sparhawk, and, forgetting the gun and the stairs like a cliff, Jerusa turned toward her father's voice. He was standing at the bottom of the stairs beside Michel, his hat in his hand as he gazed up at her.

Antoinette turned, too, and gasped when she realized it was Gabriel. "Kill him, Michel!" she shrieked in English. "He has come, my son, just as we planned! Kill him now, the monster who murdered your father!"

Her breath tight in her chest, Jerusa watched as Michel's hand hovered over the hilt of his sword. He could kill her father instantly. Gabriel's back was to him, and they stood no more than three feet apart. It could be done so fast that Gabriel wouldn't realize until it was too late.

No, Michel, please, please, for my sake and the love we share...

"Kill Sparhawk, Michel," screamed Antoinette. "If you love me as your father did, you will kill him!"

"Christian Deveaux never loved anyone but himself!" shouted Gabriel fiercely. "He was the monster, ruled by hate and evil!"

"No!" Wildly Antoinette shook her head, her whole body trembling, and as she did, the lantern slid from her wrist and dropped into the cellar. It thumped twice as it fell, the sound echoing as if it were in a well, and then shattered with a crash at the bottom. A pop, a little explosion that was barely audible, and then suddenly a bright flare rose from below where the lantern's flame had found dry palms and old timbers.

But Antoinette didn't notice, the first tears sliding down her face. "No! Christian loved me! You were the one who hunted him for years, bent on his destruction!"

"Deveaux began it, not I," shouted Gabriel, his voice rough with the need to tell the truth. "Forty years ago, I loved a girl named Catherine Langley. When Deveaux captured our sloop he forced me to watch as he did things to her that no man should ever do to a woman, and when he was done he laughed and gave her to his men, and then, at last, to the sharks."

Jerusa listened in horror, stunned both by her father's admission and the anguish that marked his face forty years after he'd lost this first love. She had always believed her mother to be the only woman he'd loved; how, she wondered with aching sympathy, had he managed to keep the memory and pain of this first girl locked so long inside?

"But maybe my Catherine was the fortunate one," he continued, his voice rising. "Though she suffered so much at Deveaux's hands, at least her pain ended with her death. She didn't have to live with the scars to prove how he had used her in the name of his wickedness. Isn't that so, *madame?*"

"Christian loved me!" cried Antoinette frantically,

through her tears. "If I suffered it was my own doing, not his! He needed to teach me, to correct me, to make me worthy of his love!"

"Oh, *Maman*," whispered Michel as a lifetime of deception began crashing around him. Now he remembered the whispered stories he'd always denied about his father, choosing instead to believe in the handsome, loving gentleman in the portrait over *Maman*'s bed. He thought of the pale scars that ringed her wrists and the others he'd glimpsed on her back as she dressed.

But the worst scars were the ones that didn't show, and Michel closed his eyes as he thought of how she'd ruled his life with her obsession for vengeance. Her beauty, happiness and love had been destroyed long ago, just as she'd always sworn.

But Gabriel Sparhawk wasn't the one who'd done it.

Michel let the hilt of his sword fall from his fingers, and for the first time he could remember, his sword hand was shaking. God help him, he had come so close to making the worst mistake of his life, and overwhelmed, he looked again up to Jerusa. She was all he had left now; she alone would be his salvation.

But the danger she was in was worsening. Gray plumes of smoke curled up through the night sky as, for a second time, fire spread through the ruined house. The flames flashed bright in the empty windows, and at the top of the white stairs Jerusa and his mother were outlined like frozen silhouettes.

"Let the past go, *madame*," said Gabriel. With his hat in his outstretched hand, he climbed the first step toward Antoinette and Jerusa, and Michel caught his breath, praying that his mother would listen. "Don't let Deveaux hurt you any longer."

"But he loves me!" wailed Antoinette. "How can I live without love!"

Gabriel climbed another step, his face flushed by the firelight. "You don't have to, *madame*," he said, coaxing. "You have a world of love right here in this lad of yours. You heard him yourself. He loves my daughter, and she loves him. What finer words can a parent hear, eh?"

"No!" Abruptly she pulled the gun away from Jerusa's head, shoving her away. Jerusa staggered on the edge of the step, fighting for her balance as Michel watched in horror.

Dear God, not his Jerusa, not now, not like this.

With a little cry she managed to twist back, lurching forward so that she stumbled down the top three steps. Michel raced toward her, leaping up the stairs to catch her.

"Oh, Michel," she said, shuddering as she wept against his shoulder. "Oh, Michel, I was so scared I'd never be with you again!"

"Hush, *ma chère*," he whispered as he held her. "It's done, *ma petite*. It's done, and you're safe."

But it wasn't over and she wasn't safe, for as he looked over Jerusa's head, he met his mother's lost, empty eyes as she slowly raised the pistol in her hand with the flames rising high behind her.

"No, *Maman*," he said slowly, his arms tightening around Jerusa as he shifted her to shield her with his own body. "Oh, *Maman*, don't do this!"

And for the first time in his memory, she smiled. "I never wanted to hurt you, Michel," she said, her words wavering through her tears. "I wanted—oh, what I wanted!"

Unsteadily she swung around to point the gun at the breast of Gabriel Sparhawk. "And you took it, didn't you?" she cried with all the anguish that overflowed her heart. "You took everything—my love, my life, now even my son—and you have left me nothing. Nothing!"

She took aim and the hammer snapped shut. But still Gabriel stood before her, unflinching and unmarked, and too late she realized the gun was empty, and even this time, the last, he had won, and she had lost.

With Jerusa beside him, Michel rushed toward her as flames licked at the back of her skirts. "Come, *Maman,* hurry!"

Wearily she smiled at him again. "No, Christian," she said softly. "It's too late for us, but not, I pray, for them."

And before Michel could reach her, she stepped back into the flames and was gone.

Epilogue

Newport
June, 1772

The windows of the Sparhawk house were open wide to take advantage of the warm summer night, and the cheers and laughter of the guests and family gathered for the old captain's birthday drifted out across the lawn into the garden. Every toast that was raised in Gabriel Sparhawk's honor carried the same theme: wonder and admiration that such a charmed, and charming, man had lived to see his sixtieth birthday, surrounded by his wife, children and grandchildren.

In the shade of the cherry tree, Michel smiled as one of his brothers-in-law thundered a particularly bawdy toast that left the men roaring and stamping their feet with approval, and the ladies shrieking. There were still some things about the English he would never comprehend or admire, but then, there were so many others he did that he wouldn't trade for all the gold in Paris.

He bent to pluck a pink rose, carefully peeling away the thorns before he handed it to the baby cradled in the crook of his arm.

"A rose, *mon fils*," he explained as the baby stared at the flower with solemn, cross-eyed consideration. "One of your grandmama's favorites, I'm told. She won't fuss if she sees you with this now, but later you might wish to keep your balls and kites and wagons out of this particular corner of the garden."

Michel touched the rose to his son's tiny, dimpled chin, and little Alexandre rewarded him with the widest of toothless baby grins. Gently Michel swept the flower back and forth, his delight equal to the baby's. He never tired of seeing the world through his son's blue eyes, and when those who saw them together would make jests about his reliving his own childhood, Michel would only smile, and silently thank God that he'd been given another chance.

"Come along, Alexandre," he said, handing the flower to the baby to clutch in his chubby fist. "It's time we joined the ladies."

He found Jerusa on the cedar bench beneath the arbor, her legs stretched languidly before her and her head resting against the back of the bench. To see her so relaxed made him smile, for she and her mother had been bustling over this party for weeks, ever since they'd arrived from St-Pierre. But then, everything about Jerusa made him smile, and that, he knew, would never change.

He bent to kiss her and he tasted her smile. With a little squawk at being ignored, Alexandre waved the rose in his mother's face.

"Why, thank you, sir," she said, laughing softly as she took the now-bedraggled flower. "You'll have every lass in town setting her cap for you if you're not careful."

"I don't doubt it will happen, *ma chère,*" agreed Michel with a sigh as he sat beside her on the bench. "And I promise you his sister will be just as admired."

He leaned across to kiss the forehead of Louisa, the second of their twins, sprawled quite peacefully in her mother's lap.

Jerusa leaned her head against Michel's shoulder. "It's gone quite perfectly, I think."

He knew she meant the party, but he couldn't help thinking of their life together. "I cannot imagine it being any better."

"At least Father seemed pleased, and Mama, too." She leaned closer and sighed contentedly. "And doesn't Ceci look wonderful? She swears the baby will be a boy, and Josh is every bit as convinced it shall be a girl."

"The baby will be what it is, Rusa, and all their fussing can't change that," said Michel with the philosophical resignation of a father of two months' standing. "Boy or girl, you only have a choice of two."

Jerusa laughed softly. "Unless, of course, you're doubly blessed."

"And we are, *chérie,* blessed in every way that matters."

Her smile faded as she saw the love and tenderness in his eyes, and when he kissed her she knew all over again that he was right, wonderfully, perfectly right.

Right as rain.

* * * * *

The Rogue's Seduction

by

Georgina Devon

Georgina Devon has a Bachelor of Arts degree in Social Sciences with a concentration in History. Her interest in England began when the United States Air Force stationed her at RAF Wood-bridge, near Ipswich in East Anglia. This was also where she met her husband, who flew fighter aircraft for the United States. She began writing when she left the Air Force. Her husband's military career moved the family every two to three years, and she wanted a career she could take with her anywhere in the world. Today she lives in Tucson, Arizona, with her husband, two dogs, an inherited cat and a cockatiel. Her daughter has left the nest and does website design, including Georgina's. Contact her at http://www.georginadevon.com

Chapter One

'Stand and deliver!'

Lillith, Lady de Lisle, recognized the voice instantly.

Jason Beaumair, Earl of Perth.

She did not need to look out the coach's window to picture him. Dark-visaged, with wings of silver at his temples and hair the colour of jet, he haunted her dreams. A scar, received in a duel over another man's wife, ran the length of his right cheek. She was—or had been—that wife.

A shiver of foreboding slid down her spine.

What was he doing, waylaying her carriage here on Hounslow Heath? He certainly did not need her jewels. He was as wealthy as Golden Ball. 'Twas a dangerous game the Earl played.

'You, Coachman,' Perth's imperious baritone ordered, 'descend with your hands empty and in the air. And you—that's right, you,' he added pointedly to the single outrider, 'drop your pistol or the driver will be sorrier for your actions.'

Lillith pulled aside the velvet window curtain in time to see her outrider drop his pistol. Perth sat at his leisure on a magnificent horse, a gun in each hand aimed at the coach. Trust the Earl to know horseflesh and not care who else knew the animal he rode was too fine for a highwayman.

At least the man wore a mask across his face. Should the *ton* get a whiff of this latest escapade of his involving her, all the old scandals would be revisited. She was not sure her reputation could withstand another assault from the Earl. The only thing that had preserved her good name the last time had been her husband's social standing. No one had willingly offended de Lisle; the man had known too many people at court.

However, as a widow, she no longer had her deceased husband's protection. And goodness knew that if her brother sought to preserve her good name both of them would be laughed out of London.

'You inside the vehicle,' Perth's lazy drawl demanded, 'come out where I can get a better look at what my labours have earned.'

He was as disreputable as always. It was his greatest fault and his greatest charm. She had thwarted him only once in her life and lived a long time regretting it.

With a sigh and a tiny smile curving her lips, she pulled her cape tight against the evening air and stepped out. Summer was nearly gone. A chill breeze caught at her silver-blond hair, undoing the intricate curls her maid had spent many hours perfecting. Her slipper-clad feet sank into the damp grass. The fine leather would be stained. No matter. A pair of ruined slippers was nothing. Great wealth was the only benefit she had gained by marrying de Lisle.

She made a mock curtsy, never taking her gaze from Perth's arrogant features. He gave her a feral grin, his strong white teeth flashing in the pale light of the full moon. At one time that look on his face had scared her. Now it excited her. She had been a child the first time she had dealt with him, ignorant and easily led by her family. She was a woman now, ready for him.

His eyes flashed. 'Come here.'

She returned his stare without flinching. 'I think not.'

Using his knees, he urged his mount forward, stopping only when he was close enough that she could smell the animal's musky scent. 'Come here,' he said again, a hint of iron underlying his words.

She shook her head. 'I am on my way home and in no mood for frivolity.'

His eyes narrowed. 'This is no frivolous matter, madam. I mean what I say.'

Without a word, he sent a shot at the feet of her coachman who had climbed down from his seat and gone to the heads of the two horses pulling her carriage. The old servant jumped back as dirt sprayed around his boots.

Anger sent Lillith a step forward. 'You go too far.'

'I don't go far enough,' Perth stated. 'Come here or the next ball will enter his flesh.'

Lillith met his hard look with one of her own. 'You are a rogue, sir, with no scruples.'

He made her a curt bow from the waist. 'You always were observant, as well as ambitious.'

The coolness of his tone set her back up. 'Be done with this and go your way. I tire of this inappropriate jest.'

''Tis no jest, Lady de Lisle. I intend to take you prisoner.'

She gasped. 'Never. Be gone.'

The grin that had been feral turned vicious, and Lillith stepped back without intending to do so. 'What dangerous game do you play now?' she asked, her voice barely a whisper.

He made no reply.

Under the protection of her cape, she searched for the tiny pistol with its mother-of-pearl handle that she always kept ready in her reticule. If he intended to threaten her with ruin and goodness knew what else, then she would protect herself. Before she could think rationally about what she intended to do, she pulled the tiny weapon out and shot.

She missed.

Furious at her own error, she threw the pistol at him. He merely leaned to one side and let it sail past. A grin of anticipation eased the harshness of his jaw, but did nothing to lessen the look of danger in his eye.

'I shall make it a personal goal to teach you how to shoot,' he drawled, that infuriating smile still on his face.

She scowled. 'You shall not be around me long enough to do so, sirruh.'

Her outrider used the fracas to make a lunge for the Earl, only to have Perth's well-trained horse shy away. The animal's action brought Perth's attention back to the servants.

'Enough dallying. Call your lackey off, madam, or I shall be forced to harm him,' Perth said through clenched teeth, the grin gone as though it had never been. His gaze never left her face.

A flush of irritation mounted Lillith's cheeks. 'Move away, Jim.'

When the servant was distant enough to suit him, Perth said, 'This is the last time I tell you to come here. The next time I will come to you.' His voice softened, although it lost none of the threat. 'And I will guarantee that you will not like it if you make me fetch you.'

Her tiny weapon was lost somewhere in the grass behind Perth. Her servants were both unarmed. Still, she did not fear Perth. He was a harsh man with a quick temper, but he would never physically hurt her.

'No.' She notched her chin up and squared her shoulders. 'If you insist on this folly, then you must fetch me. For I will not come to you, not like this.'

'You always were stubborn,' he murmured.

Without warning, he urged the horse forward. Lillith twisted in the damp grass, her foot slipping as she tried to sprint away. He was on her. His right arm swept down and around her waist so that the gun he held bit hard into her side. She took a deep breath to shout at him only to land with a cramping thump, stomach first, in front of him. She sprawled like a sack of grain across his horse's back, all the air knocked out of her lungs. Through the blood thundering in her ears, she heard her servants shouting and moving about.

'I would not if I were you,' Perth drawled seconds before shooting a pistol.

The sound reverberated through her body. If he had truly shot one of her men, she would see to it that the Earl paid.

She tried to wriggle off, determined to escape even if it meant landing face down in the dirt. A large, masculine hand settled firmly on her posterior, holding her securely in place. Heat spread through her hips until it engulfed her entire body. She might just as well be undressed and he with no gloves on, for it felt as though his bare flesh touched hers.

She bit her lower lip. Perth had always had this effect on her. Even after she wed de Lisle, she had responded like a wanton to just a glance from Perth. It was her shame.

De Lisle had called her cold. Thank goodness he had not known the truth.

As though he knew her worries for her servant, Perth said, 'Do not worry, madam, I harmed no one. Something which cannot be said for you.'

The horse lunged forward, scattering her thoughts like clouds before a winter wind. The bones of the animal's neck dug into her gut and made her feel like retching. This was an abominable situation.

'Release me,' she said, trying to shout and hearing her voice come out as a squeak.

'In good time,' Perth said, humour laced through his words.

Drat the man! He was enjoying this.

Her hair, having come completely loose from the topknot her maid had worked so long to achieve, hung in thick strands around her cheeks, providing a cushion from the hard smoothness of his boots. The breeze made by the horse's progress blew up her skirt and chilled her to the bone.

Determined to make this abduction difficult, she wrapped both hands around Perth's ankle and pulled. He lurched to the side.

'Careful, madam,' he thundered. 'You will unseat us both. Plunging from a galloping horse would not be healthy.'

In spite of the truth he spoke, she grinned—momentarily. His powerful hand smacked her rear. She was shocked more than hurt. Her cape and dress buffered any hurt and made it more humiliating than painful.

'How dare you, sirruh,' she said, keeping her grip on his ankle although she no longer pulled. She was becoming foggy-headed from being upside down.

'I dare a great deal,' he said, his voice a low growl of promise.

Her stomach felt as though it rushed to her throat. Surely they would soon be far enough away from her carriage and servants for him to stop so that she could change position. Or better yet, escape.

They came to an abrupt halt, jarring her painfully against the saddle. She released his leg and pushed against the horse's shoulder in an attempt to slip off on to her feet. Perth stopped her by jumping to the ground ahead of her and hauling her off. She landed with her back moulded against his chest, his arm wrapped around her ribs just below her breasts.

Her breath caught in a gulp. His nearness was as heady as the finest French champagne, a drink she enjoyed sparingly for that reason. The scent of musk and cinnamon that clung to him was an aphrodisiac, a strong memory of years before.

Mortification at her weakness made her furious. She twisted, trying to break his hold. Instead of releasing her, he used her momentum to turn her in his arms. Her bosom pressed tightly to his chest. Her loins melded with his. Her face met his. Only inches of cool air separated their lips.

She shuddered and turned her head away.

'Let me go,' she whispered. To her ears, she sounded breathless and vulnerable. 'Now,' she said more forcefully when he did not immediately obey her.

A chuckle started deep in his chest, the vibration reaching her through the clothing that separated them. The sound escaped him as a low rumble that should have been humourous but was not.

'You have run from me these last ten years. You will run no more—until I am through with you.'

The cool of the late summer night turned cold.

'Have you not learned that revenge is best eaten hot? Yours is cold. Let the past go and release me.'

Even as she said the words, she hoped against hope that they not apply to him. Once he had loved her enough to defy her family to have her. She wanted him to love her still.

'You always were intelligent as well as beautiful.'

'Revenge it is then,' she said softly, holding firm to the hard edge of her anger.

He nodded.

Revenge. Something inside her crumbled and died. Hope, perhaps. De Lisle had gone to his maker just over a year ago. Since that time, she had hoped against hope that Perth might still want her. And he did. But he did not love her. By kidnapping her, he showed that he intended to ruin her.

She had to escape him. Before she could think better of it, she stomped on his instep. Her soft leather slipper barely made a dent in his boot, but she took him by surprise. His grip relaxed, and she spun around out of his arms and made a dash for the road they had stopped beside.

He caught her cape and dragged her back, but she slipped the garment from her shoulders and kept going. Her feet slid in the dirt and she gasped for breath but managed to keep running.

Seconds later he had her.

He twirled her around and crushed her to him. One arm wrapped around her waist, the other cupped the back of her head.

He stared down at her, the pale light of a half-moon

glinting off his silver-streaked hair. His features were shadows and angles. She could not see the expression on his face, but there was a tightness to his body that told her more than words.

Lillith sucked air into her lungs. Her palms pressed against him. 'Do not,' she gasped seconds before his mouth took hers.

His lips were firm and sure against hers. His tongue teased her. His teeth nipped her. Hunger and desire beat at her. Shivers chased by flames chased by more shivers coursed through her body. If he released her, she would sink to the ground.

When she felt as though there was no more air left in the world for her to breathe, he let her go. She sagged against him.

The hand that had cupped the back of her head slid to the column of her neck. His fingers glided along her heated flesh and became tangled in the length of her hair. He held her secure.

'I have wanted to do that any time these past ten years,' he said, his voice a rasp.

His grip on her hair chained her to him as surely as the love she had always felt. Lillith pulled herself erect, causing his fingers to tighten their hold, and wondered what had happened to her bravado and determination to escape him. It was an effort to focus her mind on what he said. She licked lips that felt branded. Her fingers strayed to their swollen flesh without her conscious volition.

'Ten years is a long time,' she finally managed.

'I can be a patient man when needs be.'

Exhaustion came fast on the heels of his words. All her hopes and desires combined to crush her emotions. Her shoulders sagged before she realised it. If only this abduction had not happened. As soon wish for Perth's love.

Quickly, defiantly, she straightened to her fullest height. She was tall for a woman, her eyes level with his chin. 'Do you call this act that of a patient man?'

His smile, that devastating slash of teeth, mocked her. 'I call waiting ten years patient.'

He leaned into her and brought a strand of hair to his face. 'Lilac,' he murmured. 'I remember the first time I met you, you smelled of sweet lilac. Everyone else wore rose water or lavender, but not you.'

He let the tress slip through his fingers. The hair slid down her shoulder to curl along her breast where the fine muslin of her evening gown bared her flesh. His gaze followed and sharpened. Desire, hot and hungry, burned in the lines of his face. She saw his reaction and her own body betrayed her. It had always been thus with her.

'I would have forsaken my marriage vows for you,' she whispered, the words coming from a place in her heart she had thought locked away. They spoke aloud the dream she had cherished through the early months of her marriage to a man who cared nothing for her pleasure in the marriage bed. She had thought them long ago forgotten.

The fire died in his face. His eyes became chips of ebony ice. 'I don't dally with married women. Nor do I share what is mine.'

Shame at her words and her weakness goaded her. 'Is that why you fought a duel with my husband, a man many years your senior?'

His hand, which still gripped her nape, tightened. 'You were mine and I intended to have you the only way possible.' Now he shrugged as though sloughing away an unpleasant memory. 'But de Lisle was better with a sword than I. He kept you.'

His grip on her loosened and the temptation to squirm was great. She resisted. He was a strong man, and had he intended to let her go he would have released her completely.

She sighed. 'So what do you mean to do now?'

Clouds scudded across the moon, casting his face into darkness. Lillith could not see him clearly enough to read his emotions. She shivered.

'I intend to make up for the past years. My country retreat is a long ride from here. That is where we are going.'

'No.' The denial was automatic.

His cruel smile returned and he hauled her so close that she could see the night growth of dark hairs shadowing his jaw. 'What happened to your passion, your willingness to deny your marriage vows?'

She flared in anger. ''Tis one thing to give everything to a man who loves you, another to have a man throw your youthful passions in your face and turn them to revenge.'

His mouth thinned into a hard line. 'You are a fool.'

She saw no love or even liking in his eyes. He

watched her with cold determination and it made her hands feel numb with dread.

Revenge, revenge and revenge. Nothing more. He would ruin her for revenge and in the process ruin himself. She would not let him do so.

Her resolve to resist him firmed, and she began to struggle in earnest. She kicked his shin and instantly regretted it as pain shot up her leg. She flung her arms out and at him. He released her waist in time to catch one of her wrists in each hand. He held her effortlessly as she panted from exertion and frustration.

'I won't go with you,' she said between clenched teeth. 'You cannot do this to me. You will ruin me. Us.' Bitterness welled up in her. 'As you very nearly did ten years ago.'

His eyes glinted in what light from the night sky remained. 'And you have no de Lisle to save you this time. And I would wager in Brook's betting book that your brother will not do so.'

She bit her lip and looked away, twisting as far to the side as his continued hold on her wrists would allow. He spoke only the truth, no matter that it hurt. This was a night for long-buried truths and long-remembered pain. She wished to inflict some of her own.

'You are as cruel and self-absorbed as ever. Had you been a different man, my family might have let me wed you.'

She heard his sharp intake of breath and the satis-faction that she had hoped for eluded her. No matter what lay between them, she had never hated him. Far from it.

'Had I been a rich man instead of a distant cousin that no one expected to inherit, things would have been different. Your family sold you to the highest bidder, a shrivelled-up prune of a man who no more knew what to do with you than a youth faced with his first woman.'

Still more truths. He was determined to strip her of the hard-gained pretense in which she had found refuge. He laid bare between them in the cold night air all their past, even as in the doing he laid waste to any possible future they might have had.

Tears stung her eyes, and she could do nothing to stop them or wipe them away. Her fingers were not hers to command.

'Let me go,' she said, trying desperately not to choke and alert him to her turmoil. 'I promise not to run or give you further trouble.'

His hold loosened, but did not release her.

She heard a rumbling in the distance. It sounded as though a carriage came their way, but there was no light as that which would come from outside lanterns. She chided herself. If this were Perth's coach, there would be no light for others to see. Her servants would be looking for her.

The carriage came into view, a darker shadow on the road. Perth released one of her hands and stepped into the path of the oncoming vehicle. The coachman's sharp eyes spotted the Earl and the carriage halted. Without waiting for someone to approach them, Perth thrust her forward, yanked the door open himself and threw her inside.

She landed with a thump and a swirl of skirts that tangled with her legs. The cape that she had lost during her struggle with Perth quickly followed. She tried to get her balance to stand up, only to fall back against the seat when the carriage lurched forward. No sooner had the vehicle started moving than the door opened again and Perth bounded gracefully inside.

Lillith managed to get on to the seat opposite from where Perth deposited himself. Fine leather met her fingertips. Once Perth had been a captain in the Hussars, living only on his army salary. Now he was rich enough to squander money on any toy that took his fancy. Her fingers smoothed over the butter-soft leather. Had he been this rich ten years before, they would not now be sitting here, adversaries, each intent on hurting the other.

She sighed.

No inside lantern was lit, so the interior was too dark for her to see Perth's face. Yet she felt the energy he projected—an energy that excited her as much as it scared her. He would command her attention and her love, and then he would walk away from her without a backward glance.

A chill ran the course of her back. Without taking her attention off him, she leaned forward and groped along what she could reach of the floor in search of her cape. She found it and hauled it up and around her shoulders, as someone might shield themselves from an attack.

'Come here,' he said, his voice soft and dangerous.

Chapter Two

Lillith sat frozen in place.

His command echoed through her mind: *Come here.* She hugged the cape closer until the soft muslin caressed her cheeks and tickled her nose. It did nothing to ease the cold that seeped into her bones. She bit her lower lip.

'I think not,' she managed.

'We have a long ride, Lady de Lisle—Lillith.' His voice was low and thick as sweetest honey when he said her name. 'I think you will come over here sooner rather than later.'

'You always were arrogant and too sure of having things your own way. Your besetting sins.'

He chuckled deep in his chest, a mirthless sound. 'And what are yours, milady? Fickleness and faithlessness? I would rather have my own.'

She reared back as though he had slapped her. In a way he had. 'I do what I must when I must.'

She put all the conviction of her past choices into her words, refusing to let him make her despise herself for what she had had to do. Her family had depended on her. She had saved them. If her own happiness had died because of their need, then it was a price she had been willing to pay, a price she would pay today if need be.

'You do as you are bid to do,' he sneered.

Anger flared in her, setting her chest pounding and her blood rioting. 'You have overstepped the bounds of politeness, sirruh. What I did in the past and what I do in the future is none of your concern. Nor do you have the right to criticise me over something that was no concern of yours.'

'No concern of mine?' He leaned forward until she could feel his warm breath on her face. He smelled of cinnamon and cold night air. 'Who did you leave at the altar?' A harsh laugh tore from his lips. 'My twin?'

'I did my duty to my family. I could do nothing else.'

'You were sold to save your brother from the River Tick and exile to a continent where Napoleon held reign,' he said, disgust and loathing dripping from every word. 'You were nothing but a piece of goods sold to the highest bidder. Unfortunately for me, I was not the highest bidder. I was not even a contender.'

Enough was enough, and she had tired of hearing things that she could not change any more than she could change the position of the stars. She drew herself up and let the cape fall from her shoulders.

'Are you finished insulting me and my family, for I am certainly tired of hearing you?'

His eyes flashed in the dim moonlight that managed

to flicker in through the window, but he said nothing. Instead, he grabbed the cane that lay on the seat beside him and rapped the end on the carriage roof, signalling the coachman to halt. The wheels had barely stopped turning before he was out the door.

Lillith's sense of victory was fleeting at best. Without Perth she was left to her own thoughts and they were not pleasant. Too many things had happened and it seemed worse were to come.

The slowing motion of the coach woke Lillith. She blinked her eyes, trying to see better. She was not at her best upon first waking. The vehicle stopped completely, and she found herself tossed forward and caught by an arm around her waist. Her wits returned in a rush.

Perth. Abducted.

Vaguely, she remembered the carriage stopping once before, but she had fallen into an exhausted sleep, her thoughts and memories twisted into nightmares, and had not roused so much as tossed about. Then warmth and security had enveloped her, and the dreams had eased and she had gone deeper into sleep. She now realised that Perth had entered and had taken her into his arms.

Now he released her before she said a word or even tried to free herself. She nearly tumbled off the seat, but managed to scramble across the vehicle and to sit up, facing him.

The inside was dimly lit from outside light. She guessed it must be some time in the early morning.

They must have travelled some considerable distance since her abduction.

'We are stopping here to change horses and get something to eat.' Perth's voice was deeper than usual. She wondered if he had just woken up. 'Stay here. I will be back shortly.'

Before she could reply, he was gone.

Any lingering tiredness left. If she meant to flee, she had better start now. Grabbing up her cape, she scooted to the door, which she opened and jumped through. The step had not been let down, and it was a long way to the ground. She landed with a thump and twist of her ankle. Pain shot up her right leg. She sank backwards until she sat in the carriage doorway.

She took deep, slow breaths to try to still the pain. Any thought she'd had of escaping seeped away. She could not run and, from the looks of this inn, there was nowhere to run. It was a typical village pub, and a small village at that. From her limited vision, she could see several cottages, a village green and not much else. She had no idea where they were.

She gathered up her courage to try putting weight on her foot when Perth came into view. He moved with a lean looseness that she found intriguing. Dark hair, a little longer than fashionable, swept back from his high forehead. The scar slashing his cheek was pronounced in the dark haze of a face in need of a shave. His full lips were firm, with a hint of sensuality that made her remember how his kiss had felt—punishing, devastating, exciting.

He reached her, dark brows drawn in irritation. 'I told you to stay put.'

She pushed the memory aside and stood. She ignored the shaft of pain streaking from her ankle up her leg. 'I do as I wish. You are not my keeper.'

'I am the keeper of your reputation. What if someone of our circle had been here and recognised you?'

She huffed in indignation. 'And what if someone had? Is it not a little late for you to worry about my good name?'

In the heat of her ire, she stepped forward, intending to face him without hesitation. Immediately, her right leg buckled and a sharp intake of breath caught her unawares. His arms circled her and lifted her up before she could come close to the ground.

'What in Hades have you done?'

She turned her head and glared at him. His eyes met hers. Lillith blinked, and blinked again. He was too close. She shook her head.

'I turned my ankle.'

'Because you defied me. Had you stayed in the carriage this would not have happened.' His face inched closer to hers. His breath stirred a strand of her hair that had fallen over her eyes.

Fresh indignation at his arrogance swept away his appeal. 'How typical. It is all my fault because I did not do as you ordered.' She made an unladylike sound. 'If you had acted like a gentleman and let the step down and helped me out, I would not have had to jump out and thus injure myself.'

It was his turn to shake his head. 'Women. You have no logic.'

'And you have no feeling,' she shot back.

Fury mounted his features, but he did not reply to her taunt. 'Since there is no one of our acquaintance here, I have bespoken a room where you can refresh yourself. Then we can have some breakfast before continuing on.'

She nodded, not sure enough of her voice to answer him.

'I will take you to your room and look at that ankle. The last thing we need is for it to become severe and need a doctor's attention.'

Again she did not answer. Her thoughts were a jumble. Nor did the press of his chest against the side of her bosom or his arms so intimately around her waist and thighs help her concentration. They might as well be naked for the lack of barrier her dress and cape and his greatcoat and jacket provided. To her eternal shame, she had always reacted this carnally to his nearness. When she was young, her feelings for him had scared her. Now only shame mixed with her ardor, and she was not sure that shame was enough to keep her from succumbing to him.

They entered the building to a smiling, bowing innkeeper. The man was young and thin as a whippet. Perth passed him by with a nod. She smiled.

The smells of eggs, ham and freshly baked bread assailed her nostrils. Her stomach growled.

'Soon,' Perth said, a genuine smile tugging at the

side of his mouth for the first time since this adventure had begun.

He carried her effortlessly up a flight of stairs and down the hallway, ducking his head as the ceiling got lower. The building had been built a long time ago. Thatched roof and timbers spoke of an Elizabethan birth. The quaintness appealed to her.

Perth stopped before a door and kicked it open with his toe. He bent forward so that his chin was nearly in her bosom. Still, his head barely missed the lintel. But her nerves ran riot. She was sure his jaw had rested momentarily on the swell of her breast, leaving a hot brand and swollen flesh behind. He seemed not to notice anything.

He strode across the small room to the bed that nearly filled the space and set her carefully down. As his arms slipped away, she felt instantly bereft and vulnerable. If anything, she should feel safer without his body touching hers. Not so.

'Which ankle is it?' He knelt down and cocked his head up to look at her.

The hair sprang in thick waves from his forehead. The urge to comb her fingers through the rich mass was nearly her undoing. With a jolt, she realised what she was thinking. But it was too late. He had already seen her response.

His look turned knowing. His eyes took on a smouldering awareness that sent shocks coursing through her system. His hands slid underneath her skirt and his long fingers stroked down her left calf.

Her eyes widened as a tiny gasp escaped her.

'Wrong ankle,' she managed to say through the tightness in her chest.

His fingers shifted to her other leg, but not until he had thoroughly stroked the uninjured limb. His gaze never left her face, a face she knew betrayed every emotion she felt, every tremor of desire his touch elicited.

She felt heat mount her neck and flood her cheeks. Still, she watched his long, finely formed fingers skim over her injured ankle. He was gentle yet firm, watching her for every nuance. She winced when he pressed on a tender spot.

His attention shifted to her foot. ''Twould be best if you took off your stocking,' he murmured. 'Fetching as it is, I think there might be bruising with the swelling.'

She stared at his bent head and the proud jut of his jaw. He was a man many women desired. He looked back up at her, one dark brow raised quizzically. She started, caught once more in admiration of him.

'Leave the room, Perth, and I shall do as you request.' Her voice was husky, and she forced her jumping nerves to ease. 'Send a maid to bind the ankle. You have done enough.'

'Have I?'

He rose in one smooth, tightly controlled movement. The muscles in his thighs bunched and flexed, catching her attention as everything about him did. She turned her head away.

'I don't think so,' he said, his voice low and rough. 'I will bandage your ankle.'

Her head jerked back. 'No, you will not. Surely the innkeeper's wife knows better than you.'

'I am more skilled than you think. Wrapping your ankle will take but a few moments.' His eyes narrowed to slits when she opened her mouth to deny him. 'The less contact you have with others, the less likely anyone is to find out what has really happened to you. I am merely thinking of your reputation.'

'Are you?'

He gave her a ruthless smile that did not reach his eyes. 'Yes.'

'Do you honestly think my servants will remain quiet about what has happened? That no one will learn that I was abducted by a man?' She shook her head, wondering how naïve he thought her.

'I think that if they care for your reputation they will confide only in your family. With discretion, no one else need know.' A mocking light in the black depths of his eyes told her what he thought of her brother's ability to keep quiet.

'Mathias is many things, Perth, but he has always been concerned for my well-being.' That much at least was truth.

'As he sees it.' He left without another word.

Lillith instantly felt stranded, alone and vulnerable. She shook her head to clear away the inane thought. Better that she search for a way to escape than that she repine over Perth's departure. He meant her no good.

She slid from the bed, careful not to put her injured foot on the floor. On one leg, she hopped to the single window. From its height, she could see for miles around. Nothing but fields. Nothing that looked familiar. They had travelled a great distance.

With a sigh, she sank into the nearby chair. Its over-stuffed, chintz-covered cushions swallowed her. She leaned her head back and rested it on the well-padded chair, her eyes closing. Even were she uninjured, she would be hard-pressed to get away.

And did she want to?

He would hurt her. He would hurt her badly. Still, a part of her yearned unceasingly for what only he could give her. It had been this way since she first saw him, ten years ago. She feared the longing for him would never cease.

The sound of the door opening jerked her upright. Perth entered, his greatcoat gone and a laden tray in his hands.

'I have brought tea and cold meats and cheese.'

He laid the tray on a nearby table, then shrugged out of his navy jacket and rolled up the sleeves of his fine lawn shirt. From one of his jacket pockets he took a roll of snowy-white cloth.

'You play the servant well,' she said, an edge on the words as she fought to maintain her emotional distance.

The scar on his cheek twitched. 'How proper of you to remind me that, without good providence, I might be one.'

'That was never my intention,' she said, hurt that he thought her capable of trying to inflict pain. 'I merely meant that you do the job well.'

He turned so that his eyes bored into hers. 'My apologies, then. Your brother would not have hesitated to make the comparison and mean every cruel innuendo possible.'

She surged up, forgetting her ankle in her ire. 'My brother is a gentleman and would do no such thing. You may think what you wish of me, but leave my brother out of this. He has nothing to do with what is between us.'

The words were out of her mouth in a rush, followed by a sharp intake of breath as her ankle buckled under her weight. She sank with a moan back into the chair. Lillith squeezed her eyes shut in a futile attempt to stop the tears that sprang to her eyes. He was instantly beside her.

'You always did think your brother a paragon,' he said through clenched teeth as his fingers lifted her skirt enough to reveal her injured leg. 'You have not taken off your stocking.'

'No, I have not.' She forced the tears back even as one escaped to trickle down her cheek.

He reached up and caught the single drop on his forefinger. His touch tugged all the way to her toes. Her heart twisted in knots when he sucked the moisture from his skin, his eyes never leaving hers.

Tension mixed with anger and pain to create a heady sense of invulnerability. 'A maid would do better than you, Perth.'

'I have had plenty of practice wrapping sprains and mending breaks.'

'No doubt you have,' she said with a sardonic curl

on lip. 'Still, I think, for propriety's sake, a maid is better.'

'Propriety is not one of my concerns,' he said, stroking the inner portion of her calf. 'Discretion, yes.'

Tingles shot up her leg, making her catch her breath. 'Do you intend to seduce me? Is that what this is all about?'

The hot leap of desire in his dark eyes told her everything. But why?

'I am not in the habit of abducting women,' he murmured, never taking his gaze from her. 'When I do so, I have a purpose. You have discovered it,' he finished with a hard smile that twisted the white scar crossing his cheek. 'But first, we must make sure that you are capable of the pleasure when it comes.'

'Pleasure?' She raised one pale brow, not surprised by his confidence so much as irritated at his assumption that she would succumb to him.

His hand slipped higher, igniting sparks along her inner leg. His eyes never left hers. When she gasped in surprise and...pleasure...at his touch, his smile hardened. Only then did she jolt into complete realisation of what he did.

Her hand met his face in a loud smack that surprised her. It had been unconscious. His head jerked, the cheek with his scar reddened.

'I...I...' She floundered. 'You go too far, Perth,'

'I don't go far enough. Not yet.' His voice was cold. His hand dropped back to her ankle. 'Remove your stocking or I will do so.'

His change of topic took her breath away. He always had been mercurial.

'Leave the room and I will.'

Disgust twisted his mouth. 'We have been down that road before.'

Without waiting for a reply, he slid both hands up her leg to her knee. His nimble fingers caught hold of her garter and pulled it off. The stocking sagged to her ankle and he rolled the delicate silk covering from her foot. In spite of his gentleness, her ankle was swollen and the removal hurt. Lillith bit her inner cheek and held her breath to keep from crying in pain.

Perth frowned. 'This should have been wrapped immediately.'

'I shall be fine if you will leave me alone and allow me to rest.'

'You will be fine after this is wrapped and you have stayed off it for several days at the least.'

She opened her mouth to retort, but he started wrapping the roll of linen around her ankle and the agony took away all thought of what she had intended to say. For long minutes she alternated holding her breath with shallow breathing. Neither helped. She closed her eyes and tried to think of something different, something pleasant. All she could think about were Perth's eyes when his hands had slid up her leg, his passion riding him like a demon. She gave up.

She opened her eyes and noted that his no longer held emotion. 'That hurt. I am sorry,' he said quietly.

She nodded, not trusting herself to speak without crying.

He opened a flask and poured a thick liquid, then diluted it with a brown liquid and held the mixture to her. 'Drink this. It will help.'

'Laudanum?'

'You should have had it before, but somehow it did not work that way,' he said with a wry twist of full lips.

Still unwilling to speak much, she took the glass and downed the bitter drink in one long gulp. It hit her empty stomach like a bomb.

She gasped and coughed. 'What was that?' she asked when she finally caught her breath.

'Laudanum,' he said, rising in one swift, fluid motion so that his powerful legs were close enough she could run her hands down his flanks.

She shook her head to try and clear it. 'Yes, I know there was laudanum in it. But what else?'

'Scotch whisky,' he said shortly. 'The combination should take care of any lingering discomfort. We have a long way to go today and cannot afford to stay here any longer.' He cast a rueful glance at the tray of food. 'I have ordered a packed lunch and a flask of tea.'

'I shall have to be more suspicious of what you feed me,' she managed to whisper, even though the concoction threatened to spin her head.

'Yes, you shall,' he said, moving to the bed and yanking off the quilt. In several swift strides he was beside her again and threw the cover over her shoulders.

'What are you doing?' she asked, batting ineffectually at the quilt. 'I have a cape, thank you.'

'Yes, you do and it is safely in the coach. Summer is over although autumn is not yet upon us. Later this evening the air will be cool and this will keep you warm for I intend to travel straight through to our destination.'

She tried to push the thing away, but his hands held it secured at her throat as he leaned down so that his face was inches from hers. Without warning, his mouth crushed hers. His lips moved against hers and his tongue swept inside. Lillith's head fell back as he deepened the kiss. Her senses swirled out of control. Her spine arched and to her shame, she would have clasped her hands in his hair had they not been secured under the quilt.

Finally, when she thought that her mind and body were no longer hers to command, he ended the kiss. Her eyelids were heavy as leaded weights, her abdomen was a pool of lava. Yet when she forced her eyes open, his met hers with cool detachment. Her world had spun out of control while he had cold-heartedly seduced her.

Shame flooded her cheeks.

'Bas—' His fingers pressed against her lips, keeping her from saying the only word she knew that adequately described him.

'Careful, Lady de Lisle. You don't want to say things you will regret later.'

'I will regret nothing later,' she stated. *Except that kiss and my response.* She turned away from his knowing look and wished for the strength to resist him.

Before she could think of anything else to say or

try once more to free herself from the heavy folds of cloth, he swept her up into his arms. Her hair, already loose, tumbled down her back. Disgusted by her cowardice and yet unwilling to look at the faces of anyone who would see her in this wanton position, she turned her face against his shoulder and let the length of her hair cover her face.

It was not so easy to shut out the sensations that Perth's closeness ignited in her body. She felt every beat of his heart and every breath he took.

She trembled as he carried her from the room and down the stairs, the food uneaten and forgotten. Even her stocking lay unmissed in the room.

Chills set in, making her shake. Chills that no amount of warmth or covering could abate. He scared her, but her reaction to him scared her even more.

Chapter Three

The inside of the carriage was smaller than Lillith remembered. Perth sat across from her, his knees meeting hers. This had not occurred before. Her nerves jangled.

'Are you hungry?' Perth asked, opening the basket packed by the innkeeper.

Roast beef and fresh baked bread assaulted her nostrils. Belatedly, she remembered the food left uneaten in the inn and her stocking left for someone else to find. Her stomach rumbled. 'That would certainly help ease the effects of your concoction,' she said tartly, wishing something could ease the longing she felt for him.

'Food will help,' he agreed. 'You will need another dose in a couple of hours if you are to keep the pain at bay. You should eat something before then.'

She grimaced. Much as she disliked the mixture, he was right. Her ankle had hurt so badly and now it was a dull throb. She even thought she might be able to escape if the sensation stayed at this level.

He eyed her. 'I am sure you feel much better, but you still are in no shape to stand on that foot.'

Had he read her mind? Or had her face been that transparent? She had never been good at hiding her emotions.

Her much older brother, Mathias, had known instantly ten years before when she'd first fallen in love with Perth. Mathias had told her then that she should never play cards. Her face gave away every thought and feeling she had. De Lisle, on the other hand, had called her a cold fish with a face that showed nothing. Thank goodness for that. However, it seemed that, like Mathias, Perth could read her like a well-marked map.

She sighed as she took the plate of cold beef and buttered bread Perth handed across the too-small space separating them. She was ravenous. The first bites hit with a soothing effect that went a long way to calming her nerves. Several mouthfuls later, Perth handed her a heavy earthenware mug filled with steaming hot tea. She drank it in large gulps.

'Easy,' he muttered. 'You will make yourself ill.'

She continued drinking. 'I was hungry and thirsty. You are less than gracious to your unwilling guests.'

He shrugged, the greatcoat he had put back on emphasising his broad shoulders. 'You had only to ask.'

She made an unladylike face and nearly spilled what little remained of her tea. 'Yes, and you would have told me to wait until we stopped.'

'Probably,' he agreed, finishing off his large helping of food. He took a gold flask out of the side pocket in the coach and took a swig.

Lillith smelled the distinct odour of the brown liquid he had put in with her laudanum. She shuddered. 'How can you drink that barbarous stuff? It is like swallowing liquid fire.'

He eyed her. 'Have you ever swallowed fire?' he asked flatly, a jaundiced look on his face.

'Of course not. That is merely a manner of speech.'

'As are so many other words,' he said harshly. 'I happen to like whisky. It burns going down but I know what I'm drinking. It is honest. Not many things in life are.' He took another swig. 'I always know what to expect from it.'

She set her empty plate and mug beside her on the leather seat before primly folding her hands in her lap. 'Are you talking about something besides whisky?'

'We are talking about whatever you think we are talking about,' he answered.

'I don't play riddle games,' she said on a sniff.

'Neither do I—any more.'

He replaced the flask and turned his attention to the outside. Fields lay fallow. Sheep roamed everywhere. Occasionally they passed a farmhouse. The road itself was dirt and it would be a morass in the rain. Still, they kept a good pace.

'Will we be at your destination soon?' she asked.

'Soon enough.'

He did not even look at her. Frustration made her itch to thump him on the chest and demand that he pay attention to her. But she did nothing. Instead, she took several deep breaths and tried to calm herself. They did no good.

'Why are you doing this?' she finally asked. 'Why now after all this time?'

Still he did not look at her. She thought he did not intend to answer her. She was wrong.

'You are a widow now.'

Long minutes went by. Lillith waited with all the patience at her command for him to continue. She started twiddling with her fingers. Thankfully the gloves she wore kept her from picking at her nails, a bad habit she had developed shortly after marrying de Lisle.

'I have been a widow for just over a year.'

'The proper time of mourning,' he murmured. Without warning he turned and his dark eyes bored into her. 'A year would hardly be time enough to get over someone you truly and deeply loved.'

She felt under attack. She suspected there were things he was not saying. His words hinted at meanings other than those he spoke directly of. He seemed to think she should understand what he really meant and she did not. Her sense of ill usage mounted.

'What are you really talking about?' she demanded.

His countenance darkened. Instead of speaking, he retrieved his cane and used it to bang on the roof again. Within minutes the carriage came to a halt. He flung open the door and jumped out. His greatcoat flapped in the wind and his pale cheeks took on a ruddy hue. He signalled to his groom and was soon mounted on the horse he had ridden while abducting her.

Her sense of ill usage intensified until she wanted

to stick her head out of the window and scream at him. What kind of understanding could they reach when he would not talk to her?

None. Absolutely none.

Time passed and Lillith struggled under its slow hand. Never one to remain idle for even short periods, this enforced inactivity for long hours was trying. A book, her needlework, even mending would be welcome. Anything to occupy her mind and keep her from brooding on Perth and his intentions, which she knew to be dishonourable.

What had been a dull throb in her ankle had increased to nearly the original pain. That did nothing to improve her disposition. Nor did having to admit to herself that Perth's remedy of laudanum and whisky had worked and would very likely work again.

With a sigh of defeat, she picked up the gold-handled cane Perth had discarded on the seat across from her and rapped the roof. The Earl, drat his sense, had been right in that she needed to mend quickly and constant pain did not help achieve that end.

The carriage rolled to a reluctant halt. The wheels had barely stopped when Perth pulled open the door and scowled at her.

'Are you worse?'

His voice was deep and, if she had not known better, she would have said worried. She frowned at him, not wanting to tell him she wanted another draught of his concoction, but knowing it would be for the best.

She had never been good at defeat—no matter who her opponent was.

'Yes.' She watched his black brows raise in sardonic acceptance.

'Do you want another draught?'

Her frown deepened. 'Are you going to stoop so low as to make me beg?'

'I am simply looking for clarification.'

She gripped her hands together. 'You are plainly looking to provoke me, which you are all too ready to do. Yes. Yes, I would like another measure of that swill you call a remedy. Is that clear enough? Are you satisfied?'

He made her a mock bow and entered the carriage and pulled several vials from the leather pocket on his side of the seat. Knowing she could have made the medicine herself had she known where everything was did not make her feel better. Within minutes he handed her the earthenware mug. She took it with ill-concealed ire.

She gulped down the whisky and laudanum in two gulps. Her eyes watered. In spite of her intention to remain stoic while the mixture burned its way down her throat and to her ankle, she ended up coughing.

'Some tea would help,' Perth said almost gently.

She gasped in deep breaths. 'Please.'

He took the mug from her unresisting fingers and filled it. She took it back and sipped at the soothing drink. She had never been one to drink strong alcohol. Her father and brother's examples had been enough for her to see the harm. She was not even fond of ratafia, its sweet almond flavour cloying to her sense of smell and taste. Thus the strong liquor went right to her head.

'That should help the pain and allow you to sleep,' Perth said.

She looked at him with jaundice. 'In a moving carriage?'

'You did once before.'

She could not argue the fact. 'How much longer?' she asked, thinking from a distance cushioned by the alcohol that she sounded much like a child.

He answered her with the obvious patience one would show to a recalcitrant child. 'One more change of horses and then we should arrive by midnight.'

'You planned well,' she muttered. 'Posting spare horses.'

His lips twisted. 'Wealth has its privileges.'

Even in her present haze, she could not mistake the bitterness in his tone. Somehow it hurt her to hear him this way. 'You were not always so jaded.'

'Ten years ago I was young and idealistic. Today I am much more experienced.' His voice was cold as a Scottish winter wind.

'We are back to words within words,' she said. 'Ten years ago I married de Lisle. Is that what you are referring to?'

'Ten years ago you left me waiting.' He leaned his head to one side. A ray of late afternoon sunshine caught the scar on his right cheek and turned it fiery red. 'I waited until evening, thinking you had been unable to escape.'

'Mathias was supposed to meet you and tell you that I was no longer able to wed you against the wishes of my family.'

His laugh was short and hard. 'The family that sold you to a shrivelled-up old man with enough money to pay your brother's gaming debts.' His voice deepened. 'Well, Mathias did not arrive till late.'

Her first inclination was to defend her family. But he was right as far as it went. She had jilted him for an older, wealthy man and for the reason he said. And, if Perth were to be believed, Mathias had not acted as quickly as he had assured her he would.

'I did nothing that is not done every day by members of our class.' Her words slurred slightly and in spite of their argument, her eyelids were heavy. The medicine was making her drowsy despite the acrimony that flowed between them. She wondered if a wish to escape from this hurtful airing of truth was also behind her creeping exhaustion.

'True.' His voice now held no emotion. It was as though, having had his say, all the emotion that might have held sway over him was gone.

'And I did not know that Mathias took so long to reach you. For that I am sorry.'

He continued to scrutinise her. There was an ugly gleam in his eye that made her wonder if she had mistaken his lack of emotion. She wondered if there were things she did not know. Mathias had never told her about that meeting. She had never been brave enough to ask.

'Don't be. It was a salutary lesson in the workings of your family.'

She was the first to look away. Much as she had tried not to think too deeply on it, she knew her family had not treated him well. Leaving him at the altar of the small country church where she had promised to meet him to be married by special licence was not done. Her only balm had been to know that eloping with her lover was not acceptable either. No, she never should have embroiled herself with a penniless young army officer, no matter how much she had loved him. Her family had never made any secret of the need for her to marry well. She had let her emotions rule her for a brief, bitterly regretted period.

Now she was reaping the harvest her rash actions had sown. No, not just now. She had been doing so for the last ten years. De Lisle had never trusted her and had made her life a misery because of that. Nor had the *ton* ever accepted her. A woman who jilts one lover and then has a duel fought over her between that lover and her new husband is never accepted. That taint was still with her. This abduction, when word got out as it inevitably would, would ruin her completely. Perhaps that was Perth's intention. And perhaps it no longer mattered. She preferred the country.

When she glanced back at him, his head was turned away. He lounged back, his beaver hat at an angle that shaded his eyes. His hands rested in his lap. His legs stretched across the space separating their seats. His dusty Hessian boots were scant inches from her slip-pered feet. Perfectly at his ease, he appeared to have fallen asleep.

All the emotional turmoil of the last minutes seemed to have been sloughed from his shoulders like so much baggage that is disposed of without a second thought. How she wished she might forget the past ten years.

She woke at the sudden cessation of sound. She sat up and looked out. Flambeaux illuminated a small, boxy and symmetrical building made of what appeared to be butter-coloured stone. She wondered if they were in the Cotwolds. They could have reached here in the time they had been travelling.

Perth opened the door before she had the chance to notice much else. He extended his hand to help her down.

For an instant, she thought about resisting, but the firm line of his jaw told her plainly that he was in no mood to countenance defiance. Very likely he would merely reach in and haul her out.

She took his hand and allowed him to help her. A good thing, too. Her head ached from the whisky and laudanum. She told herself that was the reason the feel of her gloved hand in his gloved hand had felt so intimate. But she knew it was only a sop. She had always been attuned to him physically and emotionally.

When he released her, she managed to stand without his help, most of her weight on her good leg. The medicine had not been good for her head, but it had helped her ankle. She took a deep breath and looked

around, determined not to feel so acutely Perth's nearness.

Immaculate lawns stretched out like a velvet skirt
in the silver light of the moon. Birch trees ringed the
circular drive. Roses in their last gasp decorated the
borders, their scent perfuming the air.

'Your hunting box?' she asked.

'My retreat,' he countered. 'This is not hunting
country.'

That did not tell her much.

Without a word, he went to talk with his coachman.
His words drifted to her on the breeze.

'Take the horses and men back to town. I will notify
you when I want you to return.'

He was stranding them here. She took a step toward
them, intending to tell Perth she had no intention of
staying here indefinitely, but her bad leg buckled
again. She caught herself with a painful gasp.

'Stubborn,' Perth said, striding to her side and
swinging her up into his arms—again.

'I am heartily sick of this position,' she muttered,
angling her head so that she did not look at him.

'But I am not,' he said, holding her a little tighter.

She suppressed a moan. Even through the layers of
their clothing, it seemed that his body burned into hers.
The scent of him assaulted her senses. She remembered the first time she had been this close to him. She
had been intoxicated by delight.

They had only just met the night before at Almack's. He had asked her to dance two country dances
and then left. Now he was calling on her, along with

several other gentlemen. But he was the only one she could remember, the others having vanished into the past. He had leaned over to take a cup of tea from her and the hint of cinnamon had wafted over her. With a quizzical look, she had met his eyes—and been lost.

His warm breath moved over the nape of her neck sending little currents of excitement skidding down her spine and bringing her back to the present in a sensual rush. This compromising position had to end.

She twisted in his hold. 'Let me down. I am perfectly capable of standing on my own.'

He mounted the last steps and entered the house. 'Of course.'

He set her down abruptly. His arm fell away from her legs first, leaving them wobbly. Then he released her back. She was on her own, standing in the elegantly furnished foyer of his house.

'Milord,' a man said, coming hastily in through a side door.

He was short, slim and bandy-legged. His hair was brown peppered with grey. A short beard, neatly trimmed, spoke of independence. It was not fashionable to have a beard. He wore a serviceable country jacket and breeches that had seen newer days. Still, he had an air of dependability about him.

'Fitch, I trust everything is ready?'

The little man drew himself up ramrod straight. 'I should hope so, milord.'

For only the second time since Perth had abducted her, she saw him genuinely smile. 'A manner of speech only, Fitch. I never doubted for a second your ability.'

Only slightly mollified, the servant looked at her. His lively gaze took in everything about her. He nodded as though agreeing with his own assessment.

She held out her hand. It was not the accepted thing to do with servants, but she sensed there was more between this man and Perth than servant and master.

'I am Lillith, Lady de Lisle,' she said.

Fitch took her hand and bowed over it. Very continental. 'I am Fitch. His lordship's batman.' He released her hand.

'Batman?' she asked.

'And general factotum,' Perth said. 'He has been with me since I first entered the army.'

Lillith's smile faded. And he undoubtedly knew exactly what had happened ten years ago. She was to be held prisoner by two men who had no reason to care about what was best for her.

'I have dinner almost done and her ladyship's room ready,' Fitch said, stepping back.

'Roast beef and potatoes,' Perth said.

'If you wanted French food, then you should hire yourself a Frenchie to cook it,' Fitch said. 'I am an honest Englishman and I cook like one.'

'With a Gaelic man's sensibilities,' Perth said, a spark of humour in his grey, nearly black eyes. Changing the subject, he said, 'I will take Lady de Lisle to her room so she can freshen up and then we shall be very glad of supper.'

Lillith edged away, refusing to grimace as her ankle made itself known. 'Lady de Lisle will take herself.'

Both men looked at her. Perth dark and sardonic, Fitch with his brows pinched in worry.

She gritted her teeth and hobbled to the staircase. The solid mahogany wood was a burnished auburn. Taking a deep breath, she leaned on the banister so that it took her weight and hopped up the first step on her good leg. Three stairs later, she stopped to catch her breath. Looking up she nearly groaned. It seemed that the next floor was in the sky. Her stubbornness had gotten her into difficult scrapes before, but none this physically trying.

'Perhaps you would care to lean on me, my lady,' Fitch said from where he stood at the bottom of the staircase.

Three steps and she was winded and her good calf threatened to cramp. 'Perhaps I would, Fitch,' she said, measuring each word for they cost her dearly. At least it would not be Perth helping her.

She glanced at the Earl. He stood where she had left him. His hooded eyes watched her like those of a bird of prey that was keeping in sight its next meal. From somewhere, she found enough energy to toss her head in defiance. Her hair swirled around her shoulders, but when all was done the small act of rebellion did nothing to make her feel better.

Fitch was beside her, his shoulder fitted under her arm, and still Perth did not move or say a word. As she continued up the stairs she felt his gaze on her back. A scorching awareness engulfed her and would not leave no matter how she tried to put him from her mind or how she panted in exhaustion.

'We are nearly there, Lady de Lisle,' Fitch said, his nasal voice pitched to give encouragement. 'Not much more and you will be able to rest. I will prepare a nice hot bath for you. That will help.'

She nodded. There was not enough air in her lungs to speak. Her left leg burned with exhaustion. For a fleeting moment she allowed herself to imagine being carried by Perth. He might excite her and make her unsure of herself, but he never made her so tired she wanted to collapse and cry in frustration.

They reached the first-floor landing long after Lillith had decided she could go no further. And she still had to get to her room. A sigh escaped her clenched lips.

'Enough,' Perth said from right behind her.

Lillith started. She had been so focused on preparing herself for the next ordeal that she had not heard him follow.

'Enough what?' she panted. 'I will say when I have had enough, not you. 'Tis bad enough that I am here against my will.'

She felt Fitch stiffen, but the man said nothing. Just as well. She was rapidly descending into a horrible mood and Perth did not look any merrier. He never had liked having his will thwarted. For that matter, neither did she.

'You will hurt yourself worse if you keep this up.'

'I will do as I please.' She lifted her chin and took a deep breath. She would hop to wherever her room was. 'Where do I go?'

Perth made a sound that she chose to ignore.

'It is this way, Lady de Lisle,' Fitch said, once more extending his arm.

'Don't be any more stupid than you must,' Perth growled. 'Use this.' He thrust the cane from the carriage into her right hand. 'It is not ideal, but it is better than what you intended.'

She suppressed a sigh of relief. Much as she desired to show the Earl that she would do as she pleased, she had not looked forward to more hopping. Her fingers curled around the gold knob. She had large hands for a woman, but the handle of the cane was nearly too big. But then Perth was a tall man.

With Fitch guiding her, Lillith started down the carpeted hallway. Her right shoulder ached abominably from using her right arm so much for support and her left leg felt ready to crumble for the same reason. Somehow she held her back straight. Fortunately, they did not have far to go. This was not a large house by aristocratic standards.

Fitch opened the door with an economy of motion and followed her in. The room was delightful. Mellow yellows and creams graced the walls and curtains. A large bed took up most of one wall. Burl walnut furniture, a table and two cosy chairs, grouped around a cheery fire. Her spirits lifted.

'Here, Lady de Lisle,' Fitch said, moving to her side. 'Let me help you now. His lordship has stalked off to his room. You have no need to further tax yourself.'

This manservant was a knowing one. She slanted him a look. 'Your master is overbearing.'

'He does have that habit, my lady. It comes of being in the army for so many years.' He deposited her in a cream-coloured chair before moving to one of the three doors in the room and opened it. 'This is where your clothes are, my lady. And if you will be so kind as to rest, I will have your bath prepared shortly.'

'A bath?' Just the thought was divine. The pleasure was fleeting as she remembered his other words. 'Clothes? Those are not mine.'

So Perth used this house to entertain women. She should not be surprised or hurt by that. Many men did the same thing. Her brother was one. Still, knowing that Perth considered her no better than one of his lightskirts hurt—hurt badly.

She told herself she was a fool, but that did not ease the tightness in her chest. He had abducted her and kept her with him for nearly an entire day against her will. This latest was nothing. Nothing, she told herself.

'Pardon me, Lady de Lisle,' Fitch said, interrupting her internal tirade. 'But his lordship had them specially made and brought from London for you.' There was a kindness around his brown eyes. 'Lord Perth does not bring women here. This is where he comes to be alone. You are the first woman he has entertained here.'

The vise around her chest seemed to loosen and breathing was just a little bit easier. Once more she was being a ninny where Perth was concerned. When would she learn? Still, she felt better.

Her innate graciousness surfaced. Fitch was not responsible for his master's actions. 'This is a delightful room. And I should be very grateful of a hot bath. It has been a long journey.'

Fitch nodded. 'I know, my lady. I will have everything quickly.'

As soon as the door closed behind Fitch, Lillith let herself completely relax. Her head fell back to rest on the stuffed chair and her eyes drifted shut. Even her ankle seemed to ache less. She dozed off.

Too soon she heard a loud knock. 'Come in.'

Fitch stood in the doorway, wrestling with a hip tub. 'I am sorry that we don't have anything larger, my lady, but this is all I can handle. His lordship has sent away all the servants except me.'

'Whyever for?' she asked. 'This is a great burden on you.'

Fitch pushed the tub across the rug until it sat directly in front of the fire. With the expertise of practice, he draped large towels around the tub.

'His lordship does not want word of your presence to leak out.'

She made a very unladylike noise. 'He should have worried about that before he kidnapped me.'

Fitch did not reply. 'I shall be right back with several buckets of hot water.'

'Your master should be helping you,' Lillith shot back as Fitch closed the door behind himself.

'I intend to do so,' Perth said.

Chapter Four

'Wha—?'

Lillith twisted around to see one of the three doors opened and Perth standing on its threshold. He filled the space and made her nerves jump.

Suspicion raised its ugly head. 'Where does that door go?' she demanded.

He smiled, a brief stretching of firm lips. 'To my room.'

The breath caught in her throat. 'I might have guessed,' she said bitterly. 'You are determined to make this as unpleasant as you can for me.'

His look turned thunderous. 'I don't have to try. You are already doing everything possible towards that end.'

He pushed off from the door jamb and sauntered towards her. His jacket was gone and his cravat missing. The white lawn shirt he wore had the top two buttons undone.

Black hairs curled enticingly over the edges of his shirt. She could imagine how crisp they would feel against her fingers. Her right hand lifted before she realised what she was doing. She dropped it to her lap with a lack of grace that was unusual. A blush suffused her face.

How many times must she make a fool of herself over this man? It seemed too many.

'Do you not know how to knock?' she said, putting all her frustration at herself into the words. Petty as her demand had sounded, it did stop his progress towards her. That was a great relief to her strained nerves.

'When it pleases me.' His gaze ran over her. 'You are exhausted. As soon as your bath is over we will eat and then you will go to bed.'

Go to bed.

Chills chased up her spine followed closely by lightning. This was the situation she had both dreaded and desired. For too long, she had wondered what it would be like to make love with him. But not like this. Not for revenge.

Before she could think of something to say, there was a knock on the door to the hall. 'Come in,' she said, her voice a little too husky.

Fitch entered with two pails of steaming water. He glanced at Perth on his way to the tub. Just seeing the hot water and smelling the lilac-scented soap that Fitch pulled from one pocket momentarily took Lillith's focus off the earl.

Longing must have shown blatantly on her face for Perth said, 'I will go with you, Fitch. Lady de Lisle seems ready to dive into the two inches of water and it would be better if she could submerse herself.'

Both men left. Lillith gave herself several deep breaths before forcing her weight up on to her good foot and the cane. She crossed to the hip bath and picked up the soap. She smelled the creamy bar. She had been right. It was lilac. Perth had remembered what she wore.

Her heart did a painful flutter. Such a small thing, and yet to her it spoke of deeper emotions than she could have hoped for. Carefully, she set the soap back onto the special ledge built into the tub and then moved to the door Perth had entered through. She stopped on the threshold.

Her eyes narrowed as she examined the room. This one was masculine to her feminine. Deep forest green and beige curtains covered the window and the same colours lay on the wood floor in a thick carpet. Heavy mahogany furniture—a large bed and chairs and a table—took up most of the room. A toiletry stand was in a corner where the morning light would hit the attached mirror. He spent time here.

His coat, greatcoat and muddy boots were cast aside. Fitch had not been here to tidy.

'Do you find my room interesting?' Perth's deep voice said from directly behind her.

She whirled around, taken by surprise, and the cane twisted from her grasp. She hastily gripped the side of the door and her free hand went to her throat. She had been so engrossed in examining his room that she had not heard him return.

Instantly on the defensive, she demanded, 'Why are we in adjoining rooms?'

He smiled, slow and lazy with a nearly feral gleam. 'For every reason you imagine.'

The pulse at her throat pounded. 'You are fantasising if you think I will participate in anything with you.'

He took a step closer. 'Once you would have done anything I asked.'

She drew herself back, wishing she could disappear because she knew in her heart that what he said was true. She lied. 'You always did think highly of your skills. It seems little has changed.'

He chuckled, but it was not with mirth or with kindness. 'I know you, Lillith. You might have left me at the altar because of your brother's need, but that does not change the fact that you wanted me then and you want me now.'

He took another step towards her. This time she had to edge back. His scent threatened to overpower her as his maleness already overwhelmed her. Somehow, she managed to hold herself high as though she had not just retreated from his assault.

'Right now all I *want* is a bath.' She consciously dropped her hand from her throat. 'If you will move, I will go back to the chair and rest until you and Fitch are done.'

The manservant entered her room just then with more water. For the first time, she noticed that Perth also held two pails. The effect he had on her was not reassuring.

He made her a slight, mocking bow before taking his buckets to the bath and emptying them. Fitch did the same. Steam rose from the little tub.

Longing expanded in her chest. She needed that bath. She felt filthy and tired and utterly exhausted.

Perth must have seen her need. 'We will bring one more round and then it should be ready for you.'

She nodded, not trusting her voice to sound nonchalant. This time when they left, she made her slow, painful way back to the chair. Laying the cane on the floor beside her, she bent over and pulled off her slippers. The delicately embroidered leather was beyond repair. They would do for the present, but she would never be able to wear them in public again. Little matter. She had dozens of shoes, as she had dozens of everything. She had married for money and made sure that she enjoyed what it could provide.

Knowing Perth and Fitch would return soon, she quickly undid her one remaining blue satin garter and then unrolled her silk-knit stocking from her left leg. The stocking was dust-stained and frayed around the top. The last night and day had brought heavy use to her clothing. Next she gingerly unwrapped the linen from her right ankle. The lack of support when she was finished made her ankle start to ache again. Still, the swelling was down and she did not think it looked as bruised.

No sooner had she neatly folded the stocking and wrap and placed them with the garter than Perth returned. This time he said nothing, merely casting a glance at her, before he dumped the water. Fitch followed suit and left.

She raised both silver-blonde brows when Perth remained. 'I intend to thoroughly enjoy this comfort, Perth, but not until you leave.'

He set his buckets down on the fireplace's hearth. 'How do you intend to undress?'

Nonplussed, her mouth dropped. 'Not with your help!'

That knowing, dangerous smile returned. 'You have no lady's maid.'

'I am not a cripple. I can take care of myself.'

'Can you?' He leaned back against the mantel so that his broad shoulders rested comfortably against the creamy marble. 'I did not know you were a contortionist.'

She drew herself ramrod straight, or as straight as the overly-cushioned chair would allow. 'I do not need your assistance. And if I did need help, it would not be you I would turn to.'

'Fitch?'

She glared at him. 'Before you, yes.'

'I see.' He pushed away from the mantel and left the room.

Her eyes widened at his abrupt and unexpected departure. She had routed him too easily. Still, she did not intend to waste any more time.

Without more ado, she twisted her arms up and back and strained her fingers to reach the tiny buttons that held her gown closed. The first three buttons were easy. She swallowed a growl of frustration. Rearranging her arms, she undid the buttons at her waist and below. The ones smack in the middle of her back remained securely closed.

The temptation to rip the gown off was strong. But dirty as it was, she would rather wear it again than anything Perth had bought for her. She willed herself to calm down.

She would stand up and try pulling the gown up enough that the buttons were higher on her back. It worked.

The fine muslin evening dress fell from her body and puddled in a dingy white heap. Only her chemise remained. Fastened with silk ties, it was easily discarded.

Once more using the cane, she hobbled to the tub. Somehow she managed to get in. A sigh of unadulterated pleasure left her as she sank into the steaming hot water. A pillow, another dose of Perth's medicine and she could stay like this all night.

She let the heat soak some of the soreness from her muscles. Even her ankle felt better for the hot water.

With arms gone soft from relaxation, she lifted her hair so that it fell down her back and into the water. Clean hair would add to her comfort. It did not matter that she could not dress her hair afterward. She would braid it.

Quickly she lathered with the lilac soap and rinsed off. When she was done, the room was engulfed in scent. She allowed herself to rest her head on the part of the tub designed for that and closed her eyes. Soon the water would be too cool for comfort, but for the moment it was bliss. Later she would have to wrestle with getting out.

She dozed, only to waken with a mouthful of soapy water. Taken unawares, she flailed at the water, sending sprays onto the surrounding towels. Coughing assailed her.

Strong hands hooked under her arms and pulled her up and out of the tub. A large drying sheet fell on her shoulders and hung to her bare feet. Water dripped unheeded on to the floor.

Still coughing, she pushed back a strand of damp hair with one hand and held the sheet at her neck with the other. Only one person would be in here. Cinnamon assailed her even as intense awareness made the hair at her nape stand up.

Perth.

The urge to turn so that she found herself in his arms was great. She felt the heat of his body, so close to hers that any movement would cause them to touch. She was so weak where he was concerned.

She did not turn around. 'Please go.'

His hands caught her shoulders and gently turned her, the way she had just wished to move. She lifted her chin in defiance of him and of her reactions to him. His mouth was close enough that she could touch it with hers by standing on tiptoe.

Her ankle started throbbing again. She shifted her weight to her good leg.

'Go away,' she said, unable to keep her petulance out of her voice. Things with him were so incredibly difficult. 'I do not feel well.'

He did not budge. 'You need more medicine. And food.'

'What I need is for you to leave me alone.' She sighed, gripping the sheet around her as though it were the only thing that kept her safe. 'If you truly want to help me, then let me eat alone and give me another draught of your concoction and then let me be.'

The sharp blackness of his unfathomable eyes clouded. His gaze lowered and his face took on a tension that sharpened the angle of his jaw. She looked down and saw that the sheet was damp and clung to her like a second skin, leaving nothing to his imagination. He took a deep breath that shuddered through his body and released her so suddenly that she stumbled.

'Not now. Not yet,' he said in a voice uneven from suppressed longing. He dragged his attention from her body. 'I will bring you food and medicine, but I will not leave you alone. Not yet.'

She gripped the edge of the tub and started to shiver. He mistook it for cold. He went to the fireplace and stirred the coals into a blazing heat. Several swift strides later and he was in the room with the clothing. He returned with a royal purple robe made of brocaded silk. He laid it on the nearby chair and left without another word.

Lillith gaped. His departure had been too easy to be permanent. She quickly dried and donned the robe. It fit as though it had been made to her measurement. She belted it securely. Only then did she look around for a brush, knowing there would be one. Perth had thought of everything so far, she did not think he would fail here.

She was right. A gold-embossed brush with matching comb and mirror reposed on a woman's dresser. She hobbled to it and then back to the chair. She was beginning to think of the overstuffed seat as an old friend that welcomed her with cushioned arms. She sank into it and began to carefully untangle her fair hair.

She had barely finished one strand before Perth returned with a laden tray. He set the food and beverage on the table and moved everything closer to her. The aroma of mutton and mint sauce made her stomach growl.

Serviceable plates, flatware and mugs made place settings. Simple and sturdy like a man would use if he did not care what others thought of the table he set. Nothing was monogrammed with his coat of arms.

She watched him like a mouse watches the cat before it springs. The brush slipped from her fingers and fell to the carpet where it lay ignored. The urge to jump up and pace the room made her fingers knot into the folds of the robe. The inability to release some of her tension tightened her mouth.

'Drink this.'

Perth held out a mug she knew contained his cure-all. The strong, musty smell of Scotch assaulted her. The drink would ease some of her anxiety as well as help her ankle. She took it and swallowed quickly, only to nearly cough the liquid up.

'Wha-what did you do? Double the dose?' she gasped.

The mug dangled from her forgotten grip and Perth caught it just before it fell. 'I decided that you need a good night's sleep more than I need what I brought you here to have.'

She gulped hard and her eyes watered. She felt as though someone had ignited a bomb inside her ribs. But there was more. Tendrils of excitement twisted through her limbs. Her mouth turned suddenly dry.

She took several more deep breaths and pushed her palms against her stomach in an attempt to stop it from somersaulting. She picked her words carefully.

'You intend to spare me your attentions?'

That was not what she had meant to say. The last thing she needed to do was provoke him, yet here she was doing that exact thing. What had got into her? But she knew. Desire. Desire for him. Only for him.

His mouth thinned into a sword-sharp line. 'For tonight.' He spun on his heel and went to the door that separated their rooms. 'But this is a respite only.'

All she could do was stare. A sense of bereavement moved over her like a reluctant breeze. No matter what she told herself or told him, she wanted him. She always had and always would. Still, before she slept, the door between their beds would be locked and a chair wedged under the handle. She would do the same thing under the knob for the door to the hallway.

Whether the precautions were to keep him out or keep her in, she would not even consider.

Chapter Five

Light streamed onto her face, waking Lillith and giving her a blinding headache. Her ankle added its complaint before she struggled to sit up. With blurred vision, she looked around the unfamiliar room and wondered where she was. Her sight finally focused on a man lounging at his ease in an overstuffed chair.

Perth.

Memory rushed back.

'How did you get in here?' she demanded, pushing thick strands of nearly white hair back from her face.

He eyed her steadily with no softening of his expression. 'Do not again attempt to lock me out of a room in my house.'

He did not raise his voice, but the total lack of inflection was like a whip. Instead of intimidating her, his order infuriated her.

'It is rather early for you to act the high-handed lord and master.'

Instead of having the effect she had hoped for, Perth's gaze lowered. The coldness that had made him

look formidable quickly became heated desire. She
blanched. Belatedly, she realised that the night rail she
wore was fine muslin, so fine that it was nearly translucent, and that the sheets were around her waist. She
yanked the covers to her chin.

His eyes met hers. Hot, liquid and nearly overpowering need forced her to an awareness of him that she
had tried so hard to ignore throughout the long night.

She licked lips gone dry. One hand gripped the
sheets until her knuckles turned white. The other rose
to the rapidly beating pulse at the base of her neck.

'Why?' she asked, the cry torn from her. 'Why are
you doing this?'

He rose in one lithe motion. Before she could blink,
he was on the bed, his hip a hot brand against her side,
his mouth too close to hers.

'Because I must,' he said.

She closed her eyes to the desire in his that went
beyond need to obsession. Every emotion she saw in
his face she knew to be a mirror of that in her own.
A soft moan escaped her just as his lips took hers in
a kiss that punished even as it rewarded.

His fingers tangled in her curls, holding her head
for his plunder. His tongue demanded a response. She
could not resist. They met in a battle of sensation that
set her body afire.

Her back arched and before she knew it, her fingers
dug into the thick waves of his hair, holding him as
he held her. Her mouth moved beneath his, an open
invitation to anything he asked.

Nothing mattered but the feel of him against her and in her. Nothing. She had waited too long.

She heard him groan as his mouth slipped from hers to trail down her jaw to the place where her neck and earlobe met. His tongue slicked along her skin, leaving shock and delight in its trail. Her hands fell to his shoulders where her fingers kneaded at the hard muscles. Sensation after sensation buffeted her. Desire rode her.

He shifted so that he lay lengthwise beside her. Her head fell back, giving him full access to the gentle swell of her neck and bosom, the sheet once more at her waist.

With mouth, tongue and teeth, he traced the line of her gown, never going beneath its gossamer protection. He teased her with skill and passion. She responded like a woman starved. Her body was beyond her conscious control. Instinct drove her.

Unable to withstand his assault without completion, she gripped him and pushed his mouth where she needed it. His lips closed over one breast and pulled. His teeth nipped lightly, followed by his tongue. Sharp stabs of excruciating delight shot to her gut and lower.

'Jason.' She breathed his Christian name as passion consumed all else.

He lifted his head so that his eyes, black with hunger, met hers. His nimble fingers undid the laces of her nightgown as he watched her face. With stroking movements that sent thrills along her skin, he skimmed the material from her bosom. His thumbs plucked at her nipples. Her eyes shut.

Nothing separated her flesh from him. His mouth closed over one aching breast as a hand slid down her rib cage to her thighs.

She gasped, then moaned as ecstasy caught her in its talons until a scream was torn from her lips. Not until she lay limp and replete did he stop.

Reality came back to her slowly and shamefully. Unable to meet his gaze, she flung an arm over her eyes and turned her head to the side.

'Go away,' she finally managed through lips swollen and sensitive from his kisses. 'Have you not done enough? Proven your mastery over me? Must you stay and gloat as well?'

'Look at me, Lillith.' His voice was low and harsh and full of dissatisfaction. 'I am in too much discomfort to gloat. I want you too badly, and not in the way we just shared. I want to be inside you. I want to have what you just experienced, but I want to be buried in you when I do and to feel you as you reach your pleasure with me.'

Heat that she had thought dissipated through release and shame rushed back, tightening her belly. The ache he had only just appeased started anew, stronger and more demanding. How could this be? How could she be so wanton, so…so…

'You make me your harlot,' she whispered, the words barely audible.

'No,' he denied her. 'I make you my woman. As you should have been ten years ago. I intend to claim you, to brand you with my body and my passion until no other man can satisfy you. Only then will I release you. Only then.'

Not looking at him, she did not see him move. His hand caught her wrist and pulled her arm down. His other hand threw the covers aside. No gentleness this time.

He ripped the gown from her and pillaged her. He was a pirate, raiding every secret she possessed. She rose up to meet him: passion for passion, need for need, pleasure for pleasure.

When he finally entered her, it was one powerful surge that brought them together in a meeting of male and female that took her breath away. He moved forcefully, filling her and overwhelming her. What had gone before was nothing compared to the contractions ripping her apart now.

Her back arched, her pulse pounded and a scream ripped from her. He increased his motions and covered her mouth with his, his tongue imitating their other joining. She went up and over, her release sending him to his.

Only later, as the late morning sun entered the room where they lay covered in sweat, their legs joined, did she come back to sanity. Now that he no longer made love to her.

Never had she experienced such a total and complete surfeit of physical desire. Just knowing that he could bring her such an experience again, in moments, made her desire him once more.

Her shame was tenfold. The anger she had felt upon

first awakening and realising that he had somehow broken into her room resurfaced. Only this time it was aimed at herself for her weakness, but she lashed out at him for what he had done to her and for what she had begged him to do.

'You are a rutting beast.'

The warmth that had heated his eyes turned to the sharp coldness of obsidian. 'And you are better?'

His mocking question infuriated her more. 'Get out.'

With lithe grace that took no note of his nudity, he rose from the bed and gathered his clothing. He gave her not a backward glance.

In spite of her anger and her need to have him gone, she watched him hungrily. Their passion had been white hot, with no time to savour one another. Now she drank her fill of his tall, broad-shouldered form, his lean well-muscled hips. His legs were shaped so that many a woman would sigh at the sight of them.

The only mar to his physical beauty was a series of scars criss-crossing his back. At some time he had been badly whipped. Probably while he was in the army.

The urge to go to him and run her fingers in soothing strokes over the scars was nearly irresistible. Only the knowledge that such action would end in more lovemaking stopped her.

He pulled the chair from beneath the doorknob and disappeared into his room. She felt cold and alone. No satisfaction accompanied her privacy.

She rolled to her side and curled into a tight ball.

If she squeezed herself hard enough and long enough, she might find comfort or, lacking that, the strength she needed to resist him. He had vowed to make her desire him above all else, and she already did so. Now she had to keep that from him.

Knocking, knocking, knocking. In her dream she knocked on Perth's door, demanding that he let her in. Her need for him was something she could not resist.

Knocking…

Lillith roused. This time she came instantly awake. Someone knocked on the door from the hallway. It had to be Fitch.

She pushed up in bed. Instantly, the aches from her morning activity assailed her. She was long unaccustomed to the acts she and Perth had performed.

The sheets twisted around her naked body. Her torn nightgown lay on the floor like a discarded rag. And her ankle began to throb.

'Come back later,' she managed to get out through a throat that felt swollen and sore. 'I do not feel well.'

The knocking stopped. 'I will be back, my lady, with some food and a posset.'

'Thank you, Fitch, but there is no need. I just need rest.' Exhaustion ate at her, brought about by physical exhaustion and mental dismay.

'His lordship will not agree, my lady.'

'His lordship can go—' *to hell*, she finished in her mind.

There was no answer so she assumed Fitch had left. She collapsed back on to the pillows. She needed

Perth's concoction for her ankle, a cup of strong hot tea and another bath. She needed the moon.

She forced herself to sit on the edge of the bed. The cane was propped against the wall where she had left it after climbing into bed the night before. She gripped the golden handle and gingerly lowered herself to the floor. The pain that shot up her ankle was like a slap across the face. If she had been even slightly dazed from exhaustion, she was now very much aware.

The curtains billowed into the room, the breeze from outside filling them like a ship's sails. She had closed the window before going to sleep.

She hobbled to the window and looked out. A large, old oak tree grew up the side of the house, its branches reaching close enough that an agile man could gain entrance to her room. So that was how Perth had entered. Tonight she would make sure and latch the window so that it could not be opened from the outside.

If she did not get away before then.

Moving more steadily, but no less painfully, she returned to the bed and used the cane to hook up the torn nightgown. With a snarl, she wadded it into a tight ball and stuffed it into a drawer that was filled with silk stockings and ribbon-encrusted chemises. Last night she had marvelled at all the gowns for bed, each one as gossamer as a butterfly's wing. She had wondered if Perth intended to keep her captive long enough to wear each of them. Now she wondered if one would even last a night if he gained access to her room.

A shiver of desire coursed through her. She deliberately stepped on her bad foot. The excruciating agony sent all thought of the Earl and what he might do from her mind. Biting her lip, she collapsed on to the bed. That had been a very stupid thing to do.

She fought back tears.

If only she had married him. Things would not be like this. But that was not what had happened. Long ago she had schooled herself not to look back. It only brought regret.

A knock heralded Fitch's return.

Lillith took a deep breath and pulled on the dressing gown that also lay near the bed. She was naked underneath, but there was no helping that. The way she felt right now, she could not dress herself.

'Just a minute,' she managed. Getting to the door was torture. Her abused ankle screamed at her. Before she moved the chair and unlocked the door, she asked, 'Are you alone?'

'Yes, my lady. The Earl has gone for a ride. He will not be back for some time.'

She breathed a sigh of relief.

But not until she had taken the whisky and laudanum mix and had several strong cups of tea did she relax. Fitch brought her food and she ate. He brought hot water and she washed. He found a gown she could don without help and she did so.

The situation tempted her anger to resurface. It would be so easy to become furious again, but it would accomplish nothing. She had to heal and she had to get away from Perth before he stole all her strength from her.

* * *

Perth rode like the Wild Hunt chased him. And if regret and anger and passion made up the Hunt, then it did hound him.

He had accomplished what he had set out to do. He had made her desire him, and he had made her beg for him. But that was no longer enough. He wanted more. He wanted everything she had to give. And then he wanted it to never end.

He groaned. His body was in no condition to be riding. His desire was unquenchable and though she was not near, he reacted as though she lay naked in front of him.

He laughed harshly, the sound mingling with the wind that tore at his hair and blew his coat out behind him. His gelding responded by running faster. A fence loomed ahead. They took the obstacle in one jump and continued their reckless, headstrong rush.

Only once before had Perth ridden this passionately with such disregard for his or his mount's safety. That had been ten years ago. He cursed himself for his weakness where *she* was concerned. But it did him no good.

His desire for her rode him like he rode this horse, unrelenting and without thought for the consequences. He wanted her more than he had ten years before. Ten years before he had not made love to her, felt her surround him and take him inside her body. Ten years before he had lost his heart. Today he had lost his soul.

He had to have her.

* * *

He found her sitting on a bench in his garden. The fish pond was at her feet and rabbits hopped through the grass that surrounded her. Rose bushes shaded her, the last of their flowers scenting the air.

Lillith watched him stride towards her. His hair was windblown and there was a wild glint in his dark eyes. The scar that ran the length of his right cheek stood out white and fierce.

'What are you doing here?' he demanded, sitting beside her without asking permission.

The narrow bench was barely large enough for both of them—it certainly provided no distance between them. Still, Lillith edged away until she was nearly unbalanced. It was not far enough. He radiated heat, and the smells of horse and the outdoors mingled with his cinnamon and musk.

She looked away, focusing on the distance. 'Who landscaped the grounds?'

It was an inane question, but she dared not let him pick a topic of conversation. The dark hunger in his gaze told her all too well what he would pursue.

'Capability Brown.'

A curt answer. She waited for more, sensing that nothing would be forthcoming. She licked her lips and still did not look at him. 'He achieved a fine result.'

'I think so.'

She sighed. 'I think I will go in now. It is becoming hot.' She took up the cane she had used to walk out here and levered herself to a standing position.

'How is your ankle?' he asked, standing with her.

'Better,' she answered as curtly as he had.

'Look at me,' he ordered, his voice low and demanding.

'I think not,' she said, wishing her voice did not sound so breathless.

She tried to move around him, but he gripped her wrist. His free hand cupped her chin and before she could do anything, he angled her face so that she had to look at him or close her eyes. She looked at him.

His gaze roved over her, devoured her with his intensity. She felt a flush rise up her bosom to her neck and mount her cheeks. Still, she would not relent before his onslaught and look away.

'Once is not enough,' he said, his voice low and raspy. 'I have waited too long to let you go now.'

She did not pretend to misunderstand him. 'So, you intend to continue keeping me against my will. I had thought better of you now that you have got what you set out to get.'

He flinched as though she had hit him. 'That sharp tongue of yours. I like better what you did with it this morning.'

The blush that had suffused her deepened, and once more she spoke to hurt. 'A gentleman would not mention that.'

His face whitened. 'I am not a gentleman, as we both know too well.'

Was there pain in his words? Looking at the hardness of his face, she thought she was mistaken.

'What do you intend to do, then?' she asked.

He still held her wrist. His eyes still held her captive. 'I intend to make love to you until we both can stand no more.'

His bold statement hit her like a flood and filled every empty part of her body and heart with desire for him. Somehow she managed not to fall into his arms.

She took a deep breath and shook herself as though trying to rid herself of a sensation too great to bear. 'I am hungry. Fitch said he would have dinner ready by the time you returned from your ride.'

His eyes narrowed and bitterness tinged his words. 'Nothing I have said means a thing to you.'

She glanced away from him and forced the lie to her lips. 'Nothing.'

He released her and she hobbled away, refusing to look back at him. If she did such a weak thing, he would know instantly that she had not spoken the truth.

Fitch waited inside the French doors that opened into the library. He had lit a fire that took the chill out of the air. Books lined every wall and where the shelves did not go to the ceiling, portraits filled the spaces. Warm woods and rich reds made the room cozy.

'If it pleases your ladyship, I shall serve dinner here. It is only a cold collation.'

'That will be perfect,' she said, making her way to one of the couches that flanked the fireplace. She sank deep into the burnt-red brocade cushions. 'And tea, please.'

Fitch drew himself up. 'Of course, my lady.'

She smiled. Her butler had much the same way

about him. His dignity was every bit as great as any duke's, and if the truth was told, the servant probably held himself more upright.

Fitch was barely out of the room when Perth entered. 'I take it that this is where we will be eating.'

He did not wait for an answer but moved a large table so that it stood between the two couches. Next he pulled up a straight-backed leather wing chair and sat down. Silence fell.

Outside a bird chirped. Inside the fire crackled and the mantle clock ticked. She looked everywhere but at Perth. Several books lay on the side table near her: Cicero, Scott and Byron.

'Have you read these?' she asked, attempting to ease the silent tension that engulfed them.

He glanced at the books. 'When I cannot sleep or the weather is too nasty to go out.'

'I have read Scott and Byron,' she replied.

'Everyone has read them,' he said. 'Both are lionised.'

Fitch returned with the food, putting an end to a conversation that was fast running out of steam. Perth thanked him and then waved him away.

'I will serve Lady de Lisle and myself. Go do something you would enjoy.'

Fitch looked at both of them then thought better of protesting. 'As you wish, my lord.'

Perth quirked one dark brow. 'I am not going to devour her.'

'As you say, my lord.'

Lillith studied the servant's bland face. She wondered if he meant to be as impertinent as he sounded.

'Be gone,' Perth said.

Fitch bowed himself out, but there was an air of defiance about him. He might have done as ordered, but Lillith sensed that the servant did not approve of what was going on.

They ate in silence. The hunger she had felt earlier had long passed. Nerves always affected her thusly.

Instead of ringing for Fitch when they were through, Perth cleared the table himself. He would not be gone long and Lillith decided to wait. If she went to her room, she did not doubt that he would follow. That was the last place she wanted to be with him.

When he returned, he was scowling as though he had been through something unpleasant, but he made no mention of it and she did not ask. He sat down in the same chair and stared at the fire.

'Do you play chess?' he asked without looking at her.

'Occasionally,' she answered, gratified when he gave her an irritated look.

'Will you play against me now?' he asked, his tone mocking.

''Tis better than some games we might play,' she said, striving to keep her own tone as cool as his.

He rose and fetched a chessboard and a satinwood box that held marble pieces. She watched him set up the game. His long fingers moved with a sure deftness that brought back memories of them moving over her skin. The nails were clean and well kept, as was all of him. His skin was smooth yet without softness. He was not a dandy.

When her body screamed to be touched as he touched the chess pieces, she forced her attention elsewhere. 'Twould do her no good to continue desiring him. There had to be more between them than their bodies.

'You may start.'

His deep voice startled her. She had been too intent on her emotions and had lost track of what he did.

'Oh, yes,' she muttered, reaching for a pawn and moving it recklessly.

He looked from the pawn to her face. 'You must not play much.'

Within three moves he had that pawn and a knight. Not long after he had two more pieces. She was going to lose without ever having given him a fight. Their chess was like their lovemaking. Her hackles rose at this idea. Somehow, some way, she had to resist him. He checkmated her easily.

'I will play you another game,' she said fiercely. This time she would concentrate and consider each move.

He eyed her with surprise. 'You want to be bested again? I have never taken you for a woman who likes to lose.'

She sat up straighter and scowled at him. 'I don't. I intend to win the next game.'

His smile was a lazy act that lent a slumberous slant to his eyes. The breath caught in her throat.

Without a word, he set the pieces in order once

more. This time she refused to watch him. She had no intention of being distracted.

He rose and went to a side table where a decanter of liquor sat with two glasses. 'Would you care for a drink?'

'No,' she said curtly, wrinkling her nose.

He sauntered back to his seat. ''Tis just as well.'

She glared at him. 'For once you are right. My brother drinks enough for ten men, as did my father. I know what too much alcohol can do.'

He saluted her with a finger to brow and took a sip. 'We both know.'

His words were a knife. Her face blanched and she looked down at the chessboard. Too much drinking and too much gambling had put her brother into the type of debt that had forced her to marry de Lisle in order to get a settlement to bail Mathias out of the River Tick. Perth was never going to let her forget that she had chosen another man over him and why. Never.

She took a deep breath and moved her first piece.

Two hours later she had him in check, but not mate. He leaned back in his chair and took a sip of his third glass. He studied the board.

'You have improved vastly,' he drawled. 'Somehow I thought you might.'

She gave him a tight, cool smile.

'Still,' he said softly, 'I think that I win.' He moved a piece. 'Checkmate.'

She frowned and her fists tightened. A low growl escaped her clenched teeth. 'Drat. I did not see that.'

He finished the drink and leaned back in his chair. 'It is getting late.'

His words and all that they implied sent a shiver up her spine. She looked at the French doors and was surprised to see that it was dusk outside. It would be dark soon.

'Let us play cards,' she said hastily. Anything to keep them in this room and away from their connecting bed chambers.

A predatory grin slashed his face showing strong white teeth, teeth that could nip her skin with great tenderness or with tantalizing provocation. Her fingers went involuntarily to her throat where the breath seemed to be trapped.

'A game of whist,' he said, gathering the chess pieces and returning them to their box.

She stared at his hands and then at nothing since everything about him roused her senses. 'That would be fine.'

He rose and put the chessboard and pieces away. Then he lighted a branch of candles and set them on the table between them before fetching a pack of cards. He sat down and shuffled them.

'Shall we play for straws?' she asked, thinking that was a safe wager.

'Scared?' he taunted her.

'I have played cards nearly since I could crawl,' she retorted. She felt much safer playing whist than she had chess. She had a chance to beat him at this game.

His heart-stopping grin returned. 'I think the stakes should be higher.'

'A shilling a point.'

His eyes became heavy-lidded. 'A piece of clothing.'

Chapter Six

'What?' She gasped, not sure she had heard him correctly. 'I won't play you for your clothing. Nothing of the kind. A shilling or I will...'

She did not want to say go to her room. She knew from the look on his face that he would follow her without a qualm, whether she wished it or not. A repeat of this morning's activities was not what she wanted, or at least not what she felt was best, regardless of what her heart and body desired.

His grin turned wicked. 'I will make it easy on you, Lillith.' Her name on his lips was seductive and made her pulse pound. 'You may play for shillings. I shall play for clothing.'

She gaped at him. The urge to beat him that had driven her all afternoon as she lost at chess faltered. She knew she could not keep him from removing his clothes one piece at a time as she won. The only way to keep him dressed was to lose. Her pride rebelled, but her head knew what she must do.

She nodded.

With fingers that shook in spite of her determination that they should not, Lillith picked up her cards and fanned them. She suppressed a groan. They were better than good.

'You should not play cards when there is a wager you don't want to lose,' Perth said. 'Your face is transparent.'

Her brother had often told her the same thing so she had no doubt that she had given away the truth. She would win this hand by the strength of her cards. And she did. She closed her eyes when his fingers went to his throat.

'Don't worry,' he drawled. 'I am only going to take off my cravat this time.'

Under the lazy words was the hint of sensuality. He knew she was attracted to him against her will. He had proved that this morning. She heard the slide of material as he pulled the long cloth from his neck.

'You can look,' he said.

She told herself that what he had done was nothing. He was still fully clothed. She opened her eyes to see that he had undone the first button of his shirt. Dark, wiry hairs curled around the fine white lawn. She knew they were crisp to the touch and, if wound around her finger, would cling like a lover's kiss. Her gaze rose to his face where she saw that he knew exactly what was going through her mind. His eyes were dark as the night and as filled with flames as the fireplace. With hands that shook worse than before, she picked up the cards and shuffled. Somehow she had to lose.

Two hands later, he murmured, 'You win again. Try as you might, you cannot lose every hand.'

She averted her eyes and shuffled the cards until her fingers ached. A solitary shilling lay on his side of the table. A shilling she had borrowed from him and insisted that he fetch so there was tangible proof that he had won a hand.

The fire had burned low and the candles were a third gone. The room was cooling off in the night air. Yet, Lillith felt as though she sat on burning coals.

Against her will, her gaze returned to Perth. He watched her like a predator watches its prey. Slowly and deftly, his fingers worked down the front of his shirt, undoing buttons with ease. The fine material opened to show a V of sun-browned skin with dark hairs trailing down his chest. With the grace of a cat, he stood and stripped the shirt off.

His shoulders were as broad as she remembered. His stomach as flat and hard as the floor that suddenly seemed more inviting than a bed. The flames from the fire played along his muscles, seeming to make them ripple as though he moved. She shook her head and made herself look away from his male perfection.

Instead of sitting down, he moved to the table that held the alcohol and poured another glass. With his back to her, she watched him with a hungry intensity that made her ache. Heaven help her, she wanted him—just as he had planned.

To ease some of her need and to satisfy her curiosity, she asked, 'What happened to your back?'

He stiffened and did not turn towards her. 'Nothing.'

His curt reply told her not to pursue the topic. Whatever had happened must have hurt him greatly if he still would not discuss it. She despaired of ever reaching him emotionally.

He angled around. 'We can stop this stupid game any time you wish,' he said, his voice rasping like a man deprived of air.

She grasped at his offer of respite. 'Good. I would like to read one of your books.'

He lifted one brow in a sardonic statement. 'I did not mean that you could escape the inevitable. Merely that we would forgo this particular brand of foreplay.'

She stopped in her attempt to stand. Anger at her cowardice flared. 'Then the next time you lose, take off your boots instead of your breeches.'

He laughed outright. 'That is more like the girl I once knew and the woman I first abducted. I had thought that the injury to your ankle had taken away all your spirit. I am glad to be mistaken.'

His words said one thing, but the smouldering heat in his eyes said something altogether different. There was no humour in his gaze, only desire and need. She sank back into her chair, all her bravado fading away under the intensity of his study.

'Another hand, then,' she finally said. 'I cannot let it be said that I feared to finish what we have started.'

Even as she agreed, she wondered what she was doing. She knew where they were headed. It was inevitable, much as she tried to deny her reaction. He wanted her and he was determined to have her. Unfortunately for her peace of mind, she wanted him just as badly.

They played the next hand without speaking. Perth sipped his drink and Lillith wished for some strong hot tea. The tension between them made her crazy.

Perth played his last card. 'I believe you have won again,' he drawled.

She stared helplessly at her boss card. 'It takes greater skill to play badly than to win.'

He shrugged, the flicker of fire and candles glimmering across the expanse of his chest. 'Perhaps I am more motivated than you.'

She gave him a jaundiced look. 'Most definitely.'

He bent over and tried to pull one of his boots off and could not. One black brow raised. 'You will have to help if this is the item of clothing you intend me to remove.'

'I *intend* for you to take nothing else off. You are the one determined to undress.'

Her words dripped like acid. He ignored them.

'If you refuse to help, then I will take off something else.'

'No.'

He stood and undid the button at his breeches. She jumped up, knocking the table and nearly overturning the candles. Like lightning, he grabbed the candelabra and set it straight.

'You are too late,' he drawled, undoing the last button so that the front fell open.

'Wicked. You are wicked,' she accused, flushing

from her bosom to the roots of her hair. 'Isn't it enough that I desire you before all else, even my honour? Must you bedevil me until I can think of nothing but you and what you do to me?'

'I will do whatever I must to have you, Lillith.' His eyes were darker than hell.

He rounded the table and grabbed her. She gasped and took a step back. Her heel hit the grate in front of the fire. Heat scorched her as he grabbed her shoulders and pulled her to him. His scar stood out in livid relief against his skin. Then he bent his face to hers.

She cried out, whether in denial or a plea, she did not know.

He covered her mouth with his and she melted into the all-consuming heat of his passion. Nothing else mattered.

Desire, hot and unquenchable, drove him through the night. He could not get enough of her. Need whipped him until he drowned in his passion, her passion, their passion. No sooner were they done and lying limply entangled than his need rose again, an insatiable heat that engulfed him—them. He entered her, devoured her and was consumed by her.

It was late the following morning when he finally left her. She curled into a tight ball as his body moved away from her. The urge to stroke his palm down her flank and rejoin her was nearly impossible to ignore. Clenching his fist, he turned sharply and left without a backward glance. He knew that if he looked at her, he would never leave her.

He entered his room and shut the door quietly behind him, keeping under tight rein all the emotion that boiled inside him. Someone cleared his throat.

'Pardon me, my lord,' Fitch said. At least the servant had the grace to flush on seeing his master standing naked.

'Damn it, Fitch. If I need you, I will call,' Perth growled.

He felt no embarrassment at his lack of clothing. Fitch had seen him in worse situations. What did discommode him was the emotion he knew had been on his face when he entered the room. A naked body was nothing. A naked heart was altogether too vulnerable.

Scowling, Perth crossed the room and took the robe Fitch had picked up in spite of being told to leave. He belted the heavy silk robe about his waist.

'Well?' he finally said.

'Pardon my saying so, my lord—'

'But you are going to say so anyway,' Perth said sardonically. 'As you did last night.'

'Yes, my lord. We have been together too long and gone through too much for me to stand by and watch you do this deed without trying to stop you. The lady deserves better than you are giving her.'

Perth's scowl deepened into an angry flush. The scar running his cheek stood out like a streak of white lightning.

'You go too far.'

Fitch said nothing, just watched the Earl.

'I intend to offer her marriage.' Perth crossed the room and threw open the window. The fragrant morning air washed over him. He turned back to the manservant. 'That will take care of any wagging tongues should word of this get out.'

Seeing the harsh line of the Earl's jaw and the way the scar blazed, Fitch knew that to continue arguing would be fruitless. 'As you say, my lord.'

Fitch could not keep the disappointment from his voice. With a curt bow, he left the room.

Perth watched his manservant leave. As Fitch had said, they had been through much. And now this.

He ran his fingers through his hair, remembering against his will how Lillith's fingers had clutched hanks of his hair in order to hold his mouth to hers. Her scent still clung to him, lilacs and woman. He groaned.

Frustration was an emotion he had great experience with, but why should he suffer it now? She was in the next room and he knew that if he went to her, caressed her, she would open to him. He knew that with a certainty that threatened to send him to her.

'Damnation.'

He slammed his fist against the wall. This was not how it was supposed to be happening. This was not supposed to be tearing his gut out. She wanted him and admitted it. He intended to offer her marriage. She would accept. She would be his, to have and do with as he wished.

Nothing more. Nothing less.

* * *

Lillith sat down at the small table and wondered why she had come downstairs. Fitch would have brought her breakfast up to her. But Fitch had to do everything because all the other servants were gone. Perth had done what he could to see that none of this leaked to a member of their set.

The hunger that had brought her downstairs dissipated. She had never been concerned about acceptance. Vouchers for Almack's, invitations to all the proper balls and routs, all of that had never interested her. She attended as a matter of course. Everyone of her acquaintance attended.

She heard the door open and turned. Perth stood in the doorway, looking as though he had not kept her awake most of the night, looking as though nothing had happened between them.

She forced herself to take a sip of the tea she had prepared along with a slice of toast. 'What do you want?'

She kept her voice flat and hoped he would leave without saying anything. She did not think she could bear to hear anything he might say to her after what they had done.

He remained where he was, his stance easy. He wore a green jacket over a shirt that was open at the neck. Buckskin breeches accentuated the muscles in his thighs, thighs that had rippled under her fingers just hours before. She shook her head.

'I want to marry you.'

She dropped the cup. The fragile china shattered, sending tea splattering. She knew the hot liquid hit her hand, but it did not hurt. Nothing could hurt like the words he had just spoken. He only wanted to marry her to possess her, to continue his revenge by breaking her heart. He did not love her.

'Marry *you*?' She put her palms on the table and pushed herself into a standing position. 'After what you have done? Never.'

A stillness came over him. If she did not know just how little she really meant to him, she would have thought that her words pained him.

'What other choice do you have?'

She blanched before anger came to her rescue. 'I am a widow. I have any choice I choose to make.'

His mouth curled. 'What if word of this spreads? I have done everything I can to prevent that, but you may after all have to doubt your servant.'

Her anger turned bitter. 'Nor did you do anything to disguise the fact that you were a nobleman abducting me.'

'True. I intended to marry you when we were through.'

'When we were through?' she asked, incredulous at his assumption. 'You thought I would marry you after what you have done? Dragged me here with no consideration for my wishes, my needs. You are more arrogant than I thought.'

He shrugged and moved into the room, closing the door behind himself. 'What if you have a child from this? Have you considered that possibility?'

Because she had not, the question set her back. She

sank to the chair with a thud. A cold lump settled in her throat, but she met his look squarely.

'After nine years of marriage and no children, I don't think I need worry about that. And if I do, then it will be my problem.'

Fury twisted his face. He lunged forward and caught her shoulders with his hands before she realised what he was doing.

'You will not. Should you bear a child, it will be mine as well as yours. I will have as much to say about what happens to it as you do.'

She stared up at him, surprised by his vehemence but determined that she would do as she felt best. 'You say that now, but we will not be wed. You will not even know should that come to pass.'

He shook her, not hard, but enough that she knew her words had increased his anger. 'I will know.'

They stayed like that for long minutes, eyes locked, mouths hard lines of stubborn rejection. Her heart beat painfully and she could see his scar whiten until it stood out harshly on his cheek. Meeting him glare for glare after what they had just said was one of the hardest things she had ever done.

After an eternity, his hands fell away and he stepped back. 'I will have a carriage pick you up in one hour. It will be a hired one from the nearby village. It will take you wherever you want and no one need know you have even been here.'

'Like that?' she asked, taken aback by his abrupt change of focus. 'You are freeing me without another word?'

He nodded. 'If you will not marry me, then there is no more need for you to stay under my roof.'

Her mouth was dry and a lump had lodged in her throat, making breathing difficult. This was what she had wanted, her freedom. But this suddenly, this abruptly, after being asked to marry him and talking of a child that she knew would never exist, made her head spin.

Dazed, she watched him leave, his boots cracking against the wooded floor. The door slammed behind him. Silence reverberated through the room. She slumped into her chair.

He had asked her to marry him, and she had told him no.

Her hands shook when she tried to pour herself more tea. Somehow she managed to get cream and sugar in the cup and got the drink to her lips. The scalding heat helped ease some of the ice that seemed lodged in her chest. A tear escaped her eye and slid down her cheek.

If only he had spoken of love.

Exactly one hour later, Perth caught her hand, knowing she did not want him to touch her and unwilling to do as she wanted. He helped her into the rented carriage where she sat with ill grace. He leaned in so that whatever he said to her would not be overheard by the hired driver.

She tugged, trying to free her hand from his. He tightened his grip. 'Look at me, Lillith,' he demanded, angered by her determination to ignore him.

'Why should I do that?' she demanded. 'You will only use it to say something I don't want to hear or to take liberties I don't want to give.'

She was leaving him and the pain of that loss strengthened his resolve. 'I do what I must.' He caught her chin with his free hand and turned her face to his. 'I have treated you abominably, but I have also given you pleasure. Things would not be easy between us, but I believe we could make a go of marriage.'

She glared at him. 'I have had one marriage of convenience, I will not willingly enter another.'

His pulse quickened. 'So you want a love match.' Something tightened his chest and twisted his gut. She had hurt him too much, he would never give her that power over him again even if it meant losing her. 'Then you had best be on your way, Lady de Lisle, for I have no intention of marrying anyone for love. Lust, yes. Mutual satisfaction, absolutely. Love, never. I suffered from that malady once and have vowed never to do so again.'

Still, determined as he was to keep her from his heart, he could not resist the closeness of her. Her scent invaded his mind and the thought of making love to her very nearly had him climbing in the carriage and shutting out the world.

Instead, he held her chin steady while he took what he wanted. His mouth plundered hers. He kissed her with an intensity that surprised even him. When he finally released her, he breathed hard as though he had run a great distance. He noted that her bosom rose and fell in deep gasps. Her cheeks burned crimson. Her eyes were wide and haunted.

She did not say a word to him, but her now free hand rose to her mouth and pressed hard.

He stepped back and signaled the coachman to start. 'If you change your mind,' he said softly, 'you know where I am.'

She turned away as the carriage moved forward. He did not expect to hear from her. But did he want her enough to follow her? He feared that he might.

Chapter Seven

Lillith limped into the foyer of her dower house. An Elizabethan manor home that had once been the county seat of the Lords de Lisle, her deceased husband had bequeathed it to her until her death or remarriage. Her mouth twisted bitterly. She would die here.

'My lady.' Her impeccable butler, Simmons, hastened to meet her. 'We did not expect you. We have been worried. You have been gone for several days.' He ran to a stop, his face suffused with red at his unaccustomed outburst.

'I was…I was staying with a friend. She was in need of companionship.'

She saw by his eyes that Simmons knew she lied, but he nodded. That was the story she would tell and if her servants had not gossiped—she nearly laughed in bitterness for she knew they had—no one would be the wiser. However, she would never acknowledge anything. The *ton* would talk about her behind her back, and some of the doors previously open would close, but within a fortnight her escapade would be stale as yesterday's bread. Someone else's escapade would be the latest *on dit*.

'I will have Cook prepare you tea,' Simmons said, studiously ignoring her lack of luggage.

She took pity on him. 'My things are on the front steps.' The clothes Perth had ordered for her were packed in several trunks sitting outside. She would distribute them to the poor tomorrow or the day after. She wanted nothing to remind her of the past week.

The butler's normally passive countenance lost its tension, and the twitch at his left eye stopped. He was very protective of her. He had been with her the entire ten years since her marriage and had elected to come to the Dower House with her.

'Thank you, Simmons. I could use some very hot tea,' she said, untying the green ribbons on her chip bonnet. 'Please have it served in my rooms.'

'My lady.' He bowed. The tick at his left eye was back. 'Mr Wentworth is in the drawing room. He has been here for several days.' Lillith blanched. Mathias had travelled far.

'Have the tea served in the drawing room and in-clude biscuits and cake.' Still clutching the ribbons of her bonnet, she went to meet her brother.

She opened the door herself and waved Simmons away. Mathias stood with his back to her; his gaze focused on something in the rear gardens. A deer paused in the act of eating one of the last roses of the season.

Mathias turned. 'My dear, you are finally home. I was beginning to worry. You left no word.'

His tone was mild with just a hint of censure. His mouth was a puckered Cupid's bow. Lillith's palms began to sweat in their fine kid gloves. Mathias was half a dozen inches taller than she was and he shared her thick, nearly silver hair. That was the only trait they shared. He had a robust figure, held in check by a girdle much like that worn by the Prince of Wales.

He also gambled with the Prince and the Prince's cronies. He was welcomed everywhere in spite of his excessive gaming because his tailor might never be paid, but his gambling debts always were. They were considered a debt of honour and not a vice by England's aristocracy.

Lillith tossed her hat on to a nearby Chippendale chair in a forced effort at nonchalance. Under the best of circumstances, Mathias had an awful ability to see right through her. This was the worst of circumstances, and she could not afford for even her brother to know where she had really been. He would challenge Perth to a duel and one of them would surely die. She could not chance losing one of the two men that meant the most to her.

Somehow, she managed to fluff her hair as though she had not another thought in the world. 'I have been with a friend. Now, before you start, Mathias, I cannot—absolutely cannot—tell you who she is. That would be a betrayal. She was in need and I did what I could.'

She hoped with all her heart that one of the ladies

of the *ton* had been in the country this last week. Better yet if the woman was married and had left her husband in Town.

'I would never ask you to betray a confidence, my dear. You know that.'

Yes, she did know that. It was similar to a gambling debt. One always paid one's debts, no matter what it cost oneself or one's family.

She closed the distance between them for the hug they always exchanged. Instead of releasing her afterwards, Mathias held her and studied her face.

'You look different, Lillith. Tired. You are not getting sick, I hope.'

She pulled her hands from his and put distance between them. He was always too perceptive. Always.

She forced a laugh. 'I am tired, as you say. Nothing else. We spent long nights talking and getting little rest. I shall spend the next week catching up.'

Simmons entered with refreshments and Lillith took the opportunity to pick a seat that put her back to the light coming in from the window. Shadows would serve her best.

She prepared the strong tea liberally laced with cream and sugar as Mathias liked. 'A biscuit? Some cake?' Her goal was to keep the rest of their conversation neutral.

'Thank you, my dear. I have been too worried about you to eat properly. As soon as your servants reported your abduction, I came here.' He watched her like a hawk.

She nearly cried out in frustration. Of course her

servants had gone straight to Mathias. Why she had thought she could get away with Perth's charade, she did not now know. Still, she had to try.

'My friend had me abducted as an exciting game. You know how life becomes so boring after the Season ends.' She waved her hand in imitation of languid disregard. 'Why, the late Duke of Richmond held up his own wife and a pompous cleric. Why should we be any less intrepid today?'

Mathias sighed. 'Ah, yes, the late Duke. But that was many years ago, my dear. No one's reputation was at risk, and you are not normally so full of spirit.' He took a large sip of tea and a hearty bite of cake. Pleasure eased some of the edginess that had crept into his blue eyes. 'However, Mrs Russell says she did have you abducted as a lark.'

Lillith's mouth dropped before she could gain control of the surprise at her friend's timely ingenuity that took her, which was quickly followed by anger with Mathias. 'Why did you go to someone else looking for me, Brother? And why did you not say so at the start?' But she knew why. He had been testing her as both he and her father always had. She let go of her anger. This was just Mathias. 'Did *you* care so little for my reputation that it did not matter if word of my disappearance got out?'

He scowled, his pleasure in food momentarily forgotten. 'I feared for your safety and went to the one person I knew I could trust with news of your disappearance. But not until I had given you several days to return. Mrs Russell assured me that it was a lark, you were safe and she would tell no one.' He sipped his tea and eyed her. 'As to informing you at the beginning, I wanted to hear if you would prevaricate.'

She set her teacup down with a click and took a deep, fortifying breath. She never stood up to Mathias. He had been too much older than she. But she would take no more of his meddling. 'Twas bad enough that Perth had abducted her and kept her against her will. Her only family should not also be so cavalier towards her.

'Mathias, what I do is no concern of yours. I am a widow. In the eyes of the world, our world, I am free to come and go as I please.' That was stretching the point, but to seem weak now would only make him more inquisitive.

There was a sceptical gleam in Mathias's eyes. 'Even a widow—a respectable widow—has limitations on her freedom.' He took a large, determined bite of his cake and got back to his point. 'Mrs Russell said that she had her husband kidnap you.' After an almost imperceptible pause, he added, 'If you truly were abducted by your friend.'

'Yes, Nathan Russell played a highwayman to perfection.' The lie fell from her lips, and the urge to stand up and leave the room, ending the inquisition here and now was strong, so strong, she put weight on her feet in anticipation. Her ankle twinged and she winced.

Mathias put his cup down and rose. 'You are hurt. How did this happen when you were in the safety of friends?'

He towered over her. Once she had felt protected by his massive size; now she felt overwhelmed. All this deception that led from one lie to another. If only he would stop this interrogation and let her alone. But she knew he would not, so she had to.

She used her ankle as an excuse to escape. 'It is merely my ankle. I twisted it getting out of a carriage. Nothing more, but I should like to go to my rooms and rest.'

Not letting him nay say her, Lillith stood. This time her ankle truly protested. She gasped and reached for the back of her chair.

'Perhaps I should have continued to use the cane,' she said with a wry twist of her lips. 'But I was too vain. Now I shall pay the piper.'

Mathias scowled as he put an arm around her waist and helped her to the door. They climbed the stairs slowly, neither saying what they thought. All Lillith wanted was to reach the privacy of her rooms. With luck, Mathias would return to London now that she was home. She could only hope.

He escorted her into her rooms where her lady's maid, Agatha, waited. He waved the woman from the room.

Not releasing Lillith, he said quietly, 'I know there is more to this story than you will tell. All of London knows of the abduction—or will shortly. Servants talk. If this woman is truly your friend, she has done you no good having a man carry out her lark.' His arm tightened so that she could not ease away.

'She meant no harm. Please let me go so that I can sit down and rest my ankle.'

'Of course,' he said, abruptly releasing her.

Thankfully she stumbled on to a settee. He was furious or he would never have treated her so cavalierly.

'I shall be returning to Town tomorrow,' Mathias said, picking a piece of lint from his otherwise immaculate sleeve. 'The Prince has need of my company. I suggest that you remain here in the country for a lengthy period.'

'I fully intend to, Brother.' She lifted her chin. 'Until the Little Season begins, Town is so boring.'

His eyes narrowed, but he left without another word. She watched him with a heavy heart. They had not done well together since her marriage. Once she had thought everything of him. Now he was close to being an adversary.

Agatha's return made her focus on undressing and getting into a hot bath. She wished for some of Perth's concoction. Not only would it help her ankle, it might ease some of her emotional turmoil. But she did not truly need it for her ankle and she did not drink alcohol. Her brother and father had shown her only too well what drunkenness could do.

Only when she was completely alone did she allow herself to think of Perth's last words, said as the carriage pulled away. *If you change your mind, you know where I am.* If she changed her mind, she should be put in Bedlam, for that is where she would eventually end up if she married Perth without his love.

He would use her as he saw fit and then toss her aside. He would break her heart and then her soul.

Lillith gazed at the sheet of paper lying in front of her on her rosewood desk. Her eyesight was not strong and writing was always a strain, but today she had been sitting here an hour trying to think of what to say. Madeline Russell deserved to know what had happened between her and Mathias. The task was beyond her concentration today. 'Twas just as well. What she had to tell Madeline should not be trusted to paper.

Sighing, she stood and went to the window. Snow dusted the trees and lay on the ground in a patchwork quilt. This morning the sun shone brutally cold.

Two months had passed since her abduction. She had heard nothing of Perth. Her fingers knotted at her waist.

The Little Season would begin soon. Parliament would sit before the Christmas season and all the political hostesses would accompany their husbands to London. Perth always attended Parliament.

She watched a doe leave the safety of the nearby woods and enter her garden. Hunger drove the animal. She was much like that doe. Her hunger to see Perth, hear his voice, urged her to abandon caution. She would never contact him, but she would go to Town in the hope of meeting him.

She turned away to give the doe privacy and perhaps a measure of comfort. Lillith feared her body had betrayed her. She would never tell Perth, but the need to be near him was too great for her to resist.

She had three more baskets of food and warm clothing to prepare for her tenants and deliver. Then she would journey to London and whatever future awaited her there.

Several days later, Lillith's carriage drew up in front of the small London town house that her friend Madeline Russell shared with her husband of nearly four years, Nathan Russell. Nathan came from a minor branch of a noble family. The couple was comfortable, but far from wealthy, and their tiny home was not in the fashionable West End. But it was cosy and welcoming and the Russells were accepted everywhere.

When the butler announced her, Lillith rushed across the small sitting room that separated her from Madeline. Madeline had been her dearest friend since infancy. Their fathers' property marched side by side and the two girls were like sisters.

'I have missed you dreadfully,' Madeline said, rising and enfolding Lillith in her arms.

Lillith stood a head taller than her auburn-haired friend, the difference a source of good-natured banter and true chagrin on Madeline's part. The role of Pocket Venus had not been one Madeline enjoyed.

'And I you,' Lillith said with heartfelt truth. 'So much has happened. And I must thank you for the Banbury tale you gave Mathias.'

'Pshaw.' Madeline waved the thanks aside. 'You would have done the same for me.' Her hazel eyes lit up. 'But now you owe me the true story, for I am sure that it is juicier than anything I might have made up.'

Lillith sank into one of the overstuffed chintz cushions that Madeline loved so well and gratefully took a cup of steaming tea. She took a long swallow before staring into the milky mirror. 'Where to start? 'Tis a long story that started ten years ago.'

'Ah.' Madeline sighed. 'The Earl of Perth. I knew he still cared for you.'

Lillith's laugh was harsh. 'He desires me.'

'That is a good start,' Madeline said with a surge of the practicality that so often seemed at odds with her otherwise whimsical nature.

'De Lisle desired me,' Lillith said flatly.

Madeline shuddered and took a dainty bite out of a cake. 'That is entirely different. De Lisle was old enough to be your grandfather. Perth is a man in his prime and, if rumour tells the truth, as good in bed as he is with swords. And I don't know any man who would willingly cross him in a duel. At least not any more. Ten years of practice have made him an expert, or so Nathan says.'

Lillith's mouth twisted. Honour and reticence kept her from confirming Madeline's words. But her face must have given away her thoughts.

'He is,' Madeline crowed. 'I knew it. He abducted you and then seduced you. How absolutely delicious.'

Lillith set her empty cup down. 'This is not a fairy tale, Madeline. It is my life.'

Madeline sobered. 'I am sorry for making light of it, but not for what happened. You belong with Perth. I have thought so from the minute I first saw you together.'

'That was years ago. Even you cannot be that sentimental,' Lillith said.

'Hah. The way the two of you looked at each other that night at Almack's set my blood boiling and at that time I had no idea what a man and woman did together.' She took another bite of her cake and smiled dreamily. 'Now I do and I would not forgo that delight for anything.'

Now Lillith laughed. 'You and Nathan have a very unusual marriage.'

'True,' Madeline said, coming back to reality. 'A love match.'

'Exactly,' Lillith said drily. 'That is not what Perth offered me.'

Madeline watched her friend closely and saw the pain and disillusionment. 'Ah, he still smarts from being jilted. But surely you explained to him that you left him for the good of your family.'

Lillith's mouth twisted. 'Nothing I said mattered. He does not care why I chose de Lisle over him. He wants…he wants revenge. Nothing more.' Her fingers twisted in her lap, pleating and unpleating the linen napkin Madeline had given her with the tea. 'He offered me marriage. One of convenience. Nothing more.'

'Then take it,' Madeline said stoutly. 'Many a marriage of convenience has become one of love.'

Shame at her weakness paled Lillith's face. 'I could not survive. I want too much from him. As God is my witness, I would go insane married to Perth, knowing that he did not care for me the same. Every time he left the house, I would wonder where he went and whom he went with. He would make love to me one time and then leave my bed for his mistress's. That is what a marriage of convenience is. I could not live that life.'

Madeline sighed and reached out to take one of Lillith's busy hands. She held tight until Lillith's fingers stilled.

'Then you must not marry him, if he will make you so miserable. And there is no reason you should. You are wealthy enough from what de Lisle left you that you need never consider marrying again. You can do whatever you want and answer to no one.'

Lillith gave her friend a watery smile. 'That sounds very convenient.'

Inside, she wished that it were that easy. Her emotions threatened to drown her in their intensity and there seemed to be nothing she could do to escape them. But she knew that talking of this to Madeline only made the situation seem more immediate.

She took a deep, shuddering breath and vowed to change the subject. 'Are you going to Sally Jersey's tonight?'

Madeline, ever willing to do what she could to help Lillith, tacitly agreed to change the subject. 'But of course. Everyone who has come to Town for the Little Season will be there.'

'I had thought of not going,' Lillith said quietly, realising that even this new topic must lead back to Perth.

Madeline sat straight up and frowned. 'You most

certainly will go. No one knows what happened to you except me, Perth and you. That is, unless that brother of yours told others.'

Lillith smiled gently. 'Servants, even the best, will talk and before you know it the talk has spread to another house and to another master or mistress. Even if Mathias has managed to keep this to himself, it will be known by others.'

Madeline sat back, her auburn brows drawn in worry. 'You are right, unfortunately. However, you must on no account shun Society. As soon as you do that, everyone will know that whatever scandalous thing they have heard about you is true. Meet them face to face and spit in their eye if you must.'

For the first time in many weeks, Lillith's laughter was genuine. 'You are such a fierce little thing when you are bent on protecting your own. And you are right. The *ton* likes nothing more than gossiping about someone's mistakes. 'Tis much less fun for them if the person they are waiting to devour fights back. I will go.'

'And I will be there to stand by your side,' Madeline said, handing Lillith another cup of tea. 'Let us drink to that.'

Both laughing, they lifted their cups.

That night, Lillith entered Sally Jersey's London town house with her head held high. The soft lavender muslin gown she wore helped. She knew it was the perfect foil for her pale complexion and willowy figure. In the world in which she moved clothes did make the woman. Just as attending functions such as this assured one's place in Society. Thankfully, Sally was an old friend and would no more ostracise her than she would fail to provide Lillith with the much-coveted vouchers for Almack's.

The rooms were crowded, but with winter in the air they were not hot. Parliament was back in session and only the diehard socialisers were in Town along with the politicians.

Several women looked her way, but avoided eye contact. She had expected nothing else. Others would accept her.

She made her way around small groups, smiling and nodding to those she knew. Most acknowledged her. Madeline, present as she had vowed, saw her and broke away from her companions.

'Lillith, see how easy it was to come tonight? Although I had begun to despair that you would not.' Her laughing eyes held a hint of compassion. 'Ignore anyone rude enough to stare.'

Lillith took Madeline's outstretched fingers and squeezed them warmly. 'I have already refused to see at least half-a-dozen dowagers.' She smiled for her friend. ''Tis so much easier to stay in the country and let the London tabbies do as they please. And less tiring.'

What she did not say was that Perth had drawn her back. She could not bring herself to tell even Madeline that secret of her heart.

'Tsk. You have more energy than a full nursery— and no one rusticates all year.' She linked her arm in

Lillith's and drew her into a slow promenade around the room. 'Smile and nod like there is nothing on your mind but this moment.' Madeline followed her own advice.

It was difficult at first, but Lillith found that the more she smiled and laughed, the more she nodded to acquaintances and friends, the easier the entire charade became. 'Careful, Madeline. Before you know it I shall become a social butterfly.'

'Become?' Madeline teased. 'You are one already. Even Mrs Drummond Burrell cannot cut you after this outing. Sally will not allow it.'

'Are the rumours that vicious?'

'So I have heard,' Madeline said *sotto voce*, keeping a smile on her face. 'But, of course, no one has dared mention them to my face.'

They continued their walk and Lillith even managed to smile and nod graciously at an older woman whom she knew would be telling the worst tales about her. Unfortunately, they were very close to the truth. The only element missing was the name of the man with whom she had spent a sinful few nights. In the *ton* one could do anything, defy any propriety, ignore any convention so long as one was discreet and did not get caught. She had been as good as caught.

'Still,' Madeline said, her voice perking up, 'if you brazen this out, there will be another tale to occupy them within a fortnight.'

'Quite true,' Lillith murmured, resisting the urge to spit at the woman who had just given her the cut direct. She could not hide her flinch.

'Grace Lovejoy is poisonous, Lillith. Pay her no heed. Her mind is always in the gutter and every word she utters confirms that.'

Surprise at her friend's vehemence lightened Lillith's heart. 'Madeline, that is not at all like you.'

Madeline shrugged. 'You are my friend.'

Simple words, but from a true friend and full of support. 'Thank you. I know I can depend on you.'

Madeline hugged her close. 'Never mind. There is Nathan. He is so unfashionable. He thinks I should spend every minute with him.' Her voice held ennui, but her eyes held love.

'Two children and four years has not lessened his *unfashionable* love,' Lillith said with gently mocking humour. 'Every woman should be as lucky as you, my dear.'

Despite her liveliness, Madeline was very perceptive and caring, the trait that had first drawn Lillith. She caught Lillith's unspoken desire. 'You will find someone. You did not choose de Lisle. Some day you will have with a man what I have with Nathan, trust me on this.'

'Perhaps,' Lillith said, releasing her friend. 'Now you must go or Nathan will surely come to fetch you.'

'It would not be the first time,' Madeline said with just a touch of chagrin.

Madeline had barely left when a deep baritone said, 'Lady de Lisle, so nice to see you returned to Town.'

Lillith whirled around. She had been concentrating on Madeline and had not heard the Earl of Ravensford approach. He was a good friend of Perth's. Instantly, her fair complexion suffused with pink.

'How nice of you to say so,' she managed.

Ravensford was as tall as Perth, but there the similarities ended. Ravensford's hair was auburn and his eyes green. He was easy going and had a manner about him that could charm the chemise off a doxy— or more likely his new wife. Theirs was said to be a love match.

The smile left his handsome face and he studied her openly. 'Perth is here.'

Her eyes widened before she had control of herself. 'Really? How…interesting.'

'It could be,' he agreed. 'He is in a foul mood.'

'When is he not?'

'Where you are concerned, not often, unfortunately. He is in the room set aside for cards.'

It was her turn to study him. 'Why are you telling me this?'

He met her scrutiny calmly. 'Because he is my friend, and I do not want to see the two of you make a hash of everything. Nor do I want to see either of you do something that will add to the unsavory gossip circulating about you.'

'You are nearly as blunt as he, but I thank you.'

He nodded. She turned away. Perhaps it was time she left. There were too many pitfalls here.

She cast a glance towards the door leading to the card room and froze. Perth lounged against the frame, watching her like a panther watches a long-desired prey. Her muscles tightened and her right hand crept to her throat. She could not look away. Heaven help her, she could not ignore him.

He pushed off and moved towards her, his pace a slow saunter that drew her attention to his lean hips and strong thighs. She looked back up in time to see ardor darken his eyes and hunger sharpen the angles of his face. She took an unconscious step back.

'Lady de Lisle,' he said, taking the hand that had rested on her throat and bringing it to his lips. His eyes never left hers as he pressed his mouth to her fingertips. 'I had hoped you would be here.'

Gloves were no barriers to the passion his kiss conveyed. She gulped and pulled her hand away. 'I am just leaving.'

'Allow me to get your wrap and call for your carriage.'

'No.' The word came out like a shot. She took a deep breath. 'No, thank you. That is the footman's job, my lord Earl.'

'How kind of you to remind me,' he murmured, stepping away, his eyes gone hard and cold. 'I mistook my welcome—once again.'

He twisted on his heel and was gone before she could catch her wits that had gone begging. Lillith ignored the audience his approach had attracted. Looking straight ahead and with her shoulders back, she left. But she knew that the encounter would add more conjecture to her disappearance. By tomorrow everyone would remember the old scandal.

Later, when she was alone and safe from prying

eyes, she would allow herself to remember the feel of his lips and the sound of his voice.

She loved him so much it was an ache in her chest that refused to go away.

Chapter Eight

Perth lounged at his leisure. Ravensford sat across from him and both drank from glasses filled with Brook's finest burgundy. When Ravensford had called to invite him to Brooks, Perth had been more than happy to quit the solitude of his own house.

Lillith's snub last night at Sally Jersey's rout had not improved his mood. He had been in London exactly two days, having left his country retreat as soon as the servant he bribed at Lillith's country estate told him she had left. He still was not sure why he had come, but that was how he felt about everything involving the beautiful Lady de Lisle.

'Town is scarce of people,' Ravensford drawled.

Perth forced himself to set aside thoughts of Lillith and eyed his friend from beneath heavy lids made heavier by several bottles. 'Since when did you care about Society? I thought you considered it well gone since your marriage to the delightful Mary Margaret.'

Ravensford grimaced. 'Sarcasm always was your forte. Mixed with just enough truth to make it bite.'

Perth raised his glass. 'To a direct hit.'

Both drank.

'And what of you?' Ravensford asked, a sly grin bringing a sparkle to his eyes. 'I see that you are squirming on the end of Cupid's arrow.'

Perth studied the dregs of wine in his glass. 'Not me, my friend. Women are like wine—to be enjoyed while being consumed and then forgotten.'

'Ha!' Ravensford finished his glass and, instead of pouring another, rose. 'Let us go see what the Betting Book says about you.'

Perth raised one black brow, but stood and followed his friend. The infamous book was easily found.

Ravensford opened it to the last page and ran a finger down the print. 'Nothing. Damme, Perth, there is not a single thing about you and the elusive Lady de Lisle.'

'And why should there be?' Perth queried with an uninterest he was far from feeling.

Ravensford shot him an irritated glance. 'Because there is definitely something between the two of you. Always has been and always will be.'

He paged back and still found nothing.

'Enough of this nonsense,' Perth said. 'There are better things to do with this afternoon. I hear there is some prime horseflesh to be gotten at Tattersall's.'

'Nothing,' Ravensford said in ire. 'Both Brabourne and I were subjected to having our amorous adventures written about and bet on, but not you.' He gave Perth a suspicious look. 'But not you.'

Perth shrugged. 'With you and Brabourne there was fire with the smoke. With me there is neither.'

'Really?' A mocking grin showed Ravensford's very white teeth. 'Then instead of visiting Tattersall's you will be delighted to accompany me on an afternoon visit to Lady de Lisle.'

Only for an instant did Perth hesitate. Another man would not have noticed, but Ravensford did and grinned.

Perth scowled. 'Of course. I am sure that both she and her brother will be delighted to see us.'

'Wentworth is staying with his sister?'

'He is being dunned,' Perth said flatly, knowing that explained all.

'The man is a leech. Always has been,' Ravensford said, setting his glass down. 'But come along, old man. We have a visit.'

Refusal passed through Perth's mind but, much as he detested his weakness, he wanted to see her. At least with Ravensford along he could not seduce her or challenge her brother—or could not do so without Ravensford trying to intervene.

He set his empty glass down. 'A tame way to spend a perfectly good afternoon, but come along or we shall be past the acceptable hours for visiting.'

Lillith listened to her brother discuss his latest coat with one of her male callers while she poured tea and offered cakes to Madeline, who had come hoping for a quiet talk. Lillith was not sure whether she was glad of Mathias's company so she could not satisfy

Madeline's curiosity or not. Her horrible suspicion was fast becoming a certainty and part of her wanted to discuss the situation with Madeline. Another part of her did not want anyone to know. What to do?

For now, nothing.

She turned to answer a question from Mathias about the cut of his coat and missed Perth's entrance. His voice made her jerk around even as it shot through her entire being like lightning striking a tree and setting it afire.

'Lady de Lisle, Mrs Russell, Wentworth, Peters.' Perth's unmistakable voice greeted everyone.

There was dead silence.

'Hello, all.' Ravensford broke the silence, a look of unholy enjoyment on his handsome features. 'We told the butler not to stand on ceremony and announce us. The poor fellow was devastated, but what could he do?'

With a quick, questioning glance at Lillith, Madeline held her hands out first for Ravensford's quick kiss and then Perth's. 'Ravensford, Perth, how delightful to see you. Things were getting deadly dull here.'

'So we thought,' Ravensford said, taking an empty seat where he could watch everyone at the same time. Such diverting entertainment was not to be wasted. It was too bad Brabourne was not here to enjoy this, for the Duke had a wicked sense of humour. But he and his new bride were on the Continent.

Perth looked at Lillith. 'Lady de Lisle.' She nodded coolly at him, but did not offer her hand.

Mathias scowled at both men in turn. 'What brings

you two to call? There is nothing here that would interest rakes of your stamp.'

Madeline's gasp of surprise was the only sound. Lillith gave her brother a warning frown but Mathias ignored her.

Desperate to keep the situation from getting worse, Lillith dropped the cup of tea she had just poured. The liquid spattered the pale lavender of her gown and the fine bone-china cup shattered on the floor.

'Oh,' she gasped. 'I can be so clumsy. Mathias, please ring for Simmons.'

With ill grace, Mathias crossed to the fireplace and pulled the ribbon to summon the butler. He stayed standing where he was.

Sensing that her brother was not going to let the small matter of a broken cup and spilled tea alter his course, Lillith jumped to her feet. 'I am so sorry to end this delightful gathering—' she sent a pointed look at Perth '—and so soon after you and Ravensford have joined us, but I simply must change my gown.'

She stood and individually stared each guest down until, one by one, they rose and took their leave.

Madeline pressed her fingers and murmured, 'Do not let this distress you. Men can be such boors.'

Lillith smiled weakly.

Ravensford tossed off a casual farewell.

Perth moved forward and took the hands that Lillith had not extended. Shocks of desire and need flooded her, moving from the tips of her fingers to the tips of her toes. She straightened her shoulders, intent on resisting his pull.

'Lady de Lisle, I hope to see you again.' He lifted her right hand for the touch of his lips.

The breath caught in her throat as his skin touched her. If his touch had been electric, his kiss was a lightning storm out of control. She yanked both her hands free in a movement that lacked grace.

'My lord Perth,' she said, her voice much too husky for her liking. 'As we move in the same circles, our seeing each other from a distance is inevitable.'

A sardonic smile curved his mouth. 'I shall endeavour to do everything in my power to ensure that we not only see each other from a distance, but that we see each other much closer.'

Her blush was hot and instant, beyond her control. His smile turned knowing as he made her a curt bow.

She watched him saunter from the room. Slowly, her blush receded to be replaced by cold dread. Mathias had stood his ground as the others left.

'He is not the man for you, Lillith. He will never offer marriage.'

Her brother's cold words chilled her. Unconsciously, she lifted her hands to rub the gooseflesh that broke out on her arms. The urge to tell Mathias that Perth had already offered marriage was strong. She resisted. Perth offered a marriage she could not, would not, accept. She had married without love once. She would not do so again.

'I am the judge of who is right for me,' she said, 'and if it is Perth, then so be it.' Shock held her motionless. She had intended to agree with Mathias, not confront him and—worse yet—tell him that if she wanted Perth then she would take him. This was not like her.

Mathias crossed the room in several swift strides and gripped her elbow. 'He was not right for you all those years ago. He is not right today. See that you remember that.'

She looked defiantly up at her brother who towered over her. 'I am no longer a child, Mathias. I will choose whom I see.'

'And whom you consort with?' He sneered. 'For, make no mistake, that is all you will do with a man of Perth's ilk. He will not offer marriage. Not now. He is known throughout the *ton* as a womanising rogue who dallies where he pleases and leaves without a backward glance. Will you become his next doxy?'

The blush she had lost returned in a rush. Only this time the reason was anger, not desire. And fear. For his words came too close to reality.

'Let me go,' she gasped, yanking away from his punishing grip.

He released her and stepped back, surprise flashing momentarily across his fleshy face. 'Perhaps I spoke too harshly, but only out of concern for you.'

'Perhaps you spoke too harshly? Perhaps?' Her voice rose before she could control her fury. 'How dare you call me a doxy, or even hint that I might be one! How dare you do that to me. And *you* my brother.'

'I am only worried about you, Lillith.' His voice took a more conciliatory tone. 'Perth is a scoundrel and, while he intends you no honour, it is obvious that he still desires you. I wish only to help you stay out of his clutches.'

How many more truths would her brother utter? They were like darts that pierced her skin and left poison in their path.

She took a deep breath. 'I am fully aware of Perth's intentions. I do not plan on succumbing to him. I am a woman now, not a young girl—as I told you before.' She turned away from him so that he would not see the sparkle in her eye that hinted of tears to come. Things were so complicated.

'Please go now. I must change and then rest. This evening I am promised to Lord and Lady Holland for dinner.'

'As you wish,' he said.

She heard the door close behind her brother, but sensed that this was not the end of his objections. He would watch her closely. And he would do everything in his power to see that she and Perth were kept apart. She was not sure whether that knowledge gladdened her or made her ineffably sad.

That evening, to Lillith's chagrin, she sat across the table from Perth. Lord and Lady Holland, as usual, had invited a mixture of politicians and wits. She wondered where she fitted in. Probably as a single woman. Other hostesses were always in need of single men; Lady Holland never was.

'Do you not agree, Lady de Lisle?' Perth's deep voice asked.

Politics were not a great interest of hers and she had

no desire to become a political hostess, yet she did keep up with the trends. Even she knew that Perth's plan would not do well.

'I think your idea is honourable, but I fear you will find opposition in executing it.'

Interest sparked in his eyes, making them snap. He was so devastatingly handsome, she wondered how she could continue to resist his advances.

Lord Holland interjected. 'The returning troops are in sore need of jobs, else they will become lawbreakers and a worse burden on the country. But you are right, Lady de Lisle, Perth will face opposition in Parliament, just as Lord Alastair St Simon has.'

'Honour is not always a matter of paying one's gaming debts,' Perth said harshly. 'We, and all of Europe, owe these men a chance to find fit employment and the means to feed and clothe themselves and their families.'

She listened to him speak with conviction about the needs of the returning army. Now that Napoleon was finally defeated, men were being let go from the army and navy. Many of them had no other skills and could find no work. Many became beggars, others thieves.

The man on her right made a comment that demanded her response, and she reluctantly let Perth's words fall away from her attention. Her first duty as a guest was to entertain the people seated beside her.

To Lillith, it seemed an eternity before Lady Holland rose, signalling that it was time for the women to leave the dinner table. She rose with the other women and followed them to the drawing room, while the men

stayed behind to drink port and smoke cigars or cig-
arillos as the inclination took them.

One of the married women, Constance Montford,
sat beside Lillith. She was older and considered one
of the forthcoming London hostesses. She was also a
gossipmonger.

She gave Lillith a large smile. 'My dear Lady de
Lisle, so delightful to see you back in Town.'

Lillith returned her smile with a nod. 'Thank you,
Mrs Montford. I am delighted to be here.' She was
not going to give the woman anything to bandy about.

Mrs Montford tittered, a trait that would not do well
in a political hostess. 'One hears such malicious rumours.' If she had a fan, Lillith thought the woman
would be fluttering it. 'But of course, one knows not
to believe all of them.'

'A very wise choice,' Lillith murmured, wondering
when the woman would get to the point and mention
the *on dit* circulating about Lillith's disappearance.

'Titbits are like spice,' Mrs Montford continued.
'They enliven an otherwise dull evening.'

Lillith gave the woman a tiny smile. 'I thought you
enjoyed politics over all else, Mrs Montford. Are you
not trying to set up a saloon to rival Lady Holland's?'

It was a bold thing to say in this company, but Lillith was determined that Mrs Montford should get as
good as she gave. The woman was determined to drag
Lillith's potential scandal into the open, so Lillith
would make sure that Mrs Montford's ambitions were
discussed as openly.

Mrs Montford's eyes narrowed and her voice lowered to a sibilant whisper. 'I had heard that you flaunted convention, Lady de Lisle, even to letting yourself be kidnapped by a gentleman and then staying with him for a length of time unbecoming to a respectable lady.'

Lillith's smile thinned. 'Ah, the gloves are off. One should not believe everything one hears, my dear Mrs Montford. The *ton* is notorious for rumours that ruin a person's reputation.'

'Yes, is it not?' the other woman murmured.

A retort rose to Lillith's tongue only to be swallowed by Perth saying, 'Lady de Lisle, Mrs Montford, such beauty in one spot. May I join you?'

He sat down in a chair close by without waiting for them to invite him. Mrs Montford simpered at him. Lillith glared at him. With the *on dit* of her abduction making the rounds of the London drawing rooms, she did not need Perth's proximity. She was not sure she could hide the emotions he engendered in her. Someone would be sure to notice and talk would eventually link him to her disappearance. Their past would only hasten that conclusion.

'Lord Perth,' Mrs Montford said, 'you must come and call on us. I am holding a small gathering tomorrow. I am sure you will find many of your acquaintances there.'

'You honour me, Mrs Montford.'

Lillith noticed that he neither accepted nor declined the invitation. He had charm when he chose to use it.

'And what of you, Lady de Lisle?' he asked, turning

his dark gaze on her. 'Will you have a small gathering tomorrow?'

He was baiting her. 'I think not, my lord.'

His smile became predatory. 'A shame. The one you had this afternoon was so interesting.'

Her fingers stilled in her lap. As soon as she realised that she had reacted, she sought to dissemble. 'My brother is staying with me. His friends are always about.'

Mrs Montford's sharp gaze went from one to the other. 'Ah, yes, I had forgotten you two are acquainted.'

Perth turned back to her. 'A long-standing acquaintance.' He rose gracefully. 'If you will excuse me, ladies. Lord Holland seems to want me.'

Lillith seethed. He'd added wood to Mrs Montford's budding fire and then he left her to put it out. There was nothing else she could say to sidetrack the woman so she decided to leave.

'If you will excuse me as well,' Lillith said.

Before the woman could answer, Lillith used the arm on her chair to help lever herself up. Her ankle was much better, but it was still difficult at times to rise up after sitting for a while.

She made her way to Lady Holland and made her excuse. 'My ankle is acting up again, I am afraid,' Lillith said.

'By all means, don't think you must stay here when you are uncomfortable.' Lady Holland accompanied Lillith to the foyer. 'I see that Mrs Montford had you cornered. The woman is thoroughly unlikable. I don't blame you for wanting to get away.'

Lillith smiled and nodded. She had no intention of slandering any person to another, not even someone such as Mrs Montford. She knew only too well how harmful that could be. Her carriage arrived shortly after and she escaped gratefully.

Perth watched Lillith leave. No doubt she and Mrs Montford had come to an agreement that their dislike for one another was mutual. By tomorrow there would be fresh meat for the gossip mill.

'Be done with it, man,' Lord Holland said. 'Marry the woman.'

Perth refocused his attention. 'I beg your pardon?'

Lord Holland shook his head. 'Lady de Lisle. Marry her and get this over with. Watching you watch her is like seeing a rabid wolf eyeing a sheep. 'Tis painful.'

Perth felt himself flush. 'My apologies. I did not know I was making you uncomfortable.'

Lord Holland gave him a rueful grin. 'She feels the same about you, you know. Written all over her.'

'I see,' Perth said for lack of anything else.

'Then do something.' Lord Holland slapped Perth on the back.

'Perhaps. If you will excuse me.' Perth made his bow and his escape.

Outside his carriage waited, the horses pawing impatiently at the ground. He leapt inside and they were off before he even sat.

It was the small hours of the morning and he did

not want to go home. He was not sleepy and he would do nothing but brood about Lillith. He would go to Brook's instead.

The exclusive club was filled with gentlemen gambling, drinking and talking. Perth made his way to one of the card tables and took an empty seat. Viscount Chillings, a tall, elegantly lean man with thick silver hair, was already there. They were shortly joined by Lord Alastair St Simon, who had married Lizabeth Stone, Lady Worth, just a year ago. The three men were old friends.

'All we lack is Brabourne,' Chillings said, 'but he is on the Continent with his lovely bride. Shall we cut for deal?' He fanned the cards across the table.

'We are short,' Lord Alastair said, 'but we might as well.'

While they did that, a fourth man sat down in the last empty chair. Perth glanced up to see Mathias Wentworth. The man was as self-satisfied as ever. His silver-blond hair, so similar to his sister's, fell over grey eyes that were as red-shot as the setting sun.

Perth resisted the urge to tell Wentworth to go and instead said, 'You are just in time to draw. But I doubt that we play the stakes you are used to.'

Wentworth's mouth split into the parody of a grin. 'I think that tonight you will.'

Chillings lounged back in his chair as he flipped over his card, the ace of spades. 'I am not in the habit of wagering my inheritance.'

Perth glanced at his friend from the corner of his

eye. Was Chillings trying to provoke Wentworth? He turned his card over, the two of hearts.

'It seems I am not to start this game.'

Lord Alastair St Simon turned his over to show the ten of diamonds. 'Nor I.'

Wentworth, with the smirk still on his face, showed his card, the queen of spades. 'It seems that neither am I.'

Chillings gathered the cards and expertly shuffled them. He then offered them to Perth to cut before dealing. The play began, the stakes relatively low for men of their wealth. Lord Alastair never played for great sums since his wife's young brother had killed himself after losing a large amount of money to Lord Alastair in this very room. Perth was actually surprised to see him here.

'Where is Lady Worth?' Perth asked, knowing Lord Alastair would not be here if his wife wanted him by her.

Lord Alastair played a card before answering. 'She is with my mother. It seems they think my country house needs refurbishing.' He shuddered. 'And I am not the man to tell them they are wrong. But I don't intend to be there when they rip it apart.'

Chillings nodded. 'I know exactly. My wife did the same thing. Made no difference that the place had been good enough for my family for the last four hundred years.' He also shrugged. 'Now it does not matter.'

No one said anything. The Viscount's wife had died

two years ago during childbirth. The babe had died as well.

The game continued. The stakes mounted. Wentworth continued to throw his vouchers on to the growing pile of wagers. No one thought him capable of coming up with the amount should he lose, but no one said anything either. It was for Wentworth and his own sense of honour to know when he needed to stop.

They broke their sixth bottle of port when Perth won the last hand. Everyone drank to him, even Wentworth.

'I think it is time I left,' Chillings said, finishing his wine and standing. 'I will be by tomorrow with a bank draft.'

Perth nodded, never having expected differently.

'The same,' Lord Alastair said, leaving his port unfinished as he stood to leave.

When they were gone, Wentworth still sat across from Perth. His eyes were feverishly bright, an addicted gambler to the core. 'I will play you another hand,' he said, his voice high and excited. 'All or nothing.'

'You will?' Perth drawled, wondering what the man was about. 'You already owe me around ten thousand pounds.'

'So I do. So I do.' He rubbed his hands together. 'But I have a better prize for you, one you have coveted for many years.'

Perth's eyes narrowed, but he resisted the urge to lunge across the table and grab the repellent man by the neck. 'Do you?' he drawled. 'Somehow I doubt that it is yours to give.'

'Oh, never doubt that the prize goes where I bid it go. You of all people should know that.'

Wentworth's knowing grin and sly words were nearly Perth's undoing. Under cover of the table, his hands fisted until the knuckles turned white, but he maintained his outward pose of indifference.

'We wagered money, not lives,' he said softly.

'So we did,' Wentworth said. 'I did not know you were so fastidious. Particularly since you have been panting after her for years. Why, just this afternoon you came sniffing around.'

The urge to knack the man's teeth into the back of his throat was nearly overpowering. But that would create only more scandal than his actions toward Lillith had already started brewing.

'Apparently, I am more interested in allowing people to do as they wish than you are.' Perth paused and took a long drink of wine. 'But then we already knew that.'

Wentworth bared his teeth. 'Yes, we did. A pity. Of all the possible suitors for Lillith's hand, you would be the easiest to land and the wealthiest.'

Wentworth's crude words ignited the embers of anger that Perth had so far kept in check. 'You intend to try and sell your sister to the highest bidder—again?'

Wentworth's smirk widened. 'Plainly put, yes. Do you care to enter the fray?'

Perth's eyes narrowed to dangerous slits. 'If you

haven't the blunt to pay me,' he said slowly so that every insulting word would sink in, 'then I will pretend that we never met tonight.' He flicked a contemptuous glance over the other man as he rose. 'But I will not take your sister's life in trade.'

Wentworth poured himself another glass of wine and gulped it down. 'You want my sister and I am willing to give her to you. So why all this fuss? Why not make things easy?'

'You always were willing to give her to the highest bidder.' Perth's lip curled in contempt. 'Is that why you sat down here tonight, so that you could gamble away Lady de Lisle's freedom once again? And did you pick me because you thought I would make the trade? You are a despicable worm.'

Wentworth sneered as he poured himself still another glass of wine and gulped it down, bringing a hectic flush to his cherubic cheeks. 'You are no different from de Lisle, only younger. After that, you want exactly what he wanted. He had the money. Now you do.'

A low growl started deep in Perth's throat. It would be so easy and so satisfying to rip Wentworth to shreds. And it would accomplish nothing.

'I am not interested in playing your game. Don't pay me what you owe—or have your sister pay it. She is wealthy enough to support you for some years to come.'

Wentworth's heavy brows knitted for an instant before the man realised his features gave him away. Suspicion flared in Perth.

'What have you done, Wentworth? Are you selling her to the highest bidder because you must in order to maintain your gambling obsession?'

Lillith's brother downed his wine and stood. The creak of his stays was loud in the silence.

Perth stood as well. 'It was a mistake for de Lisle to leave her inheritance under your management. But then, I imagine that you made that deal with him long before he passed on.' In a show of indifference he did not feel, Perth poured himself another glass of wine and downed it in one gulp. 'Have you paupered her already?'

Wentworth turned away without comment. His corpulent figure weaved its way from the room. There was a horrible sinking feeling in Perth's gut. Lillith was back up for sale to the highest bidder.

Damned if he would lose her a second time.

The next day Perth received a draft on Mathias Wentworth's bank for ten thousand pounds. He stood in front of the fire and stared at the piece of paper. He was tempted to throw it into the flames. Wentworth did not have this kind of blunt, he must have got it from his sister.

But if his fears were true, Lillith did not have this kind of money either. The man was playing a dangerous game with Lillith's future.

Chapter Nine

Perth raised his quizzing glass and surveyed the crowd at the Covent Garden Opera House. Anyone who was anyone in Society was present. The Duke of Wellington sat in his box with friends. The Prince of Wales held court in his private box. And—his perusal stopped. Lillith sat with Madeline and Nathan Russell.

'Found her at last,' Ravensford drawled.

'Andrew,' Mary Margaret, Lady Ravensford, chided in a husky voice that sounded as though she had just risen from making love. Her voice had first caught and held Ravensford's interest. 'Leave the man alone.'

Ravensford took his bride's fingers and raised them for a kiss, all the while giving her a devastating smile. 'He would feel uncared for if I did not tease him.'

Mary Margaret snorted. She was a beautiful woman although not in the current vogue. She was dark where blonde was fashionable. Her figure was full-busted and slim-hipped. But her eyes were her best feature, brilliant as finest emeralds; they showed compassion and depth. Ravensford doted on her.

'Ignore him, Perth,' she said.

'Always,' Perth said, suiting action to word by rising and leaving.

On stage the dance continued. In the pit, those who could not afford seats or boxes watched for any sight of delicately turned ankles. Perth ignored it all as he made his way to the Russells' box.

His knock was curt and he entered before permission was granted. He scowled.

'Perth,' Madeline Russell trilled. 'Do join us. We are become quite a party.'

Chillings, sitting at his ease beside Lillith, waved languidly. 'All the world's a stage, as the Bard said,' he drawled.

'So it would seem,' Perth replied, pulling a chair up to Lillith's other side.

He nodded at Madeline Russell, who watched everything with an avid gleam in her eye while her husband had a more sanguine look. Perth nodded to him.

'Been following your bill in the House of Commons,' Russell said. 'Heavy going. Let me know if there is anything I can do to help.' Nathan Russell had influence in the Lower House and would be a valuable ally.

'Thank you, I will.' He turned his attention to Lillith, who laughed at something Chillings had said. 'I did not know you like the opera.'

She turned a cool gaze to him. 'There are many things you do not know about me.'

'And many things I do,' he said low, his voice a husk as memory caught his gut and twisted it.

Chillings watched the interaction between them. 'I believe I must be going.' He bowed to Lillith and looked pointedly at Perth. 'I will be at Brook's later.'

Perth nodded.

No sooner than Chillings was gone than another knock sounded on the door. The Prince of Wales entered with Wentworth in his wake. Everyone stood before the men bowed and the ladies curtsied. Behind the Prince's back, Lillith's brother smirked.

'Mrs Russell, Lady de Lisle.' The Prince took a hand of each of them. 'I could not resist such beauty.' He slanted a glance at his friend. 'And Mathias here insisted on visiting with his sister.'

Perth said cynically, 'It seems that living with her is not enough.'

Silence fell and tension mounted. Lillith, resenting the fact that once more she must play peacemaker between her brother and the man who had been her lover, said, 'Mathias has joined me in London because he knows how I hate to stay alone in a house as large as mine.'

No one said a word.

Madeline jumped into the fray. 'We are delighted to have you, your Highness. Can we offer you some wine?' She gestured to the opened bottle and empty glasses.

The Prince, never one to deny himself pleasure, accepted. When he sat down, Mathias held his arm out to Lillith.

'Come walk a moment with me, Lillith,' he said, his tone an order.

Lillith's hackles rose but, with Perth so close and ready to pounce on Mathias for any reason, she stood. Better to keep the two men apart. They had never got on well, but lately it seemed as though something had happened to make everything worse.

She laid her hand on Mathias's arm and allowed him to escort her from the box. She heard a chair scrape behind her and turned to see Perth getting to his feet. She frowned at him and shook her head. His eyes narrowed, but he did not follow and she breathed a sigh of relief.

Out in the corridors it was colder than the box. She released Mathias's arm to pull her shawl closer.

'What do you wish to discuss?' she asked, impatient with him because she knew he meant to scold her.

'You should not encourage Perth. I have told you before, he offers nothing honourable.'

Lillith's mouth thinned. Perth was more honourable than her brother allowed. It was love the Earl did not offer.

'We have been down this road before and it goes nowhere,' she said testily. 'Should I pursue Viscount Chillings? It seems that he left your party to join mine tonight. Did you suggest it?'

A gloating smile made Mathias's cheeks puff out. 'You have been widowed a year. It is time you looked to remarry. Chillings would make a good match. He is a widower, so the two of you would have something in common. And a man, once married, tends to marry again.'

A young woman carrying oranges passed them,

casting a curious glance their way. Her presence reminded Lillith that they were not private.

'This is not the place to discuss this, Mathias.'

He shrugged. 'There is never a good time to discuss matrimony.'

Still, he turned them back toward the Russells' box. He opened the door without knocking and angled Lillith in ahead of him. The Prince had already left, but Perth sat where she had left him, a brooding darkness on his face.

The Earl stood abruptly. 'Lady de Lisle, Mrs Russell, I would be delighted if you would join me for a ride in Rotten Row tomorrow. It will be cold, but invigorating.' His words included everyone, but his eyes held Lillith's.

She shivered and opened her mouth to refuse but Madeline beat her. 'Why, Perth, we would be delighted. Wouldn't we, Nathan? Lillith?' She shot Lillith a quelling glance that said louder than words that they were going on this outing.

Lillith turned away. Madeline was an inveterate matchmaker no matter who the couple was. Earlier she had tried as blatantly to put Chillings with Lillith.

'Lillith is already engaged to me,' Mathias said, his face dark with irritation.

In spite of trying to keep her face impassive, Lillith's muscles tightened in rebellion. Mathias was only trying to keep her from Perth's company, which was no bad thing. She said nothing.

'It seems that Lady de Lisle dances to your tune

once more,' Perth said, his tone dangerously close to insulting.

Silence reigned as everyone watched Mathias, wondering if he would take offence or let the tone go. He was known as a man who avoided duels. He stiffened and his hands squeezed Lillith's arm. Then he released her and stepped away.

'You would do well to remember that, Perth,' Mathias said before turning and leaving with poor grace.

Perth, a knowing look on his face, took his leave, saying, 'I shall look forward to seeing you another time, Lady de Lisle.'

Madeline, vastly enjoying herself, held out her hand for Perth to kiss in the Continental way. The Earl obliged her while Nathan Russell looked on with amusement at his wife's antics. Then, before Lillith realised what Perth was about, he took her fingers and raised them to his lips. This contact had to stop. Most Englishmen did not greet women this way. But she could no more find it in herself to deny herself this pleasure than she could root out the love she felt for him.

His eyes held hers as his mouth touched the fine leather of her gloves. The intimacy of his look intensified her unreasonable desire. She knew only too well how his mouth felt on her bare flesh. She flushed and pulled her hand away.

Perth nodded and left.

'He is devilishly handsome,' Madeline said. 'Any woman would be beside herself to receive such marked attention from him.'

Lillith frowned as she surreptitiously wiped her hand down her skirts. Somehow she had to forget the feel of his flesh on hers. 'I am not any woman,' she said acerbically.

Madeline became comforting. 'And nor should you be. He would not be so interested if you were.'

Lillith turned away from her friend's knowing eyes. If she had not wanted Perth's attentions then she should not have come to Town for she had known this would happen. She had, in fact, longed for it. Now the intensity of their meetings scared her more than when he had abducted her. She began to think that perhaps he truly cared for her since he pursued her so diligently. But no. He wanted revenge.

It was painful to remind herself that he wanted revenge for what had happened so long ago, but she had to remember. Otherwise she would fall into his arms and be miserable for the rest of her life, always loving him and wanting him to love her. For she knew him well enough to know that, where he did not love, he would not be faithful. It would kill her to be married to him and have him turn to another woman.

She sighed. That was not the life she wanted.

As soon as Perth exited the Russells' box, he left the opera. Ravensford would wonder, but he would not worry. Outside, the weather was cold and wet. Fog blanketed the streets so that not even the light from a linkboy's flambeau could provide more than ten feet of visibility. Brook's was a distance from here but, the mood he was in, Perth knew the walk would do him good. He was balked of his goal, and he was too active for this sedentary London life.

He set out with long strides, his cane swinging at his side. The night air was brisk and he needed that to ease some of the heat his meeting with Lillith had created. No matter how many times he saw her, or how he tried to win her, she resisted him.

He hit the cane against the street in frustration. She wanted things he could not, would not, give. He had loved her once, he would not make that mistake again.

He increased his pace until he turned the corner of the street where Brook's stood. Inside the exclusive club it was warm, smoky and dimly lit.

Perth shrugged out of his greatcoat and gave it to the nearby footman. Somewhere here, Chillings waited for him, if he had not misunderstood the Viscount. Rather than ask a servant for the Viscount's whereabouts, Perth set out on his own. He found Chillings ensconced in a leather wing chair in a dark corner with a decanter of amber liquid and two glasses on the table beside him. Another chair sat opposite. Perth took it.

'Whisky?' Chillings asked by way of hello. 'I had it brought specially.'

'Thank you,' Perth said, accepting the offered glass.

For long minutes, neither spoke. Each drank a glass of whisky and poured another. Someone smoked cheroots across the room. Someone else smoked a pipe. The haze curled around the chandelier and the branches of candles. A roaring fire added its particular scent and fuzz to the air.

Chillings pulled a snuffbox from his jacket pocket,

flicked open the lid and offered some to Perth. 'It is the Beau's own mix.'

Chillings had been a particular friend of Beau Brummell's and had stuck by the man even after Brummell had his falling-out with the Prince of Wales. If talk was true, Chillings had also lent quite a sum of money to the Beau and never gotten it back. He was not the only one.

'No, thank you,' Perth said. 'I am not a snuff taker.' He finished his second glass while the Viscount took a pinch of snuff and with a flick of his wrist sniffed the concoction. Never a patient man, Perth broke the carefully created calm between them. 'Why did you ask me here?'

Chillings raised one coal-black brow so that it nearly met the premature grey of his hair that hung in one rakish lock over his high forehead. 'I thought that was obvious—the lovely Lady de Lisle.'

The muscles in Perth's shoulders tightened into painful knots. His voice, however, was non-committal. 'I was not aware that we had something to discuss pertaining to her.'

'Enough prevaricating,' Chillings said. 'Life is too short to allow misunderstanding to ruin a friendship or to let pride keep one from going after what one wants.' He put the delicately enamelled snuffbox back in his pocket and took a swig of whisky. 'Believe me, I know.'

Perth set his empty glass down and waited.

'Lady de Lisle is an extraordinary woman and not at all in the common way. Any man would be inter-

ested in her—if he were not already engaged elsewhere.' Chillings met Perth eye to eye. 'I enjoy her
company, but that is as far as it goes. I was in her box
because her brother asked me to pay attention to her
as a favour. It seems she lacks for male company.' He
said the last blandly.

'Or the kind Wentworth deems appropriate,' Perth
said.

'That too.' Chillings finished his drink and stood.
He held out his hand. 'Friends?'

Perth rose and took the other's hand. 'I wish you
the best of luck with the lady who *has* caught your
fancy.'

Chillings laughed ruefully. 'I shall need all the luck
I can get. She is a high-flyer, new to Town, and not
at all interested in becoming a cyprian. I hope to convince her otherwise.'

'You will succeed. But, in the meantime, how about
a hand of cards?'

In charity with one another, they moved to a room
where groups played all manner of gambling games.
Before they could settle at a table, Chillings walked
to where the Betting Book was kept. He flipped it open
to the last page and motioned Perth over.

'I saw you in here with Ravensford several days
ago. Were you checking to see if someone had written
anything about you and Lady de Lisle?'

Perth eyed the Viscount. 'Ravensford insisted.'

'But you knew there would be nothing,' Chillings said.

'What do you mean by that?' Perth asked, careful to keep any hint of suspicion from his voice.

'Oh, I think you know exactly what I mean.' Instead of pursuing the topic, Chillings turned away. 'Are you up to faro tonight, Perth? I feel like taking a risk.'

Perth laughed. 'If I can be guaranteed a turn at being the bank, I will be more than happy to indulge your desire.'

The two made their way to the table where a game of faro was in action. Perth knew Chillings was done speaking of the Betting Book, but he still wondered how much the Viscount knew. If he knew everything, he had been very discreet throughout the past months. And if that were so, he knew he could trust the man when Chillings said he was not interested in Lillith.

But Perth knew Wentworth would stop at nothing to ensure that he married Lillith off to the highest bidder once more, a man who would be willing to pay Wentworth's debts. He intended to have her for himself, but he'd be damned if he would pay Wentworth's gambling debts in the bargain.

Days later, Lillith paced her bedchamber. The large airy room, done in shades of lavender and blue, normally eased her nerves. This morning she knew nothing would help. Her stomach roiled and she had already lost what little breakfast she had managed to eat. Each passing day made it harder to deny what her body told her.

'My lady,' Agatha said, 'your guests will be here shortly. I still need to fix your hair.'

Lillith sighed. She and Madeline and Nathan were going for a picnic in the country. Madeline had said she would invite some others to go with them, but it was Lillith's gathering and they would all be meeting here. At the time she had proposed it, it had seemed a delightful diversion and a good effort to do something that might, if only for a couple hours, keep her mind from Perth. Now she was tired and grumpy with a digestive system that refused to cooperate. She wished she might claim sickness, but dared not.

She pressed her hand to her abdomen as she sat for Agatha's ministration. She had been waking up sick for the last three weeks. She was also more tired than usual.

'Ouch,' she said, tears springing to her eyes. 'Do be careful, Agatha.' It seemed the maid was less gentle than normal.

'Pardon, my lady. I did not mean to hurt you.'

Lillith sighed. 'I know you did not.'

Her thoughts whirled around. What if her fear was true? What if she was carrying Perth's child? No. It was impossible. Nine years of marriage had never ended in this—surely three nights could not?

'Bring me the green shawl,' she said, forcing her thoughts to her toilet. 'And the bonnet trimmed in green satin and apple blossoms.'

'Yes, my lady.'

Agatha rushed to do her bidding. Lillith stood and started pacing before she caught herself. Enough of this.

She donned the clothing and swept from the room,

intent on ignoring the rumblings of her stomach, though she knew from experience that it would be lunchtime before she got relief. Right now she needed to make sure that Cook had everything packed and that the coach was ready. That would take her mind off the other things.

Agatha ran after her with the apple-green pelisse.

Thirty minutes later, Lillith was assured that everything was as complete as she could possibly make them. And not a minute too soon. She heard the knocker and the sound of the door opening.

'Mr and Mrs Russell,' the butler announced just as the knocker went again.

Lillith moved to take Madeline's outstretched hands. Nathan stepped aside and smiled as the two of them hugged.

'You are positively glowing,' Madeline gushed, moving back.

'Thank you,' Lillith said, grinning and making a short curtsy. 'You are delightful as well. Going on a picnic suits you.'

'A perfect idea,' Madeline said, releasing her light, trilling laughter. 'To go at this time of year is even more enticing. Town can be so boring during the Little Season, with so many staying in the country, that a picnic in questionable weather adds spice.' She laughed again. 'You always were one for doing the unexpected.'

Lillith laughed as well, enjoying her friend's pleasure in this unusual adventure. 'Let us hope it does not snow. Who else did you manage to coerce into taking this risk with us?' Lillith asked.

Madeline glanced at her husband and some of the laughter left her face. 'Well, you see…Nathan ran into Lord Ravensford and his wife riding in Rotten Row. Yesterday. And…'

She trailed off as the butler opened the door again and announced, 'Lord and Lady Ravensford and Lord Perth.'

Lillith blanched and her eyes held such a look of reproach that Madeline flushed bright red. 'I am terribly sorry, Lillith, I did not… Oh, dear, I have made a muddle of everything.'

Lillith's good manners rose to the fore. She forced a smile to her face and turned to her new guests. 'Ravensford, Lady Ravensford, Perth, how delightful to have you join us.'

Ravensford's eyes sparkled. 'I cannot tell you how delighted we are to be here. A rare bit of luck to run into Russell in Hyde Park yesterday.'

Lady Ravensford's eyes held sympathy. 'I hope we are not too many. Men often don't think of that sort of thing when they plan an outing, particularly when it is not their outing to plan.'

Lillith's smile turned genuine. 'Do not worry, Lady Ravensford. I asked Madeline to find some others to go with us. I am glad she found you.'

Some of the tension in the room eased.

Then Lillith shifted to greet Perth. His eyes were stark. She raised a hand to him, the pulse beating at the base of her throat.

'Perth.'

'Lady de Lisle.'

She forced a weak smile. 'We must be leaving if we hope to have any time in the country,' she said breathlessly, wishing she could resist him and knowing once again that she could not.

Without waiting for a reply, she swept from the room. The sooner she put some distance between her and Perth the better for her peace of mind—and heart.

She stood in the foyer, donning the heavy cape Simmons held when a sense of foreboding came over her. Looking up, she saw Mathias on the first-floor landing. He was watching her like a ferret watches a mouse.

He had spent the night. She thought that he was being dunned and could no longer afford his fashionable set of rooms in the Albany. But she did not know for sure. She did not ask and he did not tell.

'Going out, Sister?' For a man as heavy as he was, he moved lightly on his feet as he descended the stairs. 'Did I hear Perth?'

Just then the rest of her party spilled into the foyer. Madeline and Lady Ravensford laughed at something Nathan was saying. Lord Ravensford, one auburn brow raised, looked at Mathias while Perth ignored her brother.

In a rush, Lillith said, 'We are going for a picnic, Mathias. As you can see, we are a group.'

Instantly she regretted the last words. They sounded as though she sought to impress upon him the innocence of the situation, something that was no concern of his. At worst her words implied that there was a need for innocence, which then implied that there was more between her and Perth than she wished anyone to ever realise—especially Mathias.

Mathias stopped halfway down the stairs. His gaze swept over them and a sneer marred his face.

Perth's heavy-lidded eyes were cold and deadly.

Apprehension chewed at Lillith. Something more had happened since the incident in her drawing room several days ago. She would have to find out from Mathias when she returned. Right now, she wanted to get her party out of here before the situation became ugly.

She rushed forward and took Madeline's arm and pulled her out the door, hoping the others would follow. Outside, her coach waited. The Russells' carriage, a high-perch phaeton done in hunter green, stood behind hers. Behind them was another phaeton done in ebony and bearing the Earl of Ravensford's coat of arms. No other vehicles waited.

The tension created inside changed focus but remained. She turned and spoke without thinking. 'Where is your carriage, Perth?'

His eyes caught hers. 'I walked.'

'What? I find that hard to believe.'

He shrugged and settled his curly-brimmed beaver on his head. 'I find that after so long in Town, I need exercise. I walk a lot in the country. Besides, I live only a few streets away.'

'How do you intend to accompany us? You have no carriage and both Nathan and Ravensford have phaetons that will only hold two.'

His eyes held hers. 'I had hoped you would offer me transportation.'

'No, no, that cannot be,' Madeline said, stepping between them. 'You must ride with Nathan, Perth. I will go with Lillith.'

Relief warred with disappointment. But what Madeline said was best. She might be a widow, but that did not give her carte blanche to be alone in a carriage with a man who was not her relative. It could be done, but should not be done with the rumour circulating about them, for his name was now being linked with hers.

Perth cast her one last smouldering glance before joining Nathan Russell in the phaeton. She and Madeline got into her carriage and the coachman whipped the horses into motion.

They passed quickly through London, the cobbles sounding loud through the West End and out into the country, Richmond their destination. Soon the phaetons passed them by.

'I am so terribly sorry,' Madeline said. 'I did not know until it was too late that Nathan had invited Ravensford. Then for Ravensford to bring Perth.' She reached for Lillith, only to withdraw her hand. 'I am so sorry. I know you find his presence uncomfortable.'

Lillith smiled ruefully. 'It does not matter, Madeline. I must learn to deal better with his company, but it is hard.'

She gazed at the countryside they passed. The trees had lost their leaves and the furrows in the fields were brown. November was here and the earth was going to sleep.

Many members of the aristocracy had homes in Richmond. It was an easy travelling distance if one went by water. De Lisle had a house there, which had gone to his heir, a distant nephew, who was not much older than Lillith. The new Lord de Lisle did not care much for her, having been against the marriage from the start. Still, they managed to maintain a distant relationship of tolerance.

'Well, then,' Madeline said, her voice perkier, 'I can hope for the best. I still think you should accept his offer. 'Tis time you remarried.'

Lillith listened to her friend's ramble, nearly choking on the last. 'You would have me marry the Earl of Perth? A man who does not love me?'

Madeline shrugged, looking not a whit chastened. 'He obviously cares for you. And there is the rumour already linking you to him. A marriage would soon scotch that.'

Lillith sighed. 'Yes, there is the rumour,' she said softly. 'Somehow my disappearance has been linked to Perth and I don't know why.'

'Don't you?' Madeline raised one auburn brow. 'Surely you dissemble, something you need not do with me.'

'Why should my absence from my country house be instantly linked to Perth's absence from Town? Either one of us could have been gone for any number of reasons not related to the other.'

'You could. I agree. But no one believes it.'

'Why?' Lillith turned a puzzled face to her friend.

Madeline shook her head as though such a question had such an obvious answer that it was ridiculous that Lillith did not see it. 'Because the two of you look at each other as though you are one another's most coveted treasure. Everyone has seen it, and everyone has commented on it at one time or another. Many wonder when you will marry. Or, barring that, begin an affair. The disappearance is taken as the start of the affair.'

A soft gasp escaped Lillith. 'Why have I not heard any of this?'

'How should I know? Perhaps you have refused to hear what is being said.' Her voice softened and she added, 'But none of that really matters. You love him, you should marry him and be done with it.'

'Perhaps,' Lillith replied. There was much to consider here. 'He does not love me,' she added softly.

Madeline barely heard her friend's last words and could not suppress a comment. 'Vastly dramatic, but I think far from true.'

Hope surged in Lillith's heart only to be ruthlessly suppressed. 'He desires me,' she murmured.

'Oh, yes, he does that,' Madeline said with a delightful shiver. 'It must be infinitely exciting to have a man of his ilk want you. *I* would be ecstatic.'

Lillith laughed. 'Now I know you jest. You are madly in love with Nathan. No other man even catches your eye.'

Madeline shrugged. 'As to that, no woman can *totally* ignore the Earl of Perth. He is so dangerous looking. One can imagine him abducting one and carrying one off without a thought for what anyone else might think. A rogue.'

'Yes,' Lillith said, 'he is all of that and more. But as I have already told you, he does not love me.' When Madeline opened her mouth to speak, Lillith held up her hand to stall her. 'Desire is not enough. Not for me. I have had that before and it is a cold bedfellow.'

'Oh, dear,' Madeline breathed. She took Lillith's unresisting hand in hers. 'I am sorry. I did not think of that, only that where there is such burning desire surely love will follow.'

'But not always,' Lillith said bitterly. 'Not always.'

The carriage slowed down and both stopped speaking. They were pulling on to a dirt side road and would soon be at their destination, a small hillside on Lillith's late husband's property. It was a charming respite from the buildings and the dirt and the soot of London. Lillith had often come here for peace. Today would be vastly different.

She said to Madeline, 'We are here.'

Madeline nodded and let the previous subject die.

Soon they were all climbing out of their carriages and the servants were unloading the baskets of food. Blankets flapped in the wind and soon covered the dying November grass. No wildflowers greeted them, but a view of rolling countryside rewarded them for the journey. By evening it would be unbearably cold. As it was, Lillith's adventure was truly that. The weak November sun warmed no one. They had come more for the company than the weather. Thankfully it was not raining, or worse, snowing.

Chapter Ten

Lillith found Perth sitting beside her on the blanket, her acute awareness of him warming her despite the day being cold and the sun weak. He poured her a cup of tea, even though a footman hovered nearby ready to serve. She took the cup, her fingers brushing his, and memories of the first time he had poured her tea flooded her senses. It had been during that coach ride. She flushed hotly as her mind continued to remember the rest of her abduction.

He seemed to know her thoughts. 'We can have that again,' he murmured, his voice husky.

She lowered her eyes from the intensity in his. 'No, we cannot. And please…' she lifted her free hand to keep him from speaking '…say no more. If for no other reason than that there are others around us.'

A grim smile twisted his mouth. His scar looked pinched. He rose and went to speak with Nathan Russell, who stood some distance away looking out at the surrounding fields.

Mary Margaret, Lady Ravensford, sat where Perth had. 'He is a passionate man,' she commented mildly.

Lillith gave her a bland look.

'Sometimes you must do what your heart tells you, not what your head cautions,' Mary Margaret said gently. 'Believe me, I know that is not easy.'

'Thank you,' Lillith said. But she did not want to talk about this with her. 'Have you been here before?'

Lady Ravensford took the hint and followed. Madeline soon joined them and the three discussed the latest *on dits* with relish. Shortly the gentlemen joined them and organised pandemonium set in as the footmen served the food on specially packed china and silver. Crystal goblets filled with champagne. Laughter filled the chilled air.

'To Lady de Lisle and her fantastic entertainments,' Ravensford said, raising his glass.

'Yes,' everyone else added, following his lead.

Lillith laughed with delight, only to feel Perth's gaze on her. Drawn inexorably, she looked at him. He raised his glass to his lips and drank, his attention never wavering from her.

'To Lady de Lisle,' he finally said, his glass empty.

There was an expectant pause, almost as though the others felt momentary embarrassment at witnessing something too private. Shivers chased down Lillith's spine.

Against all sense of self-preservation, she was drawn to Perth as a moth to the flame that would destroy it. She gathered all her strength of will and looked away from him. She must return to the country soon or she would be lost.

The next afternoon Lillith found herself riding in Hyde Park in spite of the cold weather and her own exhaustion. Somehow she had allowed Mathias to talk her into this outing. They had argued when she had questioned him about the increased hostility between him and Perth. Mathias said it was nothing. She knew better.

Today, they were in a small group of three men, another woman and Lillith. The other female was Lady Annabelle Fenwick-Clyde, the twin sister of Viscount Chillings. Lillith had just met her this day.

Like her brother, who also rode with them, Lady Annabelle had prematurely grey hair and eyebrows dark as the night. She was elegantly slim in a hunter-green riding habit and dashingly fashionable in a matching military-style hat. Her blue eyes sparkled and her wit was acerbic. Lillith found her very entertaining.

'Oh, look,' Lady Annabelle said, 'the Earl of Perth. I have heard he is a devil with the ladies and a military hero.' She prodded her brother with her riding crop. 'Do call him over here, Chillings, for I don't doubt that you are acquainted with him.'

The Viscount gave a long-suffering sigh. 'There are times like now when I wish you had not returned from Cairo, Belle.'

The lady laughed heartily and winked at Lillith. 'I am such a trial to him.' She slanted a glance at Mathias's portly figure and frowning face. 'Something I am sure you are never to Mr Wentworth.'

Lillith looked at Mathias and fought the urge to tell him he looked like he had swallowed a lemon whole. After all, this outing and the people they were with had been his plan. Instead, she said demurely, 'I try not to be a bother. There are always repercussions I would rather not face.'

Lady Annabelle gave Lillith a sharp look but said nothing.

The third man of the party, Mr Carstairs, moved closer to Lillith and said, 'I cannot believe that you are ever trouble.'

Lillith smiled graciously and hoped that Perth noted the ruggedly handsome man who sat his horse so well. It would do Perth good to know that other men found her attractive. It would do her more good if she found someone attractive besides the Earl. This longing for someone she could not have for anything more than a surcease of passion had to stop.

Mr Thomas Carstairs was an East India Company nabob recently returned to England. His hair was bleached blond by the Indian sun and his face was burned a swarthy golden brown. His teeth shone blindingly white when he smiled, and the skin around his piercing blue eyes crinkled. A very handsome man.

Lillith sighed internally. Too bad he did not make her blood boil and her pulse pound. A hint of cinnamon floated on the cold November air. Perth was near.

She turned her head in his direction as nonchalantly as she could, when the urge to feast her eyes on him was nearly overpowering. It seemed that she had not seen him for longer than she could bear, although she had last been with him yesterday.

'Did I see you summon me over, Chillings?' Perth asked with cool composure.

The Viscount laughed. 'My sister wants to make your acquaintance. Englishmen are a novelty where she has been the last two years and so far she cannot get enough of meeting her countrymen.'

Perth looked at Lady Annabelle and his eyes lit with appreciation. 'My pleasure to help a lady in distress. I am Perth.'

The lady held out her gloved hand and smiled so that a dimple showed in her left cheek. 'I am Annabelle Fenwick-Clyde, Chillings's twin sister.'

Lillith watched the exchange with distress. Lady Annabelle was a handsome woman with intelligence and wit; qualities Perth admired. The lady also did nothing to hide her interest in the Earl. Lillith bit the inside of her cheek to keep from saying something, anything, to break the awareness between the two. She was spared further discomfort.

'Lady de Lisle, would you care to race to that large tree by the Serpentine?' Mr Carstairs asked.

Fearful that she could not keep her sense of gratitude out of her voice, she nodded and spurred her mare forward. It was not something she would have normally agreed to, but for the instant the freezing wind in her face was like a much-needed slap of cold common sense. Perth's flirting with Lady Annabelle was to be expected and another reason she would not marry for convenience.

She and Mr Carstairs arrived at the tree breathless. Her black velvet hat with its white ostrich plume had tilted too far back during her dash and threatened to fall. She steadied her mount and reached up to better secure the hat.

'Let me,' Mr Carstairs said. 'After all, I am the cause for its precarious position.'

It was an offer she had not expected and was not prepared for. Mr Carstairs edged his large grey gelding close to her mare and leaned towards her, his hands reaching for her head. He smelled of sandalwood and the cold, both pleasant but neither exciting. When his shoulder brushed hers, she felt nothing, neither discomfort nor anticipation. Nothing.

She thought he might have lingered longer than absolutely necessary on straightening her hat, but she was not sure. 'Thank you,' she murmured, smiling at him as she backed her mare away.

He grinned, his strong white teeth so appealing. 'My pleasure. Any time.'

The look in his blue, blue eyes and the inflection of his voice hinted that many things would be his pleasure to do with her and for her. Still she felt no excitement. She did not even blush.

She had barely put distance between them before the rest of the party caught up. She ignored Perth's obvious irritation at something, probably her, and turned to Mathias. 'Is it not time for us to return home? I believe you have a meeting later this afternoon.'

Her brother scowled at her. 'We have time enough for another canter around the park.'

She thought about arguing, but the set of her brother's shoulders told her that he would be obstinate. Her reluctance would only cause a scene. 'As you wish,' she murmured, angling her horse away from Mr Carstairs.

Unhappy with the entire situation, she urged her mare into a canter, hoping to leave the others behind. Disappointment pierced her as she heard the clop of another horse's hooves.

'You are free with your favors,' Perth said, his voice rough.

He caught up with her and for a moment she thought he intended to reach for her reins. He obviously thought better of it, but his hands clenched on his own reins.

She glanced sideways at him. 'As are you. Lady Annabelle is a very interesting woman.'

'That she is,' he murmured. 'But I have not made love to her.'

The blush that would not come for Mr Carstairs flared into existence. Heat scorched Lillith. 'Be quiet,' she ordered. 'Someone will hear.'

He glanced back. 'They are too far away. Besides,' he scowled at her, 'Carstairs might as well know now that his chances are non-existent.'

Her hands jerked on the reins, causing her mount to

prance. She leaned forward and soothed the mare with strokes along its neck. 'That is not your decision.'

The scar running the length of Perth's right cheek whitened. 'By heavens it is. You are mine, Lillith, whether you admit it or not.'

Her brows snapped together. 'I am no one's plaything, sirruh. And most definitely not yours.'

Anger turned Perth's eyes black.

'I thought I told you to stay away from my sister?' Mathias's voice separated them.

Lillith jumped. She had been so involved in her fight with Perth that she had not heard her brother approach. Anyone else from the party might have interrupted them and neither of them would have known it until the other person had overheard everything.

What was happening to her? Not even her sense of self-preservation worked when Perth was near. Heaven help her.

Perth cast Mathias a contemptuous glance. 'I do as I please, Wentworth. You should know that by now.'

'Then go and flirt with Lady Annabelle,' Mathias said with a nasty twist of his mouth. 'That seemed to please you well enough, and leave my sister alone.'

Perth's lips thinned. He nodded to Lillith. 'We shall discuss this later.'

He turned his horse and cantered back to join the other three where he positioned himself beside Lady Annabelle. Anger at Mathias mixed badly with the anger she felt toward Perth and the jealousy Lady Annabelle generated.

'Stay out of my affairs, Mathias,' she said flatly.

His face red enough to cause an apoplexy, he retorted, 'You act like a harlot around that man. How many times must I tell you he is not for you? You need to remarry and Perth will not do.'

Her hands clenched the reins. 'What I do with Perth is my concern, not yours. Nor do I need to remarry.' Her mouth twisted bitterly. 'My marriage was not so enjoyable that I am anxious to repeat the experience. And I don't have to. De Lisle left me a wealthy woman, as you should know since he appointed you the trustee of my estate.'

For a second his eyes shifted from hers before he returned his gaze to her and said, 'You are a headstrong woman, Lillith, and it will bring you nothing but trouble. Already everyone is talking about you and Perth. Will you have them decide the two of you are having an affair? Do you intend to be one of those widows who become the acknowledged mistress of a wealthy man? For that is where you are headed.'

She said nothing. There was too much truth in his words. Her fury turned inwards.

'Besides,' Mathias continued in a more reasonable tone, 'it has been over a year since de Lisle's death. 'Tis past time you remarried. Carstairs or Chillings would be perfect.'

She stared straight ahead and, even through her irritation, suspicion began to show. 'Why are you so intent on my remarrying, Mathias? I have plenty of money from de Lisle's settlement. And a new husband might not be so eager to have you live with us as has been your wont the past six months.'

It was long moments before Mathias answered, as though he considered his words carefully. 'A woman who has enjoyed the marriage bed once is more likely to seek such pleasure elsewhere if she is not wed again. And you need a man's hand and guidance. You are far too attracted to Perth for your own good. Another man would keep him from your thoughts and your side. I am only thinking of you.'

'You are saying that you think I am a trollop and too weak to manage on my own.' She gave him a hard look. 'You are insulting me.'

'No, no.' He raised one gloved hand in protest.

She studied him. He was her only living relative. Her brother. But there were times when she wondered if she was the only one of them to care that their relationship was all the family they had left. When she managed to think about Mathias with her head and not her emotions, she realised that he treated her like an object that was his to dispose of as he willed. It was not a pleasant thought and she tried to keep herself from it. Unfortunately, since Perth had re-entered her life, the knowledge had been forced upon her that she was always the one to reach out to Mathias—unless her brother had need of money. Then he came to her.

Whatever else Mathias might have said, and what she might have replied, never happened. The rest of their party caught up with them and this time she was very much aware of their coming close.

She gave everyone a false smile. 'My brother has decided to continue on his ride by himself or with the rest of you if you so please. My apologies, but I have matters to attend to at home.'

She glanced at their faces. Surprise on Lady Annabelle's, disappointment on Mr Carstairs's, consideration on Chillings's and, of course, sardonic acceptance on Perth's. Her brother she ignored. She left without another word.

Perth watched her go, noting the stiffness of her ramrod back. Whatever Wentworth had been prattling about, it had infuriated Lillith. He considered that a good thing. She was too controlled by her brother and it would do her good to stand up to him. Particularly since he had an instinct that Wentworth had gone beyond the bounds of what even a loving sister could accept—or so he hoped.

Lillith lifted her aching head from the chamber pot. Her bleeding was three months late. She could no longer deny the truth. She carried Perth's child.

She rocked back on her heels and fell backwards so she sat on the floor. One hand slipped to her still flat belly. All these years of thinking herself barren, listening to de Lisle berate her for her inability to conceive.

She was not sure if she felt joy or despair. She had always wanted children, but over the last years she had finally reached a sort of dispassionate acceptance that she would never have any. Her second hand strayed to her waist.

In six months she would have a child.

Wonder held her for long minutes. Would she have a boy or a girl? It did not matter.

But what about Perth?

If Perth learned of her condition, he would force marriage on her. He would feel it his duty and to do less would besmirch his honour. She had no doubt that the abduction of months ago would be as nothing compared to what he would do this time. She would not put it past him to hire a minister to join them against her protests. A powerful nobleman could do many things.

That was not what she wanted.

She levered herself to a standing position and crossed to the window. Outside night was descending. In what light was left, she could make out a cold drizzle. A carriage rumbled by, the inside a golden glow. Someone headed to a dinner party, and then perhaps to the opera or the theatre.

She sighed and her warm breath left a cloud on the glass. She rubbed the fog away, noting the chill that came through.

She did not want another marriage of convenience. And especially not with Perth. It would be the end of too many girlish dreams that she had cherished in spite of all the facts that said her chances for a love match with him were gone.

But what of her child? Could she condemn it to be a bastard because of her own cowardice?

She turned from the window and went to sink in a chair in front of the roaring fire. Warmth eased away some of the chill that still held her. Her hands fluttered listlessly before setting once more on her stomach.

She could go to the Continent, have the child and leave it with a couple who would care for it. She knew of women who did that. Her heart wrenched. No, she could never do that.

She closed her eyes and wished life was easier, but it was not. This child she carried was hers, and she would keep it and raise it with all the love she had to give.

But she would not go to Perth with this news.

She would go to her Dower House and wait for the birth. She would lie, tell everyone that she met and married the babe's father during the time she disappeared. If need be, she would go to the Continent in the spring, have the child and return. No one would believe her, but it did not matter. Other noble families raised bastards and the children were accepted into Society. Hers would be too.

Her decision made, she stood. 'Agatha.'

The maid looked in from the dressing room where she had been making minor repairs to some of Lillith's dresses. 'Yes, my lady?'

'We are leaving first thing in the morning for the Dower House.'

The maid nodded. It was normal for her mistress to return to the country at this time of year.

The decision made and the order to pack understood by her maid, Lillith felt a weight lift from her heart. She would go to the country, bear her child and raise that child on her own. She would not look back with regret to this choice. The child would be enough for the rest of her life.

She could not have Perth. She would have his child.

Chapter Eleven

Perth stared morosely at the fire.

A month after coming to Town, he was no nearer his goal for the returning army veterans or his pursuit of Lillith. Bitter frustration soured his mood. As did Fitch's reproachful looks. The manservant chose that moment to enter the library.

Caught in regret and guilt, Perth said testily, 'I have asked her a dozen times to marry me. Does that satisfy your pinched idea of responsibility?'

'Pardon me, my lord,' Fitch said with a voice that would have curdled milk, 'but have you told her that you love her?'

Perth drew himself up. 'I do not lie, no matter what the cost.'

Fitch made a noise under his breath. 'You have been doing a pretty good job of it for the last ten years.'

'You go too far.'

Perth's voice would have frozen another person. Fitch had been with the Earl too long and gone through too much. War had a way of forging relationships.

'I believe you have done that on your own, my lord.'

'Get out.'

Fitch did so without a qualm.

Perth rose and went to a table where a decanter full of good Scotch whisky awaited his pleasure. He poured a glassful and downed it in several gulps. The alcohol burned down his throat and exploded in his stomach. It changed nothing.

'Damnation!'

He threw the glass at the fireplace where it shattered against the brick. There was only one thing to do.

Less than an hour later, Perth stood in front of Lillith's door. The night air rifled through his greatcoat and whispered down his neck. The flambeau held by the linkboy he had hired to light his way blew out. It did not matter. He had already seen all he needed. The knocker was gone. She had left Town.

He banged on the door anyway. With luck she had left a couple of servants to care for the empty house. He had only to rouse them.

'My lord,' the boy said hesitantly.

Never one to take his anger out on someone less fortunate than himself, Perth reached in his pocket and tossed the youth a Golden boy. 'You may go.'

The youth had managed to relight his flambeau and in its flickering light he saw what he held. 'Thank you. Thank you much, my lord,' he said, his joy in such bounty showing on his face. He bowed and hurried away as though fearing Perth would realise how much he had given and demand it back.

Perth hardly noticed that the boy had left. He pounded harder. Someone had to be here. He would find them if he had to go around to the back and beat on every door there. He would break in through a window if he must.

Although, once he stopped and thought, he knew where she had to be, or where he hoped she had gone to—her Dower House. If she had gone to the Continent instead, he would be hard pressed to find her. But it was a strong possibility. Since Napoleon's final defeat, all of the *ton* was flocking to Europe. If she had gone there, her servants would know where and getting that information from them would save him weeks of time. For he would find her.

When no one answered he swore under his breath and headed for the back. All the windows were dark, making him fear that she had not left anyone here. He banged on the door and looked in all the windows. Not a glimmer of light. Nor did anyone answer his banging.

There was one other place he could go. Madeline Russell would know where Lillith was.

Not wanting to waste time going to his own house for a horse, Perth hired a carriage to take him to Nathan and Madeline Russell's small town home. Their house was lit up and through the windows he could see people milling. They might not be wealthy, but they were well liked. Some of the tension that had lent him speed seeped out and his shoulder muscles eased.

Without a qualm, he strode up the steps and knocked. He did not care that he would be arriving uninvited to what appeared to be a small gathering. The butler answered immediately.

'Tell Mrs Russell that the Earl of Perth is here to see her,' Perth said, not bothering to take off his beaver hat or hand over his gold-tipped cane.

No emotion showed on the servant's face. 'If you will come with me, my lord, I will inform Madam of your presence.'

Perth found himself in a charming little room done in pinks and baby blues. It was far from fashionable, but he found that the colours amused him. They were something he could easily imagine Madeline Russell choosing. He did not sit. Time was of the essence.

The door opened and Madeline Russell came in. Her auburn hair was curled around her face and her evening gown was fine white muslin. Unlike her very unconventional room, she was very much in vogue.

Perth forced a smile. 'Mrs Russell, I am sorry to intrude on you like this, but I need to know where Lady de Lisle has gone.'

Madeline's eyes widened. She cast a quick look over her shoulder to see if anyone had heard Perth. Relieved that no one could have, she closed the door behind her.

She looked Perth straight in the eye. 'Why do you want to know?'

Instead of the irritation Lillith's challenges always

caused him, he found Madeline Russell's directness calming. But he was not about to reveal his business to her.

'I did not come here to be questioned, Mrs Russell. I came here for information. The sooner I have it, the sooner I will leave you to return to your guests.'

Her mouth pursed. 'Lillith has had enough of your high-handed ways, Perth, and I quite agree with her. If you cannot be bothered to give me a very good reason why I should betray her confidence, then I won't.' She stood her ground.

The temptation to leave and search for Lillith without any knowledge of her whereabouts was strong. Undoubtedly she was at her Dower House. But he could not be sure.

He gritted his teeth, all calmness at the situation gone. 'You are an impertinent minx. I imagine Russell more than has his hands full with you.'

She nodded and crossed her arms over her chest. 'Flattery will get you nothing,' she replied sweetly.

'Damned if it won't,' Perth muttered under his breath, for he had had more than his share of conquests by using charm. The stubborn look on the woman's face told him it would not work this time. 'Very well, I intend to ask her to marry me.'

Madeline's face softened. 'That is all well and good and something you should do, but I am not sure that is enough.'

He ground his teeth. 'It will have to be enough. I can offer nothing else.'

She studied him, noting the way he stood on the

balls of his feet, ready to pounce. His scar was white. His eyes were hard. He needed Lillith. Perhaps that was enough for now.

'She has gone to her Dower House.'

'I thought as much,' Perth said in disgust. 'And I have wasted well over an hour making sure. Thank you, Mrs Russell, I shall be going now.'

'Tut, tut, Perth. She might just as well have gone to the Continent.' Madeline's eyes clouded. 'And she probably should have.'

Perth stopped on his way to the door. 'What do you mean by that?' But he had a sharp, tight feeling in his gut.

She turned so that she could look him in the eye. 'That is something I don't intend to divulge. If you must know, then it should come from her.'

Perth nodded curtly.

He strode from the room and out of the house. Urgency drove him now more than ever. The sharp twist of his gut intensified. Fierce pride mingled with desire and an urge to protect.

He must get to Lillith.

He stood on the pavement in front of Madeline Russell's house and swung his cane to and fro in irritation. Not one carriage had passed this way in the last fifteen minutes, and it was a long walk to his house in Grosvenor Square. There was nothing else to be done. He set off, his long strides eating up the distance.

Fog swirled around his feet. The cold night air bit through his many-caped greatcoat. Occasionally, the candle glow from the window of a passing house lit his way. He increased his pace. There was no time to lose. Always he was on the lookout for a carriage that might be for hire. He was sorely tempted to knock on one of the doors he passed and offer to pay them any amount they wanted for a horse.

He paused at a likely place. He could smell a stable, which meant there might be a horse. But there were no lights.

Footsteps sounded behind him and across the street. He had been hearing them for some time but had assumed they were someone else out on this night. He flicked a glance over his shoulder in curiosity.

Three shadows moved in the darkness between two buildings, but no one came forward. What is going on here, he thought, finally beginning to think about where he was and that he was alone. He was a brave man and not particularly afraid, but hoodlums attacked in gangs. Even he, with his cane and the sword it hid, would be hard pressed to fight off a large number of men.

'Who goes there?' he demanded, forgetting about the possibility of a horse.

He turned to face the opposite side of the street. One of the shadows separated from the others and came forward, empty hands held up in the dim light provided by the moon and stars. No gas lamps lit the road here.

'Jus' me, guv. Wonderin' if ye'd have a bit o' money for a starvin' man?'

Perth watched the man approach. The other two

shadows, men, edged outward on each side of the one coming towards him. Perth flexed his gloved fingers. His leg muscles tightened. The bite of cold air on his face, the tang of soot on his tongue and the chance of danger to his life combined to energise him. This was living for him. This is how he felt with Lillith. The realisation hit him like a blow and took his breath away. No wonder he wanted her so badly. She made him feel alive, as though his life was worth living.

The thugs moved closer, forcing Perth to pay attention to the present. 'I've nothing for you,' he said flatly. 'Take your friends and be gone before something happens that you will regret.'

The man stopped while the other two came forward and edged to either side of Perth. In one smooth slide, Perth pulled the sword from the cane. The steel shone sharply in the dim light. The advancing men paused, then rushed forward as one.

Perth backed up until the building was behind him, then stood his ground. The sword flashed as he countered the attack that had started in earnest. He felt steel hit flesh and one of the men yelped.

'Gor, 'e's got me. The devil take 'im.'

That man staggered and turned aside leaving two men. Perth's mouth twisted into a wicked grin. The odds were getting better.

'Leave now,' he said through clenched teeth, 'and no one else will be hurt.'

The two remaining thugs fell back, but did not depart. He heard them muttering and braced himself for another attack. It came as soon as he had anticipated.

The sword flashed and the one on his right dropped the cudgel that had been raised above his head poised to strike. The heavy wood hit the ground with a thud and the man who had held it whirled away, a stream of filthy language pouring from his mouth like bilge running down a sewer.

Perth watched the second man flee. 'You are by yourself now. Do you think you can do what three of you could not?'

The man slunk back. Perth stepped forward and picked the cudgel up in his left hand.

''Twas suppose ta be easy,' the man growled. 'Nothin' ta worry about. That be w'at the cove said. Damn 'im.'

'Ahh, the light dawns.' He could turn this to his advantage, Perth thought. 'I will double whatever you were offered to harm me if you will take me to the man who hired you.' Even though the light was bad, Perth would swear he could see avarice tighten the other man's face. 'That will give you my money and what the other has already paid you up front. And you will share it with no one.'

The thug rubbed his jaw. 'T'at's a idea. But w'at's to insure you'll pay me? Got the blunt on ye?'

The man was definitely greedy. Perth reached into the inside pocket of his coat and pulled out a leather bag that jangled. He tossed it to the thief. 'My first installment. Tell me when and where you are to collect the second part of your fee for tonight's work and I will meet you there. Then you will get more from me, and I will meet face to face with the man who arranged this attack.'

The scoundrel eyed Perth warily. 'And 'ow do I know you ain't just sayin' this to get away?'

Perth laughed outright; the idea was ludicrous. 'Because I could run you through where you stand without a moment's hesitation.'

The man took several rapid steps back.

'But I want positive proof of who hired you and your word is not enough. Besides which, he probably did not even give you his name. Very likely he did not even hire you himself.'

'Five this mornin',' the man said in a rush and named a place near Nightingale Inn in the East End. A very unsavoury place, but popular with the young bucks. Perth knew the area well.

'I will be there. Now be gone.'

Not until the man was well away did Perth sheath his sword. The cudgel he kept, a grim smile making him look sinister. He would take it with him to the meeting.

By the time he entered his own foyer, it was nearly time to turn around. Fitch, who acted as butler and valet, met Perth at the door.

'My lord,' Fitch said, turning his nose up. 'You are drenched.'

Perth peeled his coat off and then his gloves. His beaver hat was ruined. He handed Fitch his cane. 'This will need cleaning.'

Fitch's eyes widened momentarily, but he said nothing.

Perth grinned. 'Yes, I saw some action.'

'Luckily for you this is the first time. Some of the places you frequent are less than pleasant.'

Perth laughed out right. 'Since I have attempted to take up with Lady de Lisle, my life has been one great adventure.'

'Lady de Lisle? Surely she is not the reason you had to use this sword.' He pulled the weapon from its case and studied the dried blood. 'A good cleaning and oil will make it good as new. Although…' he held it to a candle '…it appears to be nicked. A whetstone will fix that.'

'Make it quick, Fitch. You and I have a meeting in less than an hour in a disreputable part of town and we might find that cane a life-saver.'

Fitch turned and headed to the kitchen while Perth mounted the stairs two at a time, headed for his chambers.

Inside his rooms, he stripped quickly and donned clean, dry clothes with no concern that they were not fashionably tight. 'Twas better to have loose clothing in case he found himself in a dangerous situation again, and he could easily dress himself without Fitch's help. All the time, his mind whirled.

He felt excited and alive. The sense of danger and accomplishment combined to make him aware of everything around him, the heat of the fire, the sound of the wind blowing by his window. This is how he felt with Lillith, ready to take on anything, but he had not recognised the heady delight he took in her company for the same aggressive pursuit of accomplishment he had felt in the army. No wonder he wanted her so badly.

He missed being in the army and the camaraderie along with the knowledge that he did something useful. London and the pursuits of a man of leisure had bored him, and he had not even let himself realise that. Lillith had given him a goal, something to strive for. Now this situation with her brother—for he had no doubt Wentworth was behind the attack on him—gave him another reason to win her.

He had to be right about Wentworth having spent all of Lillith's settlement from de Lisle. There could be no other reason for her brother trying to push her into marriage. But why did the man want him out of the way when he had only recently tried to marry her to him? Very likely because Wentworth knew Perth would not pay the brother's debts as de Lisle had and another man might.

He went to his wardrobe and grabbed a navy greatcoat. The less conspicuous he was the better.

Downstairs, Fitch waited with the cleaned sword replaced in the cane. Perth took the weapon and put a new beaver hat on his head at a rakish angle.

'Like old times, my lord,' Fitch said, a gleam of anticipation lightening his face.

'Have you ordered horses brought around?'

'Of course,' Fitch said, drawing up in affront. 'We might not be in the army now, my lord, but I still know how to prepare.'

* * *

The area of London they shortly found themselves in was not a place to leave two thoroughbred horses without having someone stand guard.

'Here, you,' Fitch said, motioning to a youth standing in front of the pubs. 'Watch our mounts and you will be well paid.'

'Better paid than if you steal them,' Perth added, flipping a coin toward the boy who caught the money with alacrity.

The youth bit on the metal. 'The real thing.'

'See you do as we say,' Fitch emphasised, 'or you will be the sorrier for not.'

The boy gave Fitch a scornful look, but he held tight to the reins of the two horses.

Not waiting to hear the final words between his servant and the street urchin, Perth headed to the corner where the thug had said he was to meet the man who had hired him. Along the way, Perth saw several youths he knew in passing. One of them waved at him, but Perth ignored him and kept going. The young man did not follow.

Rather than stand obviously where the meeting was to take place, Perth positioned himself back away and in the shadow. Fitch soon joined him, his hand on the pistol he kept primed in his pocket. The thief arrived shortly after, but the man responsible was late.

Twenty minutes passed. The thief began to fidget, but Perth and Fitch remained steady. Perth decided the tardiness was something Wentworth would do to a lackey he considered unimportant. He would not be surprised if Wentworth did not show. As far as Wentworth was concerned, the deed was done and to meet the thug and pay him the second half of the money would be a waste of blunt Wentworth did not have. The thief would never be able to find Wentworth so the man was safe.

After sixty minutes, Perth stepped forward. ''Tis unlikely that you will ever again see the man who hired you.'

The man had an ugly look on his face. 'Flash cove, 'e'd better 'ope he don't see me again.' His head tilted and a calculating look sharpened his narrow face. ''Ow about the blunt you owe me?'

Perth's face sharpened. 'I have already paid you as much as I intend to. The second half was dependent upon my meeting the man who hired you. That has not happened.'

The man took a menacing step forward.

'I would not do that if I were you,' Fitch said, moving from the shadow where he had remained. 'I have a primed pistol in my pocket, and I won't hesitate to use it.'

The man backed down, but greed still sharpened his features. 'W'at if I finds the cove?'

Perth shook his head. 'Not good enough. I want to confront the bastard myself.'

The thug grunted acknowledgment of Perth's desire, but did not back away.

'We are leaving now,' Perth said. 'Do not follow us.'

The man flashed a crooked grin that showed brown teeth, where he had them. 'Wouldn't think o' it, guv.'

But he watched them collect their horses and he heard one of the flash coves who frequented the nearby pub call the dangerous man Perth. Wouldn't take too much to find his lordship again, for he had no doubt the man was a lord. He was too arrogant not to be.

Perth rode silently home. Fitch followed. Not until they were inside and Perth was unceremoniously throwing clothes into a duffel did either speak.

'My lord,' Fitch said aghast. 'What are you doing?'

'I am packing.' Perth dug in a drawer for a clean shirt. 'Where did you put my shaving kit?'

Fitch fetched it from the shaving stand where it stood in perfect sight. 'Where are you going? And what are you going to do about the person who paid to have you hurt?'

Perth cinched the saddlebag. 'I am going after Lady de Lisle who has gone to the country. As for the person who wanted me hurt, I have a good idea who he is.' A fierce grin creased his cheek. 'I intend to deal with him yet.'

Fitch nodded in satisfaction. 'Wentworth is where I'd put my blunt.'

Perth gave his man a narrowed look. 'How do you know so much?'

'Has to be.' Fitch picked up one of the shirts Perth had discarded in his search for a cravat. 'You are chasing his sister, and he has never wanted you in the family.' He gave Perth a knowing look. 'He has already managed to do harm to you once before.'

Perth's face hardened. 'I was young and stupid then. Ten years have made a vast difference.'

Fitch nodded. 'Now you carry a cane with a sword at all times.'

'Just so.' Perth slung the saddlebag over his shoulder and strode from the room. 'Don't expect me until you see me,' he said.

Chapter Twelve

Lillith stood naked before her mirror. Multi-branched candelabra flanked both sides of the glass and the fire added more illumination as well as warmth. She turned so that her side was reflected and studied her profile.

Was her stomach slightly rounded instead of nearly concave as it had been? She ran her palms over what she perceived to be a slight bulge. She was over three months. Surely she showed. And soon she should feel the babe move. Perth's child. Her child. She felt a quiver of excitement.

The door slammed open.

Lillith crossed her arms over her hips and spun around, intending to severely berate whoever had the effrontery to barge into her private rooms. She gasped. Perth stood framed in the doorway.

'Oh, my lady,' Agatha begged, standing on tiptoe behind the Earl and peering over his shoulder. 'I'm ever so sorry. He barged in the front door and climbed the stairs before anyone knew what he was about. He would not wait.' She wrung her hands and tried to push past the Earl, who effectively blocked the entrance.

Lillith's teeth began to chatter with suppressed anger. She twisted around and grabbed the robe tossed across a nearby settee. She yanked it on.

'Leave us, Agatha,' she said. '*You* did nothing wrong.'

She did not order Perth gone, for she knew by the look on his face that he was not leaving. He moved into the room and carefully shut the door behind himself. That very controlled action told her how furious he really was. His hair glowed damply and water from his greatcoat puddled on the pale green carpet. His Hessians were muddy. He looked as though he had ridden a great distance without regard to the inclement weather.

'You are bold and your lack of manners more than apparent,' she said coldly, hoping to sting his pride.

He stripped off his greatcoat and threw it across the nearest chair. Fleetingly, Lillith thought the water on the garment would stain the finely embroidered upholstery but it could be replaced easily enough.

'You left without a word.'

His eyes bored into hers before his gaze dropped to her belly. He stepped forward and it was all Lillith could do not to edge back and away from his advancement. Clenching her hands in the robe's belt, she stood her ground.

'I don't owe you any explanation of my comings and goings.' She lifted her chin and hoped that the trepidation making her giddy did not show in her voice.

He did not stop advancing until he stood scant inches from her. The tang of cold air and rain mingled with the familiar awareness of him. The urge to sway into him was great, even though anger at his method of entering her house still made her jaw ache from clenching it too much and too tight. She was so weak where he was concerned.

'You are carrying my child.'

His voice was deep and dark and dangerous. His eyes were black pools. Without warning, he gripped her shoulders and pulled the robe down to her waist. Her hands on the belt kept him from stripping the garment completely from her.

'How dare you!' she said, using one hand to futilely try to pull the silk back up to cover her breasts.

'I dare a lot for you and the child you carry,' he said. 'Too much,' he said harshly. 'Too much.'

She stared at him, taken aback by the hunger and need she saw in his face.

'Does that surprise you?' he asked bitterly. 'Well, not as much as it does me. I thought I was over you.'

His gaze ravished her, moving over the mounds of her breasts and making them swell with desire. She longed for his touch, at her bosom and at her loins. But…

'Do you love me?' she finally asked, the words barely a whisper as she forced them through the constriction in her throat.

His gaze came back to her face. 'No.'

'Ah…'

The word tore from her like the moan of a dying creature. Pain ripped through her. She thought he had made her suffer before, but nothing like this final renunciation. She would slap him if she could, but her arms were pinned to her sides by the garment that his large hands still kept at her waist.

'Get out,' she said. 'Get out of my life and do not ever dare to come back.' She pulled in a ragged breath. 'Or I will have you horsewhipped.'

His face turned murderous. 'As your brother did?'

She blanched. 'You lie. Mathias has many faults but he would never do that.'

He sneered. 'You say you would. Why do you suppose he would not do the same?'

'Get out,' she ordered, wrenching from his grasp.

The shrill rip of silk filled the air. She was free from his hold, but stood naked before him.

'Get out,' she said again, forcing air into her labouring lungs. He stared at her, his gaze roving over her like a hot wave of passion.

He swallowed hard and turned on his heel and left.

Lillith watched in disbelief as he walked away. The door swung shut behind him. Silence surrounded her like a suffocating blanket. Cold assaulted her even though the fire blazed and the windows were shut and the curtains drawn. She wrapped her arms around herself and squeezed. Shivering, she picked up the remnants of her robe and tossed it into a corner. The sight of it was too disturbing. She crossed to a wardrobe and drew out another robe and donned it. Only then did she allow herself to collapse on to the settee.

Her eyes were huge as she stared into the leaping orange flames of the fire. How could she have threatened to have him whipped like a common cur? No matter what he had said to her or what he had done, he was a man.

Had Mathias really had him whipped? She cringed at the possibility. But it would explain the scars on his back.

Her head felt as though a vise tightened around it. She huddled deeper into her robe and closed her eyes.

Right now, Perth was somewhere in her house and she would have to confront him. She knew him well enough to know he would not leave until she did so. But she did not think she could bring herself to discuss Mathias horsewhipping him. That was something she was not yet prepared to do.

It was something Mathias would have to answer to, if it were true. And, painful as the knowledge about her brother was, she had no reason to believe that Perth would lie to her about something like that.

She rubbed her hand across her eyes. She still had to face Perth.

Thirty minutes later and fully clothed, she entered the drawing room with as much dignity as her anger with Perth and disillusionment with her brother would allow. Perth should be made to understand that he could not follow her and barge into not just her room, but her life. There was nothing between them. She would not let there be, even if it meant tearing her heart out.

Perth watched her cross the room, her chin high and knew she was more than angry with him. Dressed in a slate grey kerseymere gown that covered her from neck to wrist, she should have been drab. Instead, she glowed. She took his breath away.

He took a step towards her.

'Do not come near me,' she ordered, putting up a hand to ward him off. 'You have no right coming here, and especially barging into my private rooms as you did.' Her voice trembled with fury. 'I want you gone immediately.'

Knowing it would infuriate her more, he sat in one of her overstuffed chairs and crossed one muddy Hessian boot over his thigh. 'In my own good time. I believe we have something to discuss.'

The hectic flush left her face, leaving her looking like the finest porcelain and just as fragile. 'You are in error. We have nothing to discuss.'

The urge to go to her and offer her his name and his protection was great. He resisted. She must marry him on his terms for her conditions were beyond his emotional ability.

He attacked. 'You carry my child. Admit it.'

If he had thought her pale before, he was mistaken. Her skin was nearly as white as her hair. She swayed and put a hand on the back of a nearby chair.

'Ridiculous.'

But her voice was tremulous and her eyes would

not meet his. 'You lie,' he said softly, rising and pacing towards her.

She started to back away, but his hand shot forward and gripped her wrist. Slowly, inexorably, he drew her to him.

'You carry my child and you left London hoping to keep me from finding out.'

Her eyes widened and now she did meet him glare for glare. 'I left London at the same time of year that I always do. You had nothing to do with it.'

'You would sound more defiant if your voice did not shake.' He shifted his hands so that they gripped her shoulders. 'Everything you do is my business.'

'No.'

'Ah, but yes,' he murmured, sliding one hand along her shoulder to the back of her neck. 'Everything.'

He felt her heart beat and the rise and fall of her bosom. Desire, hot and powerful, rushed painfully through his body. Caution and restraint disappeared. He shifted once more, fitting her to him, breast to chest, loin to loin and thigh to thigh.

A soft sigh escaped her parted lips. He took advantage of her vulnerability. His mouth descended and captured hers. Longing flooded his senses. He wanted her, only her.

He sensed her surrender instants before her fingers tangled in his hair. It had always been this way between them. He vowed it always would be.

He drew back. The need to watch her, to see the emotions play over her face as he loved her, were too great to resist. He took one breast in his hand and gently squeezed. Her mouth puckered and a soft sigh escaped her lips. His loins tightened into an ache that demanded release.

He groaned and leaned down to take her other breast into his mouth. Even through the thick wool, he felt her nipple harden. Her hands tangled in his hair and held him tight. Elation surged through him.

He suckled her while both hands slid around her waist to the multitude of tiny buttons that marched down her back. He undid them with skill gained from much practice. Only when he could feel the fine cotton of her chemise did he raise his head and then only long enough to peel the gown down her shoulders to bare her bosom to his gaze and his mouth.

Her nipples pointed rosy and swollen through the gossamer cloth. One thumb tweaked a peak while his tongue laved the other. Her soft sighs drove him on.

With fingers as experienced with chemise ties as they were with buttons, he undid the satin bows and slipped the thin cotton down her chest and waist so that she stood fully exposed to his hungry gaze. The firelight played along her skin like a lover's touch, his touch.

He buried his face in the valley between her breasts and breathed deeply of her. Lilac and woman. Going to his knees, he edged her gown and chemise lower until her belly lay naked beneath his cheek. With a touch light as a feather, he tongued her belly button before slipping lower. Her fingers gripped his hair and held him.

'Please,' she gasped.

'Relax,' he murmured, marvelling at her response to him. Never before had a woman been as wanton with him as she was. And never before had he striven so hard to please a woman. But he found that her ache was his ache, her pleasure his pleasure.

He pulled her clothing the rest of the way over her hips and down her flanks. She stood before him in all her heartbreaking beauty.

Her nearly silver hair hung around her like a silken veil. The light of the candles turned her skin to ivory and left dark hollows that beckoned his hands, his mouth and his lust. She was everything he wanted, everything he needed. She was his.

A groan ripped from his throat as he slid to his haunches and urged her to let him touch her more intimately.

Not until she gasped and trembled in his arms did he stop and then only so that he could slide his face back up to her stomach and rest his cheek against her still-spasming flesh.

More gently than he had ever done before, he ran the tips of his fingers along the soft swell of her belly. He trailed kisses over her flesh. She carried his child and the wonder of it was overwhelming.

He rose to his feet and gathered her close. 'You are mine,' he whispered. 'Now and always.'

She opened eyes still heavy from his lovemaking and gazed up at him as though she had not fully heard his words. A smile tugged at her kiss-stung lips.

This was how he wanted to see her. Always. Drunk from his lovemaking, quiescent in his arms.

He ran his hands possessively down her side and along the curve of her hip and thigh then back up to cup one heavy breast. 'Soon this will suckle our child,' he murmured, awed by the thought.

He stroked the still-erect nipple before bending and taking her swollen flesh into his mouth. Her soft gasps excited him. His loins exploded as he lost control. Surprise caught him and ripped him apart. He gasped.

He had not even entered her and still she wrung him dry of everything he had to give her.

Shaking with a release he had never before experienced, he gathered her into his arms and took her to the couch where he lay her down. With fingers that were no longer sure, he undid the buttons of his pantaloons and freed his flesh. He parted her legs and entered her completely.

She shuddered against him. Her head fell back and her eyes closed. He watched her with shuttered eyes, determined to make her cry out for him. He pulled her closer and began a languid, slow movement that was torture but worth every long, tremulous moment as he saw her begin to shake and then heard a long, low moan of pleasure rip from her.

Driven by more than his own passion, he increased the pace until she screamed and her nails dug viciously into the skin at his shoulders. Still he plunged and still she begged for more. He gave her everything he had and more. He died in her arms and was reborn again, more powerful and more potent. And still he gave her more.

* * *

Later, much later, the fire nothing but glowing embers, they lay a tumble of limbs on the rug.

Perth pushed up on one elbow and looked down at her love-flushed skin. 'I have a special licence,' he murmured, running his palm over the slight mound of her abdomen. 'We can be married immediately. Our child needs a name.'

He was so involved in touching her that it was several minutes before he realised she lay still and unresponsive under his caresses. She caught his wrist in her hand and held him still.

'I am not marrying you.' She took a deep breath. 'I know I am weak where you are concerned, but I am not so weak as to enter a union with you that we will both regret. Not even for the child I am carrying.'

She pushed away from him and rolled to her side and got up with her back to him. She gathered her garments from the floor and pulled the dress over her head.

'Lillith,' he said, 'look at me.'

'No.' She kept her back to him. 'Not until you are clothed and we can speak like adults and not rutting beasts.'

She took a deep, heaving sigh and he was sure she cried. He rose and went to her, totally unconcerned about his nakedness. He put his arms around her and turned her to face him. He had been right.

'Don't cry, Lillith. Everything will be all right. I promise you.' He wiped her tears with his fingertips.

She closed her eyes and pushed against him. 'Don't touch me. Don't come near me. Get dressed.' Her voice rose. 'I will not marry for convenience again.' She opened her eyes and stared hard at him. 'Do you understand? I will not.'

Her continued rejection of him and everything he offered began to simmer deep within him. 'Do you think ours will be a marriage of convenience after the passion we just shared?'

He stepped away and grabbed up his clothes. He yanked on his pantaloons and twisted the buttons closed. Hands on hips, he glared at her.

'Passion,' she spat. 'Passion and nothing more.'

'It is better than what you had with de Lisle.' He leaned forward until his face was nearly in hers. 'Or do you intend to lie to me and tell me he made you feel the way I just did?'

'Why? Why must you make this so difficult?' she demanded, her voice nearly a cry. 'I will not marry you. That is final.'

He stepped back and made her a curt, mocking bow. 'I hear you. But what of our child? Will you condemn it to a life of poverty or, worse yet, a father who is not its true father?' His voice turned cruel. 'I know women of the *ton* regularly have their lovers' bastards and expect their husbands to acknowledge the child as theirs. Some men even allow the child to inherit their titles and honours. Is that what you want?'

'No. And I don't have to settle for that. I am wealthy in my own right.' Her mouth twisted bitterly. 'My marriage to de Lisle insured that.'

'Did it?' he asked softly. 'Are you sure?'

He saw doubt flit across her face before she closed

off the possibility. 'Yes, I am absolutely sure. Mathias is taking care of my estate. De Lisle left it that way. My brother would never pauper me.'

Perth laughed harshly. 'Wentworth? With his inability to stay away from the gaming tables?' He paced close to her. 'Do you know that he lost ten thousand pounds to me a couple of weeks ago? Do you know that he paid me with a draft on your bank?'

She flinched. 'He has money of his own and he keeps it in the Bank of England just as I do.'

'But are you positively sure?' He pushed her with his words and with the closeness of his body. He had to get through to her. 'What if you are wrong and your brother has spent your funds? What if you are no longer a wealthy widow? Then what will become of our child?' He saw fear enter her expressive eyes. 'Can you afford to continue refusing me when you are not sure?'

'I am sure,' she countered, arms crossed protectively across her stomach. 'Yes, I am.' She turned away and moved to the fire where she held her hand out to the embers.

He followed her. 'Check things before you send me away again. A couple of days. That is all it will take. I will wait here.' She flinched. 'Not in your home,' he assured her. 'I will stay at the inn in the village.'

She said nothing, just stared at the smouldering orange coals. She started shivering. The urge to pull her close was strong. He resisted. This was the moment she had to decide.

She angled around, her face a mask of anger and uncertainty. 'I will do as you suggest. But I am sure you are wrong.'

He did not smile. He knew what she would find.

Chapter Thirteen

Lillith made a conscious effort to appear calm as she was ushered into the office of her man of business. Mr Joseph Sinclair had been de Lisle's solicitor and was the solicitor for the current Lord de Lisle. De Lisle had left Lillith's inheritance under Mathias's control with the stipulation that the money be managed by Mr Sinclair. Until now, Lillith had not called on Mr Sinclair, trusting her brother or the solicitor to contact her if there was need.

Mr Sinclair rose when Lillith entered. He was a tall, cadaverous man with sallow skin and wire spectacles. He was a solemn man, his shoulders stooped from carrying the burden of many an aristocrat's financial future. He was very good at what he did if allowed to do as he saw best.

'Lady de Lisle, please have a seat. I am glad you have come to see me.' The pinched V between his bushy grey eyebrows deepened. 'I have sent several letters asking to arrange a meeting with you.'

Her brows rose and the smile she had worn trailed

off. 'Oh. I—' She stopped. Why had she never received those letters? Immediately she thought of Mathias. But, no, that was ridiculous. 'I never received your letters. They must have gone astray.' The solicitor said nothing. The worry she had berated herself for feeling intensified. 'Thank you for receiving me on such short notice.'

Sinclair frowned and his long, thin fingers shuffled papers as though he needed an outlet for nerves. But he was not a nervous man. 'I am glad to see you, Lady de Lisle. I did not arrive on your doorstep because Mr Wentworth said he was keeping you informed of everything and that if you needed my help, you would contact me.' He cleared his throat. 'I now realise that I should have gone around Mr Wentworth.'

Mathias had never said a word to her about her monies or that Mr Sinclair was concerned. Her nerves tightened in a very unpleasant fashion. 'Why have you wanted to see me?'

He answered her gravely. 'I prepared these papers for your brother so that he could deliver them to you.' He shrugged his thin shoulders and handed her the sheaf of papers he had been fiddling with.

Lillith took the packet and set it carefully in her lap, noting as she did that her fingers shook. This did not feel good. 'Perhaps you would tell me what these papers say. It would make things quicker, and I can ask for clarification immediately without having to wait for another appointment.'

He took a deep breath. 'There is no soft or kind way to say this, and believe me I have tried many times. My lady, you are nearly broke.' He paused and the silence grew strained. 'As Mr Wentworth knows.'

She gasped, a tiny painful sound. 'He was right,' she breathed. Despair, regret at her brother's profligacy and fury all combined to make her stomach heave dangerously. She swallowed hard, determined not to give into the urge to cry. 'Is everything gone? De Lisle left me very well off and that was only just over a year ago.'

Sinclair's brown eyes held a hint of pity. 'You have the use of your Dower House until you remarry or die. The house in London was left to you in perpetuity, but Mr Wentworth has taken out a lien on it to pay some of his...more pressing bills.' He spread his hands helplessly. 'That is one of several times I sent you a letter. I wanted to make sure that you knew what was happening.'

'Gambling debts,' Lillith interjected bitterly. 'And your letters never reached me.' Her voice chilled. 'How many have you sent?'

'Three,' he said.

She shut her eyes to block the pity in his. Somehow his notes had gone astray. Or been intercepted. How could Mathias have done that?

Finally, when she was sure she would not crumble, she opened her eyes. Her voice was even calm. 'Please continue.'

'The money in the Funds has been gone for the last six months.' He shrugged and raised his hands palm up in a gesture of defeat. 'I am sorry it is so bad.'

The pain of betrayal constricted her chest. Once

more it seemed that Mathias had used her for his own means without any regard for her best interests. Hurt warred with love. He was all she had left.

'I should have tried harder to reach you,' the solicitor continued. 'You might have been able to talk to Mr Wentworth.'

She shook her head sadly. 'No, I do not think so.'

He bowed his head in acknowledgement of her words. It was normal for a female to have her nearest male relation handle all matters of finance. He had not been surprised by her deceased husband's directive, and would have been very surprised had she managed her monies herself. But he had been saddened when he saw where Mr Wentworth was headed. The man had taken a sizeable fortune and in the space of fifteen months decimated it.

'Can I sell the London house to get funds to live? If I stay in the Dower House I can get along quite frugally.'

Again he had to tell her bad news. 'You will most definitely need to sell it, but the monies realised must go to paying the lien. If there is any left, and I doubt that there will be much, I can invest it in the Funds and hopefully realize you a very modest stipend.'

She looked down at her clenched hands, not wanting him to see the despair in her eyes. No wonder Mathias had been urging her to remarry. He needed another fortune to squander, and to him she was as good as money in the Bank of England. A sigh of despair escaped her before she pulled herself up short.

This was neither the time nor the place to wallow in self-pity.

'Well,' she said, lifting her head and squaring her shoulders, 'that will be better than nothing.' She rose and extended her hand. 'Thank you, Mr Sinclair. This has not been a pleasant meeting, but it has been an educational one. Can you keep my brother from spending whatever monies are realised from the sale of the London house?'

He stood and took her hand. 'I can petition the courts, my lady.'

'A nasty airing of family problems,' she murmured.

'Or I can take the cash in hand and give it directly to you and tell you how to invest it. That would be skirting the letter of the former Lord de Lisle's will, but it could be done.'

She nodded. 'That is much better. Thank you again,' she said, turning and taking her leave.

She walked out of the building with her head high. She was in the centre of London, near the Bank of England and other giants of commerce. Her carriage stood by the paving, the horses pawing the cold cobblestones. At least it was not sleeting. The day was miserable enough without inclement weather.

She picked up her skirts and moved proudly to her carriage. Her servant opened the door and let down the steps. 'Home,' she said, adding under her breath, 'but not home for long.'

She was inside, away from curious eyes just in time. She collapsed back against the cushions and sat in a state of shock. Nothing left. Nearly nine years of marriage to de Lisle for nothing. Everything squandered for Mathias's damnable gaming.

She pounded her fists into the leather seats and wished she were hitting her brother. He had not even had the decency to tell her. Instead he had tried to push her into another marriage of convenience—his convenience. Damn him, damn him, damn him.

The tears flowed freely now as she gave her emotions freedom. Everything she had thought was hers was not. She would have to move out of the London house immediately. She would have to let many servants go. They did not deserve that.

She took a heaving breath and it felt like her chest was on fire. Mathias had much to answer for.

She swiped at the tears still trickling down her cheeks. Enough of this snivelling, she had work to do. Then she would confront Mathias. And then, she licked her lips, then she must go back to the Dower House and Perth.

A grim smile tugged at her lips. She wanted Perth, had always wanted him. But she had known their union would not be good for her. Now, thanks to Mathias, she had very little choice. Without Perth's name, her child would have nothing. She could not do that to the babe.

The despair that weighed so heavily seconds before started to ease. What Mathias had done was beyond excuse, but…

Now she must do as her heart had always urged.

Her reason told her so. There was no other way for her child. For her child.

She must marry Perth.

Four days later, Lillith's carriage pulled into the drive that led to her ancestral home. She had not been here in a number of years. Her father had died shortly after she wed de Lisle, and Mathias had never spent time here.

She watched dispassionately as they drove by the beeches that lined the road. She had never cared for the place of her birth. Her mother had died when Lillith was three. Her father had been distant and uncaring. His first love had been gambling, like his son's. She did not even know if Mathias was here, but he was not in London and with her money gone there were not too many other places he could be.

The coach came to a stop, and she waited for the door to be opened and the stairs to be let down. She was in no hurry for what lay ahead of her.

'Thank you,' she said as she disembarked.

Before her stood a rambling house of indeterminate age. Parts were Elizabethan, some Jacobean and the Palladian front more recent. She did not remember the marble columns. Mathias must have added them in one of his flush times. Her mouth twisted. Very likely after her marriage to de Lisle.

She climbed the steps, wondering if she should knock or if there would even be a servant to let her in. She paused, gathering her anger that had given her the courage to come this far to confront the brother she had always before deferred to. She marched the last distance and pushed open the double doors without hesitation.

She stepped into the foyer she remembered not being allowed in as a child. She had always to enter and leave by the back doors. Children were to be seen, occasionally, and never heard.

There was an air of disuse about the place. The side table where a silver salver should have been was empty and in need of dusting. The black and white marble squares beneath her feet needed polishing. None of the paintings she remembered from her youth hung on the walls. Mathias had probably sold all of them.

Still, no servant arrived and no sound gave hint that anyone but she was in the house.

'Is anyone here?' she called, listening to her voice echo in the enclosed, rounded foyer. She looked up and noted the Waterford chandelier was gone.

For the first time since arriving, she heard a noise. It came from the library. She moved in that direction, wondering if all the books would be gone and the places where family portraits had once hung would now be empty spots of colour against the faded fabric of the wall covering.

'Ah, Lillith,' Mathias said when she opened the heavy oak door and stepped into the room. 'What brings you to the country and without even a note to tell me you were coming?'

He lounged in a leather-covered chair that he had pulled up to a small game table. With casual skill, he shuffled a deck of cards and began laying them out for a game of solitaire.

His nonchalance and the forever-present cards added much-needed fuel to her anger that had begun to flag during her sad perusal of her family home. 'Cards as usual,' she said, sharply. 'One would think that after all the damage they have done you would be heartily sick of them. But that appears not to be the case.'

He looked up at her and lifted one silver brow. 'You are in a nasty mood, Sister. Have a seat and I will ring for refreshment.'

She took the first chair available, a slim Chippendale. 'I am surprised you have servants to bring refreshments. No one met me at the door.'

'You did not knock either,' he riposted. 'Whatever is the matter with you?'

'I don't want refreshment, Mathias. I want satisfaction. I want an explanation.' The angry words tumbled from her. She leaned forward and glared at him. 'And for everything that is sacred, stop playing with those blasted cards.'

He was not a stupid man, just a very selfish one. 'So you have been to see Sinclair, and he has told you the deplorable state of your—our—finances.' He set the ace of spades above the rest. 'I don't suppose I should be surprised, but I am. De Lisle left me as manager of your inheritance. What made you check?'

'Why I checked is none of your business. What matters now is why you lost everything. Everything. You would not even have this...' she waved her arms to indicate the house '…if it were not entailed and impossible for you to gamble away. As it is, it will very likely crumble around you, for you have no money and no inclination to keep it in repair.'

She drew a deep breath and her eyes narrowed. 'Did you intercept Mr Sinclair's letters? For he says that he sent three and I received none.'

Mathias's gaze shifted away before coming back to rest on her. For a second she thought he intended to lie. 'Footmen can always use a little extra blunt.'

'You disgust me.'

'There is no need to raise your voice, Lillith. I can hear you very well.'

His reprimand non-plussed her. She had not realised her voice had risen. She forced herself to unknot her fingers and sit back in her chair. She also pushed aside the knowledge that there was a footman in her service whom she could not trust. It was a small betrayal compared to what Mathias had done.

She tried again. 'I am selling the London house to pay the lien on it.'

He picked up a card and flicked it between his fingers. 'Sinclair mentioned something about that. I did not want to do it. Knew my luck would change.' He shrugged. 'It did not. So the house must go. A debt of honour must be paid.'

She shook her head in disbelief and took a deep breath and the enormous sadness of it all hit her. 'Have you no remorse?' she asked softly.

Mathias shifted in his chair as though he might be

uncomfortable, but nothing showed on his face. ''Tis in m'blood. No help for it.'

Appalled at his callous disregard for all the hurt and damage he had caused and his blithe acceptance of such a destructive habit, she sat motionless and speechless. He continued playing solitaire, his fingers caressing the cards as he flicked through them and laid them out. She might as well not be here.

She took one last look around the library. She had no intention of touring the house and grounds. She was not going to return. Her future lay elsewhere.

She put her hands on the arms of her chair and pushed herself up. She felt weighted down by melancholy and regret.

'I am leaving now,' she said softly. He glanced up. 'I will be staying the night at the inn in town.' She took a deep breath. There was no sense in keeping from him her plan. He was, after all was said and done, her only living relative. 'I will be marrying Perth. It will be a small ceremony in the tiny chapel of my Dower House.' Which would not be hers after the wedding. Another loss.

For the first time since her arrival, real emotion showed on Mathias's face. He surged up, beet-red. 'Perth! I won't have it.'

The anger that had brought her here and slowly seeped from her to be replaced by sadness rushed back. '*You* won't have it? *You* have nothing to say about it. You squandered a fortune of mine on gambling and have not a shred of remorse to show for it.'

He took a menacing step towards her, knocking

over the card table. He ignored the crash. 'I have plans for you to wed Chillings or Carstairs. They are as wealthy as Perth and will be better husbands.'

She glared at him, her muscles tight with fury. 'You can go to Hades, Brother. I married at your direction once. I won't do so again. If you are so desperate to repair your fences, then find yourself an heiress and marry her—if one will have you.'

She cast a critical gaze over his person, seeing for the first time the dissolute man he had become. Once he had been slim and cut a dashing figure. Now he was a caricature of that man. He ran with the Prince of Wales's crowd and a more dissolute, debauched group would be hard to find. She had let her love for him blind her to his faults. She had made excuses for him.

She closed her eyes briefly and tried to calm herself. No matter what he had done or what he had become, he was her brother. When she thought she could speak without losing her temper, she opened her eyes and said, 'I cannot forgive you for what you have done, but you are my brother. My only living relative. At the moment I am very hurt by what you have done, and would prefer that you not visit me. You are, however, invited to the wedding so long as you accept this marriage and do nothing to disrupt it or to cause trouble.'

He stood shaking in his rage with his lips pinched tight but he said nothing. When she realised he did not intend to speak, she turned away, paused and turned back.

'Did you have Perth whipped ten years ago?'

The words left her mouth before she realised that she intended to say them. She had thought she did not want to know and that the past was better left buried. Now this.

Mathias drew himself. 'That is none of your concern. A lady does not get involved.'

Lillith's eyes narrowed. Disappointment ate at her. 'You did.'

She did not bother to stay to hear what he might say. She pivoted and left. There was only so much disillusionment she could take about Mathias, and she had reached that point. She had hoped that Perth had been mistaken.

Her hands shook as she took the hand proffered by her coachman. When she ducked her head to enter the carriage, a tear escaped. She swiped it away.

As she drove off, she took one last look back at the house she had grown up in. It stood, a dim copy of its former glory. She would never be back.

She turned her gaze forward and shivered as though a draught of cold air had rushed over her. Against all her better judgement, her future lay with Perth. She loved him and knew he would care for her and the child they had created. Perhaps in time his desire for her would turn to love. She had to hope for that. For she had no other choices.

Perhaps she could make up for some of the past wrongs done him. If she were strong enough.

Perth sat in the public room of the inn and drank his ale. Outside snow fell in soft waves of white. The village green was covered and the pond had a thin film of ice. Lillith would pass this way on her return to the Dower House.

He had been here nearly a week. Fitch had arrived on his second day with the carriage and a trunk of clothes the batman considered appropriate.

Perth finished the ale and rose. The innkeeper hurried over, wiping his hands on the apron he wore.

'Is there something else I can get your lordship?' He beamed. Perth was a good customer.

'No, thank you,' Perth said.

By now he knew everyone who frequented the pub and many who did not. He was on nodding familiarity with all in the village. He also realised that every man, woman and child in this town liked and respected Lillith. They all watched him to see if he was good enough for her.

'My lord,' a young boy yelled, rushing in from outside, his cheeks red from the cold. 'Her ladyship's carriage just passed.'

'My thanks,' Perth said, tossing the youth a coin. 'You have done a good job of watching for me.'

The child beamed before strutting off proud as a peacock.

Perth turned to his landlord. 'Have my mount brought round.'

Knowing the deed was as good as done, Perth went to his room and donned a coat, hat and gloves. He looked at the cane tossed across one chair. He was not likely to need it here.

Fitch came in from his room at that moment. 'You never know, my lord. It saved your life that one time or at least kept you from a severe beating.'

Perth glanced at his manservant. 'I doubt Wentworth is here or that he has hired thugs again.'

Fitch just looked at him.

'But you are right,' Perth acquiesced. 'There are thieves in the country as well as the city.'

The anxiety that had formed lines around Fitch's mouth eased. 'Lady de Lisle has returned.'

'Yes, and I intend to speak with her before she has a chance to think up another reason to refuse my offer. Although I have no doubt that she has discovered just how dire her situation is.'

'She is proud,' Fitch said. 'As are you, my lord.'

Perth smiled ruefully. 'Yes, and we shall have a hard go of it because of those traits.'

Perth left. Outside his horse waited. He got into the saddle just as another carriage barrelled through the narrow high road. He backed his horse on to the pavement just in time to keep from being run over. The man driving the carriage was hamfisted and in a hurry.

The cane he had decided to take in spite of its awkwardness on horseback lay on the ground where he had dropped it when his horse shied. He looked at it ruefully.

'Fitch,' he said to the batman who had followed him down and witnessed the scene, 'please return that to my room. I will be making greater haste than I had thought and carrying that will only hamper me.'

Fitch frowned, but picked up the cane. 'Be careful if you've a mind to go after that idiot.'

Feeling the self-appointed protector of this little village, Perth considered going after the vehicle and putting the fear of God into the occupant. But the need to see Lillith was greater.

'I have a more important meeting.'

He set off for the Dower House and soon became intrigued when he realised that was where the carriage headed. He slowed his pace to keep just behind the coach for now he had a suspicion of who made such reckless haste in the ice and snow.

He'd be damned if Wentworth would interfere this time.

When they reached Lillith's house, he reined his horse to a stop right behind Wentworth's carriage and dismounted. Activity erupted around them. Grooms came for his horse and to lead Wentworth's carriage to the stables.

Wentworth disembarked, saw Perth and turned white, then scarlet. He halted for a moment before continuing on toward the door. Perth cut off his path.

Perth eyed the other man with disgust. Wentworth's nose was starting to glow red in the cold. His greatcoat with its multitude of fashionable capes made him look like an over-inflated balloon instead of the dashing figure he probably thought he looked.

'What are you doing here?' Perth demanded, hands on hips. He regretted the cane he had left behind when Wentworth's carriage had nearly run him down.

'Out of my way,' Wentworth snarled. 'I need to

speak with my sister. What she plans is folly.' Bold
as his words were, he did not move forward.

A hard grin showed Perth's teeth and accentuated
his scar even as exultation filled him. Lillith intended
to marry him.

'What she plans is the only means open to her after
the débâcle you have made of her affairs.' He moved
until his face was nearly touching Wentworth's. 'A
situation you will never have the opportunity to cause
again. Mark my words, Wentworth, I will have none
of your importuning. I won't pay a single bill you have
now or will have in the future. And if you come
around, I will be sorely tempted to horsewhip you myself, instead of taking the coward's way out and hiring
someone to do it—as you did.'

His deadly calm words filled the cold, still air.
Wentworth's ruddy face blanched. Without a flick of
an eye, Perth stepped aside. Wentworth hurried past,
pulling on his cape to ensure that it did not touch the
Earl.

Perth followed at a leisurely pace. He had no desire
to see Lillith's brother again. When he finally entered
the foyer, Wentworth was gone.

'My lord,' the normally imperturbable butler said,
taking the hat and gloves Perth held out. 'We were
not expecting you. Her ladyship is indisposed.'

'Her ladyship is with her brother, and I've no desire
to interrupt them.' He strode past the butler. 'Show me
to a room where I can wait for her.'

'Um…yes, my lord. This way, my lord.' Simmons
set off down the hall.

Perth soon found himself in a small room that looked like Lillith's workroom. There was a desk littered with papers and a basket of mending set beside a large, comfortably overstuffed chair. A fire roared in the grate and the curtains were opened to show a winter garden. He found it a cosy place and made himself at home.

He and Lillith still had to discuss the terms of their wedding. He would wait patiently until she arrived, now that she was his. He did not have long.

She burst into the room, obviously agitated. 'What are you doing here? I sent word to the inn that I accept your offer of marriage.'

He rose and made her a bow. 'Your talk with your brother must not have gone well. I fear he was not in a good mood after the one he and I had in your driveway.'

She made her way to the window, her back to him. She had a slim, elegant back that the thick wool dress did not hide. He thought that perhaps there was just a little bit of widening at her waist, but that might easily be his own desire. He wanted the child she carried. The urge to take her in his arms was strong, but the tilt of her chin told him that that action would only make things more difficult. He could wait now that she was to be his.

'Why are you here?' she finally asked, her voice tired.

'Are you getting enough rest?' he asked, ignoring her question.

Exasperation pinched her brows together. 'I get

enough sleep, but there is not enough rest in the world to compensate for having my brother rant and rave at me over you and then finding out that you are here to do the same over something else.'

Her words gave him pause. He had been ruthless in his pursuit of her. Perhaps it was time to woo her. Theirs was not a love match, but he wanted more than a marriage of convenience.

'I am not here to berate you, Lillith,' he said soothingly. 'I am here to discuss the settlement I intend to make on you and our child. I thought you would not want me to discuss it with your brother, given the circumstances.'

'That is true enough,' she said bitterly. Her hands unclenched and she turned to face him. 'I want provision for our child should it be a boy or girl. I won't have any child of mine being bartered like a piece of goods.' Her mouth drooped just slightly. 'I know too well what that is like. And I want a jointure independent of you. I trust you will not make my brother the executor.'

A hard smile split his lips before he nodded agreement. 'You shall have all of that. I will also arrange for our future children to have financial independence. I also know what it is like to be considered a commodity instead of a person.'

She blushed at his words. He too had paid for her brother's machinations. 'And I will *not* sleep with you.'

He gave her a slow, sensual smile as his gaze roved over her. 'We shall see.'

'I won't.' Her voice rose. 'Agree to that term or I won't marry you.'

He turned away to conceal the anger that her insistence caused. But when he spoke his voice was cool. 'I won't force you.'

'Nor seduce me,' she added.

'I cannot promise that,' he said softly, turning back to her. His eyes held hers. 'But you can always refuse me.'

He heard her sharp intake of breath and had some measure of satisfaction. He'd be damned if he would marry her, live in the same house with her and not sleep with her.

'Well,' she said, her voice raspy, 'that is settled. We will be married tomorrow. Right now, I am tired.'

He stepped in front of her, causing her to stop her steps to the door. 'I am looking forward to our wedding, Lillith. It is long overdue.'

Her eyes widened but she said nothing. She edged around him and he let her go. He could be patient. He would be patient. Tomorrow she would be his.

Chapter Fourteen

Lillith stood in the tiny church connected to her Dower House. She did not normally take services here, preferring to go to the church in the village where she could meet the people who worked the de Lisle land. Only the vicar was present from the congregation.

Now the early part of December, the building was dim inside even though candles were lit. Outside it snowed. She shivered.

Mathias stood behind her on the left. He had stayed the night with her in spite of everything. She had not had the energy or the anger to have her servants throw him out. She was too overwhelmed by this marriage and everything it meant.

Perth stood beside her in morning dress. She would swear she could feel the animosity between the two men as waves rolling over her.

The vicar cleared his throat. Lillith focused on him. The banns had not been called. Perth had a special licence. Everyone in the village still knew they were marrying. There was to be a reception this afternoon for the town folk, hastily arranged but something she wanted to do. It was her parting gift to the people she had taken an interest in and helped where needed for the last ten years. She would miss them like she already missed the servants in London that she had had to let go and the servants here who would not be accompanying her to Perth's property. Simmons, thank goodness, would come with her.

She refused to cry.

There had been no time to have a special gown made even had she wished it. She had found a wool dress in palest pink that she had worn several winters before. It had been tight in the bust, that seeming to be where she had gained weight with the child, so she had spent several hours letting out the seams. Agatha had asked to do the chore, but Lillith had declined. Sewing soothed her. The rhythmic in-and-out of the needle calmed her frayed nerves. Tomorrow she would start on clothes for the baby.

The vicar cleared his throat again, as though something were lodged in it. He began the ceremony.

She said the words required of her and vaguely heard Perth agree to take her as his wife. No one objected.

'The rings.'

She looked at the vicar. 'I have no ring.'

He cleared his throat once more and looked away. Perth was paying him a handsome fee to perform this ceremony so quickly.

'I do,' Perth said, his voice deep and sure.

He took her by surprise.

Fitch reached into a breast pocket and pulled out a ring that flashed in the yellow light of a nearby candle. Opals and diamonds formed an oval larger than the first knuckle of her thumb. She gazed at it. Opals were bad luck if not your birthstone. They were her birthstone.

She put out her left hand so Perth could slip the ring on. It slid on as though it had been made for her finger.

'It was my mother's,' the Earl said quietly. 'I know she would want you to wear it.'

His warmth was not something she had expected. He was marrying—no, had forced her to marry him for the sake of the child they had made. She had agreed for that child's sake. The earldom of Perth was not something a woman could easily give up for her unborn child. Especially now.

'You may kiss the bride,' the vicar said, his voice wavering.

She had not expected this. She felt Perth's hand at her waist like a brand, turning her and pulling her toward him. She heard Mathias snort in irritation. Then she heard nothing as Perth's mouth touched hers and the roaring in her ears drowned out all else.

It was not a light, impersonal kiss of acknowledgement. It seared to her bones. His fingers bit into the small of her back and held her tightly to him so that she could feel his arousal. His lips moved over hers and his tongue slipped inside her. She could taste the whisky he had drunk before coming here. Surely he was not nervous? The scent of cinnamon and musk filled her nostrils. It was a lip-tingling, thigh-melting kiss that left her wanting more.

He released her and she stumbled back so that Mathias had to put out an arm to steady her. 'Your reaction is disgusting,' he hissed in her ear.

She blushed at the truth in his words. It did not help when she glanced at Perth and saw the harsh angle of his jaw and the dark hunger in his eyes. He had said he would not force her, but if just his kiss given in front of witnesses made her want him, she was doomed. He would have her and she would beg him to do so.

Somehow, she pulled her emotions together and edged away from Mathias. She lifted her chin and took the arm Perth extended. Side by side, they left the chapel. The others did not follow.

Safely away from curious eyes, Lillith snatched her hand back. 'I must go and prepare for the festivities later.' He took a step after her and she whirled on him. 'Do not follow me. Remember what I said.'

His look turned hard. 'Your words say one thing, but your body and every move you make say something different.'

'I am in control of my body,' she said, wishing it were so.

He gave her a mocking smile as though he knew how false her boast was. 'Then I will see you later.'

She hurried away, trying to push him from her mind by running down a mental checklist of what needed doing for the party tonight. She needed to talk with Cook about the food, Simmons about the beverages and Agatha about what she would wear. All her clothes were uncomfortably tight. Something would need to be let out.

Her feet kept pace with her thoughts. And still she could not keep from remembering the feel of Perth's mouth on hers.

She was doomed.

Perth raised his third glass of champagne in salute to the innkeeper who whirled past with his wife in his arms as they nimbly executed a move in the country reel being played. With sardonic amusement, he saw that Wentworth consumed as much drink as he and there was no gambling to be had. The man must be going crazy.

Seeing Lillith make her way around the crowded room, studiously ignoring him, he could easily understand what it was like to be crazy. He wanted her in the worst possible way.

She moved with a grace that few women possessed. And she was kind to everyone.

His mother had been like that. The daughter of a wealthy landowner, she had run away with the younger son of a younger son who was a career army officer. His parents had married for love and, to the best of his knowledge, they had never regretted it. He had been the only child.

Lillith passed in front of him, dancing energetically with the blacksmith. The man was twice her size and lumbered. She would be lucky not to have bruised feet.

She was well liked by the common folk.

Churlishness not being one of Perth's traits, he pushed off from the wall and went to ask one of the town's ladies to dance. He chose an older woman who would enjoy herself but not simper at him. He could not stand simpering.

Meanwhile, he would bide his time until tonight.

An eternity later, or so it seemed to Perth, he stood beside Lillith and said goodbye to the last of their guests. Wentworth had disappeared long before.

'Simmons,' she said, totally ignoring Perth, 'please see that everyone is given extra wages for tonight and before they are let go. I have letters of recommendation for everyone.'

He nodded.

She turned away with a slump to her shoulders that Perth had rarely seen. The last weeks had been hard on her.

As though she sensed his attention, she straightened her shoulders and looked at him. 'I am tired and I am going to bed. Alone.'

He crossed his arms over his chest and returned her stare. 'This is our wedding night.'

'We have a bargain.'

'You have a stipulation. I did not say I would honour it.'

She gasped. 'You most certainly did.'

'No,' he said slowly. 'I said that I would not force you, not that I would not seduce you or sleep with you. We are married.'

'This is my house, and I forbid you to follow me.' She spun on her heel and walked off.

Perth watched her, enjoying the sway of her hips and the elegant curve of her back. But she was very much confused if she thought he was not going to join her. He sauntered behind her, far enough away that she did not bolt.

'My lord—' Simmons materialised '—I will show you to your room.'

Perth glanced at the butler. 'Thank you, but I know where my room is.' He saw Lillith start up the stairs. 'And I am going there.'

He headed off, but not before he heard Simmons sputter. However, the butler was in a difficult situation and there was nothing he could do but stand aside.

Perth sauntered after his wife, arriving at her room shortly after she did. He did not knock, and fortunately Lillith had not locked the door. He could almost think she wanted him to enter, but he knew better. She had thought he would not follow her after being told not to. She had much to learn.

He entered and closed the door behind himself. She sat sprawled on a settee, her feet up and her hair down. She made his blood heat.

She shot bolt upright. 'What are you doing here? I told you not to follow me.'

He moved to a chair and sat down, crossing one leg over the other. His dancing pumps gleamed in the firelight. 'And I told you that I would.'

'Well, you can just leave.' She pointed imperiously at the door. 'Now!'

'Lillith,' he said quietly and clearly, 'I have already told you. We are married. I intend to have my conjugal rights.'

She huffed and she flushed and she looked away from the desire he made no effort to hide. 'You will have to seduce me then, for I will not walk into your arms.'

He studied her, noting the luminosity of her skin and the sheen of her hair. She held herself proudly. She was intelligent and she had spirit, both traits he valued. And he desired her with an ache that was constant and painful in its intensity.

But he was getting tired of these confrontations and recriminations. Perhaps wanting her was not enough any more. He began to think it would be nice if she would return his interest without him first having to force her into arousal.

'Perhaps you are right,' he said thoughtfully. 'As much as I want to make love to you—and make no doubt losing myself in you is something I desire above all else—I begin to think that your resistance is growing tiring.'

Her mouth dropped. He nearly laughed at her surprise, but he really did not find this situation at all humourous, just her unexpected reaction.

'You are growing tired?'

He nodded. 'A little. You see, I am not used to working so hard for my pleasures.'

'Oh.' She picked at her skirts. 'I did not think you did. That is all part of why I insist that our marriage remain one of convenience.'

'A marriage of convenience usually gives the husband the right to enjoy his wife's charms,' he said softly.

'You already have,' she retorted. 'And I am carrying your child. That is the focus of a marriage of convenience. We have fulfilled it.'

'I see,' he said quietly. 'As far as you are concerned, if you bear my son then you have fulfilled your obligation.'

She nodded.

He stood abruptly, suddenly wearied beyond bearing. 'Much as I want you, I find that perhaps it is time I spared you my unwanted attentions. After a while, even the most unobservant man realizes when his presence is not only not wanted, but dreaded.'

He had never thought he would reach the point where he would not do anything to have her. But he had.

He made her a curt bow and left.

Lillith did a slow turn, studying her suite of rooms in Perth's London town house. Rich greens and golds and browns made the large area seem warm and inviting. Heavy furniture from another era filled the space and provided comfort. In all, it was not a very feminine room but she liked it. What Perth's chamber looked like, she did not know and did not want to know.

Except that curiosity moved her towards the connecting door. She had heard him leave immediately after bringing her here, so there would be no one in side. She told herself it was not like she was invading his privacy. He would be more than willing to have her in his bedchamber.

Taking a deep breath, she turned the knob and pushed open the door. The room was dim with the curtains pulled and no fire or lit candles. Still, she could see that it was as spacious as her own and done in the same colours and style of furniture. The two rooms were mirrors of one another. How strange.

Quickly, she stepped back and closed the door. She would never know why they were decorated the same since she could not let Perth know she had been in his room while he was gone, and she had no intention of going into his room while he was in it. Perhaps the person who had decorated the rooms was a man. It was a mystery she would never solve.

Agatha chose that moment to enter Lillith's room, her arms full of gowns. 'My lady, I am glad you are here. Mr Fitch just told me that the Earl is engaged to Lord Ranvensford this evening for dinner and dancing. You will need to choose your gown and we will have to let the seams out of the bosom.'

Not only was Lillith's stomach growing, but her breasts were swollen and sore. Her nipples were constantly erect and rubbing against her chemise. Being in the family way was very disconcerting.

Lillith sank into the nearest chair. The last thing she wanted to do was face London Society. But she must. The sooner done, the sooner the talk of their rushed marriage would become yesterday's old news. And there was only a week or two left before Parliament adjourned for the winter.

'The white muslin with the pink overlay,' she told Agatha. 'While you are enlarging it, I will nap.' She still barely showed her pregnancy, but she tired more easily and was more emotional. There was no other explanation for the way she had railed at Perth on their wedding night.

She took off her dress and put on a wrapper. But before climbing on to the high four-poster bed, she wrote a quick note to Madeline and asked Agatha to have it delivered. Nothing would perk her up like a visit from her friend. That done, she fell into a deep sleep.

Lillith woke to the sounds of someone moving around. She levered onto one elbow and looked around. The room was lit only by the fire, and it took several minutes for her eyes to become adjusted.

Perth stood by the mantel, gazing down at the flames. He was dressed for evening in black breeches, stockings and pumps. A white shirt glowed in stark relief against the darker colours. He held a box in his hand.

She sat fully up and pulled her wrapper up to her neck and clenched it shut. 'What are you doing in here?'

He turned and gave her a sardonic smile. 'The last I checked, this was my house.'

Her eyes narrowed, but she did not let loose the

harsh words that sprang to her lips. 'We have an agreement. We are not sleeping with each other.'

He sauntered toward her, his gaze lowering. 'Just because I am in your bedchamber does not mean that I intend to seduce you. Although—' he stopped at the foot of the bed '—the idea does have appeal.'

The heat he could so easily arouse in her flared. She jumped out of bed, rather than lie prone. 'Then why are you in here?'

'I have brought you something,' he said, holding out the box.

She eyed it as one might eye a bomb. 'What is it?'

'A gift, Lillith. Nothing more,' he said with the tone of one sorely tried. 'It will not hurt you nor is it a bribe for your favours. It is freely given because I thought it would become you.'

'Oh,' she said, feeling ashamed of her suspicions. What made them worse was knowing that she wanted him to try and seduce her. No matter what she said, her body craved him.

She took the box, opened it and gasped. A parure of diamonds and opals flashed in the meagre light.

'Do you like them?' he asked, a note of hesitation in his voice.

This was the first time she had ever heard him sound uncertain. She looked up at him. 'They are beautiful.'

It seemed to her that his body relaxed, although until that instant she had not realised that he was tense.

'I had them made to go with the ring.'

'But why? I have plenty of jewellery. You do not need to give me more.' She spoke thoughtlessly, thinking only of the money these must have cost him. She had already cost him so much.

His voice hardened and he stepped away, putting his back to her. 'Everything you have is from de Lisle. These are from me. I expect to see them on you this evening.'

Before she could think of something to say that would compensate for her previous words, he left. The door closed behind him with a definite click. She sighed. She could follow him, but she did not think that would solve the issue over the jewellery. And it would only precipitate another situation.

Instead she set the box on the bed and lit the candles in a candelabrum so she could see the jewellery better. A necklace, earrings, two bracelets and a brooch glowed in the yellow light. The opals were multi-hued and full of fire. The diamonds that surrounded the opal cabochons were white and clean. They were truly beautiful pieces. He must have taken time and consideration over this gift.

She set the candles on the table and lifted the necklace out. It cascaded over her fingers, heavy and seductive. She took it with her to the mirror and held it to her neck. The piece flashed, a perfect foil for her pale skin and silver hair. Yes, Perth had chosen well.

She whirled when the door opened, expecting it to be Perth. Relief, followed rapidly by disappointment, swamped her when she saw Agatha.

'My lady,' the maid said, 'I have done the best I can with this bodice. I hope it will be enough.' She glanced up from the gown in her hand and her mouth dropped. 'My lady...did the Earl give you those? They are finer than anything you have.'

She gave her maid a rueful smile. 'Yes, he did and wants me to wear them tonight.'

Agatha moved closer, her gaze riveted to the necklace. 'It will be magnificent with your dress. Are they...pardon my asking, but are they because of your condition?'

She had not thought of that. 'Perhaps. He did not say.' She glanced at the delicate little porcelain clock by the bed, a feminine piece that seemed out of place in the room. 'But we must hurry.'

An hour later, Lillith stood before the mirror in all her finery. Agatha had attached the bracelets, one on each arm over her gloves, and she had put on the earrings. The necklace still lay in the velvet box. She considered seeing if Perth would come and put it on her as an amends for her earlier words.

'My lady, you will be late if we linger,' Agatha said, picking the necklace up and moving to drape it around Lillith's neck.

Lillith sighed as her maid hooked the piece. 'Twas just as well. Agatha's impersonal touch was just that. Perth's fingers at the nape of her neck, and his warm breath caressing her skin, would have only caused trouble.

Agatha draped a fine paisley shawl over Lillith's shoulders and stepped back. 'Perfect, my lady.'

Lillith eyed her finished toilet. She turned from side to side. She did look good and no one would know she was pregnant. That would come later when she bore the child five months after the wedding. Well, that was not unheard of either.

Perth waited downstairs in the foyer. When she joined him, he cast a quick glance over her.

'The jewels become you,' he said, taking his hat and cane from Simmons.

'Thank you,' Lillith replied, wondering why she felt as though something was missing. She did not want compliments from him, but she had to admit that she had expected more.

She preceded him outside and allowed the footman to help her into the carriage. Again she was disappointed. Much as she railed at Perth and at her reaction to him, it felt strange and incomplete to have someone else hold her hand as she got in the coach.

On their wedding night he had desired her above all else. Since they reached London, he had been, with a few exceptions, distant. He behaved as though they really did have a marriage of convenience. And then he gave her the magnificent jewellery. She shook her head in confusion.

'What is wrong?' he asked, sitting opposite her with his back to the horses.

She cocked her head to one side and studied him in the pale yellow light from the interior lamps. His expression was saturnine, his scar pronounced. He looked dangerous, and distant and distinctly bored.

'You have changed since we got to Town.' She spoke openly, not wanting to further complicate their relationship with lies and subterfuge.

'I have tired of pursuing you and having to wear down your resistance. Our wedding night showed me that there is no pleasure in forcing you.'

'You always did before and seemed none the less excited.' Ridiculous as it was, she could not keep a tiny hitch of hurt from her voice. She was fickle.

He looked away from her to gaze out of the window. 'That was before we married. I still want you.' He turned back to her and his dark eyes pierced her. 'But I am tired of fighting. When you are ready for more than a cold bed at night, let me know.'

His words hurt, which surprised her. This is what she had demanded. Unfortunately for her, she had never really thought he would give in to her demands. Now he had and she did not like it. But it was for the best. If he did not pursue her, she would not be tempted by him and give in.

Yes, this was definitely for the best.

Chapter Fifteen

Thankfully, they arrived at Ravensford's house shortly afterwards. The gathering was larger than Lillith had anticipated. Fifty to sixty people milled about the Earl's ballroom: some danced, some talked, and still others played cards in the alcoves.

Perth kept a light touch at her waist as he steered her towards their host and hostess. Even knowing he did not touch her with the intent to seduce her, the feel of his fingers was comforting. No matter what their marriage was, he would protect her and their child.

'Ah, Perth,' Ravensford said, breaking away from the small knot of people he had been with and coming toward them. 'And the lovely Lady de Lisle.'

'Lady Perth,' her husband said firmly.

Ravensford's green eyes widened before he smiled. 'You finally did it. Leg-shackling becomes you, Perth.' His smile turned wry as Perth grimaced. 'And you, Lady Perth,' he added, taking Lillith's hand and raising it to his lips. 'Congratulations to both of you.'

Lillith blushed under Ravensford's scrutiny. 'Thank you, my lord.'

He released her hand and stepped back. 'Make yourself scarce, Perth, I wish to speak with your wife.'

Lillith thought that a fleeting look of concern marred Perth's otherwise imperturbable countenance, but it was gone before she could be sure.

'Then I shall go and pay my respects to your wife,' Perth countered, sauntering towards Lady Ravensford and her court of admirers.

Lillith turned an inquiring look on Ravensford. He took her fingers and put them on his arm.

'A walk around the perimeter will keep us away from all but the most curious.' He guided her to the wall with the least people. 'I see he gave you the opals. I was with him the day he ordered them. He was very concerned that they be good enough for you.'

'Perth?' she asked, incredulous that her husband could be so insecure. That was not the man she knew.

'Opals were his mother's favourite gem, but the family did not have the money to buy her many. The ring he very likely gave you for the wedding was all she had, and his father spent an entire year's salary on it. A hardship for an army officer. Perth's parents were long dead by the time he inherited the earldom.'

This was a window into her husband's past that she had not expected. 'I did not know any of that.'

'You would not. He would not tell you, but I will.' He stopped her and held her gaze with his. 'He will not tell you this either, but I will. He loves you, but does not yet realise it. Give him time.'

She stared, nonplussed. 'This is too private, Lord Ravensford. Please say no more.'

He shrugged. 'I had thought you a stronger person than this. I also thought you would like to know.' His voice turned cold. 'I see that I was mistaken. Shall we return to the rest of my guests?'

He did not wait for her response, but guided her back to Perth and left her with a curt bow. Perth frowned.

'What has got into Ravensford? That is no way for him to treat you.' He took a step after his friend, but Lillith grabbed his arm. 'What are you doing?'

'I am keeping you from making a mistake, Perth. I provoked Ravensford. He is justifiably upset with me. Let it be.'

He studied her carefully for long moments. Lillith felt other gazes on them. She heard a susurration of voices. Word of their hasty wedding was spreading.

He eased and she released his arm. 'See the older woman over there by the column,' he said, his voice closer to normal.

She looked where he indicated to see a strikingly handsome woman with silver hair cut fashionably short, an ideal foil for the oval perfection of her creamy complexion. She wore Lillith's favourite colour of lavender.

'She is beautiful. Who is she?'

'The Dowager Countess of Ravensford.'

'But I thought she was against Ravensford's marriage. I would not expect her to be here.' She took a closer look. On second glance the Countess did not appear as happy as she might.

'She was against the union and is still unhappy about it, but Ravensford made it plain that he would cut her from his life before he gave up Mary Margaret. He is an only child and was the delight of both his parents. He still is paramount in his mother's affections, and she does what she must.'

Lillith felt a twinge of envy. She had never known her own mother and her father had never cared. So she had given all her love and devotion to Mathias and been betrayed.

'He is fortunate.'

Perth looked down at her. 'Our child will have that love and devotion, I swear it.'

She blinked in an effort to stop the sudden and inexplicable tears his words caused. She could not trust herself to say something in response without crying, so she turned away. She felt him move away and instantly felt bereft, but could not make herself call him back. Things were happening that she had never expected, and she was having difficulty absorbing them.

Lost in her thoughts, she wandered into one of the rooms where cards were being played. One table had four for whist. Another had a faro game. The woman who was bank smiled, the others either frowned or groaned. In faro, the odds were in the favour of the person who was bank.

She watched vouchers and coins change hands. In her mind, she saw fortunes being tossed away and futures being ruined. A hand touched her shoulder and she jumped. Only then did she realise that her shoulders had hunched and her fingers had fisted.

'Lillith,' Perth said quietly for her ears only, 'not everyone who gambles loses a fortune. Most of the people play for fun. Not one of the people here tonight is in debt or has lost his or her inheritance.'

The comfort his words brought, silly as it might seem, allowed her to relax. She leaned back into the solidity of his chest and was glad for his support and warmth.

'You are right,' she whispered. 'I just let myself get caught up in my own experience with Mathias.'

'I know,' he said softly, bringing his hand to the nape of her neck and gently massaging the stiff muscles there.

'Here are the lovebirds,' a bright voice said.

Lillith started and would have jumped away from Perth but his fingers tightened. She turned to see Madeline Russell with Nathan in tow. Lillith smiled in delight.

'I did not know you were coming,' she said, extending her hands to take Madeline's.

'I did not tell you because I knew that as Perth's wife you would be here, and I wanted to surprise you.' She grabbed Lillith's hands and pulled her into an embrace. 'I am so glad to see you looking so good,' she murmured. 'Marriage becomes you.'

Lillith looked swiftly at Perth from the corner of her eye to see if he had heard, but he and Nathan had moved off. 'Thank you for the compliment, and you are as outspoken as ever.'

Instead of looking chagrined, Madeline looked supremely satisfied. 'Now that I see you, I am glad I told Perth where you had gone.'

'So you are the one. I thought so.' But her words held no censure. Things had turned out for the best.

Madeline shrugged shoulders covered in very fashionable gauze thin muslin and spangled netting. 'He was desperate to find you. I think he knew,' she finished on a whisper.

Lillith nodded. 'A lot has happened since I last saw you.' She drew Madeline to an alcove where they stood with their back to the wall so they could see anyone approaching. 'Mathias has gambled away my settlement from de Lisle.'

'That snake,' Madeline said. At Lillith's frown, she added quietly, 'I know he is your brother, but he is lower than a snake. He is…he is…I cannot think of anything that is worse than him.'

Lillith sighed and once more felt close to tears. She took a deep breath. 'Perth would completely agree with you.' She must have sounded weepy for Madeline put her arm around Lillith's waist.

'Oh, Lillith, I am sorry to upset you.'

Lillith blinked. 'You are right about Mathias. I know that and should be beyond this. I do not know what is wrong with me, but everything upsets me more than usual. This is just one more incident.'

'Well, smile,' Madeline said firmly. 'We are being watched.' She flashed a blinding grin at two dowagers. 'As for the moods, 'tis your condition. I swear, I cried from sun up to sun down.' She laughed. 'Nathan threatened to leave me for nine months.'

Lillith laughed. 'Surely not. Nathan is besotted with you.'

'True,' Madeline said complacently, 'but even he was sorely tried.'

Feeling much better for the laugh and for having told Madeline the worst that Mathias had done, Lillith allowed her friend to lead her to where Perth and Nathan stood speaking with Carstairs, Chillings and Lady Annabelle. Noting that Perth stood beside Lady Annabelle, Lillith could not stop a twinge of jealousy.

She told herself that it was her condition that made her overreact. Then, always honest with herself, she admitted that it was not. She would be jealous of Perth's interest in any other woman—Lady Annabelle was worse because the woman was so intriguing.

'Nathan, darling,' Madeline said cajolingly as she took her husband's arm, 'be a dear and go get Lillith and me something to drink.' She cast an arch look at Perth. 'Unless you would like to do so.'

Perth glanced from Madeline to Lillith and bowed. 'I would be delighted.'

From the look on his face, Lillith knew he was far from delighted. But she was glad of Madeline's manoeuvring. The errand separated Perth from Lady Annabelle.

'Congratulations,' Lady Annabelle said, moving closer to Lillith. 'I understand that you and Perth are recently wed.'

'Thank you,' Lillith murmured.

'My congratulations as well,' Chillings said.

'And mine,' Carstairs added a trifle slowly. 'His good fortune is our loss.'

'Thank you again,' Lillith said.

Perth returned with their drinks. He handed Madeline hers with a flourish. 'Next time, I will let Russell do the honours.'

'I normally do,' Nathan said good-naturedly.

Madeline laughed.

'Would you care to dance, Lady Perth?' Carstairs asked.

Lillith flicked a glance at her husband who looked ready to step between her and the other man. Hastily, she said, 'Please.'

Carstairs extended his arm and she accompanied him to where the dancing was taking place. It was a country reel. To Lillith the music went on too long and by the time they were finished, she was winded.

'Would you care to go on the terrace for some fresh air?' Carstairs asked.

She was sorely tempted, but thought better of it. 'No, thank you, Mr Carstairs. I had best return to my husband.'

He nodded. 'As you wish. I had hoped that you would like respite.'

She paused at the tone of his voice and looked up at him. 'Why would you think that?'

His tanned skin turned a burnt red. 'I should not have said anything. My apologies.'

'No,' she said quietly. 'I truly do want to know why you think that.'

He angled her away from the direction they had been going so that they walked in enough privacy to speak. 'I overstepped the bounds of propriety, but your brother said that this marriage was not to your liking.' He stopped and waited as though trying to decide what else to say. 'At one time, he intimated that you might be open to receiving an offer from me.'

Lillith stiffened.

'I am truly sorry,' Carstairs said, his deep voice full of chagrin. 'I see now that Mr Wentworth was mistaken.'

Still more to put at Mathias's feet, Lillith thought bitterly. She kept her tone low and easy. 'I am the one who is truly sorry, Mr Carstairs. My brother can be overbearing at times when he believes that what he does is in my best interests.' She had to stop for a moment to let the lie settle. She did not like telling untruths, but in this case she could not tell the truth. 'I agreed freely to this wedding.'

'I see,' Carstairs said, his voice circumspect. 'I should return you to Perth.'

'There is no need,' Perth's deep baritone said from nearly right behind them. 'I have come to fetch my wife. It is time we were gone. She needs all the rest she can get.'

Carstairs lifted one dark brown eyebrow. He looked as though he would say something, but nodded instead. 'I hope to see you around town.'

Lillith smiled at him before allowing Perth to escort her to the foyer where he bundled her into her heavy cape and then out into the street where the carriage waited. Instead of allowing the footman to help her, Perth handed her inside.

She had no sooner settled herself than Perth demanded, 'Was Carstairs importuning you?'

His question took her by surprise. She could never tell him the truth. He would challenge Carstairs and then Mathias.

'No, he was merely allowing me to catch my breath before returning me to you. The dance was more strenuous than I had thought.' She smiled softly. 'It would seem that dancing requires more effort right now than normally.'

'I am sure there is more to it than you are saying, but I will let it drop.'

'There was nothing to it,' she said coolly. 'And if there was, so what? I am carrying *your* child.'

She had not meant to goad him. The less interest he took in the intrigues Mathias insisted on creating, the better for everyone. Mathias had much to answer for, but she did not want him hurt or killed and particularly not by her husband. But Perth's lack of interest in her lately had piqued her. Against her better judgement, she wanted him to desire her. No sooner had she realised that, than she berated herself. She was totally unreasonable! It had to be her condition.

'True, the child you are carrying is mine. As the rest will be.' He made a flat statement that brooked no contradiction.

'Well, they certainly will not be another man's,' she retorted.

He grinned at that, his teeth a white slash against

his swarthy complexion. But instead of replying, he banged his cane on the carriage roof. The vehicle stopped and without a backward glance, Perth leaped to the ground and set off walking.

Nonplussed and not a little bit angry at his desertion, Lillith fought the inclination to follow him. The urge to yell at him like a fishwife was strong. She was crazy. He was only treating her the way she had demanded. He was treating her as a man would treat a woman whom he had married for convenience. After all, she already carried his child.

Still, her hands shook uncontrollably and tears were near the surface. Things were going horribly close to the way she had dreaded they would.

The next morning, Lillith sat in the breakfast room drinking hot chocolate when Perth joined her. She could not help the frown she greeted him with. He had not come back last night, or, if he had, she had not heard him even though she had lain awake until daybreak.

'Good morning to you, too,' he said, helping himself to a large slice of ham and ale and sitting across from her. 'I am glad I caught you before you left today.' He took a bite of ham. 'I have something for you.'

'Really?' She sipped her hot chocolate and nibbled on her toast. 'More jewellery?' she asked, not really thinking so or wanting any, but wanting to needle him.

He gave her a considering look. 'If that is what you want, then I shall get you more. I have already taken the Perth family jewels into Gerrard's to be cleaned and reset. There are rubies and sapphires and some South Sea pearls.'

Exasperated at herself and at him, her reply was tart. 'Nothing of the sort. I was merely curious.'

He finished his ham and drank down the ale. 'Then perhaps you will be more pleased with today's gift than you were with the opals.' He stood and went to the door where he stopped and waited for her.

Lillith's scowl intensified. She had wanted a marriage of convenience and that was exactly what he was giving her—except for the lavish presents. She sipped the last of her chocolate and rose, moving at her own leisure in spite of his haste.

Whatever he had for her, it was outside and he was excited. Watching him practically dance from foot to foot finally eased her unhappiness with him. He swept her out the front door and stopped.

In the street, a prancing pair of grey horses were harnessed to a silver cabriolet with black trim and a black top pulled up. The door was emblazoned with the Perth coat of arms.

'This is for you,' he said softly.

She gasped. 'Me? It is fabulous. I mean, it is beautiful. Surely it is for both of us.'

'No,' he said firmly, taking her by the arm and directing her down the steps and to the coach. 'It is for you alone.'

'But...thank you,' she said, remembering how he had wondered if she would like this gift more than the last. 'It is truly a magnificent present.' She turned to him, perplexed. 'But why? I already have a carriage, and I have already had so much from you as my settlement.'

He scowled at her. 'Your other carriage was de Lisle's and it has his coat of arms. You are no longer the Dowager Lady de Lisle. You are Lillith, Countess of Perth. This cabriolet reflects that.'

'Ah,' she breathed as though she understood, but she did not. 'This is to show the world that I am your property.'

'That you are my wife,' he corrected. 'I thought you might take it to your meeting with Mr Sinclair. See how you like it or if there is something you want changed.'

She shook her head in amazement. He was showering her with very expensive things. It was disconcerting.

'That is a good idea. I must go get my pelisse and a cape,' she finally said. 'The day is cold and a drizzle starting.'

He nodded and let her go.

Lillith rushed up the stairs more to escape him and the situation than because she needed to hurry. There was still plenty of time before she needed to leave. However, the horses pulling her carriage would need to keep moving. She could take a ride around London, possibly Hyde Park, before going to Mr Sinclair's. It truly was a beautiful vehicle.

An hour later, Lillith exited her new carriage.

Her appointment with Mr Sinclair was in five

minutes. Parliament would be over in several days, and she wanted to get an update on her affairs before she and Perth left for the country.

She entered the outer office and was quickly ushered into his private room. He rose and offered her a seat close to the fire. She sat with alacrity.

'It is getting colder by the hour,' she said.

'Winter. I should imagine you and the Earl will be leaving for the country soon.'

She nodded. 'As soon as Parliament ends. The Earl has some concerns he is attempting to get Parliament to address.'

Mr Sinclair nodded. 'Yes. His bill for the returning soldiers. Many people are in favour of it, but I doubt that he will get it passed. 'Tis a shame.'

Lillith was momentarily taken aback. She knew that most of the people in their circles were aware of Perth's endeavours, but she had not realised that his name and cause were so well known that people outside of their sphere were also aware of what he did. Pride in her husband's efforts brought a lump to her throat.

'My husband has many fine qualities,' she finally managed to say around the tightness that made swallowing difficult.

'Many,' Sinclair agreed. 'And he is very generous.'

Lillith coloured and wondered if news of her magnificent jewels and new carriage had managed to travel this far. 'He is.'

Mr Sinclair smiled. 'I have the marriage settlement

papers here for you to read and sign. You will see that the Earl has agreed to far more than we asked for.'

'What?' She reached for the papers.

'He has bought your London house that was on the market and it will go to the second child you have if the first is a boy. If the first child is girl, then the house will be hers. He has also given you a very large jointure that will continue in the event of his death whether you remarry or not. And he has settled ten thousand pounds on each of your children who will not inherit the earldom. Most generous indeed.'

She gaped, only just managing to keep her eyes from widening. 'Most generous indeed,' she repeated, too stunned to think of something different.

Mr Sinclair cleared his throat. 'There is one stipulation to everything. Mr Wentworth must never be in charge of handling any of this.'

'That is a wise course,' Lillith said, instantly relieved.

The good news and the bad news in the open, she signed the papers with relish and rose. 'Thank you so much, Mr Sinclair. I know that the past months have been difficult on you, but I think you will find the future ones much more pleasant.'

He bowed over the hand she extended. 'As I hope you will, my lady.'

She left his offices with a lightness of step that she had not experienced for a very long time. And it was all because of Perth. The journey home was much more pleasant than the journey to Mr Sinclair's.

She delighted in the well-sprung comfort of her cabriolet. The soft wine leather squabs beckoned her fingers and she took off her gloves to stroke her bare skin over the fine leather.

And there was Perth's generosity to her and to their children. This might be a marriage of convenience, and Perth might be acting toward her in some ways as though it was, but his behaviour was that of a man determined to show his new wife that she was valued. He was behaving as though theirs was a love match, and he was trying to show her how greatly he cared for her security and sense of worth. Which she knew was not the case. Nor could she let herself be so weak as to think it was.

'Twas very unsettling.

Chapter Sixteen

Lillith reined her mare in. She and Perth were leaving London tomorrow and she had been busy packing; she had not wanted to come here. But Mathias had sent a note asking her to meet him in Hyde Park. He had not been to see her since her wedding and she found that she missed him, and this would be her last chance to see her brother for some time.

It was late afternoon and the sun would soon be gone. She wished he had picked a warmer spot, preferably inside. But he had said he did not want her coming to his rented rooms. None of her friends, not even Madeline, would have him in their home and his friends were mostly unmarried men.

A biting wind whipped the bare tree branches around and caused little wavelets to crest white on the surface of the Serpentine. The ducks that swam on the pond in summer were gone.

She heard the sound of horse's hooves on the hard ground, and angled her mount to face that direction. Instead of seeing her brother, she saw her husband. He rode quickly and drew his horse to a halt just as she thought he would ride her down. She knew in an instant that he was furious.

'What in blazes do you think you are doing? In the park at this time of day with the sun nearly down and no groom?' he thundered. 'Anything might have happened to you. And if you have not a care for yourself, consider our child.'

On the defensive and knowing she should have brought a groom, she shot back, 'I came here to meet Mathias, who will not come to the house—as you very well know. He is still my brother, and I do still want to stay in touch with him.'

'Then meet him somewhere warmer and safer than Hyde Park in the late afternoon in the winter when nearly no one is around.'

He turned his horse and started off as though he expected her to automatically follow. Her hackles immediately rose and she stayed put. He glanced back at her, his brows drawn.

'Come along.'

'I told you, I am waiting for Mathias.'

'And I am waiting for you,' he said coldly.

She drew herself up, prepared to resist him.

A shot rang out. Her horse reared and she slid off onto the ground, hitting it with a force that knocked the wind from her.

'Lillith!'

She heard Perth's anguished cry, but could not sit up just yet and tell him she was fine. Her lungs burned and would not seem to fill with air. He was beside her before she recovered.

'Lillith, my God, are you all right?'

He lifted her into his arms just as another shot rang out. Instantly he dropped, covering her body with his. His hands shielded her face and head. She heard the horses neighing.

'We have got to get out of here,' he muttered. 'Can you run?'

Realisation of their peril hit her like a runaway carriage. 'Yes, I think so,' she managed. 'I will have to.'

He nodded. 'That's my Lillith. Now.'

He stood and pulled her to her feet. He swung her in front of him and propelled her forward. Another shot rang out. She felt his hand slip from the small of her back but return almost immediately.

She grabbed her riding skirts in both hands, cursing their bulkiness, and ran for her life. Her lungs laboured. She heard Perth's boots pounding on the ground and felt his breath hot on her neck. They made it to a copse of trees where Perth shoved her behind the largest trunk and pushed her into a crouch.

'You make a smaller target,' he explained, kneeling beside her and shielding the part of her body the tree did not protect.

She gasped for breath and pushed her hand hard against the stitch in her side. Frantic to know what was happening, she angled so that she could look around the trunk.

'Damnation,' Perth said, yanking her arm so that her

head was no longer exposed. 'What are you trying to do, give them the perfect target?'

Instantly chagrined, she said, 'You are right. I did not think.'

He let out a long, frustrated breath. 'The best thing that could happen to us right now would be for your brother to come along. Whoever is shooting at us is bound to disappear if too many get involved.'

'But why would anyone shoot at us?'

He shrugged. 'Who knows? It has been a hard winter. Perhaps someone is desperate beyond words and willing to risk the very great possibility of getting caught.' He slanted her a dark look. 'Maybe someone was waiting here on purpose.'

His words fell between them like stones.

'Surely not,' she finally managed to get out between shaking teeth.

He shrugged again and this time he winced. She ran her gaze over him and saw the red stain on his back right shoulder that was slowly spreading.

'You have been hit,' she said, suddenly frantic with worry. 'We have got to get you to a doctor.'

'Hush,' he said, his tone gentle. 'First we have got to get away from here. Everything else can wait.'

She knew he was right, but that did not stop the icy fear that clutched her heart. 'We must at least stop the bleeding.'

She lifted her skirts and ripped at her petticoats. Another shot rang out.

'Stop it,' he said. 'The trunk of this tree is not large and all your twisting around makes you the perfect target. I would rather bleed to death than have you get hurt. Now stop.'

A shot hit the tree, sending pieces of bark ricocheting. A sliver caught her cheek. She yelped and reached up to see if the piece had stuck. It had not, but her gloves came away with a dab of blood.

Perth vowed, 'Whoever is behind this will pay dearly.'

Fierce pride filled her for she knew he meant it, and right now she wanted nothing more than revenge on the person who had shot him. No matter how he felt about her, she loved him.

It was fast becoming dark.

'We will try to escape again. They will not be able to see any better in the dark than we will. That is, if someone does not come looking for us very soon. The horses will have returned to the house and the groom will immediately tell Fitch.' He had no sooner said the words than the sounds of approaching hoofbeats came to them. 'Ah, I knew I could depend on Fitch,' he said with great satisfaction.

To Lillith's relief, it seemed that Fitch had brought a small army. Several riders held flambeaux to light the scene. Every one of them carried pistols which they had out.

'Fitch,' Perth yelled. 'Over here.'

Lillith heard Fitch tell several of the riders to fan out and look for the attackers. Men and flambeaux moved into the dusk, trailing smoke and the scent of pitch. She marvelled at Fitch's efficiency.

Quickly the remaining men surrounded her and

Perth. The orange and yellow flames from the flam-beaux shot into the sky and cast the men's shadows behind them in elongated parodies.

'I knew something was wrong,' Fitch said, dis-mounting. 'A good thing you mentioned something about coming here.' He cast a quick, involuntary glance at Lillith.

She caught him looking at her, however briefly, and knew this whole débâcle was her fault. But surely her brother had not planned *this*! Someone must have known he had sent her a note or had seen her leave the house and followed her, thinking she would be easy prey. Mathias had his faults, as she knew only too well, but this went beyond gambling away and inheritance—or even a horsewhipping. *Surely...*

'Take Lady Perth home,' the Earl said, thrusting her forward into the arms of a nearby rider. 'She was thrown from her horse and I want her examined im-mediately by a doctor.'

In a jumble of limbs, Lillith found herself sitting in front of the head groom. 'You are hurt as well, Perth. You need the doctor more than I. Come home.'

Fitch jerked and spun around. He took a step to-wards the Earl, but when he spoke his voice was calm. 'She is right, my lord.'

Perth grunted. 'I will live. I have taken worse. Right now, we must look for those scoundrels or any trace they left.' His hands fisted. 'They are not going to get away with this.'

She shivered involuntarily, the cold and his chilling words finally penetrating the numbness that had descended on her. 'Then do not lay more at their feet by staying and letting your wound worsen.'

'Take her home, Thomas,' Perth ordered the groom. To ease the harshness of that order, he crossed over and took Lillith's hand. 'I would not stay here if I thought it was endangering my life. Trust me that I know these things.'

She gazed down at him and saw that he meant what he said. It would not be so bad if she had not seen Fitch turn away in disgust. Still, there was nothing she could do.

'Take care, then,' she said, leaning down and kissing him lightly. He stepped back in surprise. 'I will have a doctor in to make sure that neither the babe nor I have taken harm. And I will have him stay to examine you.'

He stared up at her, and she knew that her spontaneous show of affection had startled him. Never before had she kissed him unless it was in passion and after he had already aroused her.

He stepped back. 'I won't be long.'

Perth turned away and motioned for Fitch to follow him. 'The shots came from this direction,' he said, striding off. As occupied as he was on finding some trace of their attackers, he still listened for the sounds that would tell him Lillith had left.

'Her ladyship will be all right,' Fitch said gruffly. 'She is a strong one.'

Perth moved into a copse of trees and squatted. 'Bring the light over here.'

Fitch arrived and crouched beside the Earl. He

grumbled in disgust. 'Nothing here but a bunch of dirt that's been scuffed up.' He shifted some of the earth through his fingers. 'And some powder. You will never find them from this.'

Perth stood, frustration in every line of his taut body. 'I know, but I had to try.' He pivoted on his heel and grunted in pain. 'I guess I had better get home and have you look at this.'

'You should have done that instead of chasing after evidence you won't find,' Fitch said sourly.

Perth eased up his pace enough to lessen the pain in his shoulder. 'I hoped for something.' He cast a sideways glance at Fitch. 'Her brother sent her a message asking her to meet him here.'

Fitch's intake of breath was loud in the cold, silent air. 'Why would he do a fool thing like that?'

'We can only guess,' Perth said, moving more slowly than he liked.

Thirty minutes later, he sat in a chair in his bedroom in front of a roaring fire with just his breeches and stockings on and cursed the doctor examining him. 'Blast it, man, do you have to prod so deep?' He ran the fingers of his free hand through his hair. 'How is my wife? Is the babe all right?'

Doctor Johnson, a young man with sandy brown hair and piercing brown eyes, kept on doing his examination. 'Your wife is fine and so is the child she carries. They are both resting. She is in better shape than you are. If you had sent for me immediately, I might not have to dig so deeply, but the ball is lodged solidly in muscle, maybe even bone. Fortunately for you, I was a surgeon before becoming a doctor. Still, you will be lucky if you don't come down with a fever.'

'I shall be lucky if I am not arrested for your murder,' Perth muttered. But the relief he felt over Lillith went a long way to making him feel more charitable towards the doctor.

From his position on the other side of the Earl, Fitch said, 'He has never been a good patient.'

'That I can believe,' the doctor muttered. 'Almost. Now hold still.'

Hold still. Perth saw lights in front of his eyes and bit down hard on the piece of leather Fitch had given him to chew. Then an excruciating wrench and the doctor held the forceps high. Between the tongs was the ball.

'Whisky,' Perth demanded.

'After I am through,' the doctor said, pouring the contents of a decanter liberally along the wound.

Perth sucked in his breath. 'You could have told me you were going to do that.'

'It would not have made it hurt less.' The doctor handed him the decanter.

Perth took a long swig. 'No, it would not.' He sank into the chair.

'You have an interesting pallor that should rival Byron's in the drawing room,' the doctor said drily. 'I suggest that you stay in bed for quite some time.'

Perth closed his eyes and took another long drink.

'Thank you, doctor. Please see to my wife before you go.'

The doctor looked over Perth's head to Fitch.

Fitch shrugged. 'Best do as he says. Knowing that her ladyship is well cared for will ease him more than anything else.' He carefully took the decanter from the Earl's slack fingers. 'I will watch over his lordship.'

The doctor nodded and left through the door connecting to Lady Perth's chamber. He had given her a light dose of laudanum to calm her nerves, and she lay quietly on the bed. But he noted that her eyes were open.

'How is my husband?' she asked softly before he had taken two steps into the room.

He closed the door behind himself and went to the bed. 'Your colour is back, and your husband has a strong constitution. I understand he has suffered wounds like this several times. That accounts for the scars on his body.' He did not mention the scars that criss-crossed the Earl's back.

She gave him a wan smile. 'Is that your way of telling me that he will be all right?'

'That is my way of telling you that he is a fool, but hopefully will take no lasting harm. Although I warned him that he might run a fever. His man says he knows what to do.' He reached the bed and took her wrist to feel her pulse. 'Your husband is more concerned about your well-being than his own, and his man says to care for you and the Earl will do fine.'

Her smile widened. Even hurt, Perth was stubborn to a fault.

Shortly after, the doctor pronounced, 'You are as well as can be expected after what you have been through. I will give you the same advice I gave his lordship: get some rest.' He frowned at her. 'I trust you will follow my orders better than he, for you have a child to consider.'

She had intended to defy him and go to sit beside Perth and watch over him, but the doctor's words chastised her. Today she had not thought much of the life she carried and had consequently endangered the babe.

She nodded. 'I will do my best, doctor. And thank you.'

'Thank me by taking care of yourself.' He packed up his bag and went to the door. 'I will be back tomorrow to see how you and the Earl are doing. I expect to see improvement.'

She waited until the door closed behind him before getting up. She would rest in a chair beside Perth's bed. The doctor had said her husband was strong, but she had also seen the anger in the doctor's eyes. She knew the emotion had been caused by Perth's disregard for his own safety.

She slipped from the bed and on bare feet went to Perth's room. She did not knock, not wanting to disturb him if he slept. To her relief he was in bed, but the light of a single candle showed his extreme paleness. Worry quickened her pace.

'He is sleeping more from the whisky than the wound,' Fitch said softly.

She had not seen him and his voice surprised her.

She whirled around. He sat in a chair by the smouldering fire.

'You startled me,' she whispered. She looked back at Perth. 'The doctor was not happy with him.'

'Neither was I,' Fitch said, getting up and coming to the bed. 'But you know how he is.'

'Yes. Stubborn and arrogant.' Tentatively, very conscious of the servant beside her, she laid her palm on Perth's forehead. 'He feels cool.'

'Right now,' Fitch agreed. 'If he gets a fever it will come later.'

'Oh. I do not have any experience nursing someone with a wound.' She took her hand back. 'My times in the sickroom have been childbirthing and illnesses.'

'Not much difference when all is said and done,' Fitch said. 'I will ring for some tea and biscuits. If you intend to stay, you will need to keep your strength up.'

She was not hungry, but knew he was right. 'I will be right back.' She hurried from the room to hers where she grabbed a thick, wool robe and belted it around her waist. She returned in time to see Fitch open the door and a footman carry in a laden tray.

She poured Fitch tea and then herself. She added biscuits. 'You are undoubtedly tired,' she said. 'I can watch him by myself.'

Fitch took a drink before answering. 'Thank you, my lady, but you have been through nearly as much today as the Earl. It would be better if I watched tonight while you rest. In the morning you can take my place.'

He made sense and she was tired, but she could not bring herself to leave. 'I am not tired.'

He frowned at her. 'You are as stubborn as he and for no good reason. If he gets worse, it won't be for some hours. You will be far more use to him then if you are rested.'

He was irritated with her and rightly so. His words made sense. With as much graciousness as she could muster, she agreed. But before she could leave, she had to check on Perth one last time.

He lay as still as before and just as pale. Unmindful of Fitch who stood behind her now, she gently smoothed the hair from her husband's face. Then she ran a soft touch over his scar. Even with the white line down his cheek, he looked somehow vulnerable.

She realised with a start that she had never seen him like this before. Every other time she had seen him in bed, he had been awake and making love to her. Now he lay here hurt, and all because of her. She had no illusions. He had taken the bullet when they had run, when his hand had briefly fallen from her back. He had taken a bullet that would have hit her squarely between the shoulder blades.

She squeezed her eyes shut. Please let the wound not fester. *Please let him not die.* He might not love her, but he cared enough to risk his life for her. That meant a great deal.

More devastating was the certainty that she could not live without him.

The next morning she woke to Agatha moving around the room. 'My lady, your brother is here to see you.'

'My brother,' Lillith murmured, sitting up in bed.

'He has been here for nigh on an hour, my lady,' Agatha said, putting down the tray with Lillith's morning chocolate and toast.

Lillith dragged herself out of bed. She had not slept well with worrying about Perth. But at least she was past the morning sickness. She ate the toast first to insure that her stomach stayed settled, then drank the hot chocolate. Afterwards, Agatha helped her into a loose-fitting morning dress of pale blue kerseymere that was several seasons out of date.

Only then did she go to meet her brother. Even so, she was uncomfortable. Tell herself as she might that he was not involved with what had happened yesterday, she could not get past the fact that he had asked her to meet him in the place where she and Perth were attacked.

Mathias sat in the breakfast room drinking coffee and eating a beefsteak. He appeared perfectly at home. He looked up when she came in. 'Ordered some food when it became obvious you were not coming down soon.' He took another bite.

She eased into a chair across the table from him and waved away a footman who offered her more chocolate. 'Perth is hurt.'

'That is what the man—Simmons, is it?—mentioned. Dreadful when Hyde Park ain't safe. And in broad daylight.' He continued eating.

Lillith watched him. 'It was not exactly full daylight. The time you set for our meeting was a scant thirty or forty minutes before dusk. Perth came after me…and you never arrived.'

He waved his fork, a piece of meat hanging precariously from the prongs. 'Got waylaid. Prinny needed my advice on a waistcoat. Could not refuse the Prince of Wales.'

Lillith's eyes narrowed, but the tale was not far fetched. The Prince of Wales was a notorious dandy, and he was possessive of his friends. He could very easily have commanded her brother's presence for nothing better than to comment on the fashion of a piece of clothing.

'So, did you come today to talk to me about what you could not speak about yesterday? Although I find it unusual that you come to our house for the first time after Perth is hurt and confined to his bed.'

Mathias's mouth thinned. 'Are you trying to imply something, Lillith? Because if you are, and if it is what I think, then you are beyond the pale. I came because I knew I had been insufferably rude not to have sent a lackey to meet you and tell you that I would not be coming. It slipped my mind.'

She accepted his apology, but did not completely accept his reason. 'Why did you want to meet with me in the first place?'

'I want to stay in your town house that de Lisle left you. Rumour says Perth bought it for you and, as his wife, you can well afford to let me use it.' His blue eyes took on an ugly glint. 'The man gives you everything and will do nothing for me. 'Tis the least he can do, through you, of course.'

She could hardly believe what he had said. Even for Mathias, the idea was outrageous. Still, he was her brother. Telling him no would be hard. Perhaps too hard.

'Why do you want to stay in town? Everyone is leaving.'

He finished his beefsteak. 'The Prince will not be leaving town for several days. He wants me around and I don't want to stay in rented rooms any longer.' He wiped his mouth with the napkin. 'I find myself unable to afford them.'

Lillith's hands clenched into white fists under cover of the table and her eyes narrowed ever so slightly. He was insufferable. But he was her brother. Much as she wanted to tell him no, absolutely no, the words stuck in her throat.

She took a slow breath and hoped her voice would not show her fury. 'You may stay there for the present. Perth is sure to find out and he will want you out.'

Mathias stood and an ugly look settled on his face. 'He has made the house over to you.'

She rose so that he would not be towering over her and shook her head. 'That is not true. It is in my keeping for our second child or first girl.'

'The same thing,' he said pointedly.

She shrugged. 'Not exactly. And if Perth wants you out when he finds out, then I will be obligated to ask you to leave.'

His mouth thinned and his face reddened. 'Already he is more important to you than your own flesh and blood. And I thought yours was a marriage of convenience. I see I was mistaken.' He sneered. 'He is giving you more gifts than a man gives his mistress.'

She stiffened. 'I think our conversation has gone on long enough, Mathias. I had hoped for something different from you, but I see it is to be the same as always.'

'Not quite,' he said. 'Normally you pay more regard to what I have to say.'

He pivoted on his heel and left. Lillith watched him, sadness replacing the anger of minutes before. He was still her only living relative. That meant a great deal to her. It hurt greatly that her brother did not have the same feelings of love and commitment. Hard as it was on her, she had to admit that she was nothing but a means to a fortune for Mathias.

She sat back down and rested her head on her hand. She was very tired this morning and Mathias's visit and the ugly confrontation between them had only exhausted her further. That was the reason tears were so close. Nor did his absence ease the ugly feelings that seemed to permeate the room.

For the first time in her life, she began to truly despair of ever having a loving relationship with her brother. All the time before she had been the one to be conciliatory and to do whatever it took to maintain their relationship. Now for the first time, she was not so accommodating and the rift between them widened with every encounter while her relationship with Perth was doing just the opposite.

She took a deep breath and stood back up. It was past time she went to check on her husband. Before coming down to breakfast she had looked in and both he and Fitch had been sleeping, Perth in bed and Fitch in a chair pulled up to the bed. She had left them to come and eat. Now she needed to go and relieve Fitch and she wanted to care for her husband.

Chapter Seventeen

Lillith entered Perth's room as quietly as possible, not wanting to wake her husband. She realised immediately that she could have entered on a horse and not woken him. Fitch sprawled in a chair not two feet from the bed and snored loudly enough to wake up the dead.

She shook her head in amusement and crossed to the batman. Gently so as not to startle him, she shook one of his shoulders.

'Wha—?' He started awake.

'Shh,' she said. 'I have come to relieve you. There are eggs and kidneys downstairs hot from the kitchen. You will feel the better for having them.'

Once awake, wide awake, Fitch stood and stretched. 'Right, my lady. I will just have some and return.'

She shook her head and put her fists on her hips. 'You will do more than that. You will eat until you can eat no more and then you will get some rest.' When his mouth set in a stubborn line, she firmed hers.

'That was our agreement last night. I kept to my part and went to bed. Now you must keep to your half.'

He looked as though he would argue, and Lillith straightened her shoulders and prepared for battle. He shrank a little bit and a huge yawn caught him.

'You are right, my lady. I did agree to that and you did do what you said you would do.' Another yawn took him. 'And I am tired.' He gave her a rueful grin. 'Two hours in a chair don't do much.'

She returned his grin. 'And you were snoring loudly enough to wake Perth.'

Fitch shook his head. 'No. His lordship can sleep through cannon fire when he is tired enough or wounded. My snoring is not enough to rouse him. Trust me on that.'

'I suppose I must,' Lillith said, believing him, having already seen the proof. 'Now go. The doctor should be here soon.'

'Call me if you need help,' Fitch said, casting one last glance at the Earl who still lay fast asleep.

'I will,' Lillith promised.

No sooner had the door closed behind Fitch than Lillith strode to the bed and looked down at Perth. His thick black hair fell in several waving hanks over his broad forehead, making him look young and vulnerable. Not even the silver wings at his temples could detract from the image. Ebony lashes lay fanned across his high cheekbones. Even his scar seemed relaxed.

Softly, so as not to wake him, she brushed the hair back. The backs of her fingers grazed his skin. She stopped. He was hot. She cupped his face in her palm. He was very hot. Worry puckered her brow.

She stepped back and looked for water. She knew from her own experiences that cool water could help bring down a fever. She found what she sought on his shaving table. She poured the liquid from the pitcher and dipped a convenient cloth in. She wrung the excess moisture from the fabric and went back to Perth.

His eyes were open and he watched her.

'You are awake,' she said inanely.

'What are you doing?' he asked, his voice barely a rasp.

'I am going to sponge you. You have a fever,' she said calmly, not wanting to upset him with her concern.

'I am thirsty,' he said. 'Is there water to drink?'

She laid the cloth on his forehead before returning to the pitcher and pouring a glass full of water. She took it to him and held his head while he finished the entire thing.

'Thank you,' he murmured, his voice a little less harsh. 'I needed that very much.'

'You are welcome,' she said, setting the glass on a nearby table. 'Now lie still and let me sponge you. You will feel much better for it.'

He gave her a smile that was almost, but not quite, lecherous. 'I am sure that I will.'

She eyed him narrowly, wondering if he felt better than she had thought. When he closed his eyes, she decided that he did not. She stroked the damp cloth over his face until the material felt warm, which was not long. At this rate, she would need to move the pitcher and bowl closer to the bed. She did so, but not without some difficulty. When she was finished and once more looked at her patient, he was watching her with a grin.

'Very diverting,' he said. 'Why did you not call Fitch to help?'

'Because he spent the night watching you. It is my turn now while he gets some much-needed sleep.'

'The two of you are trading off duty?' he asked, an unreadable look in his eyes.

She nodded. 'The doctor should be here soon to check on you.'

'And you,' he added firmly. 'How are you doing? And the babe?'

She stopped wringing the cloth out and looked at him. She saw concern. 'We are both fine. Doctor Johnson said we were doing better than you.'

'That young man was very opinionated. Fitch could have done as well.'

She turned to him, hands on hips in exasperation. 'Then why did you even bother sending for a doctor if you did not value his opinion?'

He looked as though the answer were obvious. 'Because Fitch could have cared for me, but he has no experience with pregnant women.'

'Ah,' she said sharply.

She turned abruptly away to dip the previously forgotten cloth back in the water and to hide her reaction to his words. Everything he had done yesterday had been for her and their child. First he had come after her in Hyde Park. Then he had taken a bullet in the shoulder to protect her. And lastly, he had ordered a doctor he did not think he needed so that she and the child she carried would be cared for. His concern took her breath away.

She went back to his side with the damp cloth just as someone knocked on the door. 'Come in,' she said, laying the cloth once more on his forehead.

'My lady,' Simmons said from the doorway, his nose held fastidiously high, 'there is a...person...here who says he knows the Earl.'

Lillith smiled. Her butler was a snob. 'What type of person is he?'

From the bed Perth asked, 'Is he a ruffian with several teeth missing?'

'Yes, my lord,' Simmons said barely repressing a shudder. 'And filthy.'

Lillith heard Perth chuckle, which was followed by a sharp intake of breath. She whirled around and marched back to his side. 'You are to be more careful.'

'I know what I am supposed to be,' he said, throwing the cover off and swinging his legs over the side of the bed. 'And I know what I intend to be.'

His face turned as white as the sheet riding low on his lean hips and he swayed to the side. Lillith grabbed him and held him to her.

'You may go, Simmons,' she said, not wanting the butler to see what would shortly be happening between her and her husband.

'Tell the man to wait,' Perth ordered just before the door closed. 'Or I will have your hide,' he said loudly.

On a quieter note, he said, 'That ruffian is important. He knows who attacked me several weeks ago and he might be able to find out who shot at us yesterday.'

Her brows rose. 'That is quite a responsibility for a man that Simmons would just as soon throw out the door.' She eased him to a sitting position against the pillows. 'But that is unimportant. You do not feel well and should not be out of bed.'

'Well,' he said, pushing up, 'I intend to stand on my own two feet shortly.'

She bent over him and put her palms on his chest to gently push him back. Heat emanated from his flesh even through the fine lawn nightshirt he wore. He swore as he fell backwards.

'You are going nowhere. You have a fever.' She kept her hands on him for fear that he would try and rise as soon as she removed them. 'Perhaps after Dr Johnson has examined you.'

'I will damn well do as I please, Lillith. This is not the first time I have had a fever, nor is it the first time I have been wounded. I never stay coddled in bed, and I have no intention of doing so now.' His gaze ran seductively down her. 'Unless you have something entertaining in mind that we might do?'

She flushed and her bosom ached. 'No,' she snapped.

'A pity,' he said, but with no real sound of regret. 'Now you can help me or I will do it in spite of you.'

She met his challenging gaze without blinking. She knew by the tightness of his jaw and the glint in his eyes that he meant what he said.

With a sigh of resignation she ungraciously acqui esced. 'As you demand. But let me check your ban dage for bleeding first.'

He nodded. She unbuttoned his shirt and slid it o his shoulder. He leant forward enough for her to se the back. The wound was well wrapped.

'Fitch changed it during the night,' Perth said.

'Ah, that explains why there is no blood.'

'Or none that can be seen,' Perth finished. 'Now ar you satisfied? I will even tell you how to tie a slin so that my arm does not pull down on the muscle.'

She moved back. 'You obviously know much mor about this than I.'

'As I said,' he said with seeming patience, 'I hav been through this before.'

He once more swung his legs over the edge of th bed. Again he swayed and his face blanched, but h remained upright.

'Stay put long enough for me to get Fitch,' she fi nally said, irritated with his stubbornness, but no wanting him to hurt himself further.

'No,' he ordered. 'Fitch needs his rest. You can hel me; by the time we are done with our visitor, the doc tor will be here. After he leaves, we can wake Fitch.

'That is less than ideal,' she muttered.

For the first time in days, he gave her a genuine smile. 'It is the best I can offer you. Now, I will make do with a dressing robe over my nightshirt. That wil be much easier than dressing me.'

She eyed him from the corner of her eye, wondering if the tone of his voice was meant to be seductive o teasing or both. The sharp angles of his face and the tension that emanated from him decided her that he meant both.

'Where is your robe?' she asked, backing away from the attraction he had suddenly become. Even wounded he was the most virile man she had ever encountered. She shook her head in wonder and chagrin at her physical weakness where he was concerned.

'Behind that door,' he said, indicating a door she had not noticed before.

She entered his dressing room. A small trundle bed was tucked against one corner for Fitch if he felt the need although Lillith knew the batman had his own suite of rooms, unusual as that was, on the third floor. As she had always known, Fitch was not a servant.

An array of dressing gowns hung from pegs. 'Which one do you want?' she called.

'The one you like best,' he answered, which was no help.

Quickly, so as not to test his patience which she knew to be short, she grabbed the nearest one that looked like it would be warm. It was finest black cashmere embroidered in silver silk dragons. It would be warm and regal. Whoever the person was who waited for them would be suitably impressed.

She came out of the room and went to him. He stood with the help of the bed on which he had the hand of his good arm propped for support.

'I would have helped you,' she said in exasperation.

'I am not a cripple, Lillith,' he said with an edge to his words.

She stared at him. 'Of course you are not, but you did not need to risk hurting yourself when I am perfectly capable of supporting you while you try to stand and get your bearings.'

He scowled. 'I don't like being dependent.'

'No one does,' she retorted, exasperated by his determined independence regardless of whether what he did was best.

'Some more than others,' he stated flatly, holding out his hand for the robe.

She was so disgusted with him that she threw the garment at him. He caught it with his good hand and proceeded to don it. It was small satisfaction when he pulled the sleeve up his bad arm and winced.

'I might have saved you that pain,' she said acidly. 'Let us just hope that you did not start your wound bleeding again.'

'It does not feel like it,' he said, belting the sash.

She noted that he moved with increased confidence. 'Some tea and food will help.'

He nodded. 'And I am sure that our guest would like some.' He glanced up at her after getting his slippers on. 'You could order Simmons to set the breakfast table.'

She closed her mouth on a sharp retort.

'Where is my cane?' he muttered.

Minutes later she found it in the dressing room and brought it out to him. He took it and started slowly towards the door. She followed behind, wondering if she was strong enough to break his fall should he lose his balance. In the hall, she rushed ahead to order the food and find a footman to help Perth down the stairs. Her husband had already started down when she got back.

'Let Robert help you, Perth,' she ordered.

Perth stared pointedly at her. 'Do you remember someone else using this very cane on these stairs, refusing to be helped? I do.'

'Well, I did not climb all the way. Fitch helped me.'

'I am going down, I think I can manage on my own. It is my shoulder, madam, not my leg.' He took another step down. 'You may go, Robert.'

The hapless footman looked from one of them to the other. Fuming, but knowing that Perth would do it his way, much as she had insisted on her way, Lillith said, 'Yes, Robert, go and tell Simmons we will be down shortly.'

The footman bowed himself away.

Perth continued down the stairs and Lillith followed.

The smells of ham, beefsteak, coffee, hot chocolate and toast assailed her senses as she entered the breakfast room she had left barely an hour before. She watched Perth take his usual seat. She noted beads of perspiration on his forehead, but he moved with deliberation. Once she was assured that he would do, she studied their guest.

The man was a ruffian and everything Simmons had said about him was true. At the moment, he stuffed his mouth with beefsteak and gammon at the same time. One hand curled around a mug of ale, which he slurped with a full mouth.

Perth watched him with grim satisfaction, the lines around his mouth more pronounced than normal. Simmons entered and served the Earl his favourite gammon steak and kidneys. Eggs sat on a side dish with toast. Strong black coffee steamed in a mug. Perth ate slowly, careful of his wounded shoulder when he cut his food and lifted his fork since he was right-handed, the same side that was hurt.

Lillith sat down beside Perth, their guest having taken her normal place. She took tea and a piece of toast, sipping on one and nibbling on the other. She was not hungry, but she was extremely curious.

The man took his last bite and drank his last gulp, belched and grinned in satisfaction. 'Thanks for the food,' he said, his look anything but grateful. 'I got the name you want, guv.'

Perth carefully set his fork and knife down. 'Of the man who hired you to assault me?'

'Assault? Oh, attack you. Yes.' His grin widened. 'Got more information I think you'll be wantin'. Somethin' about an attack in 'yde Park.'

Lillith jerked in surprise and her tea sloshed over the side of the cup to stain the white linen tablecloth. She noted that her husband took the extra news calmly, almost as though he had expected it.

'They were ordered by the same man,' Perth said flatly.

'That's right,' the other man said, much as one might praise a child that has guessed the correct answer. ''Ow much is the flash cove's name worth to you?'

'I already know the man's name,' Perth said quietly, his voice sending shivers down Lillith's back. 'What I want from you is to tell my wife.' He glanced at Lillith and then back to the man. 'I will pay you well.'

The ruffian named a sum that made Lillith choke. She expected Perth to say no.

'Simmons,' Perth said, 'go to the library and open the middle drawer of my desk. You will find a sheaf of bills. Bring them to me.' Simmons left. 'Now, the name.'

'First the money.'

'The name.'

''Ow do I know you'll keep your word? The other one didn't.'

Perth leaned forward, his left hand a fist on the table. 'I am not the other man.' His voice was cold. 'You will do well to remember that.'

The ruffian edged back in his chair. 'Right, guv. Right. No insult. Just can't always trust a swell cove. They got the blunt, but they don't always pay.'

Perth's eyes blazed. 'The name.'

'Right. Wentworth.' The man's grin returned. 'Rumour says 'e 'ired the men what shot at you yesterday, too. Me pal, Mike, says 'e 'eard it.'

Perth frowned in disbelief. ''Tis more likely your friend Mike was the one who shot me.'

'No, guv. No,' the other man said.

Through this Lillith sat frozen. Feeling rushed back like needles. 'No,' she murmured. 'No, you are wrong. Your friend is wrong.' But even as she said the words, doubt swamped her. It fitted. It fitted too well. 'Oh, no,' she whispered, sinking back into her chair and closing her eyes to close out the faces of the two men.

The ruffian's eyes widened and he snickered. 'Know the cove? 'E's a nasty one, 'e is. Nivver paid me what he owed me for attacking the guvnor 'ere.'

Lillith opened her eyes and stared the man down. Whether he was right or not, he did not need to gloat. The urge to reach out and slap the grin from the man's face was strong. She gripped the edge of the table instead. Her knuckles turned white and her nails dug into the cloth.

'Are you sure?' she asked.

Even as she asked, she knew his answer would not change. Mathias had done too much. But why? It made no sense.

The man's face darkened. 'I ain't uppity like the likes o' you, but I keeps me word. All I got.' He stood. 'I don't lie.'

'Do you have proof?' she demanded. 'Or are we to take your word?'

The ruffian bristled. 'Me word is me bond.'

Lillith looked away. All she was doing was taking her hurt and anger out on this man. If Mathias really had done this, then so be it, but until they had proof, she had to give her brother the benefit of the doubt.

Perth rose as well, careful not to move his right arm any more than necessary. 'I believe you,' he said quietly. 'My wife is upset. You shall have your money.'

Simmons returned then with the bills. The pile was an inch thick. Perth took it from Simmons, fanned through it and handed it over.

Surprise made the ruffian's mouth drop. 'This is more than we agreed to.'

'Take it,' Perth said. 'For your honour—and your discretion. I don't expect to hear another word of yesterday's incident or this conversation from anyone. Do I make myself clear?'

The man shot him a hard look but he kept the money. 'Yes. Thanks. I gotta go,' he added, moving around the table, careful to keep a wide berth between him and Lillith.

'Please show our guest to the door, Simmons,' Perth said.

Simmons bowed and hurried after the man who was scurrying out. Lillith watched them without conscious thought.

'He was lying,' she whispered. 'He had to be. Mathias is many things, but he is not a murderer.' She sank back into the chair and her hands dropped to her lap. Her gaze lifted. 'But I understand that you must know for sure.'

Perth watched her find excuses for her brother—again, and the anger that he felt boiled to near-explosion point. 'Why do you find it so hard to believe?' he asked harshly.

'He is my brother,' she said as though that explained everything. 'And that man just wanted money. He would have said any name. He just came up with Wentworth. He might have even known that was my brother's name. How do I know?'

'He is the brother who sold you to de Lisle, gambled away your marriage settlement and tried to sell you a second time. He had me horsewhipped while he looked on. Why should he not stoop to attacking me and nearly killing us?' he asked, his words nearly a snarl. 'Blood does not always mean love.'

She glared at him. 'He might have you attacked.' She drew a deep breath. 'I can believe that. I do not doubt that he had you whipped years ago, but he was young. He would never do that now.'

Perth's voice turned deadly quiet. 'If you believe that, then you won't mind confronting him with this man's accusations. Your brother will deny everything and you will be further assured of his innocence.'

Alerted by his ominous tone Lillith looked at him closely. 'You really hate my brother, don't you?'

'Yes. He has used you and done everything in his power to physically hurt me.'

She took a deep breath and stood. 'All right. I will send a note to Mathias, asking him to call. That way you will not have to travel. I will ask him with you in the room so you can see his reaction too.' She turned away from him and went to the door. She paused before leaving. 'Will that satisfy you?'

'Yes,' Perth said.

She did not rise when he left the room. She did not think she could lift her hand, let alone get to her feet. This felt like a nightmare with no happy ending. She had argued for Mathias, but a tiny kernel of pain and doubt made her chest ache.

Mathias had done so many despicable things. But, God, she did not want to believe him capable of this.

Chapter Eighteen

Lillith sat rigidly in a heavy oak chair. Perth lounged on a green-and-gold upholstered settee. Doctor Johnson had just left, having pronounced his patient to be doing well but having a mild fever. He had recommended bed.

They were in the front drawing room. A gold carpet covered the wooden floors and green-flocked gold curtains framed large windows that looked out on to the street. The light was good and she would be able to see every nuance on her brother's face when she told him about that man's accusations.

Neither she nor Perth said a word to each other. They had not spoken since he left her in the breakfast room. She had sent word to him about the meeting through Simmons, and Simmons had brought back Doctor Johnson's diagnosis.

She had not been capable of hearing anymore about Mathias.

The door opened and Simmons announced, 'Mr Wentworth.'

Mathias saw Lillith first and headed to her. 'I came as soon as I got your note,' he said. He saw Perth when it was too late to sit further away. 'Perth,' he managed through gritted teeth.

Perth nodded. 'It has been a while, Wentworth. Had any big wins lately?'

Lillith frowned at Perth. 'Stop that,' she ordered. He gave her a bland look, his face completely unreadable. 'Please have a seat, Mathias,' she said, turning back to her brother.

She waved to the chair closer to her than to Perth. A large, heavy table laden with books, pictures and candlesticks provided a type of barrier between the two men. She did not think that in his current condition Perth could come over the table if something went wrong. She instantly pushed the idea aside. Nothing was going to go wrong because Mathias was innocent of that awful man's charges.

Mathias crossed one elegantly shod leg over the other. 'I hope you are doing well,' he said to the air in Perth's direction.

'I have been worse,' Perth drawled. 'In fact, ten years ago I found myself bedridden for nearly a month.'

'So I heard,' Wentworth said.

Lillith looked from one to the other. They were talking about the time Perth had been whipped. It made her uneasy to see her brother talk so cavalierly about an injury he had been responsible for causing. The callousness showed a side of Mathias that she was seeing more and more of. It hurt. She took a deep, shuddering breath.

'Mathias,' she started, her voice too loud. 'Mathias,' she began again more quietly, 'I have asked you here to tell you this horrible thing an awful man, of no account, has told us about you.' She gripped her fingers tight and told herself not to worry. It was all lies. 'I know everything he said is a lie, but…'

Mathias's gaze flicked from one to the other. His jaw twitched, a nervous habit that Lillith knew only surfaced when he was wary.

'Go on,' he said.

In a rush, she told him everything.

Perth stared at Mathias. His voice was cold and so deadly soft that it was barely audible. 'This time you went too far, Wentworth. This time you endangered Lillith. No matter what answer you give here, I will see that you are ruined.'

Mathias's gaze flicked to Perth before he looked away. The only evidence that he had even heard her was the continued tick. Wentworth, debauched libertine and addicted gambler and coward, carefully picked a scrap of non-existent lint from his sleeve and made no eye contact. 'Perth knows the truth, Lillith.'

Lillith's mouth dropped. She felt as though she had been sucked dry of everything. She sank deeper into the leather cushions. All she could do was stare in dismay at her brother.

Perth watched Lillith's face blanch and her shoulders slump. Wentworth never once looked at his sister. For that alone, Perth wanted to beat the man insensate.

Still, he did nothing and said nothing. What happened next depended on Lillith. He thought she would defend her brother's indefensible actions. She had so many times in the past that he had no doubt she would do so again, no matter how much worse these last were.

Lillith's eyes shone with tears but none spilled. 'You did have those thugs attack Perth. And you did have someone shoot at us,' she finally said, her voice barely audible. 'Why?'

As though he merely spoke of the weather, Wentworth said, 'The imbeciles were to beat Perth up, hopefully warn him away from you. It had worked once before. As to the shooting, they were supposed to follow Perth and get him. They were stupid enough to shoot when he was with you. That was not supposed to happen. I truly did intend to meet you.'

She shrank further into her chair, her face pinched by pain and disillusionment. Perth nearly rose and went to her. Now, more than any time since he had known her, she needed his support. He hardened his resolve. She also needed to see her brother for what he really was.

'As to why,' Wentworth continued, gazing out the open windows now, 'I told you not to marry Perth. He was not, is not the man for you.' He looked at the Earl. 'I told you to leave her alone.'

Perth returned his look. 'I do as I please.'

'You left her alone before.'

'That was because she was married before I could do anything, and when I challenged de Lisle to an *honourable* duel that might have made her a widow, he beat me. I had no other choices.'

Outside snow began to fall. The wood on the fire cracked, sending a minor explosion of sparks into the room to die harmlessly on the carpet.

'How could you?' Lillith demanded, beginning to get some of her colour back. 'How could you do such despicable things?'

Wentworth looked uncomfortable for the first time. 'I had to. Perth has refused to help me financially. I am facing ruin and ostracism from the *ton*. De Lisle saved me before. I needed you to marry another man who would pay my debts or give you the money to do so.'

'Gambling,' she spat. 'I should have known. We have already had this discussion. I just did not realise how far you would go to support your habit.' She looked at him and disgust marred her features. 'You are despicable, Mathias.' She rose and went to stand over him. 'You are worse than despicable. You are dishonourable. Even by your warped standards, you should know that.' She sucked in air, her chest rising and falling.

'I did what I had to,' he said softly, never showing by expression or tone that he felt remorse.

The tears that had glistened before started falling. Her hands shook and she made no effort to stop them. 'Leave my home. Leave England. Not even you, my brother, a friend of the Prince of Wales, can do the things you have done and get away with them.'

Mathias managed to stand by leaning away from her

and angling behind the chair that now separated them. 'I won't go to the Continent. No one but you and Perth knows.'

'You will,' she nearly shouted. 'You had my husband attacked and then shot. He might have been badly injured. He might have been killed. You did all of that because of your gambling debts. You will go to the Continent or I will tell everyone in the *ton* what you have done. I will ruin you.'

'You are hysterical,' he said haughtily. 'You will do nothing of the sort. If you ruin me, you ruin yourself. Not even Perth's rank will save you.'

'I don't care,' she retorted. 'You *will* go. I don't want you near us where you might decide to do something else. Next time—' she took a deep breath '—next time you might kill him. Go now. Today. Or I swear I will do everything I have threatened.'

Perth rose and took a step towards them. He had never seen Lillith like this where her brother was concerned. He had never expected to. The most he had thought would happen was that she would rant and rave at him and tell him to stay away. Never had he thought she would banish him to the Continent. And especially not for him.

Wentworth stood his ground for long minutes as he and Lillith stared at each other. 'What happened to loving me because I am your brother?' he finally asked.

She swiped at her tears. 'You have gone beyond what I can accept. You nearly killed my husband and all because you wanted me to marry another man who would pay your gaming debts. Now it is my shame to be your sister.' She dropped her hands to her sides and clenched them. Her face turned stony. 'Get out of my house and do not come back. Do not go to my London house either. You are no longer welcome in any place where I am. And…if you are not on your way to Dover by tomorrow morning, I swear to you that I will tell the world what you have done.'

For the first time since Perth had known Wentworth, he thought the man felt something besides self-interest. He almost looked deflated.

'You leave me no choice,' Wentworth finally said in a voice gone dead.

She glared at him, saying nothing. After what seemed an eternity to Perth, Wentworth left. Simmons met him at the door, and Perth knew the butler would escort Wentworth to the door. Only then did Perth go to Lillith.

He went to put his arms around her, but she shoved him away and moved to the window where she could watch her brother leave. Perth heard the sounds of wheels on cobbles and knew that Wentworth drove away. Only then did she turn to him.

'Are you satisfied?' she asked bitterly.

'Yes.' There was nothing else he could say to her that was not a lie.

'Good. Then please go away so I can be miserable in private.' She turned from him again and stared resolutely out of the window, even though he saw her shiver from the cold he knew to be coming through the glass.

He took a step towards her. The long, elegant length of her back begged for his touch, his comfort. His heart begged him to touch and comfort her. Closing the distance between them was hard, but not as hard as what had to follow.

'Lillith,' he murmured when only inches separated them. 'Please look at me. I have things to tell you.'

Her shoulders hunched and she crossed her arms on her chest and still refused to look at him. 'There is nothing you can say to ease the pain of what you just forced me to acknowledge.'

He sighed. 'Did you want to remain ignorant of what your brother is willing to do? I had thought you stronger than that.'

She took a hiccuping sob and he could not help himself. He gripped her shoulders and drew her back against his chest. The need to comfort her was paramount. It was an emotion that he had thought cut out of him ten years before.

'Lillith,' he crooned, 'I am sorry for what has happened, but I cannot be sorry that you finally know. I cannot, no matter how much it hurts you.'

She stiffened under his fingers, a reaction he would have thought hard for her to do since she had already been cold as ice. 'I think I must go away for a while,' she said. 'I need time to accept what I have learned today. Perhaps I will stay here in London, in my house, while you go to the country. Yes,' she said with increasing determination, 'that is what I will do. It will be for the best.'

'No,' he said, the word a shot. 'I won't allow it.'

The patience he had hoped to have with her evaporated. He twisted her around and caught her chin in his hand. The old anger flashed in her eyes, but it brought him no familiar excitement.

He was too scared.

Sweat broke out on his brow. He knew that if he did not tell her now that he loved her, if he did not open himself up to possibly be hurt by her again, that he would lose her. She had been through too much and he had offered her too little. What he had to do, open himself to her, was the hardest thing he had ever done. It made taking a pistol shot in the shoulder seem a mere bagatelle.

Still he took a deep breath. 'Lillith, my wife. My love.' The ultimate words stuck in his throat.

Surprise, shock, wonderment moved over her face as she looked at him. The tears that had flowed for her brother stopped as she cried out softly, 'Perth. Jason, what are you saying?'

He felt her trembling in his arms. The hurt and anger of seconds before might never have existed to look at her eyes now. It humbled him to know the power he had over her happiness. It humbled him and made him very grateful.

'I...' he faltered again. 'It is easier to go into battle than to say I love you.' He smiled down at her, drinking in the love that shone in her face. 'I love you, Lillith, Countess of Perth, mother of my children. I love you more than life itself and I always have.'

'But why now?' She shook her head just a little, perplexed by what to her was a sudden change.

He shrugged. 'I have always loved you. I just refused to believe it after what happened before. But I knew I wanted you more than life itself, and when I knew you carried my child I had to have you. But...' he paused, hoping his next words would not cause a rift '...I could not allow myself to trust you as long as I knew that your brother was first in your affections. I knew he did not want you married to me and would do anything to separate us. As long as that possibility was there, I could not, would not, did not even let myself realise—that I love you.'

The flash of irritation that had entered her eyes dissipated to melting blue love. 'Oh, Jason. I am truly sorry. I never knew. Before now, I could not have abandoned Mathias. But I can promise you this: no matter what might have happened, he would have never separated us.'

He raised one brow in doubt.

'It is true,' she said. 'For I have loved you from the beginning. That is why I did not want to marry you. I did not want to see you every day, knowing you did not love me when I loved you above all else. I did not think I could stand it and stay sane. But the child changed everything.'

'For you, not for me,' he said softly. 'The child gave you a reason to marry me. I have always wanted you, but I had to get beyond my own hurt to discover that I had never stopped loving you.'

He bent down to kiss her; before he did so, he asked gently, 'Lillith, will you marry me again, for real?'

She wound her arms around his neck and pulled his mouth to hers. 'Yes, my love. Yes.'

Epilogue

Lillith gazed around at the small party gathered here at Ravensford's country seat for the Christmas season. The Duke of Brabourne and his bride were back from the Continent. She had taken a liking to the Duke and his wife almost instantly. There was something about a reformed rake that greatly appealed to her feminine side. He also treated his wife as though she were his most cherished possession. For her part, Juliet, Duchess of Brabourne, melted every time her husband so much as glanced at her.

She watched the men casually talking by the fireplace. It was obvious that they knew each other well and liked and respected each other.

'A toast to our newest newlyweds,' Brabourne said, lifting his glass of whisky, the drink of preference for all three. 'May they live long and be fruitful.'

'May we all live long and be fruitful,' Perth said with a loving look at Lillith as he drank.

'Which we are all doing our best to fulfil,' Mary Margaret said meaningfully.

Lillith laughed. All three women were in the first stages of pregnancy.

'Ahem.' Perth cleared his throat. 'I might as well make a clean breast of everything.' He gave his two friends a sly grin. 'You particularly will be interested in what I have to say,' he said to Ravensford.

Ravensford's green eyes narrowed.

'I could almost be embarrassed except that what I did turned out for the best—as all of you will agree,' Perth continued.

'What did you do, Perth, write those appalling bets about us in Brook's Betting Book?' Ravensford demanded. 'That would explain why none was ever written about you and Lillith.'

Perth gave a deprecating shrug, then burst into laughter. 'Who other? I could tell it was the only way you and Brabourne would come to the sticking point. And you would have been miserable for the rest of your lives if you had let Juliet and Mary Margaret get away.' He raised his glass again. 'I did it for the best.'

'You rogue,' Ravensford said, laughter bubbling in his voice. 'I should have known.'

Lillith marvelled at her husband. He was an arrogant, domineering man who liked his own way, but he was also perceptive enough to know that his friends had been in love and unwilling or unable to admit it to themselves. Much as Perth had been.

She rose and went to his side. 'Jason, you are incorrigible,' she murmured.

He looked down at her with enough love in his eyes to last a lifetime. 'I do what I must, madam.'

'That you do,' she murmured. She tilted her head up so that she could kiss him lightly on his scar. 'Oh!' she exclaimed. 'Oh, my goodness.'

'What is wrong,' he asked, his arm instantly around her. 'Are you sick?'

She smiled. 'I…I am wonderful.' She took his hand and pulled it tighter around her waist so that his palm rested on the slight swell of her belly. 'But our child is restless.'

A look of startled wonder transformed his features. 'Our child,' he murmured. 'Yes, I…I feel a kick.'

'Another toast,' Ravensford announced. 'To the future Earl of Perth.'

Lillith smiled. Perth beamed.

'Or the future Lady Amelia Beaumair, for that is what we will name a girl,' Perth said.

'To our child,' Lillith said simply.

'To our love,' Perth replied, kissing her.

*   *   *   *   *

Watch out for more from the Sparhawks!
Sparhawk's Angel
by Miranda Jarrett
is available next month in
Regency High-Society Affairs, Volume 8

Regency

HIGH-SOCIETY AFFAIRS

BOOK EIGHT

*These unconventional ladies will become **improper** wives!*

Sparhawk's Angel by Miranda Jarrett
The Proper Wife by Julia Justiss

On sale 2nd October 2009

Regency

HIGH-SOCIETY AFFAIRS

Rakes and rogues in the ballrooms – and the bedrooms – of Regency England!

Volume 1 – 6th March 2009
A Hasty Betrothal by Dorothy Elbury
A Scandalous Marriage by Mary Brendan

Volume 2 – 3rd April 2009
The Count's Charade by Elizabeth Bailey
The Rake and the Rebel by Mary Brendan

Volume 3 – 1st May 2009
Sparhawk's Lady by Miranda Jarrett
The Earl's Intended Wife by Louise Allen

Volume 4 – 5th June 2009
Lord Calthorpe's Promise by Sylvia Andrew
The Society Catch by Louise Allen

Volume 5 – 3rd July 2009
Beloved Virago by Anne Ashley
Lord Trenchard's Choice by Sylvia Andrew

Volume 6 – 7th August 2009
The Unruly Chaperon by Elizabeth Rolls
Colonel Ancroft's Love by Sylvia Andrew

Volume 7 – 4th September 2009
The Sparhawk Bride by Miranda Jarrett
The Rogue's Seduction by Georgina Devon

NOW 14 VOLUMES IN ALL TO COLLECT!

Regency

High-Society Affairs

Rakes and rogues in the ballrooms – and the bedrooms – of Regency England!

Volume 8 – 2nd October 2009
Sparhawk's Angel by Miranda Jarrett
The Proper Wife by Julia Justiss

Volume 9 – 6th November 2009
The Disgraced Marchioness by Anne O'Brien
The Reluctant Escort by Mary Nichols

Volume 10 – 4th December 2009
The Outrageous Debutante by Anne O'Brien
A Damnable Rogue by Anne Herries

Volume 11 – 8th January 2010
The Enigmatic Rake by Anne O'Brien
The Lord and the Mystery Lady by Georgina Devon

Volume 12 – 5th February 2010
The Wagering Widow by Diane Gaston
An Unconventional Widow by Georgina Devon

Volume 13 – 5th March 2010
A Reputable Rake by Diane Gaston
The Heart's Wager by Gayle Wilson

Volume 14 – 2nd April 2010
The Venetian's Mistress by Ann Elizabeth Cree
The Gambler's Heart by Gayle Wilson

NOW 14 VOLUMES IN ALL TO COLLECT!

M&B

He could marry her — or ruin her!

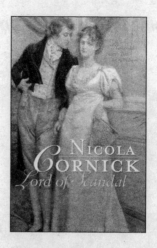

London, 1814

Scandalous and seductive, Hawksmoor is a notorious fortune hunter. Now he has tasted the woman of his dreams, Catherine Fenton, and he will do anything to make her his.

Though heiress to a fortune, Catherine is trapped in a gilded cage and bound to a man she detests. She senses there is more to Ben, Lord Hawksmoor, behind the glittering façade. She believes he can rescue her — but has she found herself a hero, or made a pact with the devil himself?

Regency romance...and revenge
by bestselling author Nicola Cornick

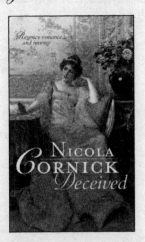

Princess Isabella never imagined it could come to this.
Bad enough she faces imprisonment for debts not her
own. Even worse that she must make a hasty marriage
of convenience with Marcus, the Earl of Stockhaven.

As the London gossips eagerly gather to watch the fun,
Isabella struggles to maintain a polite distance in her
marriage. But the more Isabella challenges Marcus's
iron determination to have a marriage in more than
name only, the hotter their passion burns. This time,
will it consume them both – or fuel a love greater
than they dare dream?

"To say that I met Nicholas Brisbane over my husband's dead body is not entirely accurate. Edward, it should be noted, was still twitching upon the floor…"

London, 1886

For Lady Julia Grey, her husband's sudden death at a dinner party is extremely inconvenient. However, things worsen when inscrutable private investigator Nicholas Brisbane reveals that the death was not due to natural causes.

Drawn away from her comfortable, conventional life, Julia is exposed to threatening notes, secret societies and gypsy curses, not to mention Nicholas's charismatic unpredictability.

"There is a dead man stinking in the game larder. I hardly think a few missing pearls will be the ruin of this house party."

England, 1887

Christmas festivities at Bellmont Abbey are brought to an abrupt halt by a murder in the chapel. Blood dripping from her hands, Lady Julia Grey's cousin claims the ancient right of sanctuary.

Forced to resume her deliciously intriguing partnership with the enigmatic detective Nicholas Brisbane, Lady Julia is intent on proving her cousin's innocence. Still, the truth is rarely pure and never simple…

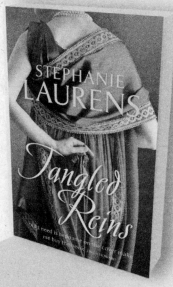

*Immerse yourself in the glitter of
Regency times through the lives
and romantic escapades of the
Lester family*

Miss Lenore Lester was perfectly content with
her quiet country life, caring for her father, and
having no desire for marriage. Though she hid behind
glasses and pulled-back hair, she couldn't disguise her
beauty. And the notoriously charming Jason
Montgomery – Duke of Eversleigh – could easily see
through her disguise and clearly signalled his interests.

Lenore remained determined not to be thrown
off-balance by this charming rake. The Duke of
Eversleigh, though, was equally determined to loosen
the hold Lenore had on her heart.

www.mirabooks.co.uk

MIRA

Immerse yourself in the glitter of Regency times through the lives and romantic escapades of the Lester family

Jack Lester had every reason to hide the news of his recently acquired fortune: he wanted an attractive, capable bride who would accept him for himself, not for his new-found riches.

But he had to make his choice before the society matrons discovered the Lester family were no longer as poor as church mice. He must convince Sophie, the woman of his dreams, to marry him as poor Jack Lester.

MIRA

*Immerse yourself in the glitter of
Regency times through the lives
and romantic escapades of the
Lester family*

Now the news was out that the Lester family
fortunes had been repaired, Harry Lester knew the
society matrons would soon be in pursuit, so he
promptly left London for Newmarket.

Fate, however, proved more far-sighted, having
arranged for a distraction in the person of
Mrs Lucinda Babbacombe. Lucinda is a beautiful,
provocative but unwilling conquest – who
to Harry's irritation cannot be ignored.

*Immerse yourself in the glitter of
Regency times through the lives
and romantic escapades of the
Lester family*

Miss Antonia Mannering and Lord Philip Ruthven
had been childhood friends who had not seen each
other for years. And although considered a very
eligible bachelor, Philip remained unmarried.

With Philip's close friend Harry Lester recently
married, Antonia only hopes that she can convince
Philip of the bliss marriage brings, that she can
run his home and not disgrace him in Society.
But is Philip ready to set up his nursery…
with Antonia as his wife?

www.mirabooks.co.uk

MIRA